ONLY IN DEATH

More Dan Abnett from the Black Library

· GAUNT'S GHOSTS ·

Colonel-Commissar Gaunt and his regiment, the Tanith First-and-Only, struggle for survival on the battlefields of the far future.

The Founding
(Omnibus containing books 1-3 in the series: FIRST AND ONLY, GHOSTMAKER and NECROPOLIS)

The Saint
(Omnibus containing books 4-7 in the series: HONOUR GUARD, THE GUNS OF TANITH, STRAIGHT SILVER and SABBAT MARTYR)

The Lost
Book 8 – TRAITOR GENERAL
Book 9 – HIS LAST COMMAND
Book 10 – THE ARMOUR OF CONTEMPT

Also
DOUBLE EAGLE
THE SABBAT WORLDS CRUSADE

· EISENHORN ·

In the nightmare world of the 41st millennium, Inquisitor Eisenhorn hunts down mankind's most dangerous enemies.

EISENHORN
(Omnibus containing XENOS, MALLEUS and HERETICUS)

· RAVENOR ·

The Inquisition fights a secret war against mankind's most deadly enemies – the alien, the heretic and the daemon – to protect the Imperium of Man and the souls of humanity.

Book 1 – RAVENOR
Book 2 – RAVENOR RETURNED
Book 3 – RAVENOR ROGUE

· OTHER WARHAMMER 40,000 TITLES ·

THE HORUS HERESY: HORUS RISING
BROTHERS OF THE SNAKE
(an Iron Snakes novel)

A WARHAMMER 40,000 NOVEL

Gaunt's Ghosts

ONLY IN DEATH

Dan Abnett

For Steve Bissett (Master of the Blood Pact)

A BLACK LIBRARY PUBLICATION
First published in Great Britain in 2007 by
BL Publishing,
Games Workshop Ltd.,
Willow Road,
Nottingham,
NG7 2WS, UK

10 9 8 7 6 5 4 3 2 1

Cover by Clint Langley.

A CIP record for this book
is available from the British Library.

Hardback ISBN 13: 978 1 84416 428 8 • ISBN 10: 1 84416 428 4
Collectors' edition ISBN 13: 978 1 84416 427 1 • ISBN 10: 1 84416 427 6

Distributed in the US by Simon & Schuster
1230 Avenue of the Americas, New York, NY 10020, US.

Printed and bound in Great Britain by
Mackays of Chatham plc, Chatham, Kent

IT IS THE 41st millennium. For more than a hundred centuries the Emperor has sat immobile on the Golden Throne of Earth. He is the master of mankind by the will of the gods, and master of a million worlds by the might of his inexhaustible armies. He is a rotting carcass writhing invisibly with power from the Dark Age of Technology. He is the Carrion Lord of the Imperium for whom a thousand souls are sacrificed every day, so that he may never truly die.

YET EVEN IN his deathless state, the Emperor continues his eternal vigilance. Mighty battlefleets cross the daemon-infested miasma of the warp, the only route between distant stars, their way lit by the Astronomican, the psychic manifestation of the Emperor's will. Vast armies give battle in his name on uncounted worlds. Greatest amongst his soldiers are the Adeptus Astartes, the Space Marines, bio-engineered super-warriors. Their comrades in arms are legion: the Imperial Guard and countless planetary defence forces, the ever-vigilant Inquisition and the tech-priests of the Adeptus Mechanicus to name only a few.
But for all their multitudes, they are barely enough to hold off the ever-present threat from aliens, heretics, mutants – and worse.

TO BE A man in such times is to be one amongst untold billions. It is to live in the cruellest and most bloody regime imaginable. These are the tales of those times. Forget the power of technology and science, for so much has been forgotten, never to be re-learned. Forget the promise of progress and understanding, for in the grim dark future there is only war. There is no peace amongst the stars, only an eternity of carnage and slaughter, and the laughter of thirsting gods.

Only in death does duty end.
– old Imperial proverb

'IN 778.M41, THE *twenty-third year of the Sabbat Worlds Crusade, Warmaster Macaroth's main battle groups advanced swiftly and thoroughly into the frontiers of the Carcaradon Cluster, driving the hosts of the Archenemy overlord ('Archon') Urlock Gaur, before them. Archon Gaur's forces seemed to fracture under the successive Imperial assaults, though it now seems likely they were in fact withdrawing to establish a defensive cordon in the Erinyes Group*

'To coreward, the Crusade's secondary battle-groups – the Fifth, Eighth and Ninth Armies – continued to combat the legions of Magister Anakwanar Sek, Gaur's most capable lieutenant. The Second Front's avowed intent was to hound Sek's rabble from the fringes of the Khan Group, and oust them from the many fortress worlds of the Cabal System.

'During this murderous phase of the Crusade, an especially bloody banishment campaign took place on the ruinous fortress world of Jago…'

– from *A History of the Later Imperial Crusades*

Day two (out of Elikon M.P.). Sunrise at four, but dust-out til later. Progress fair (23 km). Am concerned about water rations, have mentioned matter to G. and R. Dust a factor. R. repeated his 'no spit' order, ~~useles~~ frankly unworkable in my opinion. G. assures objective has its own well/water supply. We'll see.

K. has once again ~~ras~~ raised questions re: dust jamming weapons. Inspect ordered for noon halt. To follow up. Good evidence for casing all weapons during march, though R. reluctant. Casing would slow unit response in event of ambush scenario.

~~Dreams getting worse, more troubl~~

Rumour persists. Have failed to winkle out origin. Suddenly everyone's a superstitious fething idiot. Bad form. Intend to get on top of it once we're installed at objective.

Don't like this place at all. Doing best to maintain morale. Dust and rumours not helping.

Sunset seven plus twenty-one. Light winds. Saw stars for first time. They looked a long ~~aw~~ way away.

– Field journal, V.H. fifth month, 778.

ONE

The House at the End of the World

I

DURING THE SIX-DAY trudge up-country, some bright spark (and no one ever found out who) started a gossipy piece of rumour that swept through the regiment like a dose of belly-flu. The rumour ran that a bunch of Guardsmen, maybe a pioneer unit or a scout reconnaissance, had come across a ravine up in the hills full of skulls with all the tops sawn off.

The Ghosts, both old and new, were tough fethers who had seen far, far worse than a few bleached bones in their days, but there was something about the rumour, that damned gossipy piece of rumour, that stuck like a splinter under the skin, and dug until it nagged.

Like all rumours, the art was in the detail. The skulls, so it went, were human, and they were old, really old. They weren't some relic of the present war, not even an atrocity perpetrated by the Archenemy who had, until the previous spring, been the undisputed master of Jago. Old, old, old and dusty; fossil-old, tomb-old; weathered and worn and yellow, evidence of some godless crime enacted in those wild, lonely hills in ages past. It smacked of ritual, of trophy taking, of predation. The meaning was long lost, erased by time and weather and the debrading dust, so that no clear detail could be discerned anymore, and all the awful possibilities imaginable came bubbling up in the minds of the marching troops.

More than anything else, the rumour seemed to cement the dim view every last one of them had formed about the place. Jago was a bad rock, and these lonely hills were the baddest, bleakest stretch of that bad rock.

Gaunt was having none of it. When the gossip reached him, he tried to have it stamped out, quick and neat, like a bug under a boot-heel. He told Hark and Ludd to 'have issue' with anyone caught using the words 'cursed' or 'haunted'. He told them that he wanted it made known that there would be punishment duties available to any trooper found spreading the rumour.

Hark and Ludd did as they were told, and the gossip died back to a mumble, but it refused to go away.

'The men are spooked,' said Viktor Hark.

II

IT DIDN'T HELP that Jago was such a Throne-forsaken arse-cleft.

The northern mountains, an eight thousand kilometre-long range of buck and broken teeth, were possessed of three prevailing characteristics: wind, dust and craggy altitude. Those ingredients worked in concert to produce an environment that every single one of the Ghosts would have gladly said goodbye to at short notice, without regret.

The wind was cold and saw-edged, and banged around the tight valleys and deep ravines like a ricocheting las-round. It rubbed exposed flesh red-raw, and made knuckles as numb as ice. It tugged at capes, and whipped off hats without invitation. It slung itself about, and gnawed and bit and, all the while, sang like a siren; like a fething siren. It had had eons to practise its music, and it sang for the Ghosts of Tanith more keenly than any pipe or marching flute. It found crevices, split rocks, clefts, fissures and chasms, and wailed through them. It played the lonely hills like a templum organ, exploiting every last acoustic possibility of the mountainous terrain.

Then there was the dust. The dust got into everything, not least the singing wind. It sifted into collars and ears and cuffs; it invaded puttees and gloves; it clogged noses until they were thick with grey tar. It found its way into kitbags, into weapons, into ration packs, into underwear even, where it chafed like scrubbing powder. Trekking up the narrow passes, the Ghosts spat lumpy grey phlegm, rinsing their mouths from their water bottles. Rifles fatigued and ailed, polished steel scoured matt, and mechanisms jammed, until Gaunt ordered weapons to be carried cased in weather-proofs. 'Up ahead' became an opaque mist, 'behind' a trail of boot prints that was erased in seconds. 'Above' was a vague suggestion of jagged cliffs. All around them washed the haunting song of the grit-laden wind.

Quickly, they all became very grateful indeed for the brass-framed goggles they'd been issued with by the Munitorum aides at Elikon Muster Point.

Dry skulls in a dusty valley, with all the tops sawn off.

'This is going to be trouble,' said Elim Rawne.

'Trouble's what we do,' said Ibram Gaunt.

III

PART OF THE trouble was that the war was taking place elsewhere. It might as well have been taking place in another century. At night, during the intervals when the wind died back and the dust clouds dropped away, they could hear the sky-punch of the artillery and the armour divisions south of Elikon. Sometimes they saw the flashes, like lightning on a different planet, pulsing like a watchtower beacon, far away. Once in a while, dropships droned overhead – Valkyries and heavy Destriers – zoning in towards the active killing grounds. The dropships courteously waggled their wings at the thread of troopers winding along the valley floors.

Jago was a fortress world, one of the infamous fortress worlds built along the trailwards salient of the Cabal System. Nahum Ludd hadn't known quite what to expect, so his imagination had run fast and loose with the words 'fortress' and 'world'. He had conceived of a planet built like a castle, all gun-slits and machicolations; a planet with bastion towers and square corners; an improbable, impregnable thing. The truth was rather different. Jago had been fortified long before the reach of mankind's memory. Its rocky, howling, fuming crust had been mined out and laced with thousands of kilometres of casemates, bunkers and structural emplacements. Ludd wondered what manner of long-forgotten war had engulfed the place so thoroughly that such formidable earthworks had been necessary. Who had the defenders been? Who had they been fighting? How could anyone tell where one fortress line ended and the next began? Elikon had been a bewildering matrix of sub-crust forts, a labyrinth of tunnels and hard points, a maze of armoured tunnels and cloche turrets, sprouting from the landscape like mushrooms.

'So, who fought here? Originally, I mean?' Ludd asked. 'Why was all this stuff built?'

'Does it matter?' replied Viktor Hark.

'Ask the skulls with all the tops sawn off,' mumbled Hlaine Larkin, limping up the gully behind them.

IV

THEY MARCHED FOR six days, following the rough country up into the waistline of the mountains. The dust billowed around them. General Van

Voytz had been quite specific in his instructions. At Elikon, his gold braid fingered by the hillside wind, he'd climbed up onto the broad back of a scabby Chimera to address them all, like a serious but well-meaning friend. He'd been forced to raise his voice above the trundle of a passing convoy: heavy armour, troop transports, vox trailers, and the guarded cage-trucks of battlefield psykers, all rolling out towards the front.

'The Archenemy may attempt to side-swipe us here,' Van Voytz had said, his voice planed smooth by the gritty breeze. 'I'm asking the Ghosts to watch our eastern flank.'

Asking. Gaunt had smiled at that: a dry smile, for no other kind was possible on Jago. His old friend and sometime mentor Barthol Van Voytz was an expert at making the average fighting soldier feel as if any given commission was either his own idea, or a favour for the boss. *Asking*. Show some spine, Barthol. What you're doing is called *ordering*.

'There is an end-of-line stronghold called Hinzerhaus at the far east reach of the fortress wall,' Van Voytz continued. 'It's up in the Banzie Altids, a spur of the main mountain range, eight days from here.'

More like six, the way my Ghosts march, thought Gaunt.

'Hinzerhaus is your objective. Find it,' said Van Voytz. 'Find it, secure it, hold it, and deny any attempt by the enemy to cross the line at that place. The Emperor is counting on you.'

They had all made the sign of the aquila. They had all thought *the fething Emperor doesn't even know my name.*

'Do we like this job?' asked Braden Baskevyl. 'Show of hands?'

'Does it matter?' replied Gol Kolea, as the regiment struck camp.

'You boys hear that thing about the skulls, then? The sawn-off skulls?' asked Ceglan Varl, as he wandered by.

V

So THEY HAD trekked out into the back end of nowhere, into the most forgotten parts of the bad rock called Jago, into the Banzie Altids. The ravines grew deeper, the cliffs grew steeper, and the dusty wind sang for them at the top of its dry lungs.

'This is going to be trouble,' said Elim Rawne, spitting out a wad of thick grey phlegm.

'Oh, rot! You always say that, young man,' said Zweil, the old chaplain, plodding along beside him.

VI

DUST HUNG, LIKE a gauze veil, along the body of the deep valley. The wind had dropped for a moment, and ceased its singing, an eerie hiatus. Gaunt held up his hand. The fingers of his glove were white with dust.

'It's taking too fething long,' said Tona Criid.

'Give them a minute,' whispered Gaunt.

Ghosts materialised, ghostly figures, tracking back to them out of the veil of dust: Mkoll, Bonin, Hwlan. The regiment's best.

'Well?' asked Gaunt.

'Oh, it's up there all right,' said Mkoll, spitting to clear his mouth. His brass-framed goggles were covered in a residue of fine powder, and he wiped them with his fingers.

'We saw it,' said Bonin.

'And what does it look like?' asked Gaunt.

'Like the last house before the end of the fething world,' said Mkoll.

VII

THEY GOT UP and moved on; two and a half thousand troopers in a long, straggly file. The wind found its energy again, and restarted its song.

Thus it was the Tanith First-and-Only came to Hinzerhaus, the house at the end of the world.

'This is going to be trouble,' said Elim Rawne as they plodded up towards the main gate in the stinging haze.

'Any chance,' wondered Hlaine Larkin, 'any chance at all you could stop saying that?'

The wind shrieked around them. It sounded like the scream skulls would make if their tops had all been sawn off.

Day six (out of Elikon M.D.). Sunrise at four plus ten, considerable dust-out, increasing at eight (or thereabouts). Progress good (18km). Objective achieved at noon minus twenty. Can't get a good look at the place, due to dust storms. Advance moving up to secure as I write. Troop in holding pattern. G. has ordered cases off, to some general ~~cmplaint~~ complaint from the r & f.

I have dreamed again, this last night, of ~~voices noises someone who won't~~

I wonder if I should speak to Doc D. about my dreams. Would he understand? Maybe A.C.? She might be more receptive. It troubles me to reflect that, since Gereon, I have a difficulty knowing what to say to A.C. She has changed so. No surprise, I suppose. I am given to wonder where the Ana I knew went to.

It's hard to know what to do for the best. They're only dreams, after all. I'll wager if I could look into the dreams these Ghosts endure, night after night, I'd see a lot worse. I've walked the camp after nightfall. I've seen them twitch and fidget in their bedrolls, trapped in their own nightmares. ~~Still though I~~

Signals from the front. Scouts are returning.
Will record more later.

– Field journal, V.H. fifth month, 778.

TWO
Enter Here

I

THE GATEHOUSE HAS *been empty for nine hundred years. It is made of stone, close-dressed stone: floor, walls and roof alike. It is big. It has an echo that has not been tested in a while.*

The lights are still on. Glow-orb fitments sag from ancient piping, dull and white like a reptile's lidded eyes. The light issuing from them throbs, harsh then soft, harsh then soft, in tune with some slow, respiratory rhythm. The pulse of Hinzerhaus.

There is a rug on the floor. Its edges are curled up like the dry wings of a dead moth. There is a picture on the wall, beside the inner hatch. It has an ornate gilt frame. The canvas within is dirt-black. What is it a picture of? Is that a face, a hand?

Outside, through the thick bastion walls, the wind sings its siren melody.

Scraping, now. Shuffling. Voices. Scratching. Old, unoiled bolts protesting as they are wrenched back.

The outer hatch slides–

II

–OPEN.

The thick metal door swung open about half a metre and then stopped. No amount of shoving could persuade it to open any wider. Its hinges were choked with dust and grit.

Mkoll slithered inside, through the narrow entry. The wind came indoors with him, its song diminished, its dust inhaled by the gatehouse. Fine powder hung in the stilled air for a moment, as if surprised, before settling.

The rug fidgeted, tugged by the draught.

Mkoll looked around, sliding his lamp beam about him gently.

'Well? Anything? Have you been killed at all?' called Maggs, hidden behind the hatch.

Mkoll didn't dignify the question with a reply. He pushed ahead, crouching low, weapon braced, his lamp-pack chasing out all the corners and the shadows.

The shadows moved as his lamp turned. They dribbled and fell away, they altered and bent. The air was smoke-dry, not a hint of moisture in it. A pulse began to beat in Mkoll's temple.

'Chief? Is it clear?' the vox crackled. Bonin, this time, poised outside with Maggs.

'Wait…' whispered Mkoll, the pulse in his temple still going tap, tap, tap. He could feel his own nerves drawing tight. Why? Why the feth was he feeling so edgy? Nothing got to him, usually. Why did he have real misgivings about this place? Why had he suddenly got the strongest impression that–

this is going to be trouble

–he was being watched?

To his left, an alcove. A shadow. Nothing. To his right, a doorway. Another shadow. Wait, not a shadow, *a fething–*

No. Scratch that. Nothing. Just his imagination, reading shapes and forms in the gloom that weren't actually there.

'Feth,' Mkoll breathed, amazed at his own foolishness.

'Say again?' crackled the link.

'Nothing,' replied Mkoll into his microbead.

In that doorway, he could have sworn… *he could have sworn…* someone had been standing there. *Right there.* But there was no one. Just a trick of the shadows. Just his racing imagination.

This wasn't like him. Jumping at shadows? *Calm down. Calm all the way down. You've done this a thousand times.*

'Clear,' he voxed.

Maggs squeezed his way in around the hatch behind Mkoll and began to shine his muzzle-fixed lamp around. Mkoll secretly liked Wes Maggs: he liked the Belladon's spark and his wit, and admired his skill. Mkoll put up with a lot of mouth from Maggs, because of what he got back in soldiering.

But Maggs's famous mouth was unusually silent suddenly. Maggs was spooked, Mkoll could feel that. That compounded Mkoll's own edginess, because he knew Maggs wasn't like that either, ordinarily.

It took a lot to spook Wes Maggs. Six days marching through the shrieking dust, plus the–

Dry skulls in a dusty valley.

–rumour would have helped. This chamber, this dry gatehouse, did all the rest.

'Who–' Maggs began. 'Who puts a rug in a gatehouse?'

Mkoll shook his head.

'And a picture?' Maggs added, creeping over to the frame on the wall. The cone of his lamp beam bobbed and swung. Then he snapped around suddenly, his weapon up hard against his collarbone, aimed.

'Point that thing somewhere else,' suggested Bonin as he wriggled in through the hatch behind them. 'What are you, twelve? Simple?'

'Sorry,' said Maggs, dipping his gun.

'You knew I was behind you.'

'Sorry.'

'You knew I was coming in after you.'

'Sorry, all right?'

'Shut up, both of you,' said Mkoll. *This isn't like us. We're all over the place, scrappy and wound too tight. We're Ghost scouts, for feth's sake. We're the best there is.*

Bonin glanced around, and allowed his lamp beam to trickle over the walls and ceiling. 'This is charming,' he murmured.

He looked over at Mkoll. 'Shall I get the rest of the advance in?'

Mkoll shook his head. 'No.'

'Uh, why not?'

'I have a... never mind. Let's just poke about for a bit.'

Bonin nodded. 'You all right, chief?'

'Of course.'

'Look at this picture,' called Maggs. He had gone right up to the wall where the old frame was hanging, and reached out with his left hand to touch its surface. His glove was caked with dust as white as ash.

'What's it supposed to be a picture of?' Maggs asked. 'A woman, no... a man... no, a woman... a portrait...'

'Just leave it alone, Maggs,' Mkoll said.

'I'm only asking,' said Maggs, as he began to rub at the surface of the canvas with his gloved hand. The canvas shuddered in the frame. 'That's a woman, right? Am I right? A woman in a black dress?'

Mkoll and Bonin weren't looking. They were staring up at the sagging light fitments, the softly glowing, lidded reptile-eyes strung along the parched walls.

'There's still power here,' said Bonin, uneasily.

Mkoll nodded.

'How is that possible? After all this time?'

Mkoll shrugged. 'I think they're chemical lights. Chemical fed on a slow burn, not an actual generator or power cell. Anyway, they're almost dead.'

Bonin breathed out. 'Is it just me, or do they keep getting brighter, now and then?'

Mkoll shrugged again. 'Just you,' he lied.

'Hey, it *is* a woman,' announced Maggs behind them. 'It's some old dam in a black lace dress.' He'd rubbed a patch of filth off the painting with his glove. Mkoll and Bonin trudged over to his side. The pale, expressionless face of a woman gazed back at them from the blackened canvas.

'Fantastic,' said Mkoll. 'Can we get on now?'

'Oh!' exclaimed Maggs. He was rubbing at the portrait again, and the ancient canvas of the painting had suddenly perished beneath his persistent fingertips. It disintegrated like powder, and left a hole where the woman's gazing face had been. Through it, Maggs could see the stone wall the painting was hanging on.

'Happy now?' asked Mkoll, turning away.

Maggs pulled up his weapon abruptly, and aimed it at the painting.

'What the feth are you doing?' asked Bonin.

Maggs took a step backwards, and lowered his rifle. He shook his head, dismayed. 'Nothing,' he said, 'nothing, sorry. Being silly.'

'Start moving with a purpose, Maggs,' Mkoll instructed.

Maggs nodded. 'Of course. Absolutely, chief.'

For a moment, for a fleeting moment, the disintegrating portrait had appeared to bleed. Dark, clotted fluid had oozed out of the collapsed hole like black blood from a meat-wound. But it had just been trickling dust, and Maggs's imagination. He felt stupid.

Not blood. Not blood at all. Just dust. Dust and shadows and–

dry skulls in a dusty valley, with all the tops sawn off

–his own stupid imagination.

Mkoll and Bonin had crossed to the inner hatch. They began to haul on the elaborate brass levers.

'Let's get this open,' Mkoll grunted.

'Uh huh. Let's,' said Wes Maggs, as he hurried to join them.

III

'THEY'RE TAKING TOO long,' said Tona Criid. The thin song of the dust was all around them, and visibility was down to less than four metres. The forward companies had drawn up half a kilometre from Hinzerhaus, waiting for the scout advance to report back. Half a kilometre, but none of them could actually see the house.

'Just wait,' said Gaunt.

'Should I send up a support detail, just in case?' asked Gol Kolea. Like all of them, he wore his camo-cloak pulled up to protect his mouth and nose.

'Wait,' Gaunt repeated. He touched his ear-piece, took it out and checked it, and then glanced at his vox-officer.

'Anything, or am I dead?' he asked.

'You're showing live, sir,' Beltayn replied, adjusting the brass dials of his heavy voxcaster. 'Still nothing from advance.'

Gaunt frowned. 'Give them a vox-check, please.'

'Yes, sir,' said Beltayn. Pulling the phones around his ears, he unhooked the brass mic and held it close to his mouth, shielding it from the swirling grit with his cupped left hand. 'Ghost-ghost One, Ghost-ghost One, this is Nalwood, this is Nalwood. Ghost-ghost One, vox-check, please, come back.'

Beltayn looked up at Gaunt. 'Just static.'

'Keep trying, Bel,' said Gaunt.

'Ghost-ghost One, Ghost-ghost One, this is Nalwood, this is Nalwood...'

Gaunt looked over at Kolea. 'Gol, assemble a back-up anyway. Get them ready, but keep them in formation until I give the word.'

'Yes, sir.'

'Mkoll knows what he's about. This is just a vox glitch, nothing more.'

Kolea nodded, and shouldered his way back into the driving wind that was coming up the ravine. They could hear him shouting orders, and hear the clatter of men moving into position.

'This is going to be trouble,' Major Rawne growled.

'Eli, give it a rest,' said Gaunt.

Rawne shrugged a what-the-hell, but obliged.

Gaunt waited. It was slow, like waiting for his own inevitable death. He paced, head down, looking at the way his boots scooped out depressions in the dust, marvelling as they in-filled again instantly. The singing wind curated Jago. It had no desire to let anything change.

'There are certain–'

Gaunt turned around. Ludd had begun to speak and then, for some reason, had thought better of it.

'What were you going to say, Nahum?' Gaunt asked.

Ludd coughed, his voice muffled behind his cloak hem. 'Nothing, sir. Nothing.'

Gaunt smiled. 'Oh, I want to know, now. There are certain – *what*?'

Ludd looked sideways at the bulky figure of Viktor Hark beside him. Hark nodded. 'Just spit it out, Ludd,' Hark said.

Ludd swallowed hard. It wasn't just the dust in his throat. 'A-at times of stress, sir, I was going to remark, there are certain methods that may be employed to dampen a nervous disposition.'

'You think I am exhibiting signs of a nervous disposition then, Ludd?' Gaunt asked.

'Actually, sir, that was why I stopped talking. I realised, rather abruptly, that I had no business suggesting such a thing, openly.'

'Oh feth me backwards, Ludd,' Hark muttered.

'Well,' said Gaunt, 'in terms of morale and respect, you were probably correct to edit yourself. It doesn't look good when a junior ranker suggests to his senior officer that he might like to calm down.'

'Exactly my point,' said Ludd. 'I just arrived at it too late.'

'Let's hear the methods anyway,' said Gaunt, clearly in a playful mood. 'It might do some of us some good. Isn't that right, Eli?'

Nearby, Rawne inclined his head towards Gaunt, slowly. His eyes, behind his brass goggles, were hooded in the most sarcastic way.

'Y-you really want me to–?' Ludd stammered.

'Oh, Throne,' Hark breathed to no one in particular.

'I really do, Nahum. I think you should tell us all about these methods.' Gaunt looked around at the rest of them. 'Who knows? They might prove useful.'

'Could I not, you know, just shoot myself now?' Ludd asked.

'Surviving embarrassment is character-building, Nahum,' Gaunt said. 'Get on with it. Start by telling us where these methods originated.'

Ludd looked at the ground. He mumbled something.

'Louder, please.'

'My mother taught them to me.'

Tona Criid started to cackle. Varl, Beltayn and even Rawne, despite himself, began to laugh too, but it was Tona's brittle cackle that really cut the air. It made Hark wince. He knew that sound: the false laughter of bitten-down pain.

Gaunt raised his hand to quiet the chorus. 'No, really,' he said. 'Let Nahum continue. Nahum?'

'I'd rather not, if you don't mind, sir. I spoke out of turn.'

'Consider it an order.'

'Ah. All right. Yes sir. Well, there was this counting game she used to play to keep worry in check. You count one-two-three and so on, and take a deep breath between each beat.'

'In this dust?' snorted Criid. She pulled the ridge of her cape down, hawked, and spat out a gob of grey phlegm.

Ludd looked at Gaunt and lifted his shoulders. 'She used to say the words "Throne of Terra" between each count. One, Throne of Terra… two, Throne of Terra… three–'

'Can I ask you a question, Nahum?' Gaunt said.

'Of course, sir.'

'Was your mother an especially worried woman?'

Ludd shrugged. Gritty particles flecked off his leather coat. 'I suppose. She was always nervous, as I remember. Her nerves troubled her. She was frail. Actually, I don't know. I was eight the last time I saw her. I was being shipped out to the scholam. I believe she's dead now.'

Criid stopped chuckling abruptly.

'I was also young when I lost my mother,' said Gaunt. He may have been lying, but no one was in a position to refute him. 'Nahum, do I look to you like an especially worried woman?'

'Of course not, sir.'

'Of course not. But I am an especially worried commander. Do you mind at all if I use your mother's counting game?'

'No, I don't, sir.'

Gaunt turned and started back along the pass towards the invisible house.

'One, Throne of Terra... Two, Throne of Terra...' he began. At the tenth *Throne of Terra*, he turned and counted his way back to them.

The wind dropped, to a light breath. The dust sank. The sun came out.

Eszrah ap Niht, who had been silent all the while, placed his lean hand on Gaunt's arm, and nodded up the pass.

'Histye, soule.'

Ibram Gaunt turned.

They saw the house for the first time.

Elikon M.P., Elikon M.P., this is Nalwood, this is Nalwood. Objective achieved. Securing site as of sunset. No hostile contact to report at this time.

Nalwood out. (transmission ends)

- Transcript of vox message, fifth month, 778.

THREE
Ghosts in the House

I

In the ten minutes of dust-less, song-less silence that followed, the Ghosts were afforded their first proper look at the place that would later ring with the sounds of their deaths.

Hinzerhaus.

There wasn't much to see: a fortified gatehouse, built into the foundations of the soaring cliffs and, above that, several tiers of armoured casemates and blockhouses extruding from the chin of the rock-face like theatre balconies. High up, along the cliff crest, there were signs of tiled roofs; of long, linked halls and blocky towers. To either side of the house proper, the ridge line was punctuated by cloche towers and budding fortifications, like warts and blisters erupting from wizened skin.

A fortress-house. A house-fortress. A bastion tunnelled and drilled out of the impassive mountain rock.

'Feth,' said Dalin Criid.

'Quiet in the line there!' his company officer called out.

Dalin bit his lip. Every man around him was thinking the same simple thought, but Dalin was the youngest and newest Ghost, and he was still mastering the stoicism and the field drill. For a flushed moment, he felt like a complete fool.

The worst of it was, he knew they were all looking at him. Dalin had acquired a special place in the regiment, one that he was not entirely comfortable with. Touchstone, lucky charm, new blood. He was the boy who'd made good, the first son of the Ghosts.

And bad rock Jago was his first combat posting as part of the Tanith First-and-Only, which made this more like a rite of passage, an initiation. Dalin Criid had a big legacy to uphold.

Two big legacies, in fact: the regiment's and his father's.

The vox-link clicked as signals came back from the command group. Senior officers were jogging back down the ravine, relaying the orders verbally to the waiting companies.

Dalin was part of E Company, which made him one of Captain Meryn's mob. Flyn Meryn was a handsome, hard-edged man, one of the youngest captains in the regiment, Tanith-born. Word was, Meryn was a Rawne in waiting, and styled himself on the number two officer's vicious manner. Time, Dalin had been reliably informed, had mellowed Rawne's notoriously sharp edges a little... well, if not mellowed then weathered. All the while, Meryn had been getting sharper, as if he was gunning for the top bastard prize. Dalin would have rather been assigned to any other company than Meryn's, even Rawne's, but there was a matter of duty involved. E Company had a vacancy and, in the opinion of everyone except Dalin Criid himself, only Dalin could fill it.

Meryn came back down the line.

'Advancing by companies!' he shouted, echoing the sing-song of the order as it had come to him. 'E Company, rise and address!'

The company rose, in a line. Behind them, G and L companies got up off their backsides and shook the dust out of their camo-cloaks as their officers called them forwards.

'Company uncase!' Meryn ordered.

Dalin stripped the field casing off his lasrifle. He'd done it a thousand times, drill after drill, and he was no slower than the men either side of him. The case, wound up like a stocking, slipped away in his webbing.

There was noise all around him: officers shouting instructions, and the chinking rattle of troopers rising to advance. Two and a half thousand Imperial Guardsmen made a considerable row just walking.

'Keep it low!' Meryn yelled.

More noise rolled back down the ravine. The command section, supported by A, B and D companies, was already beginning its advance up the gorge towards the gatehouse.

'Stand ready to move, company!' Meryn shouted.

'Are we expecting that much trouble?' Cullwoe whispered. He was next in line, on Dalin's right.

Dalin looked in the direction Cullwoe was nodding. The heavy and support weapon crews of the regiment had begun to set up along the sides of the ravine, covering the gatehouse. Locking brackets clinked and breeches clattered as team-served weapons were bedded and assembled in smart order.

'I guess so,' Dalin replied.

'I'm still hearing yap,' Meryn bellowed, moving back down the line. He approached.

'Was that you, Criid?'

Dalin saw no point in lying. 'Yes, sir. Sorry, sir.'

Meryn glared at him for a moment and then–

oh please, no, don't

–nodded. Dalin hated that. He hated the fact that Meryn cut him slack because of who and what he was.

'Just keep it low, Dalin, all right?' Meryn said, in a painfully avuncular tone.

'Yes, sir.'

Bastard, bastard, bastard, treat me like the rest, treat me like the others, not like some... not like I'm Caffran's fething ghost...

'That's got to be a royal pain in the butt, mister,' whispered Cullwoe sidelong. 'Him doing that, I mean.'

Dalin grinned. It was a standing gag between the two of them. Khet Cullwoe was his buddy. They'd bonded early on, from the moment Dalin got himself plonked into E. Cullwoe was a Belladon, a bony, freckled, red-headed kid only four years older than Dalin. He had a grin you couldn't help but laugh with. Cullwoe was Dalin's sanity. Khet Cullwoe was the only one who seemed to get it, to get the very shitty place Dalin found himself in. 'Royal pain', in all its infinite variation, was their private, standing joke. The key was to make sure your sentence included the words 'royal', 'pain' and 'mister'.

On Dalin's left hand in the line was Neskon, the flame-trooper. He'd heard enough of the Cullwoe/Dalin interplay over the last few weeks to find it amusing. Neskon stank of prom-juice, the smell seeping out of his rind like rank, chemical sweat.

'Ready, boy?' he asked.

Dalin nodded.

The grizzled flame-trooper, his face and neck prematurely aged by the professional heat he deployed, let his tanks gurgle up and then flicked the burner. It coughed, and took with a belch of ignition.

'Happy sounds,' Neskon muttered, adjusting the fuel feed. 'You stand by me, boy. I'll see you right.'

Dalin nodded again. He felt strangely safe and looked after: a young buddy on one side, a friendly fire-ogre on the other, both of them looking out for him, because of who he was: Caffran's son. Criid and Caffran's son, brought up out of the fires of Vervunhive to be a Ghost in his adoptive father's place.

Neskon's flamer burped fuel and stammered. The flame-trooper adjusted it expertly, and brought the burn cone back to a liquid dribble.

'E Company! Make ready to advance!'

Dalin tensed, waiting for the order, the order he felt he had been waiting for all his life.

'Straight silver!' Meryn shouted.

Do it, now. Left hand down to the webbing, slide it out, spin it around, fix it to the rifle lug, *snap-snap*! Ten centimetres of fighting knife, locked in place. The trademark weapon of the Tanith Ghosts.

Dalin Criid felt a boiling surge of pride. His rifle was in his hands. He was a Ghost, and he had just fixed silver, straight silver, in anger for the very first time.

'Advance!' Meryn yelled.

'Come on then if you're coming,' said Neskon.

II

STRAIGHT SILVER DIDN'T apply to everyone. Marksmen weren't expected to fix. As the order ran down the company lines, Hlaine Larkin didn't move. His precious long-las, miraculously recovered from the swamps of Gereon, was already up to his chin and trained.

Larkin was old. With the exception of Zweil and Dorden, he was probably the oldest man in the regiment, and the best shot. Glory fething *be*, was he the best shot.

Larkin was skinny and lean, his face leathery like a tanned hide. He had been through every single battle the Ghosts had fought, and he had outlived many very good friends.

Larkin waited, sniffing the air. His head was clear for once, which made a change. He was a slave to migraines. He shifted uneasily. He still wasn't used to the foot. He'd opted for a prosthetic rather than an augmetic, but it had left him with a limp. A wooden foot brace – nalwood, thank you – Throne knew how the chief had pulled strings to make *that* happen. Larkin believed Gaunt felt guilty about the foot. It had been the right thing to do, of course, Larkin knew that, but he couldn't blame the chief for feeling guilty.

He *had* taken Larkin's foot off with his sword, after all.

Five seventy metres, panning, lock off. Larkin slowly travelled his scope. He ignored the foreground fuzz of advancing bodies, and played his sharp focus across the relief of the fortress walls and window slits instead. He was hunting for movement, hunting for danger with a well-practiced eye, hunting for the trouble Major Rawne had been so fething sure was waiting for them up there.

Larkin's breathing was very slow. Kill-shot at four thousand metres. He'd managed that once or twice. It was as if he had a special, holy angel watching over him, guiding his aim. A special angel. He'd seen her once.

Once was enough.

Larkin always believed he hadn't seen anything true until he'd seen it through his scope. As the Ghosts advanced, he watched to see what was real as much as he watched as a covering marksman.

There they went... Daur, Kolea, Kamori, driving their troops into the gate. Larkin swung his scope. There was Caober. There was Brostin and Varl. There was old father Zweil, up on a rock, using it like a pulpit to bless the advancing Guardsmen as they trudged past.

Larkin smiled. Zweil was a piece of work. Oldest man he'd ever known, and still full of it.

There was Wheln, and Melwid, there was Veddekin, Derin, Harjeon and Burone. There was Tona Criid and Nahum Ludd. There was Lubba, and Dremmond, Posetine and Nessa. There was Bragg and Noa Vadim and Bool. There was Vivvo and Lyse and sexy Jessi Banda. There was–

Wait. Pull up! Go back!

Feth, feth, feth, no–

In the midst of it all, all those moving figures... *Bragg*?

No, just a trick of the eye. A lie of the scope. A blip of the mind. Not Bragg. Some other fether. Not Bragg at all.

Come on, how stupid was *that*?

Larkin adjusted his sweep, his scope clicking.

III

Commissar Viktor Hark heaved his not inconsiderable bulk through the wedged hatch and entered the old gatehouse. Men were gathering inside, waiting, looking around, chattering quietly. Captain Daur stood by the inner hatch, despatching men from the waiting mass a few at a time into the main house.

'Quiet!' Hark said. The chatter slid away like a sheathed blade.

'Next fire-team!' Daur called out, consulting a packet of papers he'd been carrying in his musette bag.

Five Ghosts moved forward from the gathered group, C Company men led by Derin.

'Up, forty metres, take the turn to your left. Reinforce the teams in the gallery and push forward.' Daur gestured up through the inner hatch as he gave out the instructions.

'Got it,' said Derin.

'Vox anything,' said Daur.

Derin nodded. He said 'Yes, sir,' but the look on his face was all about being indoors out of the dusty wind.

'Vox anything, Derin,' said Hark, coming up behind them. 'This is not a safe place until the chief tells us it is.'

Derin and his men suddenly had their game faces on.

'Absolutely, commissar, sir.'

'You so much as hear a mouse fart, you sing it in, Derin,' said Hark. 'Watch your backs and read the signs and don't tell me anything's clear unless you can personally guarantee it on your baby sister's unblemished honour.'

There were times when Derin would have felt bold enough to remind the commissar that any baby sister he might ever have had was long dead in the ashes of Tanith. This was not one of those times.

'Got it, commissar.'

'Off you go.'

Derin's team took off through the inner hatch. Hark could hear their footsteps thudding off the stone floor.

'Next fire-team!' Daur called. More men separated from the main body and moved forward.

'How accurate's the map, d'you suppose?' Hark asked Daur.

Ban Daur wrinkled his nose and looked down at the packet of papers he was holding. Several senior officers, Hark included, had been issued with copies of the objective layouts at Elikon Muster Point.

'Well, they're old and they look like they were done from memory,' said Daur dubiously. 'Or by someone guessing. So…'

Hark nodded. 'My thoughts exactly. We're going to be running into surprises in this place.' He took off his cap and removed his brass goggles. His eyes were sore.

'You all right, commissar?' Daur asked.

'Huh?'

'You look tired, if I may say.'

'I haven't been sleeping well. Get the next team moving. We're backing up.'

Ever more troops were coming in through the outer hatch, and assembling in the gatehouse space. Hark watched and waited as Daur brought up, instructed, and sent on three more teams into the house proper. While he waited, Hark pulled out his own packet of papers, and found the central floor plan. Ban Daur's description of the cartography had been kind.

'I'm keen to locate this place's water supply,' he told Daur.

'The well?'

'Yeah.'

'Bottom of the central level, I think. Supposed to be. I sent Varl's team in to section it.'

Hark nodded. 'I'll go find them. If anyone comes looking for me, that's where I've gone.'

'Yes, commissar.' Daur glanced at the big man. 'Do you want an escort, sir?'

'Do I look like I need an escort, captain?' Hark asked.

'You haven't looked like you needed an escort since the day I met you, sir,' said Daur.

'Good answer, captain. I'll see you later.'

Hark stepped through the inner hatch.

IV

A BROAD HALLWAY led back from the gatehouse's inner hatch into the heart of the house. It had an octagonal shape in cross-section, and the floor was paved. The walls and ceiling were panelled with a dark, glossy material which Hark imagined was either a weathered alloy or some time-discoloured, lacquered hardwood. A sheeny dark brown, at any rate, like polished tortoiseshell or tobacco spit. There was the faintest suggestion of etchings or engravings on the shoulder-level sections of the walls, but nothing that eye or touch could read.

Hark walked up the hallway. Every twenty or so metres, a short flight of stone steps raised the entire tunnel a metre or so, so it was impossible to see clearly the entire length of the passage.

For the first time in weeks, Hark felt genuinely alone. For the first time in *years*, perhaps. There was no sound except for his own footsteps and breathing, and the tiny crackle of his leather coat as he moved. There was no sound of movement or voices, and he was so deep in the rock, the song of the wind outside was gone.

The lights were strange: dull white chemical glow-orbs strung from fat, withered piping that looked like diseased arteries. The light came and went in slow pulse, brighter then softer. Unnerving. The satin-brown walls seemed to soak the light up too, so that the hallway was filled with a warm, white gloom, fuzzy and softly dense, like starlight on a summer's evening.

Hark stopped and watched the slow throb of the lights for a moment. It reminded him of something else. It reminded him of the bone-deep, heavy throb of pain, which was something he'd learned all about during the battle for Herodor five years earlier. Five years. Had it really been that long?

Hark realised he was sweating. Some other memory, unbidden, had just rekindled itself, and not for the first time. It wasn't the memory of the extreme pain he'd suffered at Herodor, nor was it the nagging phantom ache of the arm he had lost there. Yet it was both of those things, too. It was linked to them, sparked off by them. It was like a dream, forgotten on waking, that flashed back later, uninvited and formless. A sense of sadness, of regret and lingering pain. Oh yes, that too.

V

HARK SWALLOWED. HE dearly wished he could pin the sensation down, identify it, perceive it clearly for once. It had been coming to him repeatedly for months, perhaps years, more and more frequently. In his dreams mostly, waking him with a start and a sense of bafflement. Sometimes, it came when he was awake, an itch he couldn't scratch, a taste in the mouth, a taste in the mind. Dorden, the old medicae, had advised Hark that serious physical trauma of the type Hark had suffered often left an indelible residue on the victim. He hadn't just been talking about phantom limb syndrome. He had meant a mental scar, the burned pathway of synapses flared and fused by the moment of agony.

'Some patients report a metallic taste, Viktor,' Dorden had said.

'You've been to the mess hall, then?'

Dorden had smiled. 'A metallic taste. Sometimes a smell, a memory of a smell, from childhood perhaps. Soap. Your mother's preferred fragrance.'

'My mother was an all-comers wrestling champion in the PDF,' Hark had replied. 'She didn't go in for perfume much.'

'You're joking,' Dorden had said.

'Yes.'

'Joke all you like, if that's how you wish to cope. Everyone develops their own strategies, Viktor. You asked me for help.'

'I asked you for your medical opinion, doctor,' Hark had said. Then he had paused. 'Sorry. Sorry, doctor. You were saying?'

'Is it a taste? A smell? A memory?'

'It's... it's a dream, doctor. Just the faded echo of a dream that I cannot actually remember. It's just out of reach. Always just beyond my ability to recall it.'

'Do you dream it? Is it an actual dream, or just the sensation of a dream recalled?'

Hark had paused before replying. 'I dream quite a lot these days, doctor. My sleep is bothered and disturbed, but I cannot say what by.'

'It may pass in time,' Dorden had assured him.

It hadn't. Hark knew it wasn't going to. Sometimes he woke up biting his lip so as not to scream aloud. Sometimes, when he was wide awake, the feeling came to him: an amorphous, incomprehensible wash of softness, like smoke, like soft-filled pillows pressing in against him. But there was always something with a hard edge hidden inside the softness, pushing at him from behind the pillows.

The lights pulsed slowly, as if the house was breathing the slow breath of a sleeper. Exactly like that, *precisely* like that. What was it? What in Throne's name was–

VI

'Hark?'

Hark snapped around, his good hand on the grip of his holstered plasma pistol.

A fire-team led by Ferdy Kolosim had come up behind him. The men hung back as the Belladon officer came forward, his brow furrowed. Hairline sweat had made tracks down through the dust caked to Kolosim's forehead.

'What are you doing, standing there?' Kolosim asked.

'Just, erm, just getting my bearings, Ferdy,' Hark replied. He took out his floor plans and shook them out.

'You sure?' Kolosim was a good man, a worthy addition to the ranks of the First-and-Only.

'Oh yes,' said Hark, forcing a smile onto his lips. 'This place... quite a place.'

'Good to be out of that bloody wind, though, right?'

'I think that's just it, Ferdy,' Hark replied. 'It's suddenly so quiet, I quite lost myself.'

'I know what you mean,' said Kolosim, lowering his rifle and looking up at the tunnel roof. 'This place feels–'

'Don't say it,' Hark advised with a grin.

'I won't. I know what Gaunt ordered. But it does, doesn't it?'

Hark nodded. 'A little bit, yes. You carry on.'

'Sure?'

'Carry on, boys.'

The fire-team moved past him and rattled away up the hall. Hark looked down at his left hand. The skin of his wrist, under the heavy black glove, itched like a bastard. He wanted to tug the glove off and scratch. Except, as he knew very well, there was no skin under that glove, just augmetic bones and sinews, just wires and plasteks and solenoids.

Hark turned, trying to ignore it, and walked on.

VII

THE LONG HALLWAY led up into the base chamber of the house. Side galleries had opened to left and right as he walked the length of the hallway;

long, drafty tunnels leading out into the base-level casemates and fortifications. The wind blew down them, thready and weak, forced in through distant apertures and slits. He could smell dust.

Hark reached a wide flight of steps. The hallway broadened out into a vestibule. The floor was no longer paved; it was tiled in the same sheened brown substance that clad the walls. It clacked under his boots, soft and gleaming, like polished leather. The steps went up under a huge wooden arch riddled with worm holes. The arch had been ornately carved, like the screen of a templum. Interlocking figures twisted into scrolling patterns, all sanded down by time until they had been rendered meaningless.

The base chamber was a circular stone vault fifty metres wide and four floors deep. A vast wooden screw-stair ran up from its centre into the upper levels of the house. At the ground floor level, and at each landing turn, hallways let out into the side sections of the house. Sentries had been placed on all the landings. The lights in the base chamber were hung from ceiling pipes, slack and heavy like eyeballs strung from optic nerves. They pulsed too: slowly, oh so slowly.

The wind was in the base chamber, gusting around from the doorways standing open on each level. It gave the air a dry, powdery smell.

'Where's that coming from?' Hark asked.

'There's a... gn... gn... shutter open somewhere, sir,' the trooper guarding the bottom of the staircase replied. Hark knew the voice and the messed-up face.

'A shutter, Trooper Merrt?'

Merrt nodded. He was cautious of the commissar. Hark had slammed Merrt down to RIP duties en route from Ancreon Sextus, though Merrt didn't hold it against him. Merrt knew he'd deserved it. As a result, Merrt had seen the Gereon liberation offensive from the sharpest end.

Rhen Merrt had once been a marksman, second only to Mad Larkin in skill. A headshot on Monthax, years before, had ended that speciality. Merrt was now the proud owner of an ugly augmetic jaw that made him look like a gruesome collision between a servitor and a human skull. The damage had ruined his aim, and he'd suffered for it. He was back at the bottom of the heap, his speciality a distant regret.

'A gn... gn... shutter, yes, sir,' Merrt said. He had trouble articulating his clumsy artificial jaw most of the time. His speech was slow and mannered.

Hark nodded. 'Well, we'll have to see to that. If any part of this fortress is open enough to let the wind blow through, Throne only knows what else it might let in.'

Merrt nodded. A couple more fire-teams clattered into the base chamber and headed off up the staircase.

'By the way, it's good to see you back, Merrt,' Hark said quietly.

'Sir?'

'This is where you belong. In the First. Try not to feth it up for yourself again.'

'I'm a gn... gn... changed man, commissar.'

'Glad to hear it. I'm heading for the well.'

'Back hatch, sir,' Merrt replied, jerking a thumb over his shoulder.

Hark walked around behind the massive staircase. There was a hole on the floor there, a brass hatch that had been levered open. Hark stood at the lip and peered down.

Darkness.

Packs of Guard equipment had been dumped on the deck beside the hatch. Hark went over and helped himself to a lamp-pack. He switched it on. The beam was hot and yellow, in strong contrast to the milky radiance of the house lights.

He went back to the hatch and played the light down. There was the rickety iron staircase. Hark lowered himself gently onto it.

VIII

'If you flick 'em, they get brighter,' Trooper Twenzet remarked, flicking one of the wall-hung lights.

'Don't do that,' said Varl.

'Why not?'

'Because... I'll shoot you,' said Varl.

'Fair enough,' replied Twenzet.

The chamber was clammy and cold. It was the lowest part of the house, deep under the crust, or so the plans said. Varl had very little faith in the plans.

He was leading a fire-team of six men from B Company, Rawne's own boys: Brostin, Laydly, Twenzet (he of the lamp flicking), Gonlevy, LaHurf and Cant. Orders, straight from Gaunt in person, had been to find and secure the objective's water supply.

Ceglan Varl was old-school Tanith, one of the first of the few. He was popular, because he was a joker and a trickster, and unpopular, funnily enough, for precisely the same reasons. Varl was lean and taut, like a pulled rope. The men with him were mostly Belladon newcomers, except Brostin, the flame-trooper, who was old-school Tanith too, very old-school.

Brostin and Varl had done Gereon together, the first time round. They'd known tough, and had spat right back in its eye.

The orders had come with plans, flimsy things on see-through paper, which had led them down to what Brostin had delighted in describing as the 'butt-hole end' of the house.

Deep down, rock-cut, clammy-deep. Dew perspired off the rough, lime-washed walls. A shaky iron staircase had led them down into this pit.

They moved around, swinging their lamp-packs back and forth like swords of light in the gloom. The house lamps down in the well room were very feeble.

The chamber was roughly oval, and cut out of the deep rock. The floor was boarded with thick, varnished planks. A big cast iron tub with a brass lid stood in the centre of the chamber. A complex system of chains ran from the lid mechanism up to pulleys and gears in the roof space.

'So that's the well,' said Varl, aiming his lamp at it.

'Well, well, well,' said Twenzet.

'I do the jokes,' snapped Varl.

'Yeah, why is that?' asked Laydly.

'Because… I'll shoot you,' said Varl.

'Once again, fair enough,' replied Twenzet.

'Get it open,' Varl ordered.

Gonlevy and Cant began to wind on the levers on top of the lid.

'It won't budge, sarge,' said Cant.

'Why not?'

Cant paused. He knew full well what was coming.

'I… don't seem to be able to move the levers, sarge.'

'Because?' Varl asked.

Cant mumbled something.

'We can't hear you,' said Varl.

'Because I can't, sarge,' Cant said.

'Oh, you can't can you, Cant?' Varl said. All of them broke up in fits of laughter, again.

'Yeah, yeah,' said Cant, who'd long ago lost sight of the funny side of the joke. 'Just bloody help us with–'

'Tweenzy's right,' said Brostin, from across the dank chamber.

'Please don't call me that,' said Twenzet. 'I did ask you.'

'Tweenzy's on the money, Varl,' Brostin insisted.

Varl switched his beam over to pick out Brostin. Brostin was hunched down, flicking one of the wall lights with a sturdy index finger.

'They do get brighter when you flick 'em,' Brostin smiled.

'Stop it!' Varl snarled. 'All of you! We're meant to be–'

'Vaguely capable?'

They all froze. Commissar Hark clumped down the staircase into the chamber.

'Sir,' said Varl.

'This the well, Varl?'

'It is, sir.'

'Got it open? Secure?'

'Not yet, sir, sorry.'

'Open it up.'

'I was just saying how the levers was stiff, commissar,' Cant began. 'We can't–'

Viktor Hark put out his left hand. His augmetic fingers closed like a vice around the winding handle.

'Can't Cant, or won't?' Hark snorted.

'Oh, not you too,' moaned Cant.

Hark's arm turned. With a creaking, shrieking complaint, the gears turned and the lid began to open. Chains clattered in the darkness above them. A foul, dry stench oozed out of the well-head.

'Was that you, Brostin?' Varl asked.

'Not this time,' Brostin groaned, fingers pinching his nose shut.

Varl, Hark and Brostin went to the side of the well and looked down. Varl shone his lamp. The beam picked up moss and treacly black lichen. The drain-stench was unbearable.

Brostin took out a spare seal ring, a small knurled brass object, and tossed it down the well.

'One, Throne of Terra… Two, Throne of Terra… Three, Throne of Terra…' Hark began.

He got to sixteen, Throne of Terra. There was no plunk, no splash, just a dry, jingling series of impacts as the ring skittered away.

Hark looked at Varl. 'You see, this,' he said, 'this is what I was afraid of.'

Day seven (out of Elikon M.P.). Sunrise at four plus nineteen, wind storm all night. Got last of regiment in just before midnight local. No sleep. Squads working to secure objective. Place is a maze. Bears ~~litl~~ little or no resemblance to schematics. Keep finding new chambers, new halls. K. found whole new wing running east that wasn't on any version of charts.

Objective feels curiously dead and alive, both at the same time. Dry, empty, but power still on, and some signs of habitation. Major problem – no water supply despite promise. Well dry. Trying to contact Elikon for assist. G. annoyed. Local water supply essential if we are to stay on station here. Rumour of secondary well, which can't be found. Not only do our schematics not agree with ~~actal~~ actual layout of place, have discovered our charts don't even agree with each other. Will send official rebuke to office of tactics for this error.

I cannot shake the feeling that there's a ~~dream trying to wanting to something in my head that~~

Medics report high incidence of eye infection amongst troops, due to dust.

– Field journal, V.H. fifth month, 778.

FOUR
Written in Dust

I

THERE WERE STRANGE echoes in Hinzerhaus, echoes that took a while to get used to. Alone in one chamber, a man might hear the footsteps of a comrade two floors up and a hundred metres distant. Sound carried.

If the wind ever gets in here, Baskevyl thought, what a song it will sing.

He was moving down through the house in search of the power room. At every turn or junction, he consulted a scrap of paper. Mkoll had written out directions to the power room for him. The charts couldn't be trusted. Daur and Rawne had gone nose to nose the night before over the location of a room marked as the 'lesser hall'. It had nearly got ugly – Baskevyl was sure Daur had been on the verge of throwing a punch – until Gaunt pointed out that, for one thing, Daur's chart and Rawne's chart were appreciably different and, for another, they were having their argument *in* the lesser hall.

Looking back on it, Baskevyl reflected that perhaps the gravest cause for concern during the argument had been Daur's behaviour. Ban Daur, clean-cut and Throne-fearing, was a model officer, the last person you'd ever expect to see swinging for a senior man.

It's because we're spooked, every man jack. Some admit it, some don't, but we're all spooked by this bad rock and this labyrinth house. There's something in the air here, some–

dry skulls in a dusty valley

–thing palpable, an oozing tension.

Whatever it was, it wasn't in the water because there wasn't any. The well was dead. They were living off their own bottles, on quarter rations. Ludd had been detailed to mark all water bottles with a piece of chalk, and write up any man drinking too much. As a result, everybody *loved* Nahum Ludd.

Baskevyl's mouth tasted as dry as a storm coat's pocket lining, and his tongue felt like a scrap of webbing. He'd snatched two hours' sleep since they'd entered the house, and all one hundred and twenty minutes of it had been a dream about a fountain, gushing pure, bright liquid.

Baskevyl checked his crumpled paper. It told him to follow the next staircase down, and he obeyed. The walls were panelled in a dark, glossy material that had been overlaid in turn by a light coating of pale dust. The white wall lights pulsed slowly.

He heard footsteps approaching, and paused to see who was coming down the stairs behind him. No one appeared. It was just another echo, relayed through the warren of halls. During his ten-minute walk from the main staircase, he'd heard all manner of things: footsteps, voices, the bump and rattle of crates being stowed. Once, he'd heard a snatch of distinct conversation, three men complaining about the water rationing. The voices had come and gone, as if the men had been walking right past him.

When he arrived at the next landing, he found two troopers standing watch, Tokar and Garond from J Company. They both visibly jumped when he walked into view, then saluted with nervous laughs.

'On edge?' he asked.

'We thought you were another echo,' said Garond.

'We keep hearing noises, then there's no one there,' said Tokar. 'Feth, you gave us a scare.'

'My apologies,' said Baskevyl. 'The power room?'

'Down there, sir,' Garond said, indicating the narrow staircase behind him.

Baskevyl nodded. 'Anything to report? Apart from noises?'

Tokar and Garond shook their heads. Baskevyl nodded again, and took a quick look around the landing space. 'What about that?' he asked.

'What, sir?' asked Tokar.

Baskevyl pointed at the wall opposite. 'That.'

'I don't see anything,' Tokar began.

'In the dust,' Baskevyl insisted.

The troopers squinted.

'Oh!' said Garond suddenly. 'It's been drawn there! Gak, I didn't see that. Did you see that, Tokar?'

'First time I've noticed it.'

'Did either of you draw it?' asked Baskevyl.

'No,' they both answered together.

He could see they hadn't. It had been drawn in the dust on the satin-brown wall panel, but so long ago the lines themselves had been covered in dust. It was just a ghost image, a human face, neither specifically male nor female, open-mouthed. There were no eyes. It had been drawn in the dust with slow, lazy finger strokes. Somehow, Baskevyl felt certain they had been slow and lazy.

'What the gak is it?' Garond asked.

Baskevyl stared at the face. It was unsettling. 'I don't know.'

'Why,' Tokar began, 'why didn't we notice it before? We've been standing here two hours.'

'I don't know,' Baskevyl repeated. He took a deep breath. 'Wash it off.'

'With what, sir?' asked Garond.

'Spit?' Tokar suggested.

'Wipe it off, then. Use your capes.'

The troopers moved forward to oblige, scooping up handfuls of their camo-capes.

Baskevyl noticed how they hesitated. Neither one wanted to be the first to touch it.

II

'Not in here, please,' said Dorden as he entered the high-ceilinged room.

Gaunt paused in the act of emptying an appreciable quantity of dust out of his boot onto the floor.

'Why not? Is there a medical reason?'

'If this is going to be the field station, then I have to keep it swept of dust,' Dorden tutted, putting down an armful of medical cartons.

'The field station?' Gaunt asked.

'Yes,' said Dorden.

When Gaunt didn't reply, Dorden looked at him. He saw Gaunt's sarcastically arched eyebrows. He saw the old stuffed leather chair Gaunt was sitting in, the ancient desk behind him, the stacks of kit bags and munition boxes.

'Not the field station, then?' he asked.

'My office, I think you'll find.'

'Ah.'

'The field station is three chambers along, on the right.'

Dorden shook his head. 'These fething maps. Are they of use to any man?'

Gaunt shook his head. 'Not any I've met.' With some satisfaction, he poured the dust out of his boot. It drizzled out in a long, smoking shower.

Dorden looked around. The room was dark and tall, fast in the heart of the house. Dirty outlines on the sheened brown walls showed where paintings had once hung. It had been impressive once, a fine state-room. Now it seemed like a cave, lit by the dim glow of the lamps.

With a slight start, Dorden realised they weren't alone. There was a third person in the room. Eszrah ap Niht was sitting in one corner, patiently reading an old book by the light of the wall lamp he had huddled up to. His fingertip was moving under the text, sticking at difficult words.

The Nihtgane had developed quite a thirst for knowledge and Gaunt had taught him his letters well. However, no one had yet convinced Eszrah that wearing sunshades indoors wasn't a good idea.

'What are you reading there, Eszrah?' Dorden called out. The old doctor still hadn't quite got the trick of pronouncing Eszrah's name.

Eszrah looked up from his book. 'Yt is ancallyd *The Mirror of Smoke*,' he replied.

'Ah,' said Dorden. He glanced at Gaunt, who was busy evacuating grit from his other boot. 'One of your favourites.'

Gaunt nodded. 'Yes, it is.'

'What's that phrase, that famous phrase? "By dying, we finish our service to the Emperor?" Or something?'

'I think you mean "Only in death, does duty end",' said Gaunt. The colonel-commissar was staring down at his bootless feet. His filthy toes poked out of the holes in his socks. He wiggled them.

'That's it,' said Dorden.

'Not original to the author, of course,' said Gaunt, preoccupied with his own feet. 'An old proverb.'

Dorden nodded. 'And rather disheartening.'

Gaunt looked up at him. 'Disheartening? Don't you intend to die in the service of the God-Emperor? Is there something you'd like to tell your commissar, Tolin?'

Dorden chuckled. 'Do you know how old I am, Ibram?'

Gaunt shrugged.

'Well,' said Dorden, 'let's just say if I'd chosen to muster out at Guard retirement age, as per the edicts, I'd have been a man of leisure for thirteen years now.'

'Feth? Really?'

Tolin Dorden smiled. 'Age-muster is, of course, voluntary. Besides, where would I go?'

Gaunt didn't answer.

'You know how I see myself ending my days?' asked Dorden. 'As a local doctor. A local doctor, serving some backwater community on a colony world. That'd be all right with me. The day comes I get too old, too slow to keep up with the pace of the Tanith First, that's where I want to end up. Leave me somewhere, would you? Somewhere I can treat sprains and flu and ague, and the odd broken bone or colicky newborn. Somewhere quiet. Will you do that for me, when the day comes?'

'You'll be with us forever,' retorted Gaunt.

'That's what I'm afraid of.'

Gaunt stared at him. 'Afraid?'

Dorden sighed. 'How much longer, Ibram? How many more years, how many more battles? We all die sometime. I saw my world die, and now I go from war to war, seeing out the last of my people, one by one. I don't want to be the last man of Tanith, Ibram, scrubbing blood off the surgery table as they wheel out the second to last man of Tanith in a body bag.'

'It wouldn't go like that–' Gaunt began.

'No, it wouldn't,' Dorden agreed. 'One day, I'll just get too old and doddery and you'll have to remove me from service.'

'Hardly. Look at Zweil.'

Dorden grinned. 'If that old fool makes a mistake, people don't die.'

Gaunt got to his feet. 'I'll find you that colony world, time comes,' he said. 'That's a promise. Maybe it'll even be the world the Tanith get to settle. Our reward for service.'

'Ibram, do you honestly believe that's ever going to happen?'

Gaunt was silent for a long time. 'No,' he said finally.

Warmaster Slaydo had promised Gaunt the settlement rights of the first world he won, as a reward after Balhaut. Gaunt had always intended to share that reward with the homeless Tanith. 'Somehow, I doubt Macaroth will honour a rash promise his predecessor made,' Gaunt said quietly.

'If he does intend to,' said Dorden, 'then just make sure we don't win here. The Tanith would lynch you if you won them this bad rock.'

Dorden looked up at the vacant places on the walls.

'I wonder what hung here,' he said.

'Do you?' Gaunt replied. 'All I seem to wonder is... who took them down?'

'What about you?' Dorden asked.

'Me? What about me?'

'How do you see your service ending?'

Gaunt sighed and sat down again. 'Tolin, we both know how my service is going to end, sooner or later.'

He gazed down at his socks. 'Do you have a needle and thread I could borrow? Of course you do.'

'You can darn, can you?' asked Dorden with a slight smile.

'I can learn to darn. This is unseemly for a man of my rank.'

'Don't you have spare socks?'

'These are my spare socks.'

'Dickerson.'

'What?'

'Dickerson, tall Belladon in Arcuda's mob. I hear he darns socks for a few coins. He's good. Used to be a seamster before the Guard. He'll probably do yours for free.'

'Thanks for the tip.'

Eszrah suddenly rose, his reynbow up and aimed. Gaunt and Dorden looked around.

Rawne entered.

'It's just Rawne,' Gaunt told Eszrah. The partisan didn't lower his bow.

'What's up?' Gaunt asked Rawne.

'Criid reckons she's found something,' Rawne said.

III

THE WARM STINK of energy greeted Baskevyl as he entered the power room.

The chamber was long and rectangular, with sloping ceilings. It was dominated by the bulk of the power hub, an iron kettle the size of a drop-pod. Power feeds ran off the kettle up into a broad roof socket, and grilled slits in the kettle's sides throbbed with a slow glow that matched the gentle rhythm of the house lighting. Baskevyl could feel the pulsing warmth. It made no sound. Whatever generative reaction was going on inside, it was a curiously silent one.

The fire-team assigned to guard the power room had been playing cards in a huddle at the foot of the entry steps. They stood when he came up, but he waved them back to their game with a smile.

'How are things here?' he asked Captain Domor.

Shoggy Domor was in charge of the fire-team detail. He walked over to the kettle with Baskevyl as the troopers resumed their quiet game. His bulbous augmetic eyes whirred quietly as they sharpened focus on the major.

'I can't really say, sir.'

'Meaning?'

'I don't know what this is. It's just running. It's been running for a long, long time, and it continues to run. I have no idea what the operating process is.'

'No idea?' Baskevyl frowned. If anyone in the Ghosts knew engineering systems, it was Shoggy.

'I think it's chemical, but I'm not sure.' Domor nodded at the pulsing, glowing kettle in front of them. 'I doubt the chief would thank me if I tried opening it up to find out.'

'There's no feed? No fuel supply?' Baskevyl asked.

'None, sir.'

'We need a tech out here, a tech-adept,' Baskevyl muttered to himself. He pressed his hands against the fat belly of the kettle, then took them away. The iron had throbbed under his touch, as if it was alive.

He looked around at Domor. 'Look, just keep watch on it, as per orders. We may not know how it works, but at least it does, and it's giving us lights. I'll get a detail down here to relieve you in... shall we say three hours?'

Domor nodded. 'What about the, er, noises, sir?'

'You too, eh?' asked Baskevyl. 'I think this place has some weird acoustic qualities. Sound carries. Just try not to let it spook you.'

Domor seemed less than convinced.

'What?' Baskevyl asked.

Domor tilted his head to indicate they should take a walk. Casually, they skirted around the throbbing kettle together and put its bulk between them and the huddle of troopers by the steps. Domor dropped his voice so his boys wouldn't hear.

'Footsteps and voices, right?' he asked softly.

'I've heard both. Like I said, I think sound ca–'

'What about the other noise?' asked Domor.

'What other noise?'

Domor shrugged. 'It comes and goes. A sort of grinding, scraping sound.'

'I haven't heard anything like that,' said Baskevyl.

'Come with me,' said Domor quietly. He stepped aside and called out to his troop. 'Chiria? You're in charge. I'm going to show Major B. the workshops.'

'Right you are, Shoggy,' she called back.

There was a door in the rear wall of the power room. Domor drew back the rusted bolts. He led Baskevyl into a series of four, small stone rooms that had once been workshops. The air within was much colder than it had been in the main hub room. It was chilly and stale, like an old pantry. Old wooden benches lined the walls, their surfaces worn. Wall racks had once held tools, but the tools had long gone. The sooty outlines of saws, pliers and wrenches hung under the old pegs.

Baskevyl peered along the row of workshop rooms. They were linked by stone arches. Domor pulled the door shut behind them.

'Listen,' he said.

'I don't hear anything,' replied Baskevyl.

'Listen,' Domor insisted.

IV

GAUNT FOLLOWED RAWNE up a long, rickety wooden staircase into the very summit of the house. They came up into a room shaped like a belfry: a circular, domed chamber into which the wind shrilled through partially open metal shutters. The wind whined like–

dry skulls in a dusty valley

–a scolded dog.

'Can't we close them?' Gaunt asked, raising his voice above the sound.

'No,' Criid called back. 'The mechanisms are jammed.'

Gaunt looked around. The base of the roof dome had eight large shutters around its circumference, all of them operated by brass winders. Years of dust had choked the gears. The shutters were frozen in various positions, like the half-closed eyelids of dying men. Eddies and scoots of dust billowed in around the sills and covered the floor like powdered snow.

'What is this?' Gaunt called.

'Criid called it a windcote,' Rawne cried back. 'Look.'

The centre of the chamber was dominated by a huge perch: a rusted metal tree of fat iron rods where things had once roosted. There was bird lime on the floor, and the remains of food baskets.

'I think they kept birds here, sir,' Criid called out, holding her cloak hem up over her mouth and nose. 'Messenger birds. You know, for flying messages.'

'I grasp the concept,' said Gaunt. He looked at the size of the shutters, imagining them wound back and fully open. 'Big birds,' he muttered.

He went over to the nearest shutter and bent down, trying to peer out of the wedged open slit. Windborne dust gusted into his face.

Coughing, he pulled back. 'This'd make a great look out, if it wasn't for that fething wind.'

Rawne nodded. He'd thought the same thing.

'That wasn't what I wanted you to see,' Criid called out to them.

'Then what?'

She pointed upwards. Something was hanging from the uppermost branch of the roosting perch.

'That,' shouted Criid.

It was a black iron face mask, swinging gently by its head straps in the swirling wind. The mask had a hooked nose and a snarling expression.

It was a Blood Pact grotesk.

Gaunt said something.

'What?' Rawne asked, against the scream of the wind.

'I said there's that trouble you were on about,' said Gaunt.

V

BASKEVYL TURNED IN a small slow circle, gazing up at the ceiling of the workshop.

'You heard that, right?' Domor whispered.

Baskevyl nodded. His mouth was dry, and it wasn't entirely due to the short-rationed water. He'd heard the noise quite clearly, a grinding scrape, just like Shoggy Domor had described. It had sounded like... well Baskevyl wasn't sure he could honestly say *what* it had sounded like, but the moment he'd heard it, an image had filled his mind, an image he hadn't really wanted. It was the image of something vast and clammy, snake-like, all damp bone and glistening tissue, like a gigantic spinal chord, scraping and slithering along some deep, rough, rock-cut tunnel far below them, like a daemon-worm in the earth.

Lucien Wilder, in days long gone, had always said Baskevyl had been born with an imagination he'd have been better off without.

'What does it sound like to you?' asked Domor quietly.

Baskevyl didn't reply. Urgently, he tried to banish the image from his head. He walked under the stone arch into the next workshop, then into the next, until he was standing in the end chamber. The walls were panelled, like everywhere else, in that satin brown material.

The noise came again. Gnarled vertebrae sleeved in wet, grey sinew, dragged across ragged stone. It slipped along rapidly, fluidly, like a desert snake. Baskevyl could hear loose pebbles and grit skittering out in its wake.

There was cold sweat on his back. The noise died away.

'Well?' Domor asked.

'Vermin?' asked Baskevyl. Domor stared at him. His augmetic eyes whirred and clicked, as if widening in scorn.

'Vermin?' he replied. 'Have you seen any vermin?'

Baskevyl shook his head.

'The place is dry and dead,' said Domor. 'There's no vermin here, no insects, no scraps of food. If there were ever any vermin here, Major B, they've long since given up on the place.'

He was right. Baskevyl felt stupid for even suggesting it. There was no point trying to fob off smart men like Shoggy Domor with patent lies.

He heard the noise again, briefly, a wriggling scratch that faded away almost instantaneously. Baskevyl stepped towards the wall, and reached out. The satin brown panelling felt warm and organic to his touch. He tapped at it, at first hearing the dead reply of the stone wall behind it.

Then, as he moved his hand along, he got a hollow noise.

He glanced back at Domor, who was watching him.

'There's nothing behind this panel,' he said.

'What?'

'There's nothing behind this panel. Listen.'

He tapped again. A hollow dullness. 'Get your team in here,' Baskevyl began. The noise came back again. Baskevyl stiffened. Throne, but he could not help visualising the awful, clammy spine-thing, snaking through the dark.

'Shoggy, would y–' he started to say.

He heard another sound suddenly: a brief, leaden *pop*, like someone cracking a knuckle. How odd. Baskevyl looked up and down, studying the sheened brown patina of the wall panel.

There was a hole in the wall at chest height just to his right, a small hole, half a centimetre in diameter, that had certainly not been there before. The edges of the hole were smouldering slightly.

'Shoggy?' he said, and then registered a sudden, sharp sensation of pain. He glanced down at his right arm. A flesh wound was scorched right across the outside of his upper arm. It had burned through his jacket and shirt, and into the skin beneath, leaving a gouge of cooked, black blood.

'Oh shit!' he announced, stepping backwards. 'Shoggy! I think I've just been shot.'

He turned around, slightly head-sick with shock. The las-round had come clean through the wall, sliced across the side of his right arm, and...

Domor was leaning back against the workbench behind them in a slightly awkward pose. He was staring at Baskevyl with his big, artificial eyes, which whirred and turned, unable to focus. He was trying to say something, but all he was managing to do was aspirate blood.

There was a black, bloody puncture in the middle of his chest.

'Oh, Throne. Shoggy?' Baskevyl cried, and stumbled towards him.

Domor, lolling sideways, finally managed to find a word and speak it. The word was, 'down.' It came out of his lips in a ghastly mist of blood.

Baskevyl grabbed Domor and dragged him over onto the workshop floor.

A second later, more holes began to appear in the satin brown panel: two, three, a dozen, twenty, forty.

On the other side of the wall panel, someone had just opened up with a las-weapon on full auto.

Elikon M.P., Elikon M.P., this is Nalwood, this is Nalwood. Hostile contact! Repeat hostile contact at this time!

Nalwood out. (transmission ends)

- Transcript of vox message, fifth month, 778.

FIVE
Vermin

I

IT SUDDENLY GOT very noisy indeed in the tiny end workshop. Bright daggers of las-fire punched through the wall panel, zipped across the shop and hammered into the opposite wall, blowing apart the empty racks and obliterating forever the smudged outlines of hanging tools.

Baskevyl tried to drag Domor in under the heavy workbench. He fumbled for his laspistol. His arm hurt like fire. Domor had gone limp, dead limp.

'Shoggy!' Baskevyl yelled.

More shots tore through the wall, shredding holes through the rims of previous holes, filling the close air with the stink of las-fire and singed fibres. Baskevyl started shooting back, one-handed, his other arm pulling at Domor's dead-weight. He wondered if he should risk reaching for Domor's lasrifle, which was lying nearby on the floor. Bad idea, he decided. He fired again, making his own holes in the wall.

'Contact! Contact! Hostiles!' he yelled into his microbead. The interlink went crazy, voices gabbling and yelling over one another.

The outer door to the workshops burst open and Domor's fire-team scrambled in, led by the redoubtable Corporal Chiria. The old battle scars across her face had long ago put paid to any looks she'd ever been proud of, but now she looked especially unlovely. Surprise and alarm, in equal amounts, had twisted her damaged features into a pink grimace.

'What the feth–?' she began.

'Help me!' Baskevyl yelled at her. He was intending for her to come and help him drag Domor out of the way.

Chiria had other ideas. She swung her lasrifle up to her shoulder and hosed the punctured wall, pricking the gloom with barbs of full-auto light.

'Get Shoggy up. Drag him back!' she yelled as she lit off. Domor was dead, she knew that much. One glimpse had been all she'd needed to know. A round to the body, heart shot.

Those bastards would pay.

Ezlan was beside her, Nehn and Brennan too. Their four lasrifles blasted furiously into the splintered panelling. They made a dull, echoing crack, like a length of cane being smacked repeatedly against a stone floor.

'Hold it, hold it! Hold fire!' Chiria yelled.

The Ghosts around her stopped shooting.

'What?' Nehn asked.

'Wait...' said Chiria.

Nothing, no return of fire, just a gusty moan of wind weeping through the hundreds of holes in the smoking, shot-up wall panel.

'Help me with him,' Baskevyl said, trying to get up and pull Domor clear. Nehn and Chiria hurried over. Ezlan and Brennan kept their weapons aimed at the perforated wall.

Baskevyl's hands were slick with Domor's blood. He'd been trying to compress the wound.

'Guard this,' he told Chiria. 'Anything stirs, you nail it. I'll carry Shoggy–'

'*You* guard this,' said Chiria, bluntly. 'I'll carry Shoggy. Nehn, get his feet.'

She handed her lasrifle to Baskevyl. He didn't argue. Sometimes, Major Baskevyl was wise enough to recognise, when it came to loyalty and bonding, orders sat better if they ran against the chain of command. It was right Chiria should carry Shoggy Domor.

Moving fast, Chiria and Nehn carted Domor's limp body out of the workshop. Baskevyl adjusted Chiria's weapon, and checked the clip. The air was full of dust, scorched and burned dust. The wall was a cratered mess of holes, like the backboard at the end of a practice range.

Baskevyl looked at Ezlan and Brennan.

'Either of you got a grenade? A tube-charge, maybe?'

'Why?' asked Ezlan nervously.

'Just asking,' said Baskevyl.

II

'HERE. OVER HERE. Set him down!' cried Ana Curth.

She'd been drawn out of the field station by sounds of commotion in time to see Chiria and Nehn struggle into the base chamber with what appeared to be the corpse of Shoggy Domor. Chiria and Nehn laid Domor down on the decking by the stairs, as instructed. Curth knelt over him.

'What happened?' she demanded as she stripped Domor's shirt and tunic off with scissors from her field satchel.

'Hostile contact,' replied Chiria, leaning on the banister and panting hard. She'd carried her captain's body a considerable way at speed. She could barely talk.

'Make sense please,' Curth snapped. 'From the top, corporal.'

'They were in the walls,' Chiria replied, gasping, her voice hoarse. 'In the walls like vermin.' She looked at Curth. 'He's dead, isn't he?'

Curth was too busy to answer. In the absence of a bone saw, she'd reached up and helped herself to Nehn's warknife. Nehn hadn't had time to object. He winced at the sight of Curth carving into Domor with his blade. Curth's hands were slippery with blood. There was an ugly crack as she sectioned the sternum. 'Chayker! Lesp! Where are you?' she shouted. 'We're going to have to get him into the field station right now!'

Chayker and Lesp, the orderlies, ran into the base chamber, lugging a stretcher and a surgical kit. Dorden materialised behind them, puzzled and half asleep.

'What's going on?' Dorden asked, groggily. He woke up very quickly. 'Sacred feth, is that Shoggy?'

'Upper torso puncture,' replied Curth as she worked frantically, tossing aside Nehn's warknife and trying to insert rib-spreaders from the kit Lesp had passed to her. 'Swabs! Forget moving him. I need swabs. Lots more of them!' she called out.

Dorden elbowed his way in beside Curth and sank to his knees.

'Oh, that's a mess...'

'You can clamp that shut with your fingers or you can get the feth out of my way!' Curth barked at him as she hastily prepped the tissue weaver from the kit.

Dorden snapped on a glove, reached in and clamped. 'There's a secondary hole in the aorta,' he began, peering down.

'Thank you for stating the obvious,' Curth replied, ripping the backing-pack off a field swab. 'These aren't going to be enough!' She looked up. 'I said I need more! More! Counterseptic too!'

Lesp took off towards the field station.

'Losing rhythm,' Dorden muttered.

'I've nearly got it!' spat Curth, trying to aim the tissue weaver.

'Auto patch it there. There, woman!' Dorden barked.

'Move your fingers, then!' Curth leaned into the bloody cavity with the buzzing surgical tool.

Calmly holding Domor's barely beating heart together as Curth heat-bonded its punctures shut, Dorden looked up at Chiria.

'How did this happen?'

'We got some hostile contact,' Chiria said.

'Where?' asked a dry voice from behind them.

Chiria looked around. Larkin limped into the base chamber towards them, accompanied by Raess, Nessa Bourah and Jessi Banda. All four of them had their long-las sniper weapons hefted over their shoulders. The marksmen had been touring the house, sniffing for decent vantage points or, better still, targets.

'Under the power room,' Chiria said.

Larkin took his long-las off his shoulder and armed it. He glanced at his fellow marksmen. 'Let's go shoot something, shall we?'

His fellow marksmen nodded.

Larkin glanced over at Curth. For a fleeting moment, she looked up from her bloody work and noticed his stare. Hlaine Larkin had believed that his precious sniper rifle had been lost forever during the grim trials of the Gereon mission. But the previous year, he'd been part of the extraction team that had finally rescued Curth from the Gereon Untill. To his amazement and delight, he had discovered that she had been keeping his beloved long-las safe for him all the while, in the hope of his eventual return.

Larkin gave her a brief nod that said he was about to make her thoughtful custody of the antique piece worthwhile.

Footsteps clattered down the staircase from above. Gaunt, followed by Rawne, Criid and a bunch of Criid's P Company, hurtled down into the base chamber, taking the steps two at a time.

'Report!' Gaunt commanded.

Dorden nodded down at the sprawled body of Shoggy Domor. 'We've been hit,' he said.

Gaunt stared at Domor's spread-eagled form. He could actually see the man's heart, beating like a red leather pump as Dorden and Curth worked on him.

'Will he live?' he asked.

'You better fething believe it,' replied Curth. 'Suture gun. Now, Chayker!'

Gaunt took a deep breath. 'Someone tell me exactly what's happened.'

'Hostile contact in the workshops under the power room, sir,' Chiria said, stepping forwards. 'Major Baskevyl is on site.'

'Show us! Go!' ordered Gaunt. Rawne, Criid, and Criid's men were already moving.

Gaunt hesitated and looked back at Curth. She'd never really regained the body mass she'd lost during her stay on Gereon. She was stick-thin frail, and her cheek bones stood out.

'Are you all right?' Gaunt asked.

'I'm not the one who was shot,' she told him, acidly, too busy to look up.

Gaunt paused, nodded, and then turned to run after Rawne and Criid.

III

CHIRIA LED THE way. Her hands were stained with her company officer's blood.

'The power room,' she repeated. 'Come on!'

'Wait! Wait!' Larkin shouted.

They all came to a halt, silent, listening.

'What?' asked Gaunt.

'Larks?' Rawne pressed.

Larkin shook his head, holding up a finger for silence.

Then they heard it: the distant crack-ping of las-fire.

'That's not the power room,' said Larkin. 'That's coming from somewhere above us.'

VI

THE LONG, DRAFTY hallway had seemed empty.

It ran as far as the eye could see: a broad, brown-panelled passageway, its roof interrupted by the domes of fortification cloches spaced at regular intervals.

The E Company fire-team was high up in the house, right under the spine of the mountain ridge, where the wind wheezed along cold, dormant hallways. Each cloche turret they came to was a dome of dead iron. The intricate manual winders on the walls were seized with grit and age. No amount of effort could induce them to turn and open the shutters overhead.

The fire-team had paused under each cloche dome in turn, gazing up at the jammed shutters, playing their lamps around, exchanging dead-end suggestions.

Meryn had inspected every set of winders they came to carefully. 'They have to open,' he announced at length. 'These winders are designed to open the shutters, so shooters can get up on the fething fire-step and aim out.' He leant on a brass handle that stolidly refused to budge. 'Feth it! Why won't they turn?'

'Because they're jammed,' said Fargher, Meryn's adjutant. It wasn't the brightest observation Fargher had ever made, but it matched his average. It would be the last idle suggestion he'd ever offer.

'Thank you, Mister Brains,' Meryn replied. 'I can see that. Why the feth would anyone build a fort this way, in this dust?'

He glanced back at the team. One of his troopers had muttered something.

'What was that? Was that a comment from you, Trooper Cullwoe?'

'No, sir,' said Dalin, 'it was me. I said maybe this place was built before there was any dust to worry about.'

'That's just daft talk!' sniffed Fargher.

'No, the boy could be right,' said Meryn, gazing wistfully up at the calcified shutter-gears of the cloche above them. 'Who in their right mind would construct a fortress with screw-open shutters in a fething dust bowl?'

'We could grease the gears,' suggested Neskon. 'I got prom-jelly. That's nice and greasy.'

Meryn thought about that.

'Maybe–' he began to say.

And just like that, like a conjuror's trick, the hallway ahead of them wasn't empty anymore.

Dalin blinked. Time seemed to slow, a phenomenon he'd once heard Commissar Hark call 'fight time'. The cold air was suddenly lousy with streaming shots: las-rounds and hard slugs, whizzing around them like a firework display. Swaythe grunted and spilled sideways as he took a round in the arm. Fargher let out a slight, sad sigh as he slammed over onto his back. As the adjutant landed, his limbs juddering, Dalin could see that Fargher's skull case had been forced out through the back of his shaved scalp in thick, white splinters. There was a black scorch mark on the ghastly, slack flesh of Fargher's forehead where the demolishing shot had entered.

Dalin started firing back several seconds before Meryn gave the order. Cullwoe joined in. Meryn's own las was up and blasting. The other six men in the team began to rake too, all save Neskon, who was frantically prepping his flamer.

There was no cover, no cover at all. Shots crisped past them on either side. Cardy smashed over onto his back with a dry cough as a las-round exploded his neck. Seerk squealed as he was hit twice in the stomach. He fell down on his hands and knees, and his shrill noises ceased abruptly as another round blew the top of his head in.

'Holy fething shit!' Meryn was roaring. 'Kill them! Kill them! Pour it on!'

They couldn't even see what they were supposed to be killing. Ahead of them, it was just dark and empty, ominously dark and empty, apart from the glittering gunfire spitting their way.

Dalin Criid crouched down and did as he had been instructed by Driller Kexie in RIP. He chased his aim towards the source of the shots, the muzzle flashes, and squeezed off round after round. Wall panels blew out either side of him. Venklin slowly backed into a wall and slid down it, blood and smoke leaking out of his surprised mouth.

'Stand back! Flames, flames!' Neskon shouted out, pushing forwards, his flamer finally prepped and raised.

'Duck and shield!' Meryn ordered. 'Flamer up!'

They dropped their weapons and put their faces in their hands. Neskon's torch sputtered for a second before it spoke, before it howled.

Brute fire surged out down the hallway in a fierce, licking cone. Dalin was sure he heard screams.

When the fire died back, dripping and sizzling off the scorched wall panels, there was silence.

'Feth…' said Meryn. He looked around. Cardy was dead, so were his adjutant, Fargher, Venklin and Seerk. Swaythe was hurt bad.

'Contact, contact, contact!' Meryn began to stammer frantically into his link. 'Hostile, hostile, hallway… where the feth are we? Fargher?'

'He's a little bit dead, sir,' Cullwoe said.

Dalin bent down and pulled the bundled schematics out of Fargher's pocket. The adjutant's dismantled head lolled unpleasantly as Dalin dragged the papers free.

'Dalin? Come on!' Meryn urged.

Dalin turned the papers over, searching for some kind of sense. 'Hallway… upper west sixteen, sir.'

'Upper west sixteen? You sure?'

'Yes, sir.'

'Hostile contact, hallway upper west sixteen,' Meryn told his microbead. 'Requesting immediate support!'

Meryn looked at the remains of his fire-team. 'Support's coming,' he said.

'What do we do now, sir?' asked Cullwoe, his hands shaking as he reloaded.

Meryn hesitated. His team strength had been pretty much slashed in half in less than fifty seconds. He was blinking fast, and showing a little too much white around his pupils.

Before he could think of something to say, they heard footsteps approaching from behind them and snapped around, weapons braced. The echo of half a dozen sets of boots rang towards them, running fast. They waited. No one came into view.

The footsteps seemed to go right past them and fade.

'What the feth?' Neskon muttered.

'Below us,' whispered Dalin. 'It must have been below us, on a lower level.'

Meryn nodded. 'Yeah, yeah. Below us. That's what it was.'

Neskon held up a grimy paw. 'Listen.'

More footsteps, further away, came and went.

'That was right above us that time,' said Cullwoe.

'Yeah, except there *isn't* anything above us,' Dalin replied quietly.

'Meryn?' a voice said. They all jumped in their skins like idiots. Captain Obel was standing right behind them, at the head of a support fire-team whose approaching footsteps hadn't echoed or carried at all. Obel and his seven troopers had just marched up behind them without any of Meryn's men noticing.

'Where the feth did you come from?' Meryn snapped.

Obel glanced over his shoulder uncertainly, as if suspecting a trick question. The open hallway behind them was long, and visibly empty.

'We came in support,' he said.

Obel glanced at the chewed up walls and the bodies of the fallen Ghosts with unsentimental efficiency. 'You decide to start the war without us, Meryn?' he asked. 'What the hell happened?'

Meryn jerked his head in the direction of the hallway ahead. '*They* happened,' he remarked acidly.

'Let's take a look,' Obel decided. Obel made swift, deft gestures of instruction with his free hand. *Advance, wary.* He left one of his men to look after Swaythe and dress his wound. The rest of them moved forwards, with Meryn and Obel at the front.

The hallway was as empty as it had been before. A sliver of wind sang in through some half-closed shutter. It moaned softly. Dust kicked and eddied along the bare floor. They could see a tidemark of burn residue on the walls and roof where Neskon's flamer had left its lasting impression.

'They fired on you?' Obel asked.

'Feth, yes,' Meryn answered.

'And you fired back, right?' asked Obel, keeping his voice low.

'Of course we did!' Meryn replied.

'Then where are the bodies?' asked Obel.

Day eight. Sunrise at four plus thirty-two, first light shows white out. Hit hard in two locations last night. Four men dead, two wounded, one critical.

Enemy unseen during both attacks.
They ~~ar ein~~ are in here with us.

Regiment on full alert condition. Defensive sectioning of Objective has begun. G. has ordered some spurs and outer tunnel/hallways closed off and barricades erected. Deep sense of unease. Like waiting for a storm to break.

G. has sent signal to Elikon requesting water supplies and reinforcement.

Have bided time touring main positions to ~~kep~~ keep morale up. Uphill battle. We may see desertions before long.

Since when did Ghosts get haunted?

– Field journal, V.H. fifth month, 778.

SIX

Shooting at Shadows

I

GAUNT TOOK THE message wafer Beltayn handed to him, read it quickly, and gave it back. He continued on his way across the base chamber to the corridor spur that led to the lesser hall.

The base chamber was bustling. Ludd, Daur and Kolosim were coordinating fresh troop deployments to the outer hallway wings. Men were trailing up out of the empty side chambers that had been designated as billets. They were dead-eyed from too little sleep and too little water. Gaunt nodded to a few as he went by. Many were lugging wooden boards and wall panels liberated from unused rooms to help bulk up barricades in the outer wings. Other details were trudging in from the gatehouse, hefting musette bags and sacking they had shovelled full of dust as makeshift sandbags. The bagging details were dusted white from head to foot, and the stack of sandbags they were building on the lower deck area resembled the loading bay of a flour mill.

The senior officers were waiting for him in the lesser hall. It was a dark, hollow room, the sagging ceiling panels supported by six large, timber posts. Something had once been bolted to the floor in the centre of the room, but there was no longer any way of telling what it might have been.

Rawne had carried in a table the night before, so they'd have somewhere to hold briefings, but the table had already gone, requisitioned for a barricade somewhere. The officers stood around in an awkward huddle.

Gaunt noted them: Rawne, Hark, Kolea, Mkoll, Baskevyl, Kamori and Theiss. All the other officers had duties that demanded they be elsewhere. This would have to do. Gaunt trusted the attending group to feed the business of the meeting back to the other officers of the regiment.

'Signal from Elikon,' Gaunt began without preamble. 'We're promised a water drop in the next twenty hours. We'll get specifics nearer the time.'

'What about additional strengths?' asked Theiss.

Gaunt sniffed. 'Nothing confirmed. The signal was terse. I think things may have got hotter up the line. Beltayn's hearing a lot of combat traffic, some serious armour duels in the main zone. Elikon requires us to make a full threat assessment before they consider releasing any reinforcements our way.'

'That could take days,' said Rawne, 'weeks, even. Don't they understand we can't even see what we're fighting?'

'I've got a direct vox to vox with Van Voytz scheduled for this afternoon,' Gaunt replied. 'I will attempt to explain the situation to him at that time.'

'I'll talk to him, if you like,' Rawne murmured.

Several of the officers laughed quietly.

'I want to make things better,' said Gaunt, 'not worse. How's Domor?'

'Stable,' Baskevyl replied.

'And Swaythe?'

'Broken limb, some tissue damage, but he's all right.'

'How's your arm?'

Baskevyl's arm had been patched, but he'd refused a sling. 'It's nothing.'

'So, any sign of the force strength that surprised Meryn's team?' Gaunt asked.

'Not a trace,' replied Kolea. 'Meryn's lads must have hit something, the response they put up, but there's no sign, not even blood stains where bodies were dragged out. I took a team right along upper sixteen personally. If it wasn't for the fact they got cut to ribbons, I'd have said they were shooting at shadows.'

'Where does upper west sixteen end?' Gaunt asked.

'It just ends in a box casemate,' said Kolea, 'about half a kilometre further on from the attack site.'

'Any access on that stretch?' asked Kamori.

'Two ladder wells and a staircase down to lower sixteen, and a ramp down to lower fourteen,' Kolea replied. 'But both spurs had men stationed on them when Meryn's team was hit. Any hostiles fleeing in either direction would have been picked up.'

'They're moving in the walls, then,' said Baskevyl with solemn certainty. 'False panels, tunnels.'

'Not any we can find,' said Mkoll. 'And we've looked. That was the first notion that occurred to me after your scrape in the power room, Bask. But my scouts simply can't find any false panels or sally ports anywhere in Hinzerhaus.'

'You'd better look again,' Gaunt told him.

There was a pause. It seemed unthinkable for Gaunt to question his chief scout's work. Mkoll, however, nodded. If there weren't any secret access points, the only alternative was something Gaunt had ordered them not to speak about.

'What about the power room?' Gaunt asked.

'Criid's ready for you to take a look,' Hark said.

II

P Company had spent several hours barricading the workshop end of the power room. They'd stacked up double lines of sandbags and planking, one to cover the door into the workshops, the other to protect the power hub kettle. Two support weapons, crew-served .30s on blunt iron tripods, watched the doorway.

The Ghosts on duty saluted as Gaunt, Mkoll, Kolea and Baskevyl entered the power room.

'Criid?' Gaunt asked.

One of the men pointed towards the workshop door. 'In there, sir.'

Baskevyl led the way with a sense of trepidation. He didn't trust the walls any more, none of them. He kept waiting to hear the scratching, slithering sound again. The little run of workshops was cold, a draught running through them. Another manned barricade had been set up in the third shop along, facing the arch into the fourth and final chamber. Criid and some of her men were waiting for them there.

Baskevyl stiffened. For a second, all he could see was the blizzard of shots popping through the wall panel at him and Domor. Then the other image came again, the ghastly, glistening snake of the daemon-worm, sliding across dry rocks in the dark.

'You all right?' Kolea asked.

'Yeah,' said Baskevyl.

The shot-up wall panels had been crowbarred away, exposing a black socket in the rock wall behind. The hole was about the size of a door hatch, and cold air gusted out of it. Sandbags had been piled up to half block it. The hole didn't seem to have been dug or cut. It appeared to be a naturally eroded void in the mountain rock.

'You just tapped along and found it?' asked Mkoll.

Baskevyl nodded. 'It was hollow. It rang hollow.'

Mkoll glanced at Gaunt. 'We haven't got a hollow response off any other wall panel in the place,' he said. 'Everywhere else is just solid. Believe me, I've tried.'

'Has anyone been in there?' Gaunt asked Criid.

Hwlan, the lead scout in Criid's company, nodded. 'Me and Febreen, sir. Not far in, just a little way.'

'And?'

'Very rough passage, sir, quite low, running west.'

'No other routes? Divergences?'

'None we could see, but we didn't think it smart to go too far just yet.' Hwlan paused. 'Strong breeze coming through there,' he added. 'I think it may go out to the surface.'

Mkoll unshouldered his rifle. 'Let's find out,' he said.

III

GOL KOLEA FOLLOWED Mkoll into the hole. Gaunt slithered in after them.

'Sir–' Criid began.

'I'm just taking a look,' Gaunt told her.

Baskevyl hesitated. He had absolutely no wish to climb into the dark cavity. He'd heard what was down there, the grunting, scratching thing in the dark. He wavered.

'Bask?' Gaunt called.

'Sir?'

'Stay here and stay sharp,' Gaunt said as he vanished from view. Baskevyl let out a long sigh of relief. He'd never refused an order in his career, but if Gaunt had ordered him to follow, Baskevyl wasn't sure exactly what he would have done.

As Hwlan had described, the tunnel was low and rough. It seemed unnaturally dark. Gaunt bent low, his boots scrabbling for purchase on a dry, loose floor. His fingertips made dust and pebbles patter down out of the tunnel walls as they groped for support. A cold stream of air touched his face, gusting up from the depths before them.

Mkoll and Kolea switched on their lamp-packs. Two ribbons of yellow light picked up the swimming dust in the air ahead of Gaunt.

'Drops away here,' Mkoll hissed back. 'Watch your step.' Gaunt heard flurries of scattering pebbles as Mkoll and Kolea tackled the slope.

It was indeed steep. Gaunt almost lost his footing as he gingerly followed them down. At the foot of the slope, Kolea turned and shone his lamp back for Gaunt's benefit.

'All right, sir?'

'Fine.'

Kolea paused, and then played his lamp beam up along the slope, tracing the walls.

'What is it?' Gaunt asked.

'This has been mined out,' Kolea said.

'Mined out? You mean *dug?*'

'Yes,' said Kolea. He reached out and touched part of the crumbling, granular wall. 'Those are pick marks.'

'And you'd know,' said Gaunt.

Kolea nodded. 'I would. Look here.'

Near the base of the wall, his light picked out something metal, then another identical object further up. They were iron pins with loop heads. They ran at intervals right back up the slope.

'They set them in as they went,' said Kolea. 'No doubt ran a cord or rope through the loops to help them scale the slope more easily.'

They turned and carried on after Mkoll. The tunnel levelled out a little and ran for another ten metres or so. It remained low, so they had to stoop all the way.

'Watch yourself here,' Mkoll announced as they caught up with him. Part of the tunnel floor and wall had caved in, revealing a deep, impenetrable cleft. A man would have to crawl head first to get into it.

'That's deep,' said Kolea. 'I can smell it. A natural fissure that fell in while this was being dug.'

They stepped carefully around the cleft.

'That suggests this rock isn't especially stable,' said Mkoll.

'It absolutely isn't,' Kolea replied. 'If this was a new working, I'd order the crews out of it until it had been properly propped and braced.'

Somewhere, something rattled. Something scratched and shirred in the darkness.

'What was that?' asked Gaunt.

IV

BASKEVYL HAD BEEN listening at the hole. He pulled back sharply.

'What's the matter?' Criid asked him.

'Nothing,' Baskevyl told her. He was lying.

He'd just heard it again.

V

HARK HAD TAKEN a walk to inspect the gatehouse. As he moved down the long hallway from the base chamber, he passed men toiling in the opposite direction moving sacks filled with dust. He exchanged a few encouraging words with them. Most were from Arcuda's company, which had been detailed to dig and fill the sacks. They were powdered white from their labour outside in the wind.

The floor of the gatehouse, and the gatehouse end of the hallway, was tracked with white footsteps and dusty drag marks. Hark could hear the wind shrilling outside the open hatch.

Arcuda's men had dug out the hatch so it would open more fully, but that had simply allowed dust to billow in more thoroughly. A curtain of camo-capes had been pegged up around the mouth of the hatch to act as a dust screen.

'Your idea?' Hark asked Maggs, who was in charge of gate security.

'It was either that or get buried in the stuff,' Maggs said. The curtain parted as several Ghosts elbowed their way in, sacks on their shoulders. Arcuda was with them.

'I don't know how much longer we can be expected to keep this up,' Arcuda said. 'Without water…'

'I know,' said Hark. He thought around for something supportive to add.

'Feth!' said Maggs suddenly. Hark and Arcuda looked around. The scout had taken off towards the curtained hatchway with his weapon raised.

'Maggs?' Hark called. 'What is it?'

The Belladon didn't answer. He pulled back the undulating curtain and disappeared outside. Hark and Arcuda glanced at one another and followed him.

Outside was a hellish white-out of dust. They fumbled to get their goggles on. The gritty wind sizzled around them and, though it was luminously bright, actual visibility was down to a dozen metres. Hark could make out the shapes of the men toiling to fill sacks in the area in front of the gatehouse. If it hadn't been for the fact there was an urgent need for sand bags, it would have been an insane activity, the whim of a sadistic commander setting some soul-destroying punishment task.

'Holy Terra,' mumbled Hark, raising a hand to stave off the gale. Maggs had gone forward, out into the open, his lasrifle up. He was hunting for something.

'Maggs? Maggs?'

Maggs dropped to his knees, inspecting the ground, as if he might determine tracks or spores.

'Maggs? What the feth are you doing?' Hark yelled as they reached him.

'I saw something,' Maggs called back. He was still looking around.

'You saw what?' Arcuda asked, raising his voice over the howling wind.

Maggs replied something that sounded like *she came this way*.

'She?' Hark yelled.

Maggs rose and cupped his hand around his mouth so they could hear him. 'Someone I didn't recognise,' he bellowed. 'They came this way from the gatehouse.'

Hark shook his head. He hadn't seen anybody. Why was he so sure Maggs had said *she*?

'Maggs?'

Wes Maggs didn't reply. He felt excessively stupid, and embarrassed that Arcuda and the commissar had witnessed his apparently irrational behaviour.

He could hardly tell them the truth. He knew they wouldn't believe him.

But it wasn't the first time he'd seen the silent figure in black, and he had the ugliest feeling he'd be seeing her again before long.

VI

Eszrah ap Niht walked into the lesser hall, scanned around once with his reynbow tucked at his shoulder, and walked out again.

Nahum Ludd was huddled up in a corner of the hall, checking duty rotas off his data-slate in an effort to forget how thirsty he was.

'Eszrah?' he called. Ludd got up and hurried to the chamber door in time to see Eszrah striding away down an east-running passageway.

'Eszrah? Wait!'

Ayatani Zweil came out of Gaunt's room and almost collided with Ludd.

'What's wrong with Eszrah, father?' Ludd asked.

'That's what I want to know, young man,' Zweil replied. 'We were happy as you like, reading. I was teaching him the pluperfect. Then up he jumps, snatches his uncouth bow from the table, and runs out.'

'Stay here, father,' Ludd said, and made off after the partisan.

'I'm not going to just stand here–' Zweil began.

'Then keep up!' Ludd called back over his shoulder.

Zweil sighed and came to a halt. 'Ah, see? You've got me there too.'

'Find someone and tell them what's going on!'

'Like who?'

'Someone useful!' Ludd shouted.

Eszrah had a good lead on the cadet, and was moving with the typical speed and stealth of a Nihtgane. Ludd realised it was no good shouting at him. Running, he managed to gain ground, mainly because Eszrah stopped to inspect a side chamber. Varl appeared out of it a moment after Eszrah had gone past.

'What's up with Ez?' Varl asked as Ludd ran up. 'He came in, aimed his bow at us, bold as brass, and then left again.' Varl's company was billeted in the side room. Several of the men were getting up off their bedrolls, bemused.

'He's seen something,' said Ludd. 'Or heard something. I don't know.' Varl grabbed his weapon and gave chase with Ludd. He called out for a fire-team to follow on the double. Ludd heard the clatter of boots coming after them.

They reached a junction. The main spur ran east, and a side hallway forked to the south. A stairwell climbed into the upper galleries.

Varl and Ludd came to a halt. 'Where did he go?' Ludd asked.

Varl shook his head. The fire-team – Twenzet, Kabry, Cant, Cordrun and Lukos – came running up the hallway behind them. Varl clicked his microbead. 'Listen up, sentries on the upper east galleries and east main. Anybody got anything? Anybody got sight of the Sleepwalker?'

There was a crackle of negative responses.

'Maybe he just had a funny turn,' suggested Twenzet.

'No,' replied Varl firmly.

'Why not?'

'Because... I'll shoot you,' said Varl.

'Oh sacred feth!' Lukos suddenly exclaimed.

Eszrah had silently reappeared out of the south-east spur without warning. He regarded them for a moment from behind his sunshades, his reynbow against his chest.

'Eszrah?' Ludd asked.

Without replying, the Nihtgane turned and started up the stairs towards the upper galleries.

'Follow him!' Varl ordered.

They ran up four flights in the weird, white gloom. The partisan left the stairs at the top, and turned east along upper east twelve, one of the highest fortified spurs on that side of the house. The spur was punctuated at regular points by casemate blockhouses and the roof domes of armoured cloches. They could feel a breeze from somewhere.

In a thunder of boots, a second fire-team joined them from the west. Six men, led by Rawne.

'Old man Zweil said Eszrah was acting up,' Rawne said bluntly.

Ludd nodded. 'He's gone this way.'

The Sleepwalker was almost out of sight. The two fire-teams started to move, jogging down the hallway. Rawne got on his link and ordered other teams to move up from the galleries below and cut off the spur ahead at the next staircase junctions.

'Where's he gone?' Varl asked. 'I can't see him anymore.' They slowed to a walk.

'He can't have got past us,' said Ludd. 'Or them.'

He pointed. Thirty metres away, a group of figures was moving towards them, evidently another fire-team, coming up and west from one of the other stairlinks.

'Then where the feth is he?' Varl asked.

'Forget the fething Nihtgane,' Rawne growled. 'Those aren't ours.'

VII

THE DARKNESS MELTED. Rough light seeped into the gloom. Gaunt could smell raw, cold air, and feel the airborne particulates pin-pricking off his face.

The tunnel grew wider as it bottomed out. There was a jagged, vertical scar of white in the blackness ahead.

'Leads right out into the open,' said Mkoll.

They scrambled up towards the jagged opening, negotiating a slope of tumbled boulders and dry, flaking earth. The wind made a low, eerie sigh as it blew into the cavity.

Mkoll reached the lip of the cave mouth, and leaned back to help Kolea and Gaunt up. They were in daylight now. A narrow shelf had choked with drifting dust in the entrance, and sprays of grit were winnowing in around the edges and chinks of the rock.

They clambered out into the open. It took them a moment to adjust their goggles and look around. They had emerged through the steep cliff wall on the far side of the crag that contained Hinzerhaus. The ground dropped away below them into a wide ravine, jumbled with boulders and scree. Beyond that, through the dust haze, they could see a broader plain of rough ground.

Gaunt turned and looked up, appreciating the northern face of the fortress rock. The cliff ran east and west, as indomitable as a city's curtain wall. He could just make out cloche towers and casemates on the cliff tops a hundred metres above. The scale was vast, far grander and more overpowering than it had been on the southern side when they'd approached the main gatehouse. The great rock ridge of the Banzie Altids dropped away like a gigantic step into the hostile flatlands behind. Flatlands – badlands, more like, badlands on a bad rock. Gaunt felt small, diminished. The three of them were just tiny specks at the foot of the soaring, dusty buttress.

Gaunt heard a dog barking in the wind, somewhere far away. He was about to remark on it when he realised it couldn't be a dog, and wasn't a dog.

It was the whining bark of a heavy support weapon.

Shots pummelled against the cliff face above them, making the brittle sound of a rock drill.

'Get down!' Mkoll yelled, but Gaunt didn't need to be told.

Elikon M.P., Elikon M.P., this is Nalwood, this is Nalwood. Requesting immediate assistance. Multi-point attack, unknown strength. This objective cannot be considered secure. Repeat, requesting immediate support at this time.

Nalwood out. (transmission ends)

- Transcript of vox message, fifth month, 778.

SEVEN
The First Assault

I

THE VOLLEYS OF shots striking the cliff face behind them were heavy and sustained. The scabby stone surface became riddled with black dents that vanished as fast as they appeared as the swirling dust retouched them. Gaunt, Mkoll and Kolea were pressed down behind a pile of loose rocks and scree. Occasionally, the enemy's aim dropped lower, and explosive impacts rattled along the top of the pile, blowing stones into fragments.

'Well, we're pinned,' groaned Kolea.

Mkoll scurried forwards on his hands and knees, searching for a way to move clear.

'No good,' he reported.

Gaunt had drawn his bolt pistol. He reached up over his head and fired off a couple of blind shots.

The enemy fire stopped. Gaunt looked at Kolea. Kolea shrugged. A second later, they both winced as the enemy fire resumed, more urgently.

'Great,' muttered Gaunt. 'Made them angry.' He clicked his microbead. 'Baskevyl? We've got hot contact. Support, if you please!'

II

BASKEVYL GLANCED AT Criid. She was staring at him.

'Read you, sir. Where are you?' Baskevyl said into his bead.

'The tunnel runs all the way to the outside,' his link hissed in his ear. 'We got caught in the open. We need cover fire from the cave mouth if we're going to get back in.'

'Understood.'

'Come carefully,' Gaunt's voice warned.

'Understood.'

Criid was still staring at Baskevyl. 'Well,' she asked, 'what are you waiting for?'

What am I waiting for, Baskevyl asked himself? What am I waiting for? Any possible excuse not to have to crawl into that bloody hole, that's what.

Criid shook her head in bafflement and headed for the hole herself, cinching her lasrifle tight around her body. 'You six, with me!' she ordered.

'Hold on, hold on!' Baskevyl called out. He drew his pistol and pushed his way to the front of the assembling team. 'Follow me,' he said.

He paused for a moment, one hand clutching the ragged edge of the hole. Darkness yawned in front of him.

He took a deep, steadying breath. 'Come on,' he said, and swung down into the blackness.

III

RAWNE WAS RIGHT.

Thirty metres away down the gloomy hall, the figures advancing towards them came to a halt. They were just shadows, half a dozen silhouettes, almost insubstantial. But they weren't Ghosts. Ludd felt that in his gut as a certainty. They absolutely weren't another fire-team responding to Rawne's order.

Rawne and Varl opened up without hesitation. Their las-rounds cracked away down the hallway. The Ghosts on either side of them began firing too. The fusillade was deafening and made Ludd's vision flash and blink. He pulled himself in against a wall and fumbled with his holster, trying to get his sidearm out. He couldn't really see the figures any more. It was as if they had gone, dissipated like smoke.

They hadn't.

Answering fire ripped towards the Ghosts. Somebody cried out as he was hit. Hard rounds and las-bolts dug into the ceiling and walls, some of them ricocheted off wildly, pinging almost comically around the tight box of the hallway like angry insects trying to escape. A wall light burst in a shower of white sparks.

'Hostile contact!' Rawne yelled. 'Hostile contact upper east twelve!'

* * *

IV

Outside the gate, in the gruelling wind, Hark turned his head sharply.

'Say again! Say again!' he yelled. The signal in his ear was little more than whooping static noise.

'Contact in the house!' Arcuda shouted, and set off in the direction of the gate hatch.

Hark turned back towards the work crews. 'Stop work! Stop work! Back into the gatehouse!'

The men could barely hear him over the wind. Some looked up, puzzled, sacks and entrenching tools lowered.

Hark waved his arms as he ran towards them. 'Come on! Stop what you're doing and get back!'

Some of them began to move, understanding his meaning at last. They grabbed tools and bundles of sacking, and started to hurry in the direction of the gatehouse.

One of them fell over.

'Get up! Come on, get up!' Hark yelled as he reached the man. Five metres away, Wes Maggs started firing.

'Maggs? What the feth are you–'

Hark looked down at the fallen man and understood what Maggs had already realised.

The fallen man was caked white with dust, but the wind hadn't yet obscured the wet, red mess in the small of his back.

'Contact!' Hark yelled. 'Contact, main gate!'

V

Baskevyl could hear the scratching in the dark. He could hear the slither of knotted skin and twisted bone, scraping on the rocks.

'Can't you go any faster?' Criid complained from behind him.

No, he *couldn't*. It was all Baskevyl could do to stop himself turning around and knocking them out of his way in a frantic effort to return to the workshops.

He told himself it was his imagination. He told himself it was the wind, or the oddly echoed noise of the gunfire outside, or the scrape of his boots curiously magnified by the claustrophobic little tunnel he was squeezing his way down.

But if it was boots, or wind, or gunfire, why could he hear snuffling? Why could he hear a slick, mucus noise of wet tissue on dry rock? Why – in the Emperor's name – could he hear breathing?

'You keep slowing down. For feth's sake!' Criid exclaimed.

'All right, all right!' Baskevyl replied. He pushed his way forwards with renewed speed.

He was going to meet the daemon-worm, sooner or later, he reasoned. It was going to find him eventually, and when it did, well, that would be that.

He might as well get it over with.

VI

HARK PULLED OUT his plasma weapon as he ran up to Maggs.

'Where?'

'All around us!' Maggs replied. 'I can't get gun sound or muzzle flash in this wind... I can't see anything. But they're there, all right!'

'Drop back. Now!' Hark ordered. 'We're too exposed!'

They started to run. Odd, truncated sounds buzzed past them: stray, passing shots they could hear for only a split-second. Hark glimpsed the bright barb of a las-bolt as it exploded the dusty ground ahead of them.

Most of the bagging crews had reached the safety of the gatehouse and bundled inside, but enemy fire had picked off two more on the way. Arcuda and Bonin were standing outside the curtain, firing off into the wind. Maggs and Hark dropped in beside them. The arch of the hatch offered them a little better cover at least.

'You see anything?' Hark demanded.

'Not a damned thing,' replied Bonin with a shake of his head. 'I think it's snipers, up in the rocks.'

'On the basis of what?' asked Hark.

'The way our guys fell down,' Bonin replied simply. 'The way they jerked and dropped... they were hit from high angles.'

'I've voxed for marksman support,' said Arcuda. 'Larkin's coming.'

'He won't be able to see anything either!' complained Maggs.

'Sometimes he doesn't have to,' replied Hark.

'Are all our boys inside?' Bonin asked.

'Yes,' replied Arcuda.

'Then who the feth is that?' asked Bonin.

Fifty metres beyond the gate, the figures of men were shambling and lurching out of the gritty storm towards them, moving as fast as they could across the thick, loose dunes of dust. Dozens of figures, charging, yelling. Hark heard the raw war cries of feral voices, and the harsh blare of battle horns.

'We're about to have a busy day,' he said.

VII

THE FIRE FIGHT in upper east twelve was a mad, brief affair. Afterwards, Ludd wondered why everyone wasn't just killed in a second. Shots spanged and spattered in all directions, a lethal combination of directed fire and hopeless deflections. Smoke swirled around with nowhere to go. Muzzle flash made the light and shadow flicker and dart. There was nothing except a battering concussion, the kind of noise you'd hear if you stuck your head in a marching drum while someone played a rapid, endless roll. Rawne was shouting orders, as if a situation like that could be tempered or controlled by orders.

'Cease! Cease fire!' Varl cried.

They stopped shooting. The Ghosts were all crowded in against the hallway walls, or lay flat on the floor where they had been firing prone. Bars of smoke rolled lazily through the quietened air.

'Either we killed them…' Varl whispered.

'Or they've fled,' Rawne finished. He voxed to the other teams on upper east twelve, warning them to guard against hostiles moving east.

Three teams acknowledged in quick succession.

'Straight silver,' Rawne ordered. They fixed their blades to the lugs under their hot barrels. Two of Rawne's fire-team were dead, and one of Varl's – Twenzet – was wounded. 'Help him,' Rawne told Ludd.

Twenzet had been hit in the ribs, a grazing but bloody wound. He grinned sheepishly as Ludd helped support him, but his brave grin was punctuated by sharp flinches of pain.

At a wave of Rawne's hand, the team advanced.

'Looky, look, look,' whispered Varl.

Now there were bodies. In contrast with Meryn's similarly tight and brutal encounter the night before, the enemy dead had not vanished this time. Four corpses sprawled, twisted and limp, on the hallway deck twenty-five metres away. Each one wore filthy, mismatched Guard fatigues and webbing. Each face was hidden behind a leering black metal mask.

Blood Pact.

'Four of them,' muttered Cant. 'I counted more than that.'

'Me too,' said Varl.

Rawne clicked his microbead and repeated his warning to the other teams further along the spur. He listened to their responses, and then glanced at Varl.

'Next team east of us is Caober's, at the top of the next stairhead. There're no exits or ladder wells between him and us, so we've got the rest of them boxed.'

Varl had been listening to his own vox-link. 'Major, there's… I'm hearing there's an attack underway at the main gatehouse. Full-on assault.'

Rawne made an ugly face, his lips curled. 'Feth! Well, somebody else is going to have to be enough of a big boy to handle that. We're committed here.'

Varl nodded. 'Close file,' he told the men. 'Slow advance.'

Rawne snap-voxed Caober's group to warn them they were coming.

'Nice and slow,' Varl repeated, his voice a whisper. 'When we find 'em, it's going to get all sudden and messy.'

'Trail us,' Rawne told Ludd.

Ludd tried to shift his grip on Twenzet so he could support him more comfortably.

'Take my las,' Twenzet whispered to him.

'No, I–'

'Take my las. I can't shoot it one-handed, and your pop gun isn't going to be worth shit when this happens. You heard Varl. We've got them cornered and it's going to be a riot.'

Reluctantly, Ludd put his sidearm away and hung Twenzet's rifle over his left shoulder.

'Blood,' reported Cant.

Spatters on the floor. A trail, winding away from them.

'Got to be close now,' whispered Varl. 'Why can't we see them?'

Rawne touched his microbead. 'Caober? Anything?'

'Negative, sir.'

Varl held up a hand. They halted.

'Forty metres,' Varl hissed, head down. 'I see movement.' He brought his rifle up to his cheek and took aim. 'Fire on three.'

The Ghosts raised their weapons and aimed.

'Three, two–'

'Wait!' said Rawne.

'What's the matter?' Varl whispered.

Rawne called out, 'Caober?'

There was movement far ahead. 'Major?' a voice floated back.

'Throne, we nearly opened up on Caober's mob!' said Kabry.

'Then where the feth did they go?' asked Rawne. 'I mean, where the feth did they fething well go?'

VIII

BASKEVYL FELT A breeze on his skin and heard a rattle of gunfire from close by. It almost, but not quite, obscured the scraping slither of the thing waiting for him in the dark.

'Get ready,' he heard Criid instruct the men behind them.

Baskevyl swallowed hard. His lamp-pack was shaking in his hand. He drew his laspistol. Treading carefully over the rough black earth of the tunnel floor, a treacherous surface almost invisible in the dark, he edged on. The tunnel dropped a little more, and then widened out.

And he could see it at last.

His breath sucked in with a little gasp. It was right in front of him, rearing up in the gloom: a giant, twisted column of white bone and gristle, uncoiling from a writhing mound on the floor. Its knotted body segments – scabby, glistening flesh the colour of pale fat – dragged against the dry black rocks as it uncoiled, smearing with dust and mould. It let out a dry, bony rattle, like a bead in a husk. He felt its worm-breath strike his face, an exhalation of cold, ammoniac vapour.

'Major?' Criid called, pushing at him.

Why couldn't she see it? Why wasn't she shooting at it? Was it just a daemon spectre meant only for him?

'Major Baskevyl!' Criid shouted.

And, just like that, there was no daemon-worm: no daemon-worm, no rearing column of ghastly, white flesh like a gigantic, animated spinal cord.

There was simply an opening to the outside world, a jagged, vertical slit of white daylight against the black cave shadow.

'The mind,' Baskevyl whispered. 'It plays such tricks.'

'What?' Criid asked.

He didn't answer. He ran towards the slit of daylight. 'Move up close, two at a time,' he called out. 'Make ready to provide suppressing fire. Follow me.'

Baskevyl ducked down in the cave entrance and peered out. The bright air outside was a dancing haze of white dust, but he could see down across the rock spoil and boulders below the cave.

'One, this is Three. Come back,' he said into his bead.

'Three, One. Good to hear from you. Position?'

'Cave mouth, so above you, I'm guessing.'

'Three, we're under you and to your left.'

'There,' said Criid, crawling in beside Baskevyl and pointing down.

Gaunt, Kolea and Mkoll were pinned behind a pile of stones about twenty metres below and to the left of the cave fissure. Streaks of fire – tracer and las – spat horizontally out of the rocky plain beyond them and struck against the cliff wall with a sound like slapped flesh.

Baskevyl looked around. Two large boulders provided immediate cover in front of the cave. Tactically, he knew he had to get as many guns out and firing as he could. The cave mouth was only really wide enough for two shooters, side by side. He wanted all eight of them, if it was humanly possible.

'Go right of the big rock,' he told Criid. 'Take Kazel and Vivvo with you. Don't fire until you hear me tell you.'

Criid nodded, and bellied her long, lean body away from him; very much like a serpent, he thought, and quickly shook the idea away. Vivvo and Kazel followed her. Baskevyl signed Starck and Orrin to take the gap between the two rocks. He glanced to Pabst and Mkteal, and beckoned them to follow him.

Baskevyl crawled up on the left side of the left-hand rock. He took a look from this improved vantage. Now he could see what they were dealing with. Belches of muzzle flash from a heavy gun, something on a tripod he presumed, winked a hundred metres beyond the chief's position. Snap shots from shooters scattered in the surface rocks added their support.

'Heavy stub, one hundred left and out,' he voxed quietly.

'I see it,' replied Criid. 'There was another one, fifty right of it. It's stopped firing now. Changing boxes or barrels, is my guess.'

'Fifteen… no sixteen… other guns,' reported Vivvo.

'Eighteen,' came Mkoll's voice over the link. 'I've been listening. Two sources to my right stopped blasting about five minutes ago. Watch for them, they're probably trying to flank us.'

'That's your task for the day, Criid,' Baskevyl voxed. 'We'll hit the firing cannon. Starck, Orrin? Just make sure everybody else ducks, please.'

'Got it,' came the vox-clipped answer.

'First and only,' said Baskevyl.

They all started firing. Baskevyl, Pabst and Mkteal trained their shots directly on the source of the heavy fire, peppering the rocks around the origin point of the chunky muzzle flash. Starck and Orrin raked punishing rapid fire across the whole area. Baskevyl saw a figure rise, twist and fall. One kill, at least, probably Orrin's to claim. Criid, Vivvo and Kazel began taking speculative, selective shots down at the right-hand portion of the scree slope, trying to flush something out.

After about a minute of sustained shots from Baskevyl's group, the heavy gun stopped firing. The sporadic shots from the rock waste around it were now coming up at the two big rocks where the newcomers were sheltering.

'Hello,' said Pabst, and squeezed off a double-snap of las. 'Well, he's dead, then,' he remarked. A few moments later, Orrin made another kill.

Then fresh gunfire began to zip in from the right. Criid hunched down, hunting the flash source. Two flanking shooters, down in the bed of the ravine. She grinned to herself. Mkoll had been right, as usual. She snuggled in her aim and waited. One muzzle flash, a burp of burning gas. That determined location and range. A second, to confirm. A slug round whined past her ear. A third.

'Bang,' she said, and unloaded a stream of six tightly grouped las-shots that blew the shooter out of cover and left him sprawled across the rock litter.

Immediately, she rolled, to prevent the shooter's partner replicating the same trick on her. Two las-bolts clipped off the side of the boulder where she had just been crouching.

'Be advised,' she voxed. 'They're good.'

'Maybe, but they're one fewer now,' Starck voxed back, flush from a kill of his own.

'Don't get over confident,' Gaunt cut in over the link.

'Oh, as if,' Criid retorted, hunting for the give-away flashes of the other flanker.

The second heavy gun started up again abruptly, mowing fire up at the boulder shielding Baskevyl, Pabst and Mkteal, forcing them to duck. Coughing bursts of dust and rock chips stitched up across the boulder and then continued to smack a line up the face of the cliff above the cave mouth as its aim was frantically over-adjusted. The bulk of the enemy fire was now targeting the cave mouth area.

'Shall we?' Kolea asked Gaunt, hearing the distinct change in the whine of gunfire.

'Of course.'

They scrambled up the pile of stones, bellied down, and began firing, bolt pistol and lasrifle side by side. Gaunt saw dark shapes moving amongst the rocks, and checked his aim. He fired again, and saw a red and black figure smash backwards against the face of a boulder and slump.

'Uh, when did you last see Mkoll?' Kolea asked suddenly.

Gaunt smiled and fired again.

IX

OUT OF THE dust, like howling beasts, the Blood Pact assaulted the main gatehouse of Hinzerhaus.

'We're going to need support here,' Hark voxed. 'As much as you can spare.' His plasma gun beamed out from the doorway, incinerating the torsos and heads of three oncoming assault troops in quick succession. Their ruined bodies dropped like bundles of sticks into the dust. Beside Hark, Maggs, Arcuda and Bonin were sowing out las-fire in tight, chattering bursts.

'I knew this was going to be a bad rock,' Arcuda complained.

'Love the Guard and it'll love you back,' chastised Bonin.

Maggs was oddly silent, as if uncharacteristically cowed by the extremity of the situation.

'Support! Support to the main entrance for the love of the Throne!' Arcuda yelled impatiently into his mic.

The Blood Pact came in like a tide along a shore. As they loomed out of the dust storm's soft white blanket, they seemed shockingly black and ragged, as if they had been cut out of some dark, dirty matter utterly inimical to Jago, where everything was stained white by the eternal dust.

They were screaming, shrieking and bellowing through the slit mouths of their awful iron masks. Torn strands of fabric, leather and chainmail trailed out behind their stumbling forms. Several of them bore vile standards: obscene, graven totems or painted banners mounted on long poles, adorned with long black flagtails that fluttered back in the wind. Others blasted raucous notes on huge brass trumpets that curled around their bodies. Some brandished pikes, or halberds, or trench axes; others lugged heavy flamers with long, stave lances. The majority fired rifles as they came on.

'You know,' muttered Hark, quite matter of factly, 'we could learn a lot from these heathens.'

'In terms of what?' Arcuda snapped, pumping out shots.

'Oh, in terms of, you know, *terror*.'

'I've learned more than I need already,' said Bonin, crimping off a double-snap that felled a charging standard bearer.

Wes Maggs said nothing. He aimed and fired, aimed and fired, with mechanical efficiency. He was watching for her in the enemy ranks, quite certain she would be there, that old dam in the black lace dress. He knew her, oh he knew her all right. He knew her business, the oldest business of all. She'd be coming, of that he had no doubt. She'd been lurking about in this rat-hole place – he'd glimpsed her coming and going ever since they'd arrived, out of the corner of his eye. She wouldn't miss a chance like this. She'd come, and then they'd all be–

dry skulls, with all the tops sawn off

–reduced to dust, like all the other poor bastards who had tried and failed to stay alive on bad rock Jago over the centuries.

Unless Maggs saw her first. Unless he saw her coming, and had enough time and courage to punch a las-round into her appalling meat-wound face.

By his side, Hark fired again and vaporised the legs of a trumpet blower. The man fell, tumbling, his horn still barking out discordant squirts of noise like the cry of an animal in pain.

The curtain behind them raked back so hard it was dragged off its pegs. Ghosts rushed out.

'At last. Make a line!' Arcuda ordered. 'Spread out!'

Guardsmen, their rifles coming up to firing positions as they moved, fanned out to meet the oncoming tide.

'Make room,' Seena yelled as she and Arilla carried their .30 out through the hatch. Maggs began to help them bed it down and fix its tripod into the dust. 'We can do it,' Arilla told him sharply, fixing the first ammo box expertly against the receiver.

'All right then,' Maggs replied, turning to fire again. 'Just make sure you shoot her if you see her.'

'Who?' asked Arilla, snapping the receiver cover shut.

Maggs didn't reply. He had returned to his position and was busy firing again, and there was too much noise for idle chatter.

The wave of attackers was close now, just ten metres. Hark knew that, despite the number the Ghosts had already picked off, they were about to reach *the Crunch*.

Arcuda knew it too. 'Straight silver!' he ordered.

The .30 opened up. It made a clinking whirr, like a monstrous sewing machine. Its clattering hail cut a swathe through the front rank of the charging enemy. As Arilla fed it, Seena expertly washed the heavy cannon from side to side. It mowed the Blood Pact down. It ripped them apart, mangled limb from mangled limb.

Hark sighed. Fight time. They were on fight time, at last. He'd been expecting it. He'd been waiting for it to begin. Everything in the world seemed to slow down. Las-rounds trembled like leaves of fire, suspended in the air. Blood Pact warriors, struck by Seena's fire, fell backwards ever so slowly, arms flung wide, fingers clawing at the air as if trying to hold onto it. Blood bloomed like flowers opening lazily in the sun. A grotesk, torn from a face, flipped over and over in the air like a ponderously turning asteroid. Even the swirling dust seemed to slow down and stagnate.

Hark braced himself. He felt curiously content as if, despite the situation, the galaxy was at last behaving the way it was supposed to behave.

At the edges of the line, beyond the .30's cone of fire, the rushing tide of Blood Pact finally met the Ghost file head on.

This was *the Crunch*. This was the point at which an assaulting enemy could no longer be fended off by fire alone. This was the point of impact, of body on body, and mass on mass.

The wave struck the Ghost line. There was a palpable, shivering clash. Straight silver met chainmail, and trench axes and spears met moulded body plating. Blades struck and dug and stabbed. Bodies were impaled, hacked down or thrown back by the impact of momentous collisions. Not every falling body was a Blood Pact warrior.

Bonin found himself in the thick of it. He speared a Blood Pact soldier on the end of his silver, and then was forced to kick the next one to death because his blade was wedged in the spinal column of the first. Twisting it free at last, he swung it hard, and slashed through a windpipe. Hot blood squirted into his face. He turned again and narrowly avoided a lunging spear. Ducking, he rolled and destroyed knees and shin bones with a burst of fire.

Hark melted a grotesk – and the skull behind it – with a single shot from his potent energy weapon. The tip of a lance plunged through his left arm, but he felt no pain, and flexed his augmetic arm sharply, breaking the spear haft. He turned and finished the business by killing the owner of the broken spear with another single burst of streamed plasma.

For a moment, in the middle of it all, he suddenly thought he could make out a distant melody, like a pipe playing. Some brazen enemy battle pipe, he decided, breaking a man's neck with a chop of his left hand.

But it wasn't. It was an old tune, a fragile thing, an Imperial hymn. No, no, a *Tanith* song...

What the f–

There was no time to ponder it. A gust of heated, tortured air swept into his face, and the two Ghosts beside him went up in fireballs, shrieking as they perished. Hark fell over, flames leaping up the tails and back of his storm coat.

'Flamer! Flamer!' someone yelled.

Hark rolled frantically in the dust, trying to extinguish himself. Somebody landed on top of him, beating out the fire.

It was Arcuda.

'Get up, commissar! They've got range with their burners!'

Arcuda heaved Hark to his feet. The commissar was dazed. Fight time had suddenly taken on a strange, unwelcome flavour. He felt dislocated, unready. His back throbbed. He was hurt. He realised he was going into shock.

Hlaine Larkin limped out through the torn curtain of the gate hatch and took a moment to observe the sheer mayhem before him. Then he knelt down and swung his long-las up to his chin, where it belonged. Through his scope, he surveyed the close-quarter fighting in front of him.

'Flamers!' someone was yelling.

Yes, there was one, squirting fire into the Ghost ranks with his long burner lance. Larkin took aim. The long-las bumped against his shoulder.

'One,' muttered Larkin.

He changed clips, one hot shot for another, and panned until he saw another long, burning stave.

He aimed. Headshot. Bump. 'Two.'

He reloaded, panned, spotted on a third flamer.

'Tank shot,' he breathed. Bump.

Twenty metres away, a warrior's backpack tank punctured and exploded, showering the Blood Pact around him with ignited promethium. Blood Pact soldiers fell, writhing and shrieking, wrapped in cocoons of fire.

'Three.'

Larkin reloaded, panned, and aimed. 'Trumpet,' he decided, and fired.

A horn blower convulsed as the top of his head blew off. He fell. His trumpet made a strange, half-blown noise.

Nothing like as satisfying as hitting a flamer, Larkin decided, and went back to that sport.

Reload, aim, fire. *Five.*

Reload, aim, fire. *Six.*

'Keep 'em coming, Larks,' a voice said beside him.

Larkin looked over at the speaker. Try Again Bragg smiled reassuringly at his old friend. 'Go on, keep it up,' Bragg said. 'Reload, aim, fire. You know the drill.'

Larkin felt his guts knot up tight with fear. He forced himself to look away from the kind, smiling face and into his scope.

'Not now,' he breathed. '*Please*, not now.'

X

'No one came this way?' asked Rawne.

'No one, sir,' replied Caober.

'I don't understand it,' said Rawne.

A thin, sharp wind blew along upper east twelve. The wall lights faded softly and then came back.

'Walk it back,' Rawne told Caober. 'Walk it back to the next set of stairs. We'll go back the way we came. Feth, they have to be somewhere.'

'What about–' Caober began.

'What about what?'

'The main gate's being attacked. From what I hear on the link, it's pretty intense.'

Rawne stared at Caober. 'Scout, if there's any chance, just so much as the slightest chance, that the Blood Pact is magically inside this place with us, defending the main gate becomes a rather secondary objective, doesn't it?'

Caober nodded. 'Put like that, Major Rawne.'

'Let's get on with it,' said Rawne.

With Varl at his side and the rest of the fire-team following, Rawne retraced his steps along the draughty hallway. Ludd brought up the rear, supporting Twenzet. Behind them, Caober's fire-team turned the other way.

They'd been walking for a couple of minutes when Varl groaned.

'What?' asked Rawne.

'Where are they?' asked Varl.

'Where are who?'

Varl gestured at the floor. 'The four dead bastards we left here,' he said.

Rawne stared at the empty deck. There was no doubting their position, but there was no sign at all of the enemy corpses they had left in their wake.

'This is beginning to feth me off,' Rawne said.

At the back of the group, Twenzet nudged Ludd.

'What's that smell?' he asked.

'Smell?' replied Ludd, finding it an increasing effort to keep the wounded trooper upright. Ludd wasn't even sure if Twenzet should be upright.

'Smells like... blood. You smell it too?' Twenzet asked.

Ludd hesitated. He didn't like to point out that Twenzet was the most likely source of the odour.

'I-' he began.

The Blood Pact warrior made a snuffling noise as he came out of the shadows towards them. His trench axe ploughed down at Ludd, but Ludd fell, letting go of Twenzet, and the jagged blade missed his ear by a very short distance.

Ludd scrabbled frantically to protect himself, and grabbed at Twenzet's lasrifle, strung awkwardly over his shoulder. He brought it up to defend himself.

The Blood Pact warrior, leaping forward, impaled himself through the neck on the upraised straight silver. His trench axe made a loud *thunk* as it dropped onto the decking. He gurgled and collapsed on his side. The weight of his body snatched the lasrifle out of Ludd's hands.

Twenzet, sprawled where Ludd had dropped him, was moaning in pain. Ludd crawled across to him, looking around, bewildered as to why no one had come to aid them.

He realised that everyone else was too busy with their own problems.

Eight Blood Pact warriors had ambushed the fire-team, pouncing out of the shadows with axes and cudgels. Everything had turned into a frenzy of movement that seemed, at the same time, oddly tranquil.

What was it Commissar Hark had called it? Ludd thought as he reached Twenzet's side. *Yeah, fight time.*

Rawne gasped in surprise as the first grotesk came out of the darkness at him. Snap instinct alone allowed him to greet it with his rifle, and the fixed blade was swallowed up by the grimacing mouth of the iron mask. Rawne kept pushing until the back of the hostile's head smacked against the hallway wall.

Varl, reacting as fast as ever, ducked under a swinging spike-mace, and fired two shots, point-blank, into its owner's belly. The hostile dropped, hard.

Varl started to yell, 'They're on us! They're on us!' He turned, but far too slowly to block the hanger slashing down at the back of his neck.

There was a sound. A *phutt*!

The warrior with the hanger suddenly staggered backwards, an iron dart embedded in his left eye slit. He half-turned and then collapsed like a felled tree.

The sound repeated. *Phutt! Phutt! Phutt!*

The Blood Pact ambusher intent on Kabry suddenly doubled up, a thick dart in his belly. Cant flinched, unable to react in time, then saw the cudgel aimed at his face drop away as the Blood Pact warrior hefting it took a dart through the neck. Cordrun felt a trench axe bite into the body armour encasing his back, and then, abruptly, felt it snatch free again as its Blood Pact owner was hurled over by a dart that transfixed the middle of his grotesk's forehead.

Rawne and Varl quickly killed the two remaining hostiles with brutal bursts of fire that left their targets splattered against the hallway wall.

'What the holy gak was that?' Varl gasped.

Eszrah ap Niht dropped lightly down in the middle of them, out of nowhere. He was holding his reynbow.

'Where the feth did you come from?' Rawne demanded.

Eszrah pointed up at the cloche dome above them, as if that explained everything.

'Ygane ther, soule,' he said.

XI

MKOLL CROUCHED DOWN behind the two Blood Pact warriors manning the heavy cannon. One was diligently feeding belts of ammunition while the other aimed and fired the antique weapon. Mkoll observed them for a while, admiring their technique and discipline, kneeling down close behind them like a third member of the gun crew.

Then he killed them and the gun fell silent.

The Master of Scouts waited for a moment, huddled down in the position amongst the rock spoil. The sound of guttural voices reached him. A Blood Pact warrior, his filthy uniform stinking of fresh sweat and the stale blood of old rituals, scrambled in along a gully on his hands and knees, arriving to investigate why the cannon had stopped shooting. Mkoll killed him. He killed the second man who came to look for the first. Then he carefully removed a tube-charge from his musette bag, plucked out the det-tape, and tossed it over in the direction of the other cannon, which had begun to chatter again.

The shock of the blast drifted back to him, along with handfuls of loose pebbles that rained down out of the air.

There was a silence that lasted for about a minute, except for wind wafting dust around the place.

Mkoll clicked his microbead. 'I think we're all done here,' he said.

Gaunt and Kolea scrambled up the slope towards the cave mouth, where Baskevyl, Criid and the fire-team were waiting for them by the pair of rocks.

'Thanks for that,' said Gaunt.

Baskevyl nodded back. 'Sorry to be the bearer of bad news, but there's a hell of a fuss at the main gate,' he said.

'Fuss?' asked Kolea.

'I'm just getting it now. A frontal attack.'

Both Kolea and Gaunt checked their earpieces and listened.

'Feth,' muttered Gaunt after a moment. 'So they're able to come at us from both sides of the objective? What kind of rat-trap has Van Voytz sent us into?'

'The worst kind,' suggested Criid.

'Is there any other?' asked Mkoll, trudging up the slope to join them.

'Good work,' Gaunt told him.

'It was nothing, sir,' Mkoll replied. He was lying. It was everything. From the moment he'd led the way into the gatehouse two days before, Mkoll had been on edge. A daemon had been stalking him, a daemon made of fear and uncertainty, two qualities generally alien to Mkoll's state of mind. He'd begun to feel himself incapable. He'd actually begun to distrust his own skills. It had been good to get out there and test himself.

'Let's get inside,' said Gaunt.

'And set charges in this cave to block it?' Kolea asked.

'Oh, absolutely,' Gaunt replied.

XII

In the end, there seemed to be no clarity or determination, no win or lose. The howling tide of the Blood Pact broke and retreated back into the dust clouds that had unleashed it.

And that was that.

Hark panted hard, his plasma pistol slack in his right hand. He was exhausted. Fight time was re-spooling back into real time, and that was always tough, especially as, on this occasion, real time brought the pain of his burns back with it.

The dunes outside the gatehouse were littered with bodies. At a rough estimate, five-sixths of them were enemy corpses. Hark looked around, recognising a few old comrades amongst the dead. He wasn't quite sure which was worse – seeing the corpse of a man you knew by name, or seeing a corpse so atrociously damaged you couldn't identify it.

There were both kinds at the gate of Hinzerhaus. Forty Ghosts dead, at least. It had been a hell of a fight for a skirmish, and Viktor Hark knew, in his heart of hearts, that a skirmish was all that it had been: an opening skirmish, a melee, a prelude.

Hinzerhaus would be the death of them all. Holding onto this place, they'd all end up as–

dry skulls in a dusty valley, with all the tops sawn off

–defunct names checked off in the Imperial annals. He shivered.

'Viktor?'

He glanced around. Curth was beside him. The medics were arriving to handle the wounded. Lesp and Chayker hurried past with a man on a stretcher.

'Viktor, you're hurt. Burned,' Curth said.

He nodded. 'Just a second. Arcuda?'

Arcuda looked up from the Ghost he was field dressing. 'What, sir?'

'Was somebody playing the pipes?'

'What?'

'Was somebody playing the pipes, Arcuda, during the attack. Tanith pipes?'

'During the attack?'

'Yes.'

'I don't believe so, sir.'

Hark turned back to Curth. 'I may be going mad,' he told her. 'Can you treat that?'

'Let me dress your wounds first,' she said, and led him back towards the hatch.

As he walked back across the blood-mottled dust, Curth's thin hand pulling at his thick paw, Viktor Hark began to shake. The wind picked up, and drove the dust at them.

'It's all right,' Curth said. 'It's going to be all right.'

Hark saw Larkin, huddled down beside the hatch, his long-las hugged against his chest, his eyes wide behind his goggles. Hark saw Wes Maggs, standing ready, twitchy, gun in hand, as if watching for something.

'No, Ana,' Hark said. 'No, it really isn't.'

Are we the last ones left alive? Are we? Someone, anyone, please? Are we? Is there anybody out there? Are we the last ones left alive?

(transmission ends)

- Transcript of vox message, fifth month, 778.

EIGHT
Bad Air

I

THE VOICE COMES *out of nowhere. It betrays no origin or source. It is only a whisper, a dry hiss that seems as old as the house itself. It sounds as if it has been mute for a long time, and is only just now remembering how to speak.*

Where is it coming from? Is it in the building's stonework? Is it imprinted in the very fabric of the house? Has contact disturbed it, woken it up, caused it to play back like an old recording? Or is it leaking into the vox from somewhere else? The past? The present? The future? Whose future?

It is a static murmur, a lisping echo at the back end of the frequency. It fades, and comes back, and fades again, incoherently. It fades and comes back in time with the harsh then soft throb of the house lighting. It pulses in tune with some slow, respiratory rhythm, the pulse of Hinzerhaus.

Are those words, or just sounds? If they are words, what are they saying? Who are they speaking to? Is the voice telling lies or some awful, vital truth?

The frequency tunes out, skipping from channel to channel in groans of noise and snatches of message. A hand reaches to the dial and turns it–

II

–OFF

Beltayn lowered his headset and sat back from his voxcaster. He swallowed.

'What the feth?' he whispered. He leaned forwards again, and switched his set back on. He pushed one cup of the headset against his right ear and listened as he twiddled.

'Hello? Who is that? Who's using this channel?'

Nothing. Just base-line static and wild noise.

'Something awry?' Gaunt asked, tapping Beltayn on the shoulder.

Beltayn jumped out of his skin.

'Sorry,' said Gaunt, genuinely surprised by his adjutant's reaction. 'Calm down, Bel. What's got you so spooked?'

Beltayn breathed out. 'Sir, it's all right. Nothing. Just a... glitch.'

'What sort of glitch?'

Baltayn shrugged. 'Nothing, really, sir. Just bad air. I'm getting ghosting on the Elikon freak.'

'What sort of ghosting?' Gaunt pressed.

'A voice, sir. It comes and goes. It's pleading... asking for help.'

'Where is it?'

'No site or status code. I think it's a vox echo.'

'A vox echo?'

'That happens, from time to time, sir. An old signal, bouncing back off something.'

Gaunt paused. 'Old or not, what does it say?'

Beltayn heaved a sigh. 'It keeps saying "Are we the last ones left alive?" Variations on that particular theme. It keeps repeating.'

'It's not Elikon?'

'No, sir. I'm getting Elikon signals layered over it. It's background. I had to tune the vox right back to sandpaper wavelengths to hear it properly.'

Gaunt frowned. 'Well, keep doing that and let me know what you find. Right now, I need my scheduled link to Van Voytz.'

'I'll get it, sir. Take it in your office.'

Gaunt wandered away across the base chamber as Beltayn began to adjust the knobs and dials of his caster.

The mood in the place was grim. It had been a bad day, and Gaunt cursed himself for missing the worst of it. Forty men dead at the gate, according to Arcuda's report, and twelve hurt, including Hark. The regiment was on alert condition red.

Varl was waiting for him at the door of his room. The sergeant saluted Gaunt as he approached.

'Major Rawne's compliments, sir,' Varl said. 'He requests your urgent attention in upper east twelve directly.'

'Tell him I'll be there in thirty minutes, Varl,' Gaunt said. 'I've only just got back in. I've got this mess to deal with, and a vox to vox with the general.'

Varl nodded. 'I'll tell him, sir. It's important, though. He wanted me to make sure you knew that.'

'Consider me aware,' said Gaunt. 'Upper east twelve? You had a scrap up there, didn't you?'

'Saw off an infiltration attempt,' said Varl. 'We think we know how they're getting in.'

'Really?' Gaunt hesitated. 'Look, I've got to make this call. I'll be with you as fast as I can.'

Varl saluted again and hurried away.

Gaunt walked into his office. There was no sign of Eszrah. The place was cold and empty. The lights faded softly and swam back up again. Gaunt wished with every fibre of his being they'd stop doing that.

He sat down at his desk. He could hear a man wailing in pain down the hall, one of the wounded in the field station.

Gaunt saw the red light winking on the vox-set on his desk. He got up, walked back to the office door and closed it, shutting out the sound of the screams. Then he walked back to his desk, sat down, and put the headset on. He pressed the connection key.

'Sir, I have the general for you,' Beltayn said, a fuzzy distortion in his ear.

'Thank you. Switch him through,' Gaunt said into the chrome mic, holding it close to his mouth.

'Hello, Elikon, hello, Elikon? Yes sir, this is Gaunt. Yes, I can hear you quite clearly...'

III

'WILL HE BE all right?' Ludd asked.

Dorden looked up at the junior commissar and smiled reassuringly. The smile fanned patterns of age lines out around the old doctor's eyes. 'Of course,' said Dorden.

Trooper Twenzet lay on the cot between them, stripped to the waist, his ribs dressed and wrapped. Dorden had given Twenzet some kind of shot, and the trooper was woozy and smiling.

'Thanks, friend,' he said to Ludd.

'It's all right.'

'Thanks for looking after me, though. Thanks. You're all right, you are.'

'Couple of days' bed rest, and Mr Twenzet will be right as rain,' Dorden told Ludd. 'In the meantime, I will keep him pharmaceutically happy and pain free.'

'This stuff's great,' said Twenzet. 'I feel wonderful. You should try it, friend.'

'It's not recreational, Twenzet,' said Dorden. 'Let's hope Mr Ludd doesn't find himself in a position where he needs to try it.'

'Course not, course not,' Twenzet nodded. 'Anyway, thanks. Thanks, friend. You're all right.'

'I've left your weapon in the store,' Ludd told the Belladon. 'You can reclaim it when you're signed off fit again.'

'No, no, you keep it,' Twenzet insisted. 'Please, friend, you keep it. You might need some stopping power to see you through this.'

Ludd smiled, believing a smile would do the trick.

'I shouldn't call you friend, though, should I?' Twenzet rambled on, suddenly troubled. 'Sorry, sorry, I didn't mean no disrespect. You being Commissariate and all that. This stuff the Doc's given me is making me all groggy and smiley. I should show you proper respect. Throne, I hope you're not going to put me on a charge for being over familiar.'

'Twenzet,' Ludd said, 'get some rest. I'll check back on you later, how's that?'

'That'd be nice, friend. I mean, sir. I mean–'

'Nahum. My name's Nahum.'

'Is it? Is it? Well, I'm Zak. Like a las-round, me old dad used to say. Zak. Like a las-round.'

'I heard the men in your squad call you Tweenzy,' said Ludd.

Twenzet frowned. 'Zak,' he said. 'I bloody hate it when they call me Tweenzy.'

'Zak it is, then. Get better. I'll come back and see you.'

Ludd moved away from Twenzet's cot. The field station was busy. Over a dozen men lay on the makeshift cots, all of them, except Zak Twenzet, casualties of the battle at the gatehouse. Dorden had moved away to help treat a man who was screaming and thrashing in pain. The man had lost a leg. The stump was jerking around as if trying to plant a foot that was no longer there.

Ludd looked away.

He saw Hark.

The bulky commissar was prone on his face on a cot in the far corner of the chamber. He had been stripped to his underwear, and Ana Curth was applying wet dressings to burns on his back and legs. His flesh was unnaturally pale. Ludd crossed to his bedside.

'Don't stand in my light,' Curth told him. Ludd stepped aside.

Hark seemed semi-conscious. Out of his clothes, his augmetic was plainly visible. Ludd recoiled slightly from the sight of it, the bulky black and steel armature of the limb that had been plugged into Hark's shoulder stump. Exposed servos whined and purred as the artificial hand clenched and unclenched. Ludd had always wanted to know how Hark had lost his arm. He had never had the guts to ask.

'How is he?' he asked quietly.

'How does he look?' Curth replied, busy.

'Not great,' said Ludd. 'I was asking for a specific medical diagnosis.'

Curth looked up at him. Her eyes were hard. 'He was caught by a flamer. Thirty per cent burns on the back and legs. He's in a great deal of pain. I'm hoping we can preserve the flesh without the need of a full graft.'

'Because?'

'Because I can't do a graft here, with these facilities. If it turns out Viktor requires a graft, we'll have to ship him out to Elikon, or he'll die. How's that for a diagnosis?'

'Fine,' Ludd replied. 'Might I point out your bedside manner leaves a lot to be desired, doctor?'

'Meh,' said Curth, going back to her dressings.

'One thing,' Hark groaned. '"He" can hear what you're saying.'

'Sir?'

Hark waved Ludd close. 'Ludd?'

'Yes, sir?'

Hark slapped Ludd's face.

'First of all, the doctor's doing the best she can, so don't harass her.'

'Understood, sir,' Ludd answered, rubbing his cheek.

'Ludd?'

Ludd leaned close again. Hark slapped his face a second time.

'Don't make friends with the troops, for feth's sake. Don't bond with the likes of Twenzet. He's rank and file, and you're Commissariate. You don't mix. Don't make him your new best friend. You have to preserve the separation of authority.'

'Yes, sir. I didn't mean to. I mean, I was only–'

Hark slapped his face again.

'I heard you. First name terms. He's a dog-soldier, and you're the moral backbone of the outfit. He's not your friend. None of them are your friends. They're soldiers and you're their commissar. They have to respect you totally.'

'I... understand, sir.'

'I don't,' said Curth, peeling the backing off another dressing strip. 'Why can't the boy make friends? Friendship, comradeship, that's a bond amongst your lot, isn't it?'

'My lot?' Hark chuckled. 'You've been around the Guard for so long, Ana, and you still don't get it.'

'Enlighten me,' she replied, tersely.

'Nahum is a commissar. He needs to command complete and utter authority. He needs to be a figure of fear and power to the troop ranks. He cannot afford the luxury of friendships or favouritism.'

'Actually, sir,' Ludd said, 'I'm just a junior commissar, so– ow!'

Hark had slapped him again.

'Ludd,' said Hark, 'do I look like I'm going anywhere fast? Curth is plastering my arse with bandages, and the chances are I'm going to die.'

'Just wait a minute!' Curth protested.

'Shut up, Ana. I'm out of action, Nahum. The regiment is without a functioning political officer. This is your moment in the sun, lad. Field promotion, effective immediate. You're the Ghosts' commissar now, Ludd. You keep them in line. I can't do it from a sickbed.'

'Oh,' said Ludd.

'I'm counting on you. Don't feth it up.'

'I won't, sir.'

'You'd better not.'

Curth ripped off her blood-stained gloves and discarded them into a pan for Lesp to collect. 'I'm done,' she announced. 'I'll be back in four hours to change the dressings.' She looked back at Ludd. 'Congratulations on your promotion, commissar. I hope you can handle the responsibility.'

She unceremoniously stuck a painkiller bulb into Hark's left buttock. 'There, that'll help you sleep.'

'Ouch,' said Hark.

'You'll take good care of him, won't you?' Ludd asked Curth as she walked away. Curth looked back at Ludd with a narrowed expression that said *are you suggesting I don't take good care of all my charges?*

'Oh. Of course you will,' Ludd said.

'Ludd?'

'Sir?'

'Do it right, will you?'

'I'll do it the best I can, sir,' Ludd said.

Hark was slipping away into the same happy void Twenzet had entered. 'Ludd?' he slurred.

'Sir?'

'Pipes.'

'What, sir?'

'Pipes. Tanith pipes. Listen for them.'

'The Tanith have no pipers, sir, not any more.'

'Listen for the pipes, Ludd.... listen... the pipes, that's the sign, the sign...'

'Sir?'

Hark had passed out. Ludd got up and walked out of the field station.

Behind him, the man without a leg was still screaming.

IV

'I BEG YOUR pardon?' said Dalin.

'I said, I need an adjutant, someone capable, now Fargher's dead,' Meryn said. 'I need a sharp man at my right hand. You read those charts in upper west sixteen yesterday, worked out where we were.'

'Sir, I–'

'Are you turning me down, Dalin?'

'No, sir.'

'It'd mean a bump in your wages, trooper.'

'Captain, that's not why I'm hesitating. I'm the most junior and inexperienced member of your company. I'm a scalp compared to the rest. Why not Neskon or Harjeon? Or Wheln?'

'Neskon's flame-troop. They're all out, bug-eyed crazy men, you know that. Harjeon, him I don't trust. Vervunhive civ. Too much of a starch arse. Wheln is old-school, but… feth, too much stiff nalwood in him. He's not adjutant material, never will be, despite his veteran status. You, you know the ropes. You're smart. I'm asking you, Dalin.'

Dalin shrugged. *And my father was Caffran and my mother is Criid and making me adjutant wins you points in the regiment, right?*

'This certainly isn't about who your father was,' said Meryn. 'I mean, get that idea out of your mind right now. I don't care who your fething dad was, or who your fething mum happens to be. I want you because you're the best choice.'

'I just hope this decision won't come around and bite you on the backside,' Dalin said.

Meryn grinned. 'Then make sure it doesn't, adjutant,' he said.

V

'THIS OBJECTIVE–' GAUNT repeated.

'Ibram, bear me out,' the vox said back to him. 'All I'm asking you to do is watch the eastern flank.'

'Barthol, please understand me. This is a doomed enterprise. The Blood Pact has already scaled the fortress wall. We just took a hit on our main gate. Our main southern gate.'

There was a pause. 'Please confirm your last remark.'

'I said we have just been attacked on the southern side of the objective. The enemy is surrounding us. We're holding an objective that is already compromised.'

The link was silent for another long moment. There was just the wheeze of dead air.

'Are you still there?' Gaunt asked. 'Elikon, are you still there?'

'Sorry, Ibram, I was consulting the tactical officers. Look, it's not going well, this banishment campaign. The bastards are holding their line with depressing success. We're pushing hard from here, but the front is broadening and they don't seem ready to break.'

'That's bad news, sir,' Gaunt said into the mic, 'but that's not the problem I'm left looking at here. The intelligence you based our orders on must have been inaccurate or out of date. The eastern line is already porous. The Blood Pact had penetrated the mountains long before we secured the objective. I don't believe the enemy is here in any great strength yet, but it won't be long. A week or two, they'll sweep west and hit you from the side, and this fortress will not be the instrument you were hoping would stop them.'

'I understand your predicament, Ibram. To be frank with you, I feared as much.'

Gaunt didn't reply. *You as good as knew you were sending us to our deaths, Barthol. Didn't you, you bastard? The intelligence wasn't inaccurate or out of date. You knew.*

'Ibram? Are we still linked? Confirm?'

'I'm still here, sir. What are your orders? Do we have your permission to withdraw at this time?'

'Uh, negative on that, Ibram. I simply can't conscience leaving the eastern flank open.'

'We're just one, small regiment, Barthol–'

'Agreed. I'll get you some support.'

'Please elaborate.'

'I can't. This link may not be safe and we've said too much already. Stand by as you are. Consider your mission profile as changed. Explore all possibilities offered by Hinzerhaus and its surrounding geography to harass and delay the enemy.'

'You want us to... keep them busy?'

'As best you can. I'm asking this as a personal favour, Ibram. Keep them busy. Delay them.'

'And you can't tell me any more?'

'Not on this link.'

'Understood. But I need stuff if we're going to survive.'

'Define stuff?'

'Water. And support, as I said. Heavy support.'

'I've organised a water drop for you tonight or tomorrow. Further information will be conveyed at that time.'

'All right. My men will be grateful for water, at least.'

'I have to go, Ibram. The Emperor protect you. Keep the bastards busy.'

'If it's the last thing I do,' said Gaunt.

But the link was already dead.

VI

UPPER EAST TWELVE was cold and breezy, and stank of expended las-fire and an underlying, organic odour that Gaunt had been around long enough to recognise as burnt blood.

As he strode along the hallway, under the cloche domes of the useless defences lining the roof space, Gaunt saw the blast marks and wall scars of the recent fire fight. Ludd and Baskevyl walked with him. Their clattering footsteps echoed back dully in the flat-roofed stretches of hallway, and rolled over them with a sharper sound as they passed under each cloche.

'Officer approaching!' Baskevyl called out.

Up ahead, a waiting fire-team turned to greet them: Rawne, with Varl, Mkoll and a dozen Guardsmen.

'Barthol send us his warmest regards, then?' Rawne asked.

'I'll fill you in later,' replied Gaunt. 'What did you want to show me?'

'We've identified how the enemy is slipping in and out up here,' said Mkoll.

'Wall panels, right?' asked Baskevyl. 'I knew it. I knew it was wall panels.'

'It's not wall panels,' said Rawne.

'Tap at the walls, if you like,' Mkoll offered. It was the closest thing to sarcasm anyone had ever heard from him. Not like Mkoll, thought Gaunt. Not like him at all. If Oan Mkoll's bent out of shape, we'd better put our gun barrels in our mouths now and say goodbye.

'Not the walls, then?' asked Gaunt. 'So?'

Mkoll turned his eyes upwards at the cloche above them. The wind outside blew skims of dust in around the slits of the almost, but not quite, closed fighting hatches.

'It's so horribly obvious, it's not funny,' said the chief of scouts quietly.

'Except, you have to laugh, don't you?' said Varl. No one seemed likely to. 'Or not,' Varl added glumly.

'I was told the shutters didn't work,' said Gaunt. 'I read Meryn's report. The winding gear is seized with dust.'

'The winding gear *is* seized with dust,' said Mkoll. 'That's not the same thing. I'll show you. Rawne, give me a boost.'

'Of course,' said Rawne, not moving. 'Varl?'

Varl sighed, slung his rifle over his shoulder, and bent down with his hands locked in a stirrup.

Mkoll placed a foot in Varl's hands and hoisted himself up into the dome of the cloche. He reached above his head and pushed his hands against the nearest shutter cover. It swung outwards without protest. Mkoll took a grip, and lifted himself up and out through the shutter. The shutter swung back shut.

'Holy Throne,' murmured Gaunt. 'It's that fething simple?'

Rawne nodded.

'The gears are jammed, see?' said Varl, pointing at one of the winding mechanisms on the collar ring of the cloche. 'But they've been disengaged from the shutters. The shutters themselves swing free.'

'All of them?' asked Baskevyl.

'No,' replied Varl. 'Nothing like, and not on every cloche, but a good few, right down this hallway. And the other fortified hallways too, probably.'

'We have squads checking,' said Rawne.

'They've systematically been in here and disengaged gears to provide themselves with entry and exit points?' Gaunt asked, wide-eyed at the notion.

'They must have been in here for weeks, months maybe,' said Varl. 'Tinkering with the winding gears, poking about.'

'Am I the only one worried about what else they might have "poked about" at?' Baskevyl asked.

'You're not,' said Gaunt. He shook his head. 'This place is like a sieve. A sieve would be easier to defend. Throne of Earth, and I thought this was a bad job already. How the feth does Barthol Van fething Voytz expect us to–'

'Expect us to what?' Rawne asked.

'Never mind. How did you find this?'

'As a consequence of our recent action against the Blood Pact up here,' said Rawne.

'Oh, tell the man the truth!' Varl snorted. Rawne glared at Varl. 'Eszrah Night found it,' Varl told Gaunt.

'Eszrah?'

'Yeah,' said Rawne. 'He got the spooks in his undershorts and came up here. We followed him.'

'I followed him,' said Ludd, quietly. No one paid much attention.

'I think Ez heard something,' said Varl. 'You know, that sleepwalker fifth sense.'

'Fifth, Varl? How many senses do you have?' asked Gaunt.

'Ah, I mean sixth, don't I?'

'I fething well hope so,' said Rawne.

'Anyway, we got jumped,' Varl went on. 'Blood Pact all over us like a camo net. Then Ez just drops in out of nowhere like... well, like a Nihtgane, really. Reynbowed their arses to the wall, he did.'

'He'd gone out through a shutter?' Gaunt asked.

'He'd figured it,' said Rawne, grudgingly. 'He came back in the way they did. Ambushed their ambush.'

Gaunt smiled. Beside him Ludd stepped forwards, gazing up at the dome. 'So that's it?' he asked. 'I was still trying to work out where Eszrah had come from.'

He looked at Gaunt. 'If they've been in here, the Blood Pact, I mean,' he began, 'if they've been in here all this time, why didn't they take the place?'

'What?' asked Rawne, scornfully.

'Why didn't they take the place?' Ludd asked, turning to stare at the major. 'They had all the time in the world. Why didn't they secure it and occupy it? We could have marched up that valley three days ago and found Hinzerhaus fully defended against us.'

'I don't know.'

'Ludd's got a point,' said Gaunt.

'Maybe they wanted to play games with us?' Varl suggested.

'Maybe there's something in here they don't like,' said Baskevyl. 'Maybe there's something in here they're scared of.'

'That's just crap,' said Rawne. Baskevyl shrugged.

'If there's something in here the Blood Pact is scared of,' said Varl, 'we're totally fethed.'

Gaunt looked up at the dome. 'I want to see. I want to see where Mkoll went.'

'I don't think–' Ludd began.

'That was an order, not an idle reflection.'

Rawne clicked his microbead. 'Mkoll? The boss wants to take a look for himself.'

'I expected he might,' the vox crackled back. 'All right. We're clear out here. Goggles, no hats.'

Gaunt took off his cap and handed it to Ludd. He put on the brass-framed goggles Baskevyl handed to him.

'Rawne? Give me a boost,' he said.

'Of course,' said Rawne. 'Varl?'

Varl sighed, slung his rifle over his shoulder again, and bent down with his hands held ready.

'Major Rawne,' said Gaunt. 'Give me a boost.'

Varl straightened up, disguising a grin. With malice in his eyes, Rawne bent over and linked his hands.

'Thank you, Eli,' said Gaunt, and hoisted himself up.

VII

THE SHUTTER FLAPPED shut and Gaunt was gone. Standing below the dome, looking up at it, they waited.

'So, I understand you're acting commissar, what with Hark hurt and everything,' Baskevyl said conversationally to Ludd.

'Uh, yes, that's right, Major Baskevyl.'

There was a long silence.

'That can't be easy,' said Baskevyl.

'No, sir,' replied Ludd.

The wind blew.

'So, er, you men had better start behaving yourselves,' Ludd added.

Varl started to twitch, as if afflicted with a tickling cough or an itch. It took about ten seconds for the twitch to turn into a full blown snigger.

'Sorry,' Varl said. 'Sorry! I just–'

The snigger turned into laughter. The Guardsmen behind Varl started to laugh too.

'Would you like me to shoot them,' Rawne inquired of Ludd sweetly, 'for discipline's sake?'

'That won't be necessary,' Ludd said, and turned away.

VIII

IF THERE WAS a forever on bad rock Jago, you could see it from there.

Gaunt got to his feet. The wind, as if anticipating his entrance, had dropped to a whisper. The dust had died. In the west, down along the spiny backbone of the Banzie Altids, a goblin moon was rising. The sky was a dirty yellow, the colour of wet peat. Clouds gathered in the north, low and banked like meringue. Down below the vast cliff of the mountain range, blankets of white fog covered the landscape.

It was cold. Gaunt moved and his feet skittered away loose rocks that tumbled off down the sheer wall into the blanket of dust far below.

'Watch your step,' said Mkoll, appearing beside Gaunt and placing a steadying hand on his arm. 'You want to see this, you do so on my terms.'

'Understood.'

On previous excursions out through the shutters, Mkoll had pegged a network of cables around the cloche. He clipped a safety line to Gaunt's belt. Mkoll was supported on one of his own.

'It's a long drop,' he said.

'It is, it really is.'

They stood for a moment and looked out over the canyon behind the mountain ridge into the dust-swathed badlands.

'You sort of have to admire their balls,' Mkoll said.

'Yes,' said Gaunt.

'We found evidence of some climbing tackle, some pinned-up stuff, but they've been pretty much coming up here and getting in by fingertips and effort alone.'

'Right.'

'That's got to be some ugly upper body strength.'

'Definitely.'

The drop was huge and the rock wall sheer. Gaunt looked down. The distance was immense and dizzying. Just a few hours before, he had been at the bottom end of this aspect, pinned down with Mkoll and Kolea. He remembered looking up. If he'd been trying to take Hinzerhaus from the north, the last thing he'd have suggested to his men was scaling the cliffs. He wouldn't have expected them to even think of it, let alone try it. The tenacity of the Blood Pact was an object lesson. They had no fear, or limitation on their endurance.

So how are we supposed to stop them? Or even delay them?

He looked to his right. The top of the sharp ridge curled around, slightly north and then in a slant to the south-west. Its length was dimpled with cloche turrets and casemates, iron domes and boxes that dotted away for at least two kilometres. On the outside, the cloche turrets, like the one he was secured against, were worn matt and rough by the scouring action of the wind and grit.

Gaunt looked to his left. There, the ridge rose up to a peak. Cloche turrets and casemates dotted up the rise of the peak and down the other side. At the apex he saw the windcote from the outside, a brass cupola, the summit of Hinzerhaus. The windcote supported a broken finial of metal. A proud flag or standard had once flown there, Gaunt thought.

'You don't like this place, do you?' Gaunt asked Mkoll.

Mkoll sighed. 'Not at all. I honestly can't think of another site I'd care to defend less. There's something about it.'

'And that something's getting to you?'

'You noticed? Yeah, this damn place makes me edgy, I don't know why. Never known a place get under my skin like this. I didn't think I was the sort of bloke to get the spooks. Now I've got 'em, it's making me doubt myself.'

'I know.'

Mkoll looked at Gaunt. 'I feel sloppy and off form. I keep second guessing myself, and jumping at shadows. I hate that. I can't trust myself. This place is making a fool out of me. And fools die faster than others.'

Gaunt nodded. 'If it helps, it's not just you. Everyone feels it. Well, except Rawne maybe, as he feels nothing.'

Mkoll smiled.

'There's something about Hinzerhaus,' Gaunt went on, 'and it's playing on our nerves. We just have to learn to ignore it. It's just an old fortress at the arse-end of nowhere.'

'Perhaps,' said Mkoll. 'I just wish I could shake the feeling that none of us is going to be getting out of here alive.'

'Would it trouble you to know that I have the same feeling, Oan?'

'It would, sir, so you'd better not tell me.'

IX

THEY HEARD A cry, like the cry of a bird, and Gaunt thought for a moment that the denizens of the windcote might have returned.

But it was a human voice, hollowed out by the wind. Three figures appeared beside a cloche a hundred metres west of them.

Gaunt squinted. 'Ours?'

'Yeah,' said Mkoll. 'I've had men searching the outside of the ridgeline, cutting free any traces of Blood Pact rope work.'

They detached their safety lines and edged along the natural rampart of the rock towards the others. Gaunt felt relief every time they reached another cloche or gunbox, where he could hold on and steady himself for a moment. The alarming drop into distant clouds reminded him of Phantine and the view down into the Scald. Despite the chill, he was beginning to sweat. He had no wish to be where he was, especially untethered, if the wind rose again.

A long five minutes of concentrated effort brought them over to the others. The scouts Caober and Jajjo nodded greetings as Mkoll and Gaunt joined them. Eszrah ap Niht waited silently behind them.

'Found much?' Gaunt asked.

Jajjo pointed to the west. 'A whole network of rope ladders and tether lines, about half a kilometre that way. Bonin and Hwlan have gone to cut them free.'

'Question remains, what do we do with the fortifications?' asked Caober. 'I mean, they're weak links unless we crew them.'

'We could try blocking them off,' suggested Jajjo.

'We crew them,' said Gaunt. 'If this place is a fortress, let's occupy it as such. Let's man these defences. If the enemy comes creeping back up here, he'll be in for a surprise.'

Gaunt looked at Eszrah. The partisan, wearing the sunshades Varl had given him long before, was staring up at the malevolent yellow moon.

'That was good work,' Gaunt said.

'Soule?'

'Good work, learning about the shutters. And I think Rawne's fire-team owes you a debt too.'

Eszrah shrugged his shoulders slightly.

'There was something else, sir,' said Caober. He led them around the grit-burnished rim of the cloche to the southern side of the mountain rampart. They were overlooking what Gaunt thought of as the front of Hinzerhaus. There was the narrow pass that led to the gatehouse, though the gatehouse was hard to make out at that distance. Immediately below them, the main sections of Hinzerhaus grew out of the sloping mountain face: sections of old tiled roof, the tops of casemates built into the cliffs, and small towers.

'There, sir,' said Caober, pointing. Gaunt could see something a long way down the slope, in the lower area of the house's southern aspect. It looked like a large, square roof surrounded by other, red-tiled roofs on two sides, and mountain rock on the other two.

'You see?' asked Caober.

Gaunt took out his scope and trained it for a better look. It wasn't a square roof at all. It was a paved courtyard, open to the sky.

Gaunt lowered his scope. 'Has anyone reported finding a courtyard so far?'

'No,' replied Mkoll.

'So there's a courtyard slap bang in the middle of the lower southern levels, and we didn't know about it?' Gaunt paused. 'That means there are still parts of this damned place we haven't even found yet.'

Day nine. Sunrise at four plus forty-one, white-out conditions. It has been explained to me that I am expected to maintain this field journal while H. is incapacitated.

Day's activities two-fold. Teams are continuing to secure the objective, which includes taking up defensive positions in the upper fortifications + those casemates covering the main approach/gatehouse. Other duty sections resuming search of objective to find 'hidden' areas, including some sort of courtyard space.

My own concern is my singular lack of authority. I cannot blame the men for it. I have followed on H's coat-tails so far, and exercised his authority. Until now the men only had to tolerate or ignore me. I frankly do not know what to do. I wish to discharge my duties as political officer, especially at this trying time, but I cannot force the men to respect me. Have considered consulting G.

Water drop now overdue.

— Field journal, N.L. for V.H. fifth month, 778.

NINE

034TH

I

THE WIND SKIRLED around the gunslits of overlook six. Larkin had propped the main shutter open with a block of wood. Goggles on, his mouth and nose wrapped up behind the folds of his camo-cape, he trained his scope out into the dust storm.

'See anything?' asked Banda snidely. She'd given up watching, and had retired to the back of the casemate to brush the dust out of her scope. Her long-las leaned against the stone wall behind her. It was cold in the bunker, especially with the shutter lifted, and dust blew in, filling the air with a faint powder. Banda shivered. She took a swig of sacra from her flask. A lot of Ghosts had begun filling their empty water bottles with liquor from contraband supplies. Something to drink was better than nothing, now the water had all but gone.

'Want some?' she asked Larkin, holding the flask out. Larkin shook his head. 'That stuff'll just make you more thirsty,' he said from behind his dust-caked muffle. 'Rot your brain if you dehydrate and keep supping it.'

'Yeah, well,' said Banda with a shrug, and took another sip.

'Plus, you won't be able to shoot worth a damn.'

'Gonna write me up, Mister Master Sniper? Huh? Gonna put me on report?'

Larkin didn't answer. He didn't especially care if Jessi Banda went crazy drinking still juice. He certainly didn't want the bother of writing her up. What good would that do?

Overlook six was one of the main casemate towers above the gatehouse on the southern slope of Hinzerhaus. When the dust dropped back, it afforded an excellent, marksman-friendly line down the throat of the pass. When the dust rose, it afforded feth all.

Kolea came in through the hatch. Banda hurriedly tucked her flask away.

'Larks?'

'Hello, Gol.'

'Anything?'

Larkin shrugged. 'I think I saw some dust just now.'

Kolea managed a smile. Like most of them, his lips were cracked and dry, and dust infections were reddening his eyes. There wasn't enough fluid in the place to mix up counterseptic eye wash.

'Beltayn just got a squirt on the vox. We think it may be this mythical water drop, but he can't fix the signal.'

'I can't help you,' said Larkin. 'Sorry.'

Kolea nodded and turned to go. 'Make sure you don't work too hard there, Banda,' he remarked as he passed her. As soon as he was out of sight, Banda extravagantly gave him *the root*, a hand gesture popular amongst disenchanted Verghastites who found words failing them.

'Hey,' said Larkin suddenly. He set his scope up at the shutter again, focusing it. 'Hey, Gol! Gol!'

Kolea ran back in. Banda had risen to her feet. 'What is it?' Kolea asked.

'Wind just dropped,' said Larkin. 'We've got a calm. Air's clearing fast. Thought I saw... wait...'

His scope whirred.

'Yeah,' Larkin said with relish. 'Two contacts, airborne, about eight kilometres out, inbound from the south-west.'

II

'THIS IS NALWOOD, this is Nalwood. Say again, over.'

Beltayn listened hard to the crackle and hum of his vox set. Gaunt, Daur, Criid and Kolosim stood behind him, waiting. Sections of troopers, forty in all, armed and ready to move, were congregating below them in the bottom level of the base chamber.

'Nalwood, this is Nalwood. Please re-transmit,' Beltayn said. The set snuffled like a snoring baby in a pram.

Kolea came clattering down the main staircase and ran across to Gaunt. 'We've got visual contact. Lifters heading this way.'

Gaunt nodded. 'Bel, can you–'

Not looking up, Beltayn raised his hand sharply for quiet.

A voice crackled out of the caster's main speaker grille. 'Nalwood, Nalwood, this is transport K862 inbound to your location. Estimate four minutes away. Water drop as requested, over.'

There was a raucous cheer from the Ghosts assembled on the staging below. Gaunt and his officers exchanged smiles.

Beltayn adjusted his caster. 'K862, K862, this is Nalwood, this is Nalwood. Good to hear you, over.'

'Hello, Nalwood. Need you to define LZ. Please advise. Pop smoke or display mag beacon, over.'

Beltayn glanced up at Gaunt. 'What do I tell him?'

'I've got smoke and a mag beacon ready,' said Ban Daur. 'What's it doing out there?'

'The wind's dead. We've got a clear window,' said Kolea. 'Let's not muck about. We'll bring them in outside the main gate and team the supplies inside, double time.'

Gaunt nodded. 'Go,' he said.

Kolea, Criid, Daur and Kolosim ran to join the sections waiting below at once, calling orders. The men began to file out towards the gatehouse.

'K862, K862, be advised we are popping smoke as requested,' Beltayn told the mic. 'Watch for it at the head of the pass. LZ is flat area in front of main gatehouse, repeat flat area in front of main gatehouse, over.'

'Thank you, Nalwood. Inbound, over.'

Gaunt clicked his microbead. 'All sections, this is One. Drop coming in, main gate. Full alert, full cover. This is going to get noticed. Any sign of trouble, you have permission to loose off.'

A FIRE-TEAM LED by Corporal Chiria was opening the outer hatch as Daur and the others arrived. 'Sections one and two, you're on portables,' Daur called out. 'Three and four, spread and cover as per brief.'

Daur stepped through the hatch and began to run out into the open. The sunlight was pale and bright, and only the faintest breeze stirred the surface dust. His heels puffed up plumes of the stuff as he ran.

He felt horribly exposed. Pieces of Blood Pact armour and weaponry still littered the dust from the day before, although the enemy had recovered their dead under cover of night. He was running right out into the open. The beige cliffs and outcrops of the pass loomed around him. In his imagination, they were full of enemy skirmishers, drawing aim. Daur was uneasily convinced his imagination wasn't wrong.

He couldn't see the transport, but he could hear the pulsing whine of lifter jets echoing around the tops of the cliffs.

Fifty metres from the gate, he dropped to his knees and swung the satchel off his shoulder. He pulled out the metal tube of the mag beacon, twisted the nurled grip and set it going. It began to emit a little, repeating chirrup, and a small light on its facing began to wink. Daur dug it into the dust, upright. Then he removed the smoke flares from the satchel, and pulled their det-tapes one by one, tossing the smoking canisters onto the ground in a crude circle. The smoke billowed up in bright green clouds and trailed off away from the gate.

'Ban, they're coming,' Criid voxed. Daur turned and jogged back towards the gate. The jet noise grew louder.

Two aircraft suddenly came into view, rushing in over the cliff top. Their hard shadows shot across the white basin outside the gate. They banked east around Hinzerhaus, disappearing from view for a second, and then swung around again in tight formation, dropping speed and altitude.

The larger aircraft was a big Destrier, a bulk lifter, painted drab cream and marked with a flank stencil that read 'K862'. It was making the most noise, its big engines howling as the pilot eased it down in a ponderous curve.

The other aircraft was a Valkyrie assault carrier, a hook-nosed machine one-third the size of the heavy lifter. The Valk was painted khaki with a cream belly. Its tail boom was striped with red chevrons and the stencil 'CADOGUS 52'.

'Get up and get ready to move!' Daur shouted through the hatch at the waiting men. The downwash from the fliers was creating a Munitorum dust storm in front of the gate area, and the green smoke was being forced upwards into the air in a strangely geometric spiral.

The Valkyrie stood on a hover at about thirty metres, and let the Destrier go in first. The big machine descended gently and crunched down in a fury of dust-kick, its cargo jaws immediately unfolding with a shrill buzz of hydraulics.

'Go! Go!' shouted Daur.

The sections led by Daur and Kolea ran out from the gatehouse towards the big lifter, heads down. They carried their lasrifles strapped across their backs. The other two sections, under Criid and Kolosim, simultaneously fanned out around the edge of the landing site, weapons in hand, watching the rocks for movement or attack.

Daur was first to reach the lifter. The idling engine was raising a tumult of dust, and the air stank of hot metal and exhaust. Three Munitorum officers stood on the payload area, manhandling the first of several laden pallets out through the cargo jaws.

Daur waved at them. 'How many?' he yelled.

'A dozen like this,' one of the handlers shouted back. The pallets were thick, flak board bases with rows of hefty fluid drums tight-packed and lashed onto them, twenty drums on each pallet.

'You got no cargo gear?' the handler yelled.

Daur shook his head. 'Gonna have to move them by hand!' he shouted back. Daur took out his warknife and sawed through the packing twine lashing the first pallet's cargo together. As his men came up, they each grabbed as many of the heavy, sloshing drums as they could manage, and headed back towards the gate. Most could carry two, one in each hand. A few of the biggest men, like Brostin, could just about lift three. It was a struggle. Everyone knew speed was of the essence.

'Let's go! Second load!' Daur yelled. He and Kolea tossed the empty first pallet clear as the handler crew slid the next one out through the jaws.

Too slow, too slow, Daur thought. The first troopers carrying drums had only just reached the gatehouse. The sheer weight of the drums, combined with the soft dust underfoot, made the process of unloading truly punishing.

Men came rushing back from the gate, empty handed, to take up the next load. They were already out of breath and flexing strained and tired arms.

'Come on!' Kolea shouted, taking the drums Daur passed to him and handing them out to each man in turn.

With the Destrier down, the Valkyrie came in to land to its left. It landed with a squeal of jets, inside Criid's perimeter.

'Derin! Watch those rocks!' Criid yelled, and jogged over into the dust-wrap surrounding the Valkyrie. A crewman had slid the heavy side door of the passenger compartment open and two men had jumped out into the dust under the hooked wing. They came forwards, bent down in the wash, hands shielding their eyes. One was dressed in khaki, the other in black. The man in black was carrying a heavy bag.

'This way!' Criid shouted, gesturing.

They hurried towards her. As they approached, Criid raised her arms and flashed a signal to the Valkyrie pilot. She saw him in his cockpit, his brightly painted helmet tipping her a nod.

The Valkyrie took off again, thrusters wailing as if in pain. It rose sharply, climbed hard, and began to turn at about three hundred metres, nose down.

Criid saluted the men as they came up to her. The one in khaki was short, slim and fair. For one awful moment Criid thought it was Caffran, back from the dead.

'Major Berenson, Cadogus Fifty-Second,' he yelled above the noise. 'This is my tactical advisor. I present my compliments to your commander, and request audience.'

'Criid, First-and-Only,' she replied, shaking his hand. 'Follow me, sir. We're a little exposed out here.'

She turned and ran towards the gate. The two men ran after her.

* * *

III

THEY WERE ONTO the third pallet. The Munitorum boys were shoving it out through the cargo jaws. Daur glanced at his chron. Four minutes. Too slow, still too slow. The men running back to collect the next load of drums were already panting and exhausted.

Kolea cut the twine with his knife, and started to pass out the drums as they slid loose, heavy and stubborn.

'Let's go, let's go, let's go!' he urged above the noise of the Destrier's engines.

Daur turned. 'What was that?' he asked.

'What?' Kolea shouted back, still handing the drums off to the relay of men.

'I heard a noise!' Daur yelled. It had been a dull thwack of a noise, a dense impact.

'Feth,' Daur murmured. 'We've got a leak here!'

Water, bright and clear, was squirting out of one of the drums on the third pallet, spattering copiously into the dust like a fountain jet.

'We've got a damn leak!' he yelled again, reaching the drum and trying to stopper it with his fingers.

There was another thwack. A metre to Daur's right, another drum began to hose water out of its side. Out of a *puncture* in its side.

Daur looked around at Kolea. 'We're–' Daur started to shout.

A las-round ricocheted off the cargo-jaw assembly. Two more spanked into the side of the Destrier. One of the Munitorum officers rocked on his feet as a red mist puffed out behind his back. He fell hard, crashing off the pallet and into the dust. A Ghost, a drum in each hand, turned and fell sideways, the side of his head shot off.

'Contact!' Kolea bawled. 'Contact! Contact!'

IV

RHEN MERRT TURNED. Something was up. He was part of Criid's section fanned out around the perimeter. The bulk lifter behind him was making one hell of a noise.

'What was that?' he yelled at Luhan.

'What?' Luhan shouted back.

'Kolea gn… gn… gn… yelled something!'

'I dunno,' yelled Luhan.

Merrt saw sparks in the rocks ahead of him. He knew what that was. They were taking fire from the crags of the pass. They couldn't hear the crack of discharge because of the lifter's engine noise.

'Contact!' Merrt yelled. He raised his rifle and blasted at the rock slope. Nothing happened. His lasrifle had jammed.

Shots whipped in across them. The enemy wasn't aiming at Merrt and his section. They were targeting the heavy lifter. Merrt saw las and tracer rounds sizzling through the air above him. He struggled to clear his weapon.

Merrt's lasrifle was a particularly battered and unreliable piece. He'd picked it up during the savage street fighting on Gereon after he'd lost his own. It was well-worn, and had a faded yellow Munitorum stencil on the butt. It was ex-Guard issue, but Merrt had a sneaky suspicion the weapon had been used by the enemy for a while.

A captured, recaptured piece, and not in particularly good order. He despised it. Merrt sometimes fancied that the time it had spent, literally, in enemy hands had left a curse on it. It was four kilos of bad luck swinging on a strap. He knew he should have exchanged it for a new issue at the Munitorum supply. He should have told the clerks the weapon's history and had them destroy it. But he hadn't, and he wouldn't have been able to say exactly why he hadn't if asked directly. Deep down, there was an unformed thought that he and the gun somehow deserved each other, an unlucky rifle for a fething unlucky man.

He worked to unjam it. It seemed to cooperate. Merrt trained it and fired. There was a jolt. The lasrifle emptied its entire load in one disastrous cough of energy. The blast threw Merrt down on his back. The blistering ball of discharge hit rocks twenty metres away and exploded like a tube-charge, throwing a drizzle of earth, dust and grit into the air.

Merrt rolled over, and looked around, dazed. He saw a Ghost go down, one of the men in the relay team running between the gate and the lifter. Full, heavy drums of water landed hard and askew in the dust either side of the body. Another member of the team fell as he was winged, got up, and fell again as a second shot burst through one of the drums he was carrying and into his hip.

Merrt got up and grabbed his las. He ejected the clip and forced home a new one.

'Work!' he snarled 'Gn... gn... gn... *work*!'

V

ENEMY FIRE WAS zipping and pinging in around them. The cargo jaws had been badly dented and the third pallet of water, half unloaded, was spraying out its contents through dozens of shot holes.

'We can't stay here!' one of the two remaining Munitorum officers yelled at Daur.

'You have to! We need this water!'

The officer shook his head. 'Sorry! The pilot says he's pulling out! Get back!'

'No!' Daur shouted, losing his footing. The Munitorum officers shoved the third pallet clear of the cargo-jaws and ducked back inside the lifter. The jaws whined shut and the Destrier lifted off in a storm of dust, shots thumping against its hull.

'No! Come back, you bastards!' Daur howled.

'Ban! Forget it!' Kolea told him, grabbing his arm and pulling him to his feet. 'We're dead out here! Get back to the gate!'

Daur ran, Kolea at his heels. The relay teams and the covering sections were scurrying back towards the gate, chased by shot. Above them, the southern casemates and gunboxes of Hinzerhaus had opened up. Heavy fire raked down from the open shutters and ploughed across the jumbled rocks of the escarpment.

Daur blundered up to the gate hatch. 'How much did we get?' he gasped. 'How much?'

'Two and a half pallets,' Kolosim replied.

'Out of a dozen?' Daur snapped. 'Feth's sake, that's not enough! We left half a fething pallet out there in the dust!'

'That's where it'll have to stay, Ban,' Kolea said quietly. 'We've got no choice. Get inside. We need to shut the hatch.'

VI

'K862, K862, WE need that load, over,' Beltayn said into the vox.

'I appreciate that, Nalwood, but the LZ is not secure. Am circling.'

Beltayn looked at Gaunt. Gaunt held out his hand and Beltayn put the vox mic into it.

'Destrier K862, this is Colonel-Commissar Gaunt, commanding this position, over.'

'I hear you, sir, over.'

'We're out of water and we need what you're carrying, over.'

'No doubt in my mind that you do, sir, but that landing site was compromised. Heavy fire. It cost me one crew member. Another thirty seconds on station, and I'd have taken a round through my engine core. I couldn't stay there, over.'

'We need that water, K862, over.'

'Suggest we try an alternative drop point, sir, over.'

Gaunt glanced at Beltayn.

'Out the back, sir? Through the tunnel from the power plant workshops?'

'We sealed it last night,' Gaunt told his adjutant. He spoke into the mic. 'Stand by, K862.'

'Circling, Nalwood. Be advised fuel load will allow me to remain here for another six minutes only. Then we're out, over.'

'What about that courtyard?' Beltayn asked.

Gaunt raised the mic. 'K862, K862, suggest you try a courtyard in the lower southern face. You can see it better than we can from up there, over.'

'Turning in, Nalwood. The dust just blew up again.'

'K862?'

'Hold on, Nalwood, it's blowing up hard suddenly. All right, we see it. Coming around, over.'

'Thank you, K862, over.'

They waited. A wind rose and gusted through the base chamber.

'Nalwood, we have your courtyard in sight. Too small for a landing, over'

'K862, can you drop, over?' Gaunt asked.

'Not ideal, but we'll try, Nalwood. Stand by, over.'

Gaunt looked at Beltayn. They both waited in silence. It was taking forever. 'One, Throne of Terra... Two, Throne of Terra...' Gaunt began to whisper.

The vox coughed. 'Nalwood, Nalwood, this is K862, this is K862. We have dropped cargo at this time. View from here is that some of it may have burst. Did the best we could, over.'

'Thank you, K862. Go home, over.'

'Understood, sir. Hope it works out for you. K862 out.'

Gaunt handed the vox mic back to Beltayn. 'So... all we have to do now is find that blasted courtyard,' he said.

VII

'I'M A LITTLE busy right now,' said Beltayn. 'What was it you wanted?'

Beltayn had been on his way out of the base chamber to work on charts in Gaunt's office when Dalin had stopped him. Dalin waved his hand. 'Nothing, adj. Just wanted to pick your brains.'

'Because?'

'Captain Meryn has appointed me as his adjutant and I'm not sure what I'm supposed to do, exactly. I thought I could ask you for advice.'

Beltayn shook his head. 'Meryn made you his adjutant? You poor bastard. What happened to Fargher?'

'He died,' said Dalin.

'Oh, yeah. Right. I heard that.' Beltayn looked Dalin up and down, thoughtfully. 'Can I ask you something, Dalin?'

'Of course.'

'Do you think Meryn asked you to do this because of who you are?'

'Are you kidding? I think it's safe to assume that was uppermost in his mind.'

Beltayn grinned. 'You don't care?'

'It irks me. It bothers me that no one can talk to me without the thought of who I am in their heads. On the other hand, I'll die of fatigue if I keep fighting it, so I'll live with it.'

'All right, then,' said Beltayn. 'So, apart from that, why do you think Meryn asked you to be his adj?'

'Because he knows I'm smart. Because he knows I can make him look good. Because I can read a map a feth of a lot better than he can,' Dalin replied.

'Read a map, eh?' Beltayn thought about that. 'You're good with charts?' he asked. 'Follow me.'

VIII

MERRT SLUMPED DOWN amongst the other members of his section. All four sections had been ordered back from the gatehouse into the base chamber. The sections that had been running the relay flopped down in exhausted heaps. Some had to move aside as the wounded were carried through by stretcher parties. From the upper levels of the fortress house, they could hear the crack and thump of continuing gunfire from the casemates.

Merrt sat and stared furiously at his rifle. The wretched bastard thing had jammed twice during the fire fight. It *was* cursed, and it was jinxing him. He desperately wanted to get rid of it, but he knew he couldn't. He still had a lot to prove to the senior ranks, to men like Hark. Merrt was on unofficial probation, and he was determined not to screw things up. He'd promised Hark as much. If the likes of Hark, or Gaunt, or Rawne discovered he was carrying a weapon tainted by the Archenemy's touch, if he admitted it, and they found out he'd known about the rifle's dubious lineage all along, that would be it. He'd be lucky if he made a penal regiment.

And Rhen Merrt was not a lucky man.

He didn't know what to do. He was afraid of the gun, and was convinced it was enjoying his fear. *Don't be stupid, it's just a gun.*

He rubbed at the half-faded yellow Munitorum stencil on the butt. He hadn't really paid the stencil much attention before. It was just a Munitorum serial code, half worn out.

Except it wasn't. It said 'DEATH'.

Merrt blinked. He felt a cold anxiety fill his dry throat like a rod of ice. 'DEATH'. It actually said 'DEATH'. It–

No, it *was* just a Munitorum code. 034TH. Half flaked away, the numerals appeared to read 'DEATH'.

Merrt closed his eyes and rested his head back against the cold wall. *You stupid idiot. 'DEATH'. You idiot, scaring yourself. You've got to shake this off.*

You've got to forget this nonsense about the gun being cursed. It's just a gun. It's just a piece of junk. Merrt heard voices and looked up.

'Good work, boys,' Captain Daur was telling them, walking down the line of them. 'Good work. That was tight, but you did well. I've just been told the rest of the water drop has been delivered. Drinks on me.'

Merrt ignored the insufferably good-looking Daur and placed his untrustworthy rifle on the floor beside him. He looked down at it warily, sidelong, as if it was a poisonous snake.

We'll see, 034TH, we'll see. I'm going to beat your jinx and break your will. I'm going to master you and prove myself. Or you're going to be the death of me.

IX

'Sir, this is Major Berenson,' said Criid, 'and this is Tactical Officer Karples.'

'Welcome to the fun,' Gaunt said. He shook hands with Berenson and took a quick salute from the aide. 'Let's talk in my office. Thank you, Criid, that will be all.'

Criid nodded and watched the three men walk out of the base chamber into one of the connecting hallways. Nearby, she saw Kolea staring at them too.

'Uncanny, isn't it?' she asked.

'Sorry, Tona, what is?'

'That Berenson. Dead spit for Caff, don't you think?'

Kolea raised his eyebrows. 'Gak, that's what it is! I couldn't put my finger on why he spooked me so much.'

'Dead spit. Could be a brother.'

Kolea looked at her. 'You all right?'

'I'm always all right,' she replied. 'So where's this water, then?'

'We're working on it,' Kolea said.

'I wasn't expecting a personnel transfer,' Gaunt said as he led Berenson and the tactical aide into his office. In one corner of the room, Beltayn was working on a pile of maps spread out on a small table. Dalin, Rerval, Fapes and Bonin were huddled in with him.

'Do you need the room, sir?' Bonin asked.

'Please,' said Gaunt.

The group gathered up their charts, locators and wax pencils and left the office. Dalin cast an oddly lingering look at Berenson as he went out.

Gaunt led Berenson and the tactical officer over to his desk and offered them seats. Berenson and the tactical sat down on two mismatched wooden chairs. Gaunt perched on the edge of his desk.

'We can probably offer you some caffeine in a while, once we've found something to brew it with.'

'That's fine, sir,' said Berenson. He took off his cap and brushed the dust off the crown. Gaunt suddenly understood Dalin's lingering fascination. The man bore a startling similarity to Caffran.

'As I said, I wasn't expecting a personnel transfer.'

'Last minute thing,' Berenson explained. His voice bore the traces of a clipped accent. 'Elikon command was concerned about appraising you over the vox.'

'We've had penetration of code,' the tactical aide said bluntly.

'It was agreed I should follow the supply drop in and bring you up to speed in person,' Berenson continued.

'I appreciate that. We feel rather cut off out here.'

'I can see why,' said Berenson with a half-smile. He looked around. 'This is a curious hole, this Hinzerhaus. I must say, it has the most peculiar atmosphere. Not entirely pleasant. Sort of... menacing.'

'Its a bad place on a bad rock,' said Gaunt. 'I presume you were briefed by Van Voytz.'

Berenson nodded. 'He's fully aware of the plight he's placed you in, sir. Fully aware. He sends his regrets. In fact, he was most particular about that. The tactical summaries left something to be desired.'

'The enemy dispositions are hard to read,' the tactical officer put in, uncomfortably. 'We are revising.'

'Karples thinks we're getting at his department for doing a bad job,' Berenson smiled. 'I keep telling him it really wasn't Tactical's fault. The enemy surprised us all. They were disguising massive troop deployments along the Kehulg Basin.'

'Show me,' said Gaunt.

Karples got up and produced a hololithic projector from his bag. He set it on the desk and aimed the caster lens at the back wall of the office. The device hummed, and projected a hazy three-dimensional graphic into the air. Karples walked into it and began to point towards certain features.

'The main elements of our opposition were identified by early orbit sweeps and sat-scatter as accumulated here in the Jaagen Lowlands, and here in the lower provinces. Elikon was chosen as the optimum beach head for landing and dispersal. Fierce fighting at armour brigade level has been taking place here, and along here, and into the Lowlands. There was some concern that enemy elements might swing east and attempt a penetration through the Banzie Altids, which is why the Lord General deployed you to this site.'

Gaunt nodded. 'But that's not how it's playing out, is it? We've seen that much for ourselves.'

Karples looked back at Gaunt, his pinched, rodent face layered in streamers and patches of coloured light from the display.

'No, it's not, colonel-commissar. Undetected by the sat-scatter drones, the enemy had massed considerable forces here, here and here before we made planetfall, the Kehulg Basin in particular. These forces have swept around out of cover and achieved a pincer around the Elikon front.'

'That's seriously bad news, sir,' Berenson put in. 'The fighting along that stretch of the line is wicked. Be thankful you're out here.'

'I'm not that thankful,' said Gaunt. 'The enemy's here too.'

Karples nodded. 'Far more advanced than we first suspected. We now believe they have been planning this for months. Successive, surprise strikes along our eastern flank were the actual basis of their strategy. Hinzerhaus is the furthest projection of their swing attack, but crucial. They are not attempting to counter-strike here, sir. This is the path of their main offensive.'

'Imagine how pleased that makes me feel,' Gaunt said, sitting down in his chair.

'Clearly, we've disposed and positioned ourselves badly,' Berenson said. 'I'm here to tell you this isn't going to be your problem for much longer.'

'Really?'

Berenson smiled. So like Caff, Gaunt thought. 'The Cadogus Fifty-Second has deployed in total strength configuration. Twenty thousand men, plus armour and artillery, along with battlefield psykers. As luck would have it, we were delayed in transit, otherwise we'd have been placed along the Jaagen zone. Thank the Throne we weren't. It gives our side tactical flexibility. My regiment is operational and moving rapidly into the field east of Elikon, with the intention of meeting the enemy offensive head on. Show him, Karples.'

'Here, also here, here and here,' the tactical aide said, pointing at the 3-D light.

'The main business is likely to be at Banzie Pass,' said Berenson, 'but we can't ignore Hinzerhaus and its environs. Five companies of mechanised infantry will be arriving in the next three days. Full support. We'll take over from you then. We'll greet them and hit them hard. All your... Ghosts, I believe they're called... all your Ghosts have to do is hold this position until then and keep the enemy contained and occupied.'

Gaunt nodded.

'And I'm here to help you with that,' said Berenson brightly.

'I hope you can shoot, then,' said Gaunt.

Day ten. Sunrise at four plus fifty-three, white out conditions, or so I'm told by A.C. Bored out of my skull here in the field station. ~~WE~~ Wish I could move. Back hurts.

Face down on a gurney. This is how I will see out the rest of my career. L. comes in to visit me, once in a while. I can tell he's not happy. I imagine the men are being less than cooperative. Poor bastard.

There was a water drop yesterday, but it seems no one can now locate the damn water. I am so parched, it's killing me. My throat hurts worse than my back, and A.C. tells me I do not want to see my back.

Bad night. I ~~had the dream suffered the voices in my head the pipes~~ slept badly, and woke up a lot. Kept ~~hearing the pipes playing in my head~~ waking, troubled. There's something going on. G. came to see me, but he wasn't saying much.

Shoggy Domor died during the night. Twice. D. brought him back both times with cardiac paddles. I am scared for Shoggy. He needs proper care in a Guard hospital. Out here, in this cellar, he doesn't stand a chance.

Have begun to hate Hinzerhaus. Am increasingly convinced it is trying to kill us all.

– field journal, V.H. fifth month, 778.

TEN

Five Thirty-Seven

I

It was early, very early. The house was cold and the lights seemed especially dim. Outside, the wind murmured.

The old dam in the black lace dress, she of the maggoty, meat-wound face, was walking about again. Maggs could hear her footsteps, and feel the chill of her.

Throne, how she wanted them dead, all of them. That was her business. When he closed his eyes, he could see her face, a face that wasn't a face any more.

Maggs had been sent to sit the small hours watch in a gunbox on upper west fifteen. At first, the six-man team had taken turns watching the shutters while the others rested, but there was nothing to see outside except dust, so they'd given up on that. They'd closed the shutters and rigged tripwires so they'd know if anyone was trying to prise them open from the outside.

Footsteps rolled along the quiet hallway behind them. Slow, shuffling steps. Maggs looked up, raising his gun.

'What's the matter?' Gansky asked him.

'Nothing,' said Maggs. He couldn't hear the footsteps any more. He got up and checked the tripwires.

'What time is it?' he asked.

'Five twenty-two,' said Lizarre, checking his chron sleepily.

Maggs walked down the hallway and looked around. Nothing, not a sign of anyone.

That was all right, though. He really, really didn't want to come face to face with her.

II

BASKEVYL WOKE AND rolled over with a groan. The floor beneath his bedroll was hard and unforgiving.

He remembered where he was.

Baskevyl sat up. He knew something had woken him: a noise. He wasn't sure if the noise had been in his dream or real.

He got up and left the billet chamber. A few Ghosts grumbled in their sleep as he picked his way out. There were sixty other men in the chamber, and he knew they needed all the rest they could get.

Out in the hall, he leaned against a brown satin wall and took out his water bottle. The water that had been taken in through the gate during the previous day's abortive drop had been carefully rationed out. It had tasted wonderful, but there was very little left in his bottle now. Another ration was going to be issued at breakfast. Estimates varied, but the reckoning was that, at strict ration levels, the water they had would last four days. No one had managed to find the bulk of the drop, or the elusive courtyard where it lay. Gaunt had already sent a request for supplementary supply drops to Elikon, a message that had not been answered.

The glow of the wall lights slowly faded. They seemed to take a long time to come back. Baskevyl watched them with fascination. The fade and return got slower at night, as if the house was breathing more slowly because it was asleep.

Something wasn't asleep. He heard a noise and knew it was the same noise that had woken him. He listened and heard, very far away, a scraping sound: a soft, wet, slithering sound coming from the depths of the earth.

It was still down there, the daemon-worm. It was still down there, and it was snuffling around, trying to get his scent.

III

'ARE WE–' THE link began to ask, and then the words were lost in a squall of loud vox-noise.

Beltayn adjusted his dials, the phones clamped to his sweaty head. 'Say again, source?'

Static. A drifting buzz.

Beltayn tried again, patiently. 'Elikon, Elikon, this is Nalwood, this is Nalwood. Requesting response to earlier transmission regarding future water drops, over?'

More static. When the dust blew up at night, it chopped the legs out of the vox link.

Beltayn sat back and took off his headphones. It was five twenty-three. He'd promised Gaunt he'd rise early and check the vox.

The grand base chamber was empty and quiet around him. He could just hear the footsteps of a sentry moving about on one of the landings above. Soft, shuffling footsteps. The poor bastard is tired, Beltayn thought. We're all tired.

He kept looking at his water bottle. Half of his last night's precious ration was still in it. He was pacing himself.

'Adj?'

Beltayn looked around and saw Dalin wandering in, yawning. Dalin was holding a bundle of charts in his hands.

'What are you doing up?'

'Couldn't sleep,' said Dalin, sitting down beside Beltayn. 'Been thinking about the maps all night.'

'Oh, don't,' said Beltayn. The frustration of the previous night's efforts had almost driven Beltayn to snapping point. With Dalin, Bonin and a few of the other most accomplished adjutants and pathfinders, he'd gathered up all the maps of Hinzerhaus issued to the regiment and gone over them line by line, looking for the fabled courtyard. That's what they had begun calling it. *The fabled courtyard.* The true nonsense of the maps had quickly become apparent. None of them matched. Some looked like plans of entirely different fortress complexes. Beltayn wondered what the feth Tactical had thought they were playing at. How could they issue a dozen different schematics of the same objective? Hadn't they noticed?

Beltayn's team had worked on it for hours, sometimes walking the halls only to end up wandering aimlessly around in futile circles. Mkoll had joined them, trying to employ that ineffable Tanith woodcraft to the task. They knew where the *fabled courtyard* should be. They knew where it *had* to be, given the sight of it the scouts had got from the ridge two days before. But they just couldn't find the *fabled* fething *courtyard*, or any sign of a hall or spur that might lead to it.

Sleep had caved them in at last and they'd given up. 'The water's not going anywhere,' Mkoll had said, stoically. 'Let's get some rest.'

Beltayn had been particularly disarmed by Mkoll's manner. He had realised the chief scout simply hated being useless, and since when had Mkoll not been able to find anything? It was as if the house was deliberately hiding the courtyard from them.

That, of course, was utter nonsense, because to believe that, you'd have to believe the house was somehow... *alive*.

Dalin spread some of the maps out on the deck beside Beltayn's vox-caster. 'I had an idea,' he said. 'What if they're *all* right?'

'What? You need some sleep, lad.'

'No, no, listen. What if they're all correct? I mean, what if they all have some *parts* correct, as much as they all show stuff that's wrong too. We should look at the bits that agree, and that agree with the actual layout of this place.'

'We tried that,' said Beltayn, 'Remember?' He wasn't in the mood for this. The boy was trying hard to impress, and Beltayn had to give him credit for that, at least, but Dalin was wasting his time.

'Hear me out,' Dalin insisted. 'This was keeping me awake. No matter how wildly different the charts are, they have certain features in common. Gaunt's map shows the base chamber and the halls along here, so does Rawne's. Hark's has got them too, but not the lower hall or these galleries here. Kolea's got galleries all over the place that aren't marked on any other charts. All of them show the well, and six of them show the power room, although–'

'You have been busy.'

'Thanks. Daur's shows the power room on the wrong level, but that is the only chart that shows an area that could be the courtyard.'

'The fabled courtyard. Dalin, we worked out that Daur's chart was the craziest of the lot last night. Apart from a couple of details, it might as well have been made up. It might as well be a different fething site altogether.'

'Yeah, I know, but what if they're *all* correct?'

Beltayn sighed. 'You keep saying that. What do you mean?'

'How old is this place?'

'I don't know.'

'But old, right? Really old?'

'Yeah,' Beltayn conceded.

'It's probably been changed and altered and rebuilt a lot. Just suppose that all of these charts were correct and accurate... when they were drawn.'

'I thi– *What?*'

Dalin grinned. 'Maybe each chart accurately reflects the layout of this place at the time it was made. Maybe *this* one–' Dalin picked a map at random. 'Maybe this one is two hundred years old, and this one five hundred. Who knows? Anyway, none of them show how things are *now*, just how things looked when the particular map was made.'

Beltayn hesitated. 'That's actually not the maddest thing I've ever heard,' he began.

'Yeah, Dalin's got a point there,' said Mkoll.

Both Beltayn and Dalin started. They hadn't heard him approach.

'Feth, you scared me!' exclaimed Beltayn.

Mkoll nodded. 'Good. I haven't completely lost it then.' He sat down with them. His face was drawn and pale, as if sleep had been eluding him for months. He reached out and took some of the charts from Dalin.

'So you're suggesting these were made at different times, in different periods? A gallery on this chart, let's say, may have been built after this other chart here was made?'

Dalin nodded. 'That's what I was thinking. Bits get built, or demolished and closed off. Rooms get added or changed. Plus, of course, there may be genuine mistakes. These are hand-drawn.'

'That's good thinking,' said Mkoll.

'The boy's sharp,' said Beltayn.

'Takes after his dad,' said Mkoll.

'It still doesn't explain why we were issued with them,' said Dalin.

Beltayn shrugged. 'An archiving error? Tactical requested maps of Hinzerhaus for our use and someone pressed the wrong key code, so we got the history of the place in chart form, rather than a dozen copies of the most recent version.'

Mkoll nodded. 'Makes sense – actual, practical, non-spooky sense. Feth alive, I'm glad *something* about this tomb is starting to make some sense.'

'Don't say tomb,' said Beltayn.

'Sorry.'

'So... can we use this?' Dalin asked. 'I mean, can we make practical use of this?'

'Yeah,' said Mkoll. 'Dalin, go wake up Bonin and get him to assemble a scout detail.'

Dalin paused. 'Wake Bonin?'

'That's right.'

Dalin swallowed. The idea of trying to rouse a Tanith scout from slumber seemed vaguely suicidal.

'All right, I'll do it,' said Mkoll. He got up. 'Meet me on west four in five. Bring the charts.'

He left the base chamber. Beltayn looked at Dalin. 'You did good, Dalin. Mkoll's impressed.'

'He is? He didn't really show it.'

'Are you kidding? That was as close as the chief gets to whooping and thumping you on the back. Mark my words, you've made a good impression.'

Dalin grinned.

Beltayn got to his feet. 'Well, come on, then. Grab those maps.'

Dalin began to gather up the unfolded sheets of paper. Beltayn turned to check his caster. He saw that one of the needles on an input gauge was jumping. He scooped up his headset, tuning.

'What is it?' Dalin asked.

'Got something at last. A signal,' said Beltayn, tweaking a dial. He listened.

'Are we the last ones left alive?' the vox whispered into his ear.

Beltayn froze.

'Who are you, sender? Who are you?'

'Are we? Are we the last ones left alive?'

'Respond! Please, respond!'

The voice faded. Beltayn took off his headset.

'Did you get something?' Dalin asked.

'No,' said Beltayn. 'Nothing important.'

IV

034TH LOOKED HIM in the face, in the *ugly* face. Merrt got up, gripping his las-rifle.

It was early, five twenty-five. The house was as quiet as a graveyard, but there was something in the air. Merrt had a gut feeling, a vague glimmer of the old combat smarts he'd once been so proud of. Just the taste of that lost instinct made his heart sing.

He'd been awake for hours, staring at the 034TH stencil in the half-light of the billet chamber.

He walked out into the hall and waited. A figure loomed out of the shadows to his left, moving with a soft, almost silent shuffle.

It was the Nihtgane. He approached, his reynbow ready in his hands. Eszrah regarded Merrt through his sunshades.

'You too, eh?' asked Merrt.

Eszrah nodded.

'Gn... gn... gn... let's go,' Merrt whispered. Eszrah nodded again, but Merrt had actually been speaking to his gun.

V

BRAGG HAD SAT with him for an hour or two through the middle part of the night, just like he'd always done when the pair of them had pulled night watch.

Bragg hadn't said anything, and Larkin hadn't spoken to him. Larkin hadn't even looked at him. Larkin had just sat there in overlook six, watching the shutters as the wind outside tugged them, aware of the presence behind him. His back had gone cold with sweat. He'd been able to hear Banda snoring from the back of the room, as well as his own amplified pulse, along with a third sound of breathing, slow and calm, comfortable.

Bragg. Definitely, unmistakably Bragg. Larkin had recognised the smell of him, the sacra in his sweat, the particular musk of his body odour. It had been such a long time since he'd seen his dear friend, part of him wanted to turn and greet him, to embrace him and ask him where he'd been.

But Larkin knew where Bragg had been, and he didn't dare turn around for fear of what he might see. Bragg had been dead since the Phantine operation, killed by a rat-bastard monster that Larkin had finally plugged with his long-las on Herodor. Bragg simply couldn't be there behind him in the overlook. He *shouldn't* be. It was against all the laws of reason, but Larkin could smell him and hear his breathing anyway.

Larkin had missed his old friend over the years more than he could say. The idea of meeting him again was wonderful.

But not like this. Not like this, please Throne, no.

Not like this.

Just before five, Larkin had heard Bragg get to his feet with a grunt and walk out. Larkin had waited a while, then slowly turned. There was Banda, asleep in the corner. No one else.

Larkin got up and eased his leg stump. He'd been sitting far too long, pinned by fear.

He saw the bottle. It was sitting on the gritty floor of the casemate a few metres behind him. He limped over and picked it up, uncorking it.

Sacra. Sweet and wonderful, the very best. No fether in the regiment had cooked sacra this fine in years. Larkin knew what it was: a gift.

'Thanks,' he said, and took a little sip.

Glory but it was good.

Banda woke up and looked at him. 'What's going on?' she mumbled.

'This yours?' Larkin asked, showing her the bottle.

'No.'

'Didn't think so. Go back to sleep.'

She did so. She was strung out and hungover. She began to snore again. Larkin took one last little sip, then re-corked the bottle and put it into his musette bag. He sat down again.

He checked his chron. Five twenty-six.

Someone leaned into the casemate behind him and called out, 'Get ready, then!'

Larkin looked around. There was nobody there, but he had known the voice.

Clammy fear blew up and down his spine. In his whole life, he'd only known one person who'd been that cheery and wide awake at five twenty-six in the morning; only one person who'd been up to do the rounds, prep the picket and check on sentries; only one person who had owned that voice.

That person's name had been Colm Corbec.

VI

'WHAT'S THE TIME?' Hark asked.

'It's... it's five minutes since you last asked me,' Ludd replied. 'It's five twenty-seven.'

'Oh,' said Hark. The field station was quiet around them. The other casualties were asleep naturally, or were mercifully drugged up against pain. From where he was sitting at Hark's bedside, Ludd could see one of the orderlies, Lesp, asleep in a chair. Ludd knew the medicae personnel had been up most of the night.

'Look, this is too early,' said Ludd. 'You should be sleeping. I can come back at a better hour.'

'No, no, sit down,' Hark replied. 'I only asked because the time passes so slowly in here. It moves like a glacier. I'm glad of the company. I don't seem to sleep much.'

'All right then.'

Hark lay face down on his bed, a thin sheet rudimentarily propped up over his back and legs to provide some warmth. Ludd could see the dark shape of soiled dressings through the sheet, and smell the odours of burn-cream and charred flesh.

'Finish your report, Ludd.'

'There's not much left. No one needs writing up, general discipline is good, despite the situation.'

'Are they giving you a hard time?'

'What? No, sir.'

'Is that because you're not putting yourself in a position where they can give you a hard time?'

Ludd didn't answer immediately.

'You can't be meek, Ludd. You've got to get up in their faces and keep them tight.'

'That's... that's my intention, commissar.'

'They'll walk all over you if you don't,' said Hark. 'I mean it. They'll walk all over you. You have to show them who's in charge.'

Ludd nodded.

'What?'

'Nothing, sir.'

'Oh, give me something to think about, for feth's sake!' Hark exploded. 'Give me a problem I can solve while I'm like this!'

Curth stepped into the field station and looked disapprovingly at Ludd. Ludd raised a hand to her and smiled. She frowned and left again.

'You'll disturb the others,' Ludd whispered.

'Then talk to me.'

Ludd sighed. 'You said I had to show them who's in charge. Well, Gaunt's in charge... Rawne... Kolea... not me.'

'The officers will support their commissar,' Hark said.

'The officers think I'm just a kid. They laugh at me.'

'Who laughs?'

Ludd shrugged.

'Rawne?'

'Yes, and he's malicious. The others, even Gaunt, I don't think they mean to be disrespectful, they just can't help it. I have no authority.'

Hark shifted on his cot, wincing. 'That's just weak talk, junior commissar. Give me some paper and a pen.'

'Sir?'

'Give me some paper and a pen, and something to lean on.'

Ludd handed the items to Hark. He gave him the field journal to lean on. Hark lay on his belly, writing furiously on the slip of paper and grunting with the effort. Ludd could see raw burns on Hark's exposed, organic arm.

'What are you writing, sir? May I ask?'

'Shut up.'

Hark finished, folded the paper up and handed it back to Ludd with the pen.

'Next time you feel unable to exert your authority, give that to Gaunt.'

'May I read it?'

'No. Just give it to him.'

Ludd put the pen and the folded paper away in his coat pocket.

'Have this too,' Hark said, tossing the field journal aside.

'Ah, I wanted to ask you about that, sir,' Ludd said.

'About what?'

'The field journal, sir. I've been trying to keep it up to date, as instructed.'

'And?'

Ludd swallowed. 'I read back, naturally, to acquaint myself with your method and style of content. I noticed... how can I put this?'

'Soon?' Hark suggested.

'I noticed some scratchings out. Some changes, where you had written and then changed your wording.'

'It's a journal, Ludd,' said Hark, 'that's how it works. The final draft report will be clean.'

'But I couldn't help reading... some of the things you had excised. The words were legible. About your dreams, sir.'

'They were private remarks that I deleted because they had no place in the record.'

'Still, they concern me. Your comments about the dreams, and your disquiet. You said you couldn't sleep and–'

'That's enough, Ludd. Forget what you read. It isn't your concern.'

Ludd got to his feet, saluted, put his cap on, and turned to go.

Then he sat down again. 'Actually, you know what? I'm going to take your advice. Yes, it *is* my concern. It's my concern as the acting senior political officer that you are troubled by your dreams so much you can find no release. For the good of the regiment, I require you to explain yourself.'

There was a long silence.

'Finished?' Hark asked.

'Yes.'

'Go away.'

'No, I don't believe I will.' Ludd leaned closer, his voice a hard whisper. 'What's going on, Hark? What's been troubling you, from before we even got here?'

'You have no right to ask–'

'I have authority, Hark, over you. You gave it to me, remember? Now start talking!'

Hark began to chuckle. 'That's good. That's actually quite good, Nahum. I'm impressed. That's how you stand up to Rawne and the others.'

'Thank you. I'm still waiting.'

Hark went quiet.

'Do I have to write you up?' Ludd asked.

Hark turned his head and looked sidelong at Ludd. His dark eyes were darker still from lack of sleep and something else.

'I haven't slept well in years, Nahum. On and off, five years, at least. Dreams come to me and ruin my sleep.'

'Nightmares?'

'No, nothing so grandiose or obvious. Just a bad feeling. The pattern has varied. There have been periods without it – wonderful, clear patches, months on end. But it's been back again of late, these last few months, and it's grown worse since we put into Jago, worse still since we got here, to this damn place.'

'Go on. Can you remember anything about the dreams?'

'No,' said Hark, closing his eyes. 'It's like... when you remember a dream, hours after you've woken up?'

'I know that feeling.'

Hark nodded. 'Like that. A sudden memory of sadness and pain.'

'Have you told anyone?'

'I've talked to Dorden. He thinks it's a trauma effect from when I lost my arm.'

'How did that happen?'

Hark opened his eyes and stared at Ludd again. There was a brooding misery in his pupils. 'The battle of Herodor, fighting alongside the Saint. We were jumped by loxatl mercenaries. They blew it off.'

'Oh.'

'You never asked me before, Nahum.'

'I never liked to, sir.'

Hark shifted on his belly, looking away. 'Well, anyway, it's not that. It's not the arm. I wish it was. It's something else. Sometimes, more frequently in these last few weeks, it's come when I'm awake too. Out of nowhere, while I'm awake. That's when I hear–'

'Tanith pipes?' Ludd asked.

'You're sharp, Ludd. Did I tell you that?'

'When you were drowsy from the drugs, sir.'

'Tanith pipes,' Hark sighed. 'I hear them, and when I hear them, I know that killing is about to start.'

There was a long silence. One of the casualties across the station aisle woke up and started to moan.

'What's the time, Ludd?' Hark asked.

'Five thirty-one,' said Ludd.

'Go do your rounds.'

Ludd got up.

'Before you go,' Hark said. 'Give me back that piece of paper.'

Ludd took the slip out of his pocket, unfolded it, and read it.

It read, in scratchy handwriting, 'To Colonel-Commissar Gaunt. If Nahum Ludd gives you this note, it indicates he is hopelessly unable to execute his duties as your regimental commissar. Please shoot the sorry fether through the head and throw his miserable carcass out for the carrion birds. Yours, V.H.'

'That's funny,' said Ludd.

'I meant it,' Hark replied.

'That's why it's funny.'

'Give it to me.'

'Oh no,' said Ludd. 'I don't want you passing it to anyone else. I think I'll keep it. And maybe, just maybe, I won't write you up for it.'

Ludd could tell Hark was laughing, even though his head was turned away.

'I'm going to give you an order,' Ludd said, bending down over Hark.

'Oh, really?'

'Yes. By my authority as regimental commissar, I order you to stay here. Think you can do that?'

Hark told Ludd exactly where his order might be inserted.

Ludd smiled. 'Good. I think we both know where we stand,' he said, and left the chamber.

VII

The tripwire pulled tight for a moment, then slackened. It pulled tight again.

Wes Maggs rolled over to find a more comfortable part of the wall he was sleeping against.

VIII

Mkoll raised his lamp and shone it ahead of them. The wall lights in that stretch of the house seemed to have died completely.

'Well?' he asked.

Dalin and Beltayn rifled through the charts they were carrying by the light of the lamp-pack Dalin held in his hand.

'Hold on,' Beltayn said. 'Something's awry.'

'Again?' asked Bonin, stifling a yawn. 'You woke me up for this?'

'Just wait,' Mkoll told him.

The five-man scout detail, led by Hwlan, reappeared from the hallway ahead.

'There's nothing there, chief,' Hwlan said, wearily.

'But the chart–' Beltayn began.

'Maybe it's hidden, a hidden door,' said Dalin. 'We could try tapping on the walls.'

'Oh, not you too,' said Mkoll. 'You're as bad as fething Baskevyl.'

'Wait, wait, wait!' Beltayn said. 'This is east eight central, right?'

'East nine central,' said Bonin.

'No, east eight,' Hwlan objected.

'Shut up, shut up!' Beltayn cut in. 'Look here, match these two up.' He held out two of the charts for their inspection. 'There should be a junction right here, to the south.'

'There's nothing!' Mkoll growled.

Dalin flinched. He hated the idea of getting the chief of scouts riled, and this had all been his idea.

'Nothing!' Mkoll barked again, slamming his fist against a satin brown panel. 'See?'

'Er, chief?' said Bonin.

Mkoll turned slowly and rapped his knuckles against the satin brown wall panel again.

It gave off a hollow sound.

'Oh, Holy Throne,' Mkoll said, swallowing hard. 'I don't believe it.'

'Pry bars!' Bonin called out. 'Pry bars, right now!'

IX

Five thirty-three. Larkin went to the shutters of overlook six and raised one of them. Outside, the wind had dropped to a vague murmur. The dust was gone. He played his scope around. He could see right down the approach pass clearly, the crags backlit by a cold, rising sun. Everything was hard shadow and as still as ice.

Down there, something–

No, just the remains of the water drop, left in the open from the day before. And some bodies, the frozen corpses of friends and comrades.

Larkin limped back to the doorway of the gunbox and looked out, left and right. An empty hall, the lights coming and going softly. No Bragg. No Colm Corbec. No ghosts at all.

He picked up his long-las, clacked his scope into place on its foresight lock, and kicked Banda.

She stirred.

'Get up,' he said.

'Gak off.'

'Get the feth up. It's coming. I can feel it.'

'Uh-huh, feel this.'

Larkin pulled out his water bottle, sloshing around the last of his ration from the previous night. He tossed it to her. 'Drink that, for feth's sake. You need to hydrate. I need you sharp.'

She drained the bottle and got up. Larkin was already at the shutter.

Banda slid her long-las up next to his and unpopped her scope's cover.

'What did you see?' she asked, huskily.

'Nothing yet. Just keep watching.'

X

West three central, just off the base chamber, was quiet. Merrt crept his way along the hallway to the junction, 034TH in his hands.

It twitched suddenly.

Merrt snapped around sharply and aimed his weapon from the shoulder.

'Gah!' cried Ludd, appearing around the corner and coming to a sudden, startled halt. 'What the bloody hell are you playing at?'

Merrt's bulky, augmetic jaw made a guttural sound as he quickly swung his rifle away.

'Gn... gn... gn... sorry, sir.'

Ludd took a step backwards, blinking. 'I asked you a question, trooper. What the feth did you think you were doing?'

'I gn... gn... gn... heard something.'

'Yes, me,' snapped Ludd, tapping his own chest with an index finger. 'Trooper, who gave you permission to stalk the halls with a lasrifle... an armed lasrifle, I notice... at fething daybreak?'

'I heard something,' Merrt repeated.

'You'll have to do better than that,' Ludd exclaimed. 'You could have shot me.'

Merrt knew he could have. Or, at least, 034TH could have. 'I was concerned there was some gn... gn... gn... activity. I was investigating.'

'And you didn't think of voxing it in straight away?'

Merrt stood up straight and lowered his weapon to his side. It twitched again. 'No. That was remiss of me, I realise.'

'Trooper Merrt, right?' asked Ludd. He knew full well who Merrt was. Ugliest bastard in the regiment with that jaw. During transit to the

Gereon liberation, Ludd had worked alongside Commissar Hark to get Merrt out of gambling troubles on the troop ship's swelter decks. As a result, Merrt had ended up on RIP duties.

Ludd had always felt sorry for Merrt, sorry for his injury, sorry for his bad luck, sorry for the RIP detail and the inflexible ordinances of the Commissariate that had demanded that punishment.

Ludd didn't feel particularly sorry now.

'I could discipline you for this, Merrt,' Ludd said, summoning up some force of anger into his voice. 'I could. Right now, summary discipline.'

Merrt stared at him. 'Yeah, right.'

'I'm acting commissar, Merrt! You will address me correctly and with respect!'

'Oh, shut up, you're just a gn... gn... gn... boy.'

Ludd felt a singular rage. He'd left Hark's side full of buoyant confidence. Merrt had picked the wrong moment to disrespect him. If Ludd had thought about it, he would have recognised the irony of Merrt's unerring bad luck. But Ludd wasn't thinking. He was fired up. He pulled out his pistol. 'Get up against the wall, trooper!'

Merrt didn't move.

Ludd aimed his pistol. What was it Hark had said? Be firm? Exert and emphasise his authority? *You've got to get up in their faces and keep them tight.* As a commissar he had every right to shoot this man where he stood. The list of charges was more than enough: Lack of respect for a senior officer. Failure to obey a direct order. Demeaning a senior officer. Endangering a senior officer with an armed weapon. Carrying an unsafe weapon in post without permission. Failure to signal a suspected alert... more than enough. But–

'You're not gn... gn... gn... gonna shoot me, boy.'

That last 'boy' did it. Ludd snapped. 'By the authority of the Holy Throne, I–' Ludd began.

Eszrah swooped out of the shadows behind Ludd and pinned him against the wall. Ludd squirmed, but Eszrah somehow managed to pluck the pistol from his hand.

'Ow! Ow!' Ludd cried.

'Be thee quiet, soule,' Eszrah said. 'Lysten...'

XI

BASKEVYL TURNED AND walked back down the hallway. The scuffing, scraping sound was growing louder. It was coming, burrowing up under him.

The worm in the dark that–

Shut up! Baskevyl willed. He drew his laspistol anyway.

* * *

XII

'Now can you see them?' Larkin said, squinting into his scope.

'Oh yeah,' Banda replied.

'Poacher one, poacher one,' Larkin said into his microbead. 'Poacher one to all watches. Contact main gate. Time is five thirty-seven. Move your arses.'

He glanced at Banda.

'Shall we? On three?'

XIII

The tripwire pulled tight, and the cloche shutter slowly lifted open, prised up from the outside. A face peered in at them. For a moment, it looked like the meat-wound face of the old dam in the black lace dress.

But it wasn't. It was the cruel, glaring iron grotesk of a Blood Pact warrior.

Wes Maggs shot it anyway. The face exploded.

XIV

Mkoll stepped over the shredded strips of satin-brown panelling and peered into the hole.

'I smell air,' he said.

'So? Let's go,' said Beltayn.

'He gives the orders around here, Bel,' Bonin told the adjutant.

'It's open air,' remarked Mkoll. 'Dust.' He looked at Dalin. 'I think you might have found it, lad.'

Dalin smiled.

His elation was short-lived. Mkoll brought his lasrifle up to his chest suddenly and looked at the roof.

'That was las-fire,' he said.

'Oh, yeah, without a doubt,' Bonin said.

'Move!' yelled Mkoll.

XV

'Here they come,' Larkin murmured, settling himself in for his first shot.

'Oh Throne, there are so gakking many of them!' Banda gasped.

'Just take them down one at a time,' said Larkin, and fired.

Day ten, continued,
I heard the pipes again. It's five thirty-six. I think
we are about to be ~~ttacked~~ attacked.

Please, Throne, make me wrong.

– field journal, V.H. fifth month, 778.

ELEVEN
The Second Assault

I

IN THE COLD, early light, the Blood Pact hit the House at the End of the World on two fronts. A force of over three thousand men came pouring out of the crags on either side of the approach pass and charged en masse towards the gatehouse and the southern elevation. Simultaneously, an assault force numbering at least four hundred attacked the cloches and casemates of the summit galleries from the north side, having scaled the steep cliffs behind Hinzerhaus.

Waking rapidly from a light sleep, Gaunt pulled on his storm coat and assessed the situation as rapidly as Kolea's adjutant, Rerval, could feed it to him.

'C company forward to the gate,' Gaunt ordered. 'H and J to the upper west line. Any spare support weapons to the southern casemates.'

Rerval relayed the orders quickly into his voxcaster. Streams of running Guardsmen thundered through the base chamber, heading for both upper and lower levels. The house was waking up with a jolt. There was a lot of shouting.

From outside and above, there was a lot of shooting too.

'Conditions?' Gaunt asked.

'Clear, sir. Dust dropped away just a few moments before the attack began,' replied Rerval.

'Why the hell did they wait for a clear patch?' Gaunt asked out loud. 'The dust is their main advantage. They could have moved up under cover and jumped us.'

'I believe that may have been their intention, colonel-commissar,' Karples said, arriving in the base station with Berenson.

'Explain?'

'The principal attack on the gate was probably scheduled to commence only when the assault elements scaling the northern cliffs had signalled they were in position and ready,' said the tactical aide in an off-hand tone. 'Scaling the cliffs may have taken longer than predicted because your scouts cut away their lines and ladders. By the time the assault elements had achieved position, the sun was up and the dust had died. They evidently decided to press on anyway.'

'Let's hope that compromise costs them,' Berenson grinned. He was clutching a brand new, short-pattern lascarbine with a bullpup grip. 'Where do you want me?'

'Where I can see you,' Gaunt replied distractedly. 'Kolea?'

'Moving!' Kolea yelled back from the floor of the base chamber.

'Rawne?'

'Units heading to station!' Rawne replied with a shout from the main staircase.

'You've got the front door, Eli!' Gaunt cried. 'I'll take the attic!'

'Live forever!' Rawne called back as he vanished up the stairs with his men.

Rerval was packing up his caster to follow Kolea.

'Where's Beltayn?' Gaunt asked him.

'I don't know, sir. His caster's here, though, where he set it up.'

'I need a vox with me,' Gaunt said, exasperatedly.

'I can manage that,' said Karples.

'Good. Grab that caster and move with me. Criid!'

'Sir!'

'Scramble your company and follow me up top!'

II

Deep in the heart of the house, Mkoll stopped running and turned.

'Go back,' he said.

'Gaunt needs me,' Beltayn objected.

'I'll square it with Gaunt,' Mkoll said. 'No matter what's going down, we need to secure that water. Take Dalin and go find that fething courtyard while we take care of business. Bonin, go with them. Hwlan, Coir, you too.'

Beltayn and Dalin turned with the three scouts and headed back the way they had come.

'Let's move with a purpose!' Mkoll told the remainder of the team.

They reached a stairwell and ascended two levels. On the second landing, the roar and chatter of gunfire from above them became alarmingly loud.

'Upper west,' Mkoll said. 'Attic levels.'

They ran on, taking the stairs two at a time. When they reached the landing that linked with the spur of west three central, they met L Company moving upstairs. They stood aside to let the troop body move up.

Mkoll saw Ludd, Merrt and the Nihtgane tagging along behind the unit.

'Commissar!' he called.

Ludd ran over, dodging in and out of the hurrying stream of troopers. 'Sir?'

'I'm going aloft,' Mkoll said. 'Beltayn may have found the water drop we've been searching for. Might I suggest you back him up and make certain?'

'Of course,' said Ludd. He was secretly pleased that the chief of scouts was addressing him with proper respect. There was no question in Mkoll's manner that Ludd was anything but the regiment's commissar. 'Where is it?'

'Mklane!' Mkoll called to one of his scouts.

'Chief!'

'Show the commissar the way.'

'Yes, sir.'

'We need that water,' Mkoll said quietly to Ludd. 'Men can't fight dry.'

'I understand,' said Ludd.

'Excellent news, sir.'

Ludd smiled and hurried after Mklane.

Mkoll nodded to Eszrah as the Nihtgane whispered past him. 'Look after Ludd,' Mkoll hissed.

'As a certayn thing, soule,' Eszrah breathed back with a look of mutual understanding.

Mkoll turned and gestured to his remaining scouts to follow the deploying company up the house.

'Where should I gn... gn... gn... go, sir?' a voice asked.

Mkoll looked over his shoulder. He saw Merrt.

Mkoll shrugged. In his experience, there wasn't much the poor bastard was good for, these days. 'Stick with the commissar. He could probably use some muscle shifting water drums.'

'Yes, sir,' Merrt replied.

Merrt turned. Mkoll and the scouts had already disappeared up the staircase, and the last of L Company was following them.

He was alone. The sound of distant gunfire echoed down the empty hallway. Merrt raised his rifle and headed down the stairs the way Ludd had gone.

III

THE SOUTHERN CASEMATES and towers of Hinzerhaus were lit up wildly with discharge flashes. Torrents of concentrated shots streamed down from the firing slits in the cliff face fortifications and hammered into the oncoming infantry ranks.

The Ghosts exacted their price for the surprise assault. In the first four minutes of action, the marksmen, gunners and support teams positioned inside the defence buttresses mowed down the charge. Hundreds of Archenemy troopers fell. Crew-served weapons, pumping and chattering out of casemate slots, cut down entire platoons. Bodies toppled and sprawled onto the pure white dust. Launchers spat squealing rockets down into the wave assault, and those rockets tossed burning figures into the air every time they struck. The hot shots of the expert snipers zipped into the charging host and took out warriors one at a time, blowing the running figures apart.

For about ten minutes, the fortress of Hinzerhaus performed its role admirably. Secure inside its ancient casemates, the Ghost defenders made a killing ground outside the front door, and slaughtered each wave that came rushing in.

'I'm out!' Banda cried, dropping back from the firing slit. 'Ammo!'

'Use mine,' Larkin spat, dropping down too. His long-las had just refused to fire. Time to change barrels.

Banda grabbed four of Larkin's clips and slammed the first one home. She resumed her fire position and banged it off.

'Shit!' she said.

'Miss?' Larkin asked, rummaging in his field bag for a fresh barrel section. 'Focus, you silly bitch. And learn... don't drink on watch.'

'Shut the gak up!' Banda replied, clacking in another hot shot load.

She fired again. 'Oh shit! Shit! Shit! Shit!'

'You're wasting ammo,' Larkin snarled as he slid a fresh barrel into position. He wound it tight. 'Don't be so useless, or I'll strip you of that lanyard.'

'Gak you, Larks,' she returned, reaching for another clip. 'I can do this.'

'So show me,' Larkin replied. He checked his weapon. Ready to go. 'Ammo here!' he yelled, over his shoulder. 'Barrels too! Move it!'

He loaded from one of the handful of specialist clips remaining, and swung up to the gunslot. He took aim and dropped his breathing rate.

The long-las bumped at his shoulder. A howling standard bearer, far below, jerked backwards and fell spread-eagled on the dust.

'That shut him up.'

'Bang!' Banda announced beside him. She slid her weapon back in through the slot and beamed at Larkin. 'See? See that? Clean kill.'

They both reloaded.

Trooper Ventnor, who was acting as ammunition runner on level six, burst into the overlook through the hatchway behind them. He was panting, out of breath. He dumped a heavy musette bag on the floor. 'Clips!' he announced.

'And barrels?' Larkin asked, taking aim and not looking around.

'No,' replied Ventnor.

'I need barrels! Move!' Larkin ordered. *Bump*. Another fine headshot.

'Keep your fake foot on,' Ventnor spat, exasperated, and disappeared.

'Bang!' said Banda with a great deal of satisfaction. 'See that? See him go over?'

'Yeah,' Larkin replied, slotting in his next clip and chasing for targets through his scope. 'Good.'

'Gak. My barrel's carked,' Banda announced, dropping back from the slot.

'Two more in the bag there. Get one,' Larkin replied. *Bump*. Over went a Blood Pact officer, sword raised, mid-yell. No amount of labour would ever piece that iron mask back together.

Banda knelt down and struggled to unwind her burned-out barrel.

'Hurry up,' Larkin called out, taking another shot. Too low. he'd misjudged. A Blood Pact warrior lost a pelvis instead of a skull. Still…

'Gak!'

'What?'

'It's jammed in! It won't pull out!'

Larkin turned from the slot to help Banda. Her exchangeable long-las barrel was truly spent, and the carbon scoring had fused it into the body of her weapon. They fought with it until it came free.

Banda screwed a new barrel home.

'Ammo and barrels!' Larkin yelled out. 'Ventnor? We're down to our last one!'

Banda and Larkin chocked clips in simultaneously, and went back to the slot. *Hunting, hunting…*

'Bang!' Banda rejoiced.

Bump went Larkin's long-las.

The runner burst into the gunbox behind them again. 'Barrels!' he yelled.

'At last,' Larkin said.

'Get down,' the runner added.

Larkin turned. 'What?' he began. His voice drained away.

Colm Corbec grinned at him. 'Get down, Larks. Get the lovely lass down too, all right?'

'Oh feth,' Larkin groaned. He threw himself at Banda and smashed her away from the slot in a clumsy body tackle.

'Hey! Ow!' Banda complained as she landed.

A second later, the top of the casemate, right above the gunslot, took the full force of the first artillery shell.

IV

AT THE SUMMIT of the fortress, along the cloche and casemate domes of the ridge line, the fight was a much closer affair.

The Blood Pact raiders had tried at first to enter the shutters quietly, the way they had done many times in the previous days. They found the cloches manned, armed and ready. The waiting Guardsmen did not hesitate. As shutters flew open, small-arms fire blazed out, cutting down the nearest raiders at point-blank range. With nowhere to run to, and just a sheer drop at their backs, the enemy tried to rush the domes and overcome them with weight of numbers.

Inside each strong point, the noise and smoke was hellish. The Ghosts had hastily constructed stages and firesteps during the night, most often out of flak board laid across sand bags, so that they could present at the shutters at head height. Unit officers had little visibility, and were forced to rely on voxed commentaries from the men firing frantically through the wedged-open shutters. The officers attempted to create zones of fire between adjacent cloches and casemates to deny the assault, but most of the strong points, especially those on the upper west levels, were quickly choked with mobs of Blood Pact warriors and mounds of corpses.

Where the ridge defences were stepped, with three banks of cloches overlooking the cliff drop in some places, the men posted in the higher levels attempted to range their fire down onto the raiders attacking the lower positions. There was, however, little opportunity for proper, directed fire. The summit fight was frenzied: a frantic whirl of desperate shooting and hasty reloading.

About seven minutes into the brutal confrontation, the enemy achieved penetration. A Blood Pact warrior, already wounded, leapt from behind the piled dead outside a cloche on upper west sixteen and managed to launch himself onto the dome. Rolling forwards on his blood-soaked belly, he lobbed a bundle of stick grenades in under the flap of the nearest shutter.

The blast killed all eight Ghosts manning the dome. Before the thick, sweet fyceline smoke had even begun to clear, Archenemy raiders were pouring in through the blackened shutter slots and spreading out along the interior hallway. In the confusion, they took out the Guards manning the next cloche along, cutting them down off their makeshift firestep from behind. A second entry point was created as a result.

Two minutes later, a lucky grenade deflected in through a shutter on upper west fourteen and blew the defenders off their platform. Once again, the enemy came scrambling inside, slaughtering the Ghosts maimed and dazed by the explosion. Fierce fighting, some of it bloody hand-to-hand business, was now boiling along two separate spurs of the summit galleries.

By the time Gaunt reached the upper levels of the house, the Blood Pact had sunk its teeth in and was biting down hard. Gaunt moved down upper west sixteen with Criid's company, bolstering each cloche he came to with sections of Criid's force. He had to shout to be understood. The rain of shots pummelling the lid of each dome sounded like hail striking sheet tin. A backwash of discharge smoke had built up like smog in the ancient hallways. Every few seconds there was the dry, gritty *crump* of a grenade detonation, and hot air billowed down the confined spaces, driven by over-pressure. The voices of men, shouting in dismay, or confusion, or pain, were as loud as the gunfire.

'Did you hear that?' Berenson yelled.

Gaunt glanced at him, scowling at the notion there was anything except total noise around them.

Berenson's face was wide eyed. 'Listen!' he shouted.

Gaunt heard them. Distant sounds, contrapuntal to the incessant din of war nearby: *whistle-krump, whistle-krump,* the unmistakable signature of shelling, coming from the southern face of the house.

Instantly, the vox-link was alive with shouts and reports.

'Rawne?' Gaunt called urgently into his microbead. 'Rawne! Two, Two, this is One, this is One.'

'–barrage coming in!' Rawne came back, his signal crumpled by distortion. 'Artillery ranging us from the pass. Repeat, artillery re–'

'Two? Two? Say again!'

'–in hard. Really hard! Feth, we–'

The link went dead, flat dead, no signal at all. Gaunt heard more shells striking the other side of the fortress. This time, he felt the floor shake slightly.

'Dear Throne,' said Karples. 'This is madness–'

He began to add something else, but Gaunt could no longer hear him because Criid, Berenson and some of the other troopers alongside had started firing. Screaming out their uncouth warcries, warriors of the Blood Pact were rushing towards them along the smoke-filled hall.

Gaunt drew his sword, the sword of Heironymo Sondar. It had been gifted to him after his successful defence of another bloody siege: the hive clash at Vervunhive.

'Men of Tanith!' he bellowed.

There was no time to say anything else. With trench axe, billhook, bayonet and pistol, the enemy was upon them.

V

DALIN COULD SMELL fresh air. He could also hear the wail and blast of artillery shells a lot more clearly than Gaunt could.

'They're giving us all kinds of feth,' he said.

'Sounds like it,' replied Beltayn. 'Keep moving.'

Dalin glanced at Bonin, Coir and Hwlan. The three scouts Mkoll had sent back with them were exchanging uneasy looks. Dalin knew they were dearly wishing they were somewhere else, somewhere they could be useful. They were three of the regiment's finest, and they were missing a full-on battle in order to run what was, essentially, a supply mission.

'Why don't you go?' Dalin suggested.

'What?' Bonin asked.

'Beltayn and me, we can find the water drop. Why don't you get going?'

'Mkoll gave us an order,' said Coir.

'But–'

'Mkoll gave us an order,' said Bonin. 'That's the start and the finish of it.'

They had passed through the hole where the wall panels had been pried away earlier, and had entered a corridor that had not seen life in a very long time. It was dry, and the polished floor was covered in a thick layer of undisturbed dust. There was something odd about the wall lights in this section. They were of the same style and arrangement as the wall lights in other parts of the house, strung along the wall panels almost organically on their heavy trunking, but these lights shone with an unremitting amber glow, not fading and returning. They burned like old lamps reaching the clamped-end of their wicks.

'Guess how much I don't like this?' Beltayn murmured.

'Guess how much I don't care?' Bonin replied.

They walked forward slowly, leaving five sets of footprints in the dust behind them. The air stirred like a cold breath. From somewhere ahead of them, they heard the rich, reverberative blasts of falling shells. The sound was not in any way baffled or dampened by intervening walls or doors.

'This match anything on the charts?' Hwlan asked.

Dalin studied the collection of maps he was carrying. 'It's hard to say…' he began.

Hwlan glared at him.

'I'm sorry,' Dalin said.

'Sorry's not good enough,' said Hwlan.

The hallway ahead bent to the left and widened slightly. They went down a short flight of steps. The walls were clad with the same satin brown panels that lined all of the house's walls, but there were more engravings and markings along the shoulder-height strips.

Beltayn ran the beam of his light along them. None of the decorations made any sense.

'I wish I knew what those meant,' he said.

'I wish you knew what those meant too,' said Bonin.

'Doors,' Hwlan said.

Up ahead, at the very limit of their lamp beams' reach, there were two doors, one on either side of the hall.

'Let's look,' said Bonin, his voice down to a whisper.

They approached the door on the left. It was solid and wooden. Bonin went first, his lasrifle cradled in a one-handed grip as he reached for the door's brass handle. Coir moved to his right, his own weapon up and aimed. Hwlan stayed behind Bonin, a grenade ready in his hand.

Bonin threw open the door and rolled inside, coming up onto his knees in a firing crouch. Coir swept in behind him, aiming up. Hwlan had their backs.

'Feth!' Bonin muttered, rising to his feet and lowering his aim. 'Look at this! Bel?'

Beltayn and Dalin scurried in past the scouts.

'Oh my word,' Beltayn gasped.

The chamber was long and high, and slanted slightly to the south halfway along its length. It was lit by the steady amber glow of the wall lights. From floor to roof, the room was lined with shelves, shelves laden with dusty books, manuscripts and matching volumes. Reading tables ran down the middle of the chamber.

'It's... it's a library,' Beltayn said.

They entered, looking around, playing their lamps up into the corner shadows of the roof, where the amber light did not reach. Slow dust billowed and twinkled in the beams of the lamps.

Thousands of books, slates and curling scrolls were stuffed onto the slumping shelves.

'So, not a courtyard then?' asked Bonin.

'No, but quite a discovery,' Beltayn said, peering at the spines of the books on the nearest shelf. 'We have to–'

'We have to find the water,' said Bonin.

'Now wait,' Beltayn said. 'This is–'

'We have to find the water, adj,' Bonin told him. 'Books are books are books. They'll still be here when we're done fighting.'

Beltayn scowled at Dalin. 'Check down there,' Bonin instructed, and Coir and Hwlan went down the room on either side of the reading tables, searching for doors.

'Dead end,' Hwlan called back.

'No other way out,' Coir agreed.

'All right then, the other door,' Bonin ordered, and Coir and Hwlan headed back to the exit.

'We really should check these books,' Dalin began.

'Why?'

'We might learn something about this place,' Dalin said.

Bonin smiled at Dalin. It wasn't a very friendly smile. 'We've learned all we have to. This fething place is a death trap, and we're all going to die here unless we secure some basics like water and a decent perimeter defence. Let's learn about the history of this place later, Trooper Criid, when we're not getting our arses shot off.'

'But–'

'Oh, don't "but" me again, or I'll smack you.'

Dalin shut up quickly.

'The lad's right,' said Beltayn.

'Same thing applies to you, adj,' Bonin told him. 'Hwlan?'

'Ready, Mach.'

Hwlan and Coir had taken up positions either side of the door across the hall.

'Take it,' said Bonin, with a nod.

Hwlan burst through the second door, Coir behind him.

'Feth me! It's an armoury, Mach.'

'A what?'

'An armoury. Come and see.'

Bonin crossed the hallway with Dalin and Beltayn in tow, and entered the second room behind Coir and Hwlan.

Lit by the same amber glow, the long gun room was high-ceilinged and lined with racks. Rows of ancient guns, most of them huge, the size of .50s, waited upright in the wooden racks for long-dead warriors who would never return to use them. The middle space of the room was taken up with armoured bunkers.

Hwlan took one of the old weapons down, grunting with the weight of it. 'What the feth is this?' he asked.

'Las?' Bonin asked.

'Yeah. I think so,' Hwlan replied, opening the action of the gun he was holding. 'Single shot charge, old style, like a las-lock. Feth, this thing is heavy.'

'Wall guns,' said Coir.

'What?' Bonin asked.

'Wall guns,' Coir repeated, taking one down from the racks for himself. Dec Coir was well known in the regiment for his knowledge of antique firearms. He carried a single shot las-lock pistol as a back-up piece.

'Hmm. Big and clumsy. Definitely wall guns,' he said, examining the weapon. 'Rampart guns is another name for them. Big, heavy, long range bastards used for battlement defence.'

'That makes sense,' said Dalin. 'I mean, given the nature of this place.'

Coir nodded. 'The casemates were built for firing these bastards. They were built with an army *armed* with these in mind. I mean, that's what this place was constructed for.'

'To defend against what?' Bonin asked.

'I can't begin to imagine,' said Coir. He was studying the hefty weapon in his hands, intrigued. 'Throne, these would have kicked. And killed. Slow rate of fire, mind you, but the sheer kill power...'

'Ammo?' asked Bonin.

Hwlan had prised open one of the bunkers. It was full of pebbles, brown satin pebbles the size of a human eyeball. 'Is this the ammo?' he asked.

'Yeah, it is,' said Coir, gazing into the open bunker almost sadly, 'but it looks dead, inert. Too long in the box, I guess.'

Dalin took one of the pebbles out. It was heavy. As he held it, it began to glow faintly.

'Feth!' he exclaimed.

'The warmth of your hand is heating up the volatile core,' Coir said. 'Put it down, please, Trooper Criid.'

Dalin put the pebble back down in the bunker, and the light in the pebble died away immediately.

'This still isn't the water,' Bonin said.

'Yeah, but–' Coir began.

'Yeah, but nothing,' said Bonin. 'Put that down. Let's get on.'

Reluctantly, Coir put the rampart gun back into the rack. Hwlan did the same.

Bonin sniffed. 'Let's move towards fresh air,' he suggested.

VI

Furious Blood Pact artillery slapped Hinzerhaus hard in the face. Orange flashes of fire, hot and rasping, lit up the southern cliffs as shells struck and burst. Parts of the casing rock blew away like matrix and exposed the hard corner angles of previously buried casemates. Two gunboxes suffered direct hits, and their fortified rockcrete frames cracked wide open. The fury of the barrage forced many of the Ghost defenders back from their firing slits into cover.

Suddenly, only a trickle of defensive fire was falling on the enemy's infantry charge in front of the main gate. The enemy took full advantage.

The first Blood Pact wave finally reached the gatehouse. A second wave rushed in behind them and began to clamber up the lower fortifications of the house's south face. A third wave came up, several dozen of them dragging a huge iron battering ram in across the white dust. They set it against the main hatch, teamed and lashed to forty men, and began to swing it.

The impacts sounded like the chime of a doom bell. Inside the gatehouse, and the long entrance hallway running back to the base chamber, sections of Ghosts waited, crouching against the walls, guns ready, wincing at the sound of every strike. Kolea, Baskevyl and the other company officers tried to keep their men in line.

'Hold steady,' Kolea yelled above the deep, booming clangs. 'Hold steady. They're not going to get past us.'

'The hatch will hold, won't it?' Derin asked.

'Of course it gakking will,' replied Kolea.

Clang! Clang! Clang!

Kolea looked at Baskevyl. 'Get the flamers up,' he said. Baskevyl nodded and turned to see to it.

They could all feel the concussive power of the shells striking the house above them. Dust and grit trickled down from the ceiling with each muffled blast. Some of the men moaned in alarm when excessive spoil poured down. Roof panels split or came away at their corners, as if the cliff above them was about to collapse.

'Keep it together!' Kolea yelled.

The shelling stopped.

The men packed in the tunnel exchanged wide-eyed looks. There was no sound except the trickle of dirt pattering from the roof and the *Clang! Clang! Clang!* of the ram driving against the outer hatch.

'Rawne?' Kolea said into his microbead. 'Rawne? Watch out up there. Rawne?'

VII

MAJOR RAWNE COULDN'T hear him. One of the first shells to strike the south face had thrown him off his feet and trashed his microbead.

'Give me a link! I need a link right now!' he had yelled to no one in particular as soon as he was back on his feet, and had spent the next few minutes running blindly from casemate to casemate. The air was thick with smoke, and shells were hitting every few seconds. Rawne blundered into panicking Guardsmen in the choked dark, and tried to get them contained. He stumbled through one doorway and saw a gunbox blown open to the sky, forming a broken, blackened cave littered with chunks of human body. Another shell struck nearby, and Rawne reeled back, sprayed with grit.

'Get on your feet!' he yelled. 'Get back to the slits!'

'They're shelling us, sir!' a trooper protested.

'I am fething well aware of that, you idiot! Get back to your position!'

He clambered into another overlook gunbox. The roofline above the gun-slot was sagging loosely, internal steel reinforcement exposed through the broken rockcrete. Trapped smoke swirled around the tight confines of the wounded casemate.

'Larks?'

'I'm all right!' Larkin called back. He was dragging Banda's limp body back across the floor of the gunbox.

'Feth! Is she-?' Rawne began.

'Stunned. Just stunned. She'll be all right.'

'Are you all right?' Rawne asked, catching Larkin's arm and helping him move Banda. Blood was streaming from a wound across Larkin's scalp.

'Yes, I'm all right.' Larkin looked at Rawne. 'We're going to die, aren't we?' he said. 'We can't fight this.'

They ducked down as another shell whined in and exploded, perilously close.

'Forget the fething shells,' Rawne said. 'It's the foot troops we need to worry about.'

'Oh, right,' said Larkin, almost laughing.

Rawne ran towards the damaged gunslot and peered out.

'You think I'm kidding?' he asked.

The shelling stopped suddenly. Larkin joined Rawne at the slot and peered out.

'Oh, feth,' he said.

VIII

THE ENEMY WAS coming up the south face of Hinzerhaus, swarming like ants. The distant artillery had been suspended so that it wouldn't vaporise its own assault troops.

The Blood Pact raiders were equipped with spiked, folding ladders, like coils of barbed wire that they shook out before them as they came. The thin anchor-teeth of the ladders bit into the stern, rock face of the house and held firm. As soon as each ladder was secure, crimson-clad raiders came grunting up them towards the lower casemates and gunslits. The ladders squealed and jangled as they dug into the stone beneath the weight of the men mounting them.

Blood Pact warriors clambered up to the first few gunboxes and stormed them. Their buck-tooth axes and sabre-knives made short work of the few, dazed Ghosts they found inside. Gore dripping from their weapons, the raiders began to press in through the lower casemate halls.

Initially deafened and baffled by the shelling, the Ghosts rapidly woke up to the intrusion. Fire fights lit up along the lower halls as outraged Ghosts responded to the masked killers surging into their midst. Daur's company found itself in the thick of the brutal close action, killing raiders as they loomed out of the smoke and attempting to drive them back out through the casemate slits.

'Contact and intrusion!' Daur yelled into his microbead. 'Contact and intrusion, level four!'

He pushed his way along the support tunnel, coughing, smelling blood and las-smoke. He was half blind. His eyes were wretched with tears from the fyceline stink. 'Come on, you men!' he bellowed at the figures around him.

They weren't all Ghosts. A scowling grotesk came at him out of the haze and an axe swung towards his throat.

IX

RAWNE PEERED DOWN out of the gunslit. Through the grey pall of smoke, he could see the red-clad figures clattering up the spiked ladders towards him. He reached out and attempted to push one of the ladders away. It was too deeply dug in, held in place on its spikes by the bodies struggling up it. Las shots whined past him, fired vertically.

'Larks!' he yelled.

Larkin appeared beside him, throwing the top half of his body out through the damaged gun slot. Larkin aimed his long-las down and fired. The shot punched through the chest of the Blood Pact warrior climbing towards him, and the corpse fell back, knocking the two Archenemy troops below it off the ladder as it dropped. Larkin reloaded and fired again, hanging right out of the slit. He'd aimed his second hot shot at the spiked ladder, and had blown through several rungs and one side of the ladder frame. The remaining upright broke under tension with a loud *ping*, and a large stretch of the ladder tore free. Eight raiders tumbled away into the smoke below.

Larkin had over-extended himself. Arms thrashing, he began to slide. 'Grab me! Grab me for feth's sake!' he cried.

'I've got you,' said Banda, wrapping her arms around his legs and pulling him back through the slot.

'There're more!' Larkin cried.

'I know,' replied Rawne, moving to the slot's lip with a tube charge in his hand. He leaned out and pulled the det-tape.

'Thanks for coming!' he called, and dropped back into cover as the tube charge fell away.

It bounced off the helmet of the Blood Pact warrior uppermost on the second scaling ladder and went off as it spun over his shoulder. The searing blast killed three of the ascending raiders outright, and sheered through the ladder, so that it broke and fell away like an untied rope, casting a dozen more raiders down to their deaths on the rocks below.

Rawne looked at Larkin. 'Is your link working?'

'I think so.'

'Send for me. Authority Two/Rawne. Kill the ladders. Priority.'

Larkin keyed his microbead. 'Listen up, you lot…' he began.

X

UPPER WEST SIXTEEN. The name would, in time, be added to the roll call of the Tanith First's most hard-fought and savage actions, and take its place alongside the likes of Veyveyr Gate, Ouranberg or the Fifth Compartment as a name to be remembered and honoured by those who came later.

Gaunt was right in the thick of it. Tunnel warfare was the worst discipline a soldier could know. It was claustrophobic, insane, uncompromising. The confines of the location drove foe into foe, whether they wanted to engage or not. Reaction times dropped to the merest fraction of a second. Everything depended on instinct and reflex, and if either of those things failed a man, he died. It was that simple. There was no margin for error, no space to correct or try again. More than once, Gaunt glimpsed a Ghost miss his first shot or first blow at an enemy foot soldier and die before he could manage a second.

There were no second chances.

Fighting in a box added its own hazards. Not only was there fire, there was deflected fire. Ricochets danced their lethal dance in and out, often caused by the nerve spasm release of a dying man, firing as he fell. Obeying their own occult dynamics, shots also hugged the walls or slid around corners, in apparent defiance of the laws of ballistics.

Gaunt's bolt pistol had serious stopping power and he used it to full effect. Those raiders who came at him were hurled backwards by his bolt rounds, knocking down the raiders at their heels like bowling pins. Where the flow of the fight descended to its most barbaric, the level of straight silver and trench axe, his power sword sliced through arms, blades, helmets and grotesks.

His Ghosts had one advantage. The enemy had effectively penetrated at two points in the summit galleries, which meant they were boxed in with Ghosts on either side of them. As best he could, given the frenetic circumstances, Gaunt pulled his defenders tight, trying to pin and crush the insurgencies. It was a task beyond the limits of his microbead, but Karples relayed his commands via Beltayn's powerful caster.

Not that there was much time or opportunity for orders. Gaunt remembered that Hark had once observed a phenomenon he had called fight time. That state ruled now. Gaunt fired, moved forwards, hacked with his blade, and allowed others to come forwards with him and blast at the enemy surge as he reloaded.

Fight time was relentless, breathless, barely any time to think or move, but also slow, like a pict-feed set on frame capture. It was almost hypnotic. Gaunt saw las-rounds glide by him like paper aircraft. He saw arterial spray hanging in the air in undulating droplets. There was no sound any more except the beating of his own heart. He felt a las-round crease his left arm. He watched a bolt-round he had fired centuries before meet a grotesk between the eyes and fold it up like a closing book, pulped flesh and pulverised bone expanding out around it like the petals of a ghastly pink flower. He witnessed a las-round, fired straight up by a man falling on his back, glance off the roof and then walk away down the hallway, deflecting ceiling to floor, ceiling to floor, like a bouncing cursor on a cogitator screen, until it finally buried itself in the neck of a raider.

Crimson beasts, stinking of blood, ran at him, ponderously slow, it seemed, wet tongues poking out of their leering metal lips, blades flashing in the furnace gloom. He cut a head in half with his sword, and shot another raider in the chest.

Then he realised, quite calmly, that this was how he was going to die.

XI

TONA CRIID HAD lost sight of her commander. The fight had become such a storm of confusion she barely had any idea which way she was pointing.

'Gaunt? Where's Gaunt?' she yelled.

The trooper beside her smiled at her and didn't reply.

'Where's Gaunt?'

Still smiling, the trooper slumped against her, his body falling open where it had been split by a fighting axe. She stumbled backwards, spitting rounds from her lasrifle into two raiders who had come out of nowhere. They jerked back, arms flailing, and dropped. Ghosts moved past her. She looked down at the dead Guardsman and wished she could remember his name.

'Forwards! Forwards!' she yelled at the men shoving up around her, and then tagged her microbead. 'This is Criid! Where the feth is the commander? We have to protect the commander!'

It was useless. There was no way of imposing order on this madness. The two Ghosts ahead of her crumpled and fell on their faces, killed so fast they hadn't even been able to scream or utter a word. All Criid could see was the grotesk coming for her, sabre-knife raised.

She brought her rifle up and impaled the raider on her straight silver. The raider took a flapping, quivering moment to die, dragging her gun down under his weight. Criid put her left foot against him to try and pluck the blade free.

Something struck her on the side of the head.

It struck her so hard, she slammed sideways into the hallway wall, and bounced off the blood-speckled brown satin panelling.

Her vision went. She tasted iron, heard wild, dulled sounds, knew she was on the floor but–

'Get up!'

'What?' she murmured.

'Get up, girl! Get up! They're all over us!'

'What?' Tona still couldn't see. She knew she ought to be moving, but she'd forgotten how her legs worked.

'Oh, come on!' the voice yelled. 'Is that how a Vervunhive gang-girl fights? Get up!'

Her vision returned. The side of her head felt sticky. She heard the chatter of a lasrifle on auto.

Caffran was standing over her, guarding her, spraying las from the hip into the enemy.

He picked off the last two with perfect aim and bent over her.

'Tona? My love?'

'Caff–'

'Gonna be all right, girl. You took a knock there.'

'Caff?'

She looked up into his eyes. They were as kind as she remembered, as kind as they had been when she had first seen them all those years ago on Verghast.

'You died,' she said, simply.

'How's Dalin?' he asked. 'I've missed him. How's Yoncy?'

'You *died*,' she insisted.

'Sergeant? Sergeant Criid?'

'Caff?'

Berenson was bending over her. 'Are you all right? Can you hear me?'

'Major?'

'I said you've taken a knock. You're dazed. Fall back.'

'I saw Caff,' she said.

'Who's Caff?' he asked. 'Look, fall back. Get yourself to the field station. Criid? Criid?' Berenson looked around. 'Trooper! Someone! Help me here!'

* * *

XII

'DOWN HERE!' DALIN yelled. He ran down the short flight of steps towards the glow of morning light. Firm hands grabbed him from behind.

'Don't just rush out there, you little fool!' Bonin hissed in his ear.

'Sorry,' Dalin replied.

'Weapons?' Bonin asked.

'Check,' said Hwlan.

'Check,' said Coir.

'Uh, check,' added Dalin. The three scouts ignored him.

'Let's go, gentlemen,' Bonin invited.

Dalin glanced at Beltayn. 'Follow them,' Beltayn advised.

From the old, worn steps, they advanced out under a carved wooden archway into the open air. The courtyard was paved with grey stones, and surrounded on two sides by wings of the house. The face of the cliff formed the yard's other two sides. The archway they had emerged from was built into a cliff face.

The tinny whine and flat crack of fighting echoed through the open air. Despite that, it was almost tranquil in the courtyard.

'Feth me backwards,' Bonin smiled. 'See that?'

They had all seen it. Nine pallet loads of water drums sat in the middle of the yard. They hadn't arrived cleanly; there was evidence on part of the tiled roof opposite that suggested the heavy cargo load had bounced at least once on its way down. Some drums in the lower part of the cargo had burst on impact, and the courtyard floor was soaked with their run out.

'It's mostly intact,' Beltayn cried.

'Glory fething be,' said Bonin. He ran to the side of the heap, pulled a drum free and unscrewed the cap.

'Drinks on me,' he grinned.

They all came forward. 'Canteen cups, one at a time, come on,' Bonin said.

They each produced their tin cups in turn and Bonin filled them all, careful not to spill a drop from the heavy drum.

The water was the most delicious thing Dalin had ever tasted. He drained his cup too fast.

'No more,' Bonin told him. 'We've been on short rations so long, I let you guzzle and you'll be shitting yourself silly come evening.'

'Besides which,' said Hwlan, 'this has to be shared out.'

'Of course it does,' Beltayn smiled, treasuring his cupful.

'Good job, you two,' Bonin said to Beltayn and Dalin. Then he fell over.

He fell on his face and landed hard across the heap of water drums. He lay still.

'Bonin?' Dalin asked, baffled.

The second shot blew the canteen cup out of Dalin's hand. The third punctured a drum beside Hwlan.

'Contact!' Coir yelled out, raising his weapon. His lasrifle was almost to his shoulder when he abruptly jerked backwards and fell.

Dalin looked up, fumbling for his rifle.

Blood Pact raiders were scurrying over the red-tiled roofs towards the courtyard. Some of them were standing up to shoot. Las-rounds whistled in at them. Dalin heard the dull *thukk* as more drums punctured.

'Oh no you don't,' he growled, and returned fire.

Day ten, continued,

All hell is breaking loose without me. Casualties are flooding in. Someone just told me we were under attack from both sides of the objective.

I can't stand the helplessness. Tried to get up just now, but A.C. ordered me back into my bed. In truth, I don't think I would've got very far. Pain more than I can manage.

I believe A.C. may have stuck me with something to keep me quiet. Feeling quite

– field journal, V.H. fifth month, 778.

TWELVE
The Last Bloody Minutes

I

THE RAM BEAT against the outer hatch, heavy and relentless. Through the gatehouse and along the entrance tunnel, the assembled Ghosts waited. There was no chatter, no whispering. The men sat in cold silence, every one of them flinching slightly at each beat that rang against the hatch. The house lights faded and came back, faded and came back.

Baskevyl realised they were doing so in time to the beat of the ram. Though the shelling had ceased, dust and grit continued to dribble down from the roof in places. The little falls made scratching, scuttling sounds, sounds that were unpleasantly familiar to Baskevyl. A little voice in his skull told him it wasn't a ram beating at the gate. It was the worm, flexing and striking with its massive, armoured head, trying to dig its way in.

Kolea had brought the flamers to the front. The gatehouse reeked of stirred promethium. The small blue ignitor flames burning at the snout of each weapon made a serpentine hissing. Baskevyl could see the tension in the flame-troopers, the slight twitch and shiver in their limbs.

The ram struck again.

'The frame's buckling!' someone cried from the front of the gatehouse.

'Hold the line!' Kolea called. 'Keep your formation and stand ready!'

'It's definitely buckling!'

Baskevyl looked at Kolea. 'Don't let them past you,' he said quietly.

'I won't if you won't,' Kolea replied.

II

Daur's gun was dry. He'd drained the entire cell with one long pull on the trigger. There was no one left alive in the support tunnel except him. The bodies of raiders lay all around him, including the bastard that had nearly taken Daur's head off. He'd just experienced the most intense fifteen seconds of his life.

He shook himself out of his daze, ejected the clip and slammed in a fresh one. Gunfire rattled and cracked around adjacent halls and chambers. He moved forwards.

The tunnel joined a main hallway. That too was littered with bodies and fogged with smoke. The ugly, jumbled corpses were Ghosts and Blood Pact, side by side in death. *Only in death*, Daur thought.

He snapped around as figures appeared. He saw Meryn moving up the hall with men of his own company and some from Daur's.

'Daur!'

'What's the situation?'

'I was about to ask you that,' Meryn snapped. He was filthy and there were beads of blood across his cheek. 'Where have you been?'

'Busy,' Daur replied.

'They're coming up the fething walls,' Meryn said. 'Rawne wants every man available to the gunboxes to keep them off. We've just cleared lower eight and nine.'

'All right. You keep moving that way. I'll take anyone from G Company with me and head back to east seven.'

Meryn nodded. 'See you in the happy place, Daur.'

Daur took his men back down the tunnel. They heard a flurry of rapid fire behind them. Meryn's group had met something coming the other way.

Haller looked at Daur. They'd known each other for a lifetime, since their days in the ranks of the Vervun Primary. Daur understood what the look meant.

'We keep moving,' he told Haller. 'They have to handle it.'

They emerged onto lower seven, a stretch of hall that connected a row of overlook casemates. Sounds of shooting rang out of each casemate hatchway. Peering into the first, Daur saw Ghosts at the slot, firing down at sharp angles.

'Spread out,' he told his men. 'Go where you're needed. Keep them out.'

III

'Can I just say how much I'm not enjoying this?' Larkin remarked.

'No,' said Rawne.

Along with Banda, they'd been holding the overlook for a full ten minutes since the ladders first came up. It was nasty work. They had to lean right out of the gunslit to fire at the raiders below or knock ladders off with charges. Leaning out made a person vulnerable. Snap shots kept screeching up past them from the base of the cliff. Larkin had been creased twice, and Rawne had taken a deflection in the front of his chest armour that had split the plate in half.

In the last few minutes they had been joined by two of Rawne's men and a Belladon from Sloman's company. That allowed them to rotate at the slot and reload, and still keep the pressure on.

'I think they're losing momentum,' Rawne said.

'You think?' replied Larkin.

'A storm assault needs momentum, otherwise it just fizzles out. If they'd had us in the first few minutes, they'd be in control now, but they didn't.'

'They look like they're still trying to me,' Banda put in, pausing to reload. 'We need more ammo. The bag's almost empty.'

Larkin limped towards the door of the casemate. He'd called twice in the last ten minutes for a runner, but there had been no sign of Ventnor, or anyone else. All the other overlooks and boxes on their level were packed with Ghosts free firing from the slits, and the ammo drain was considerable.

'Ventnor?' he yelled. 'Ammo here! Runner!'

He waited for a moment, and then Ventnor came into sight, lugging a heavy canvas sack.

'What do you need?'

'Standards and specials, and a few barrels.'

'No barrels,' Ventnor replied, pulling a few clips of standard from his sack. 'I sent Vadim down to the stockpile ten minutes ago for barrels, but he hasn't come back. There's a lot of fighting in the lower levels. The bastards got inside.'

Larkin nodded. 'I trust we booted them back out again?'

'It's a work in progress,' Ventnor replied.

'What about up top?'

Ventnor shrugged. 'I haven't heard anything, except that it's hell on legs. Someone said–'

'Someone said what?'

'Nothing, Larks.'

'Someone said what?'

Ventnor sighed. 'I dunno. Someone said Gaunt was down.'

'Is that a joke?'

'No. There was a major frenzy in upper west sixteen, that's what I heard. Gaunt was in the meat of it, as usual. And, well, he didn't walk away.'

'Where did you hear this?'

'Ammo runner I know on eight heard it from a bloke who'd heard it from this other bloke who'd been on stretcher duty coming down from the summit. One of the wounded had told this bloke and–'

Larkin held up his hand. 'That kind of story, eh? Don't spread it, Ventnor. It's wrong and it's bad for the men. Now get on. I hear other boxes calling for you.'

Ventnor nodded.

'No barrels?' Larkin added as Ventnor moved off.

'Sorry.'

'Then you'd better find me something to shoot with!' Larkin yelled after him.

Clutching the ammo packs in his arms, he turned to re-enter the overlook.

'He *is* dead,' said a voice. Larkin froze. He knew the voice, and it made him gulp in fear. He forgot how to breathe. He shut his eyes. 'Gaunt, he is dead,' the voice went on, low and soft. 'We know, because we are the ones who've been sent to get him. Sure as sure.'

Larkin opened his eyes. There was nobody there. Shaking, he backed into the overlook.

IV

DORDEN TOOK A second to breathe deeply. The field station was in a state of pandemonium. The rate of casualties coming in through triage was way beyond their capacity to cope. It broke his heart to see these broken men, the last of his kind, carried in alongside the comrades they had made in the years after Tanith.

Foskin's last estimate was two hundred and seventy-two injured, of which thirty-eight were critical. The number was rising with every passing minute. Men were going to die because Dorden couldn't help them fast enough. They'd already had to open up a second chamber to accommodate the waiting wounded, and a third to house the dead.

I am too old to witness this, Dorden thought, so old, this is too painful to bear. I should have died years ago, with Mikal, with my dear son. That would have ended this pain before it overcame me.

A stretcher arrived in front of him, and Dorden shoved his anguish aside.

'Where do you want her, doc?' asked one of the bearers, panting and sweating with effort.

Dorden looked down. Tona Criid lay on the stretcher, unconscious, the side of her head matted with blood.

'Oh Throne,' Dorden said. 'Here, over here!'

The bearers slid Criid onto a bunk and hurried away with their stretcher rolled up. Going back for more, Dorden thought.

He checked the side of Criid's limp head carefully. It wasn't as bad as it had first appeared, thank the fates. She'd be all right, provided the wound was cleaned and properly tended.

'Tolin! I need you here!' Curth yelled frantically from the other side of the station. A man was screaming a deep, dire pain-scream.

'A moment!'

'Now, Dorden!'

'Can I help?' asked a voice beside him.

Dorden glanced around. Zweil stood there. Like the medicaes, the old ayatani priest had been brought to the station for the usual duties. He had a flask of blessed water in his thin hands and a look of grief burdening his eyes.

'There are men who need your rites, Zweil,' Dorden said.

'The dead will stay dead until I get to them. The living need more urgent help. Is there anything I can do?'

Dorden nodded. 'Take this and this. Bathe her wound and clean away all the blood and dirt. Do it gently, and use that stuff sparingly. We're low on fluids.'

'Tell me about it. I'm quite parched.'

Dorden hurried away. Zweil knelt down and began to clean Criid's head wound.

She stirred.

'You're all right, Tona. You're all right now,' Zweil crooned.

'He's dead,' she murmured.

'Who is?'

'He's dead.'

'Who's dead?'

'Gaunt,' she breathed.

'What did she say?' called the trooper in the next cot along. 'What did she say, father?'

'She's delirious, Twenzet, calm yourself.'

'She just told you Gaunt was dead, didn't she?' Twenzet cried.

The noise in the station dropped away. Heads turned in their direction. Muttering began.

'Get on with it!' Zweil growled. 'She's delirious.'

Activity resumed, but there was an undercurrent that hadn't been there before.

'How delirious is delirious?' Hark asked.

Zweil looked up. Hark stood behind him, wrapped in a sheet. He was not entirely steady.

'I'm not a doctor,' Zweil replied. 'Should you be up?'

'You're not a doctor,' Hark said.

'She said Gaunt was dead,' Twenzet said.

'You can shut up,' Hark told him.

Zweil rose to his feet stiffly and looked up into Hark's eyes. 'She's delirious,' he said quietly, 'but if she's also right, well, Viktor, we knew this day would come. We will manage. We will cope. We thought Ibram was dead on Gereon for a year or more, but he came back. He's hard to kill.'

'But not immortal.'

Zweil nodded. 'Then you'd better start preparing what you'll say to the men.'

Hark was breathing hard. 'I wouldn't know where to begin. You're right. We thought he was dead on Gereon, and the regiment grieved and moved on. It won't be that easy a second time. Not if there's–'

'If there's what?'

'A body.'

'Ah,' said Zweil.

'Missing presumed dead on Gereon was one thing. There was always hope, and that hope was fulfilled. But here...'

Zweil looked at him. 'It will break us, won't it?'

'It will break us,' said Hark, 'and we will die.'

V

MAGGS COULD SEE her, moving amongst the Blood Pact raiders at the far end of the hall, her long black skirts swishing through the smoke. The old dam with the meat-wound face had come to them. She had come to claim someone. Maggs prayed it wasn't him.

The fire fight along the cloche tunnel was frenetic and fast. Maggs was low on ammo and had been forced to switch from his favoured setting of full auto to conserve. He hugged himself against the bottom of a short flight of steps and rattled away at Blood Pact storm troops, ten metres distant, obscured by drifting smoke. He aced one, that was certain, maybe a second.

His skin crawled. He'd lost sight of the old dam in the black lace dress, but he could still hear her footsteps above the gunfire, and feel the chill of her breath.

Leyr dropped in beside him and started to fire.

'How many?' Leyr asked.

'I counted eight, but you can bet your arse there're more,' Maggs replied. 'Did you hear?'

'Hear what?'

'Ten minutes ago on upper west sixteen. Gaunt.'

'What about him?'

'They got him, Wes.'

'Shit, are you sure?'

'It's what I hear,' Leyr said. 'It was murder up there, and he was right in it.'

'Who saw it?'

Leyr shrugged.

'It's wrong,' said Maggs. 'They're wrong.'

They began firing again.

They got him. Leyr's words circled Maggs's head. *No,* they *hadn't. She had. That was why she was here. She only came when a truly great man was destined to fall.*

The old dam with the meat-wound face had made her kill and they would all suffer as a result.

VI

DALIN THREW HIMSELF into cover behind the heaped pallets of the water drop. He hated to do it, because it would only draw fire onto the drums, but there was nowhere else to go in the courtyard. He fired back at the crimson raiders scurrying along the rooftop. He kept missing. He was being too hasty with his aim.

Coir was dead, dead on his back on the courtyard stones with a black pool of blood surrounding his head like a halo. Bonin was dead too.

Hwlan and Beltayn had dragged themselves behind the water canisters with Dalin and were hammering off return fire.

The worst part of it all, it seemed to Dalin, was the spatter of water leaking out of the punctured drums.

Hwlan rose a little, took a decent line, and smacked two of the raiders off the roof with squeeze-bursts. Another turned, exposed, and Dalin caught him with a group of three shots.

There was a loud bang. Dalin looked around, wondering where the noise had come from. He saw that a smoking hole had appeared in the tiled roof beside the south-east corner of the courtyard buildings. Blood Pact warriors were dropping into it.

They'd blown the roof with grenades to gain entry. They were inside the buildings.

'Watch it!' Dalin yelled. 'They're in! They're going to be coming from the yard doorways now!'

'I see it!' Hwlan called back.

Five Blood Pact raiders emerged from the yard's corner doorway, firing and running out into the open. Their shots forced Dalin, Beltayn and Hwlan to duck. Rounds smacked soundly into the drums of the precious water cargo. Water spurted.

Gunfire ripped into the raiders from the side, dropping three of them. Ludd, Eszrah and Scout Trooper Mklane appeared at the rear archway, blasting away. One of Eszrah's reynbow bolts took a raider right off his feet. Hwlan, Beltayn and Dalin immediately resumed their shooting from behind the water cargo.

A vicious gun battle kicked off between the two groups of Ghosts and the Blood Pact on the roof and inside the corner buildings. Las-shots criss-crossed and deflected off walls.

'Can we rush them?' Ludd asked Mklane in the shadow of the archway.

'Rush them? And you've been insane since when?'

'That water is vital!' Ludd protested. He paused. 'Where's Eszrah?' he exclaimed.

The Nihtgane had run out into the open. Ignoring the fire coming his way, he dashed to a wall and scaled it, hand over hand, his fingers and toes gripping the edges of the stones. He hauled himself up onto the roof and began to run along it straight towards the enemy.

They fired at him, bemused by his efforts and his native appearance.

Still running sure-footedly across the tiles, Eszrah swung his reynbow up and shot it. A raider went down, and slid clumsily off the roof. Eszrah reloaded, still running, and shot again. Another raider doubled up and fell backwards. Eszrah had shot two more of them dead before he reached the hole in the roof.

'He's making us look useless!' Hwlan roared, and got up, blazing away at the enemy. Dalin joined in, and together they shot another three Blood Pact raiders off the roof line. By then, Eszrah had dropped down into the hole.

'Come on!' Hwlan cried.

They left cover and ran towards the far corner of the yard. Ludd and Mklane quit the archway and came with them. In the corner doorway, they met two Blood Pact, but Mklane and Hwlan dealt with them quickly.

'Stay back!' Hwlan spat, looking at Dalin, Ludd and Beltayn. 'Guard the water!'

'But–'

'Guard the water!'

'May I remind you–' Ludd growled.

'No, you may not!' Mklane replied.

Ludd's head sank. 'Just go, then,' he said, bitterly.

Hwlan and Mklane pushed on. Dalin, Ludd and Beltayn returned to the water dump.

Bonin suddenly got to his feet.

'What did I miss?' he asked.

They stared at him.

'What?' he asked, reaching round to touch the back of his neck. His fingertips came away bloody.

'Oh. I got shot, didn't I?' he asked, and sat down again hard. Dalin ran to him and pulled out a pack of field dressings.

'That's nasty. Why aren't you dead?'

'I dunno, boy. Lucky?' Bonin suggested and passed out.

Dalin tried to make him comfortable.

'What about Coir?' he called out. Ludd was bending over the other scout. He shook his head. 'He's gone. Poor bastard.'

'Something's awry,' announced Beltayn behind them.

'What did you say, adj?' Ludd asked, searching Coir's pockets for his tags.

'Move!' Beltayn was yelling. 'Get into cover!' Dalin and Ludd turned, struggling to rise.

Four Blood Pact warriors were charging out across the courtyard towards them, roaring death cries in their ghastly alien tongue. They were big brutes, their shabby clothes stained with blood, their masks curved in cruel grins. They were already firing.

Ludd felt the super heated shock of a bolt hiss past his cheek. He was fumbling with his weapon. Beltayn, defiantly standing his ground, was shooting his autopistol at the oncoming raiders, apparently oblivious to the squall of las-rounds that miraculously streaked past on either side of him. Dalin saw the adjutant kill one of the raiders, and knew with sad certainty that it was the last thing Beltayn would ever do.

Dalin tried to squeeze off a burst, but was lurched violently sideways as a las-bolt splintered off his chest plating. The shocking impact knocked him off his feet and punched the air out of his lungs. He was on his back, looking back up at the colourless sky. Las-rounds whipped past above him. Rolling, gasping, he heard the brittle crack of sustained las-fire, accompanied by a bark of pain. That was Beltayn gone, surely Ludd too. Dalin tried to get up, gulping air into his winded body, braced for the kill shots he knew were about to find him.

He rose in time to see one of the raiders flopping over on his back, a hole through his chest. A second was already down, drumming his heels spastically against the flagstones as the life left him.

The remaining raider turned in time to meet a streaking las-round face on. His head blew apart in a cloud of blood and metal, and his body dropped.

'Any more for any gn... gn... gn... more?' Merrt inquired, walking out of the archway with O34TH in his hands.

Ludd nodded at him. 'Never thought I'd be pleased to see you, trooper,' he said, wide-eyed and pale with shock.

'No one ever is, sir,' Merrt replied, 'in my gn…gn… gn… experience.'

'You old bastard,' Beltayn chuckled, slowly lowering his pistol and blinking in stunned disbelief as he realised that not a single part of him had been shot off.

'Good timing, Merrt,' said Dalin with a broad grin of relief.

Merrt nodded back and patted the stock of his weapon. 'That's more like it,' he whispered.

VII

THEY WERE ALL dead. Every single Blood Pact trooper that Hwlan and Mklane found was stone dead, with a crude iron quarrel transfixing him. As the two scouts advanced through that unexplored part of the old house, they counted thirteen kills.

'Got to hand it to the Nihtgane,' Hwlan said.

'You fething have,' Mklane agreed.

A shadow twitched in front of them. Hwlan and Mklane brought their weapons up.

It was Eszrah.

'Peace, soules,' he said. 'Yts dunne.'

VIII

THE RAM STRUCK the outer hatch with a hammer to anvil shock.

Then silence fell.

The Ghosts waiting in the gatehouse entry shifted nervously.

'Stay ready, stay ready,' Kolea whispered to them.

He waited. All noise had dropped away, even the distant rattle of gunfire. The anxious breathing of the assembled men became the dominant sound, like the soft rustle of sliding material, like a lace dress brushing against the floor.

Nothing happened. Gol Kolea waited a moment longer until nothing had definitely happened again.

He glanced at Baskevyl and raised his eyebrows.

Baskevyl clicked his bead. 'This is Gate. Can I get anyone on overlook, anyone?'

'This is Daur, overlook nine, copy.'

'We're blind here, Ban. What can you see?'

There was a pause.

'Not much, Gate. Dust is suddenly coming up extra hard. But they're falling back en masse. Repeat, the enemy has been driven off.'

'Understood, good news. Thank you.'

Baskevyl looked back at Kolea.

'I think we got off lightly,' he said.

Day ten, continued,

I barely care to maintain this journal any more, but I know I am bound to. I don't know what to write.

I don't know what I'm going to say. Z. was perfectly correct. I have to say something. I have to say the right thing.

~~I can't believe~~ I find I have some difficulty fully appreciating this circumstance. I should be coping better. I have been well trained, and ~~prt~~ part of that training was to prepare for this. I suppose it may be the pain I'm experiencing, but it's weakness to blame my body for something my mind can't do.

I simply don't know what I'm going to say. I don't know if there's ~~anyting~~ anything I can say to make this any better.

I need to be sure. I need to see a body, I suppose.

– field journal, V.H. fifth month, 778.

THIRTEEN
Dead and Dying

I

'THIS AREA'S NOT secure!' Varaine called out. All around, men were coughing in the accumulated smoke, or moaning and weeping where they lay.

'Look at my face,' Dorden told Varaine as he walked past.

'Doctor!'

'You heard him, Varaine,' Rawne growled, following Dorden down the ruined upper hallway.

Night, the night of the tenth day, was closing in, and the dust was up outside. The wind swirled around the cloche domes and squealed in through the slits of hastily closed shutters.

With the shutters on the summit levels closed, they were locked in with the after-stink of battle. A trapped stench built up quickly in the armoured hallways, a smell composed of blood, smoke, fyceline haze, piss and burned meat. Rawne wrinkled his nose and wrapped his cloak up tight. Dorden, without breaking stride, popped a surgical mask over his nose and mouth.

The medicae was walking quickly, amazingly quickly for a man so old.

'You don't have to do this,' said Rawne.

'I fancy I do. I'm senior medicae regimentum.'

'Then slow down,' said Rawne.

'I don't think I will,' Dorden replied.

'Slow down for me, then,' complained Zweil, lagging behind them.

Dorden paused and allowed the old priest to catch up. The old man took the older man's arm.

'He'll laugh when he sees our faces,' Zweil said.

'Of course he will,' Dorden replied, his unsmiling mouth hidden by his mask.

II

THE SUMMIT LEVELS of the fortress had been devastated. Ignoring the mounting storm outside, men from five of the Ghost companies were attempting to clear and secure the levels. The raiders had been driven out after the most brutal of efforts, but pockets remained. Distant, sporadic gunfire echoed sharply down the hallways.

The satin brown panels on the walls were gouged and scored. Some had been blown away, revealing bare rock. Half the lights had been shot out. Bodies littered the ground, piled high in places. Corpsmen were recovering the friendly dead and the few remaining injured. Armed Ghosts with lamp-packs moved through the devastation, killing anything that moved and wasn't one of their own with quick, sure shots from their laspistols. Smoke wove shapes in the lamp beams. Condensation, stained pink, dripped off the steaming ceiling plates. Blood coagulated in pools at the foot of steps, or dried black as it dribbled slowly down the wall panels.

'How many, do you think?' Zweil asked.

Rawne shrugged. 'If we've lost four hundred, we should count ourselves lucky.'

'We're going to lose half that without water and better medical supplies,' Dorden said, still walking. 'The wounded are going to die quickly. Add that to your tally.'

'It's not a tally I started, Dorden,' Rawne replied.

Dorden didn't reply. He kept walking.

III

MAGGS HEARD SLOW, shuffling steps approaching along the hallway. His eyes were sore with the smoke. His heart ached.

Come on, then, if you're coming.

'Put that away, Maggs,' said Rawne.

'Sorry, sir. Can't be too careful. We think we've driven them all out, but there may be some survivors.'

'Understood. This is upper west sixteen?'

'Sir, yes sir. It's... it's a mess.'

'We'll see for ourselves, lad,' Dorden told Maggs, patting him on the arm as he pushed on.

* * *

IV

FAMOUS BATTLES DID not leave dignified remains. That had always been Tolin Dorden's experience. Battle, under any circumstance, was a savage, thrashing mechanism that ripped bodies asunder indiscriminately and left an unholy mess for men like him to clear up.

The sort of battles that might win a place in the records – famous battles – well, they were the worst. Dorden had found, to his distress, that any combat that was destined to be remembered and celebrated left in its immediate wake the most atrocious debris of all.

The rumours had already begun to spread: upper west sixteen, a place of heroes, toughest fight there ever was, locked in the tunnels, man to man, blade to blade. Dorden knew there would be more stories later on, and maybe decorations to cement their authenticity. Upper west sixteen had been a finest hour for the Ghosts, a make or break that would be honoured for as long as the regiment existed.

There was nothing heroic about the scene that greeted him.

The stretch of hallway was a charnel house. It looked as if a mad vivisectionist had gone to work and then burned all of his findings. The air was filled with steam and smoke. The smoke issued from the burning corpses and the steam from the wet. The floor was coated several centimetres deep with blood and mushed tissue.

Dorden took the lamp-pack from Rawne. Zweil moaned and covered his nose with a handkerchief. The lamp beam moved. There was not a single intact body. Bodies lay burned to a crisp, grinning out of blackened, heat-stiffened faces. Bodies lay burst like meat sacks, trailing loops of pungent yellow intestine across the soaked floor. Parts of bodies littered the floor space: a hand, a chopped off foot in a boot, a chunk of flesh, the side of a face, half a grotesk.

'Feth take you and your war,' Dorden whispered.

'It's not my war,' Rawne began.

'I wasn't talking to you.'

There had been flamers, at the end. Parts of the hallway were burned back down to the rock, and blood had cooked to sticky treacle in places. The soles of their boots adhered unpleasantly as they advanced.

Ghosts were picking through the dead, searching with lamp-packs and – once in a while – firing rounds. Dorden was fairly sure it wasn't just the Blood Pact they were finishing cleanly.

Mercy is mercy, he told himself.

'Can you help me?' asked a voice. It was Major Berenson. He had been shot through the right shoulder and his arm was hanging limply.

Dorden moved towards him. 'Let me see–'

'Not me, medicae. *Him*.'

Berenson nodded down at the man slumped beside him on a pile of corpses. The man had lost both legs to a chainsword or the like. The exploded remains of a voxcaster set was still attached to his back.

Dorden bent down. 'Kit!' he yelled. 'Tourniquets! Don't waste your time, medicae,' whispered Karples, blood leaking out of his mouth. 'I know I'm done.'

'I'll be the judge of that,' Dorden replied, reaching out for the medical pack Rawne handed to him.

'I am not a stupid man,' Karples gasped. 'I know I can't be saved. Is there an officer here? A Tanith officer?'

Rawne knelt down and bent in close. 'I'm Tanith.'

'He deserves a medal.'

'Who?'

'Your– *guh*! Your colonel-commissar,' Karples gurgled. 'He led the way, all the way. I have never seen so much–'

'So much what?'

Karples opened his mouth. Blood rolled out of it like lava from a volcano.

'Karples!' Berenson cried out.

'Shame,' sputtered Karples. 'Shame to give a medal posthumously.'

'What are you saying?' Rawne exclaimed.

Karples didn't answer. He was dead.

V

Maggs led them on by the light of the lamp-pack fixed under his rifle muzzle. They wandered past Ghosts despairing and weeping as they searched for evidence of the living.

A figure moved in the dark under a cloche dome ahead of them. Maggs started, raising his weapon. He saw a meat-wound face and a black lace dress.

He was about to fire when Zweil rammed his rifle aside.

'You idiot!' Zweil yelled. 'That's Varl!'

VI

'It was something,' Varl said. He was so completely covered in blood, it looked as if he had been deliberately painted. The whites of his eyes seemed very white against the red, the pupils very black. He was shaking. Dorden helped him to sit down.

'Where are you hit?' Dorden asked.

'I don't think I am,' Varl said. His voice was oddly quiet. He looked up at Rawne.

'It was going to happen one day, wasn't it?' he asked.

Rawne made no reply.

'What happened?' Zweil asked. 'Son?'

Varl shrugged. 'I can't really tell it as a story. It was all so mad, everything happening at once. I know he was hit. He was beside me and he was hit. I heard him cry out. He told me to keep going. Next thing... next thing I know, he's gone down. I tried to protect him, but I got pushed back down the hall by the bodies shoving forwards.'

Varl wiped his mouth. 'When we regained ground, he wasn't there any more. It was all a bit confused, but then I saw him. I saw him. The enemy had him. Six of them were just carrying his body away. I suppose they recognised his rank pins and decided to take a trophy. That's what I thought at the time.'

He shook his head sadly. 'I wasn't having that. I fething well wasn't having that. I went at them, me and a couple of the lads. We really got into it. It was just a blur for a bit. Then I saw him again. They were lifting him out through one of the shutters.'

Varl stopped talking.

'Finish the story,' said Rawne in a voice that seemed as old and tired as the house around them.

'I followed them,' Varl said bitterly. 'I fought my way in and followed them out of the shutter onto the peak top. The dust was up. I could barely see at first. There was fighting still going on in and out of the cloches. They were lugging him over onto their climbing ropes to carry him down the cliff. That was when I saw why. He was alive. He was still alive. He saw me. I tried to get to him, but there were too many of them. They were dragging him down, they had a rope on him. I think he knew what was going on. I think he knew what kind of fate awaited him if they took him away.'

Varl looked up at the men listening to him. 'He shouted to me. I don't know what he said. He still had his sword. Somehow he still had it. He killed one of them with it, but they were all over him. So he... he took his sword and cut the ropes.'

No one spoke.

'That was it,' said Varl. 'The whole lot of them just went. He took them all with him. They just went back over the edge and that was it.'

'Are you sure?' Rawne asked. 'Are you sure it was him?'

Varl lifted something up. They'd all assumed it was his lasrifle he'd been carrying, but it wasn't. It was the power sword of Hieronymo Sondar.

'This was left on the ledge, right on the edge of the cliff,' Varl said. Tears were running down his face, making tracks of white skin in the plastering blood. 'Gaunt's dead.'

Elikon M.P., Elikon M.P., this is Nalwood, this is Nalwood. Reporting loss in action of commanding officer. Repeat, commanding officer regimental has perished. Objective remains secure at this time.

Nalwood out. (transmission ends)

- Transcript of vox message, fifth month, 778.

FOURTEEN
Death Songs

I

It took another four hours to make Hinzerhaus secure. A scattered handful of the Blood Pact, unable to retreat with their main forces, laid low in sub-chambers and the dark ends of lonely galleries, and dished out hell to any search teams that discovered them. None died without a bloody scrap. Those were the cruellest Ghost fatalities, Rawne thought. The battle was done and still his men were dying.

His men. The thought made him light-headed. After all this time, they were his men now.

II

As the night drew out, Jago's furious wind screamed around the house, unleashing the worst dust storm the bad rock had yet inflicted on them. Dust invaded through the many broken and damaged shutters, despite efforts to seal them. The wind moaned along the hallways and galleries, clearing out the smoke, making men shiver. It sounded like grief, like the moaning despair of a widow or an orphan.

Somewhere in the noise, late in the night, Tanith pipes began to play. Hark heard them calling, plaintive and clear. His bed had been shifted to a side chamber when the field station had become full. Pain had overcome him, he'd stood for too long. The flesh of his back throbbed.

When he heard the pipes, he tried to rise. A hand touched his shoulder gently and a voice urged him to lay still.

'I can hear the music,' he said.

'It's Caober,' said Ana Curth.

'Caober doesn't play,' Hark said. 'No one in the Tanith plays the pipes any more.'

'Caober had an old set,' she said, 'and he's playing them now.'

Hark listened again. He realised it wasn't the same music that had been haunting him. It wasn't very good. There were bum notes and poor shifts of key. It was the work of someone who hadn't played the pipes in a long time.

He was playing the old tune, the old Tanith marching song, but he was playing it so slowly, it was a dirge, a lament.

'They all know,' Hark said.

'Everyone knows,' said Curth.

III

RAWNE WALKED INTO the room that had been Gaunt's office. Charts lay on the desk, and Gaunt's pack was leaning against the wall. A few personal items lay around: a data-slate, a button-brush, a tin of metal polish, a tin mug. A bedroll was laid out neatly on the small cot. Under the cot, by one of the legs, lay a pair of socks in desperate need of darning.

Rawne put the power sword down on the desk. Then he sat down heavily. He picked up the tin mug and set it on the desk in front of him. He took out his water bottle, unscrewed the cap, and half-filled the cup with water.

They had water now, a tiny little success almost lost in the day's bad business. Ludd and Beltayn had been so proud of their achievement. Rawne had taken no pleasure in wiping the smiles off their faces and the triumph out of their hearts.

Gangs of Ghosts had spent three hours lugging the water drums into the house from the courtyard. A great deal had been lost, but there was enough for full rations, enough for washing wounds and cleaning bodies, enough to make up eyewash to treat the sore and dust-blind.

Rawne took a sip. The water tasted of disinfectant, of Munitorum drums, of nothing at all.

There was a knock at the door.

'Come.'

Baskevyl looked in. 'Company reports are coming through, sir,' he said. 'Casualty lists and defence reports.'

'Field them for me, please,' said Rawne. 'Gather them all in and then report to me.'

Baskevyl nodded. He hadn't said a thing about Gaunt all night, nor commented on Rawne's elevation to command. Under other circumstances, Baskevyl might have had every right to be considered. But Rawne knew that Baskevyl understood that it had to be him. It had to be Tanith.

'Berenson would like a moment,' Baskevyl said.

'Ask him to wait, please.'

'Sir.' Baskevyl closed the door behind him.

Rawne took another sip of water. He was numb, and painfully aware that he had no idea what he was supposed to do now. It was hard to think.

'Thanks a lot,' he said to the power sword on the desk, speaking to it as if it was Gaunt. 'Thanks so very much for leaving me to deal with this shit.'

Rawne had no expectations of a happy ending anymore. Another assault like the one they had just been through would probably finish them. Gaunt had informed Rawne of Van Voytz's instructions. *Keep them busy*. That amounted to *stay there and die.*

There was another knock.

'Go away!' Rawne yelled.

Hlaine Larkin limped into the chamber and closed the door behind him.

'Are you deaf?' Rawne growled.

Larkin shook his head. 'Just disobedient,' he replied. He came over to the desk and sat down facing Rawne. His prosthetic was clearly rubbing sore, because he winced with every step and sighed as he sat.

'Finish your water,' he said.

Rawne hesitated, and then swallowed the last of the water in the cup.

'Is there a point to you being here?' Rawne asked.

'A point? No. An angel responsible? I'd have to think so. You and me, Eli. There aren't many of us left now. Fewer with each passing day. Do you remember the Founding Fields, outside Tanith Magna?'

'Yes.'

'Seems so long ago,' Larkin said, pulling a tin cup out of his pocket.

'It was a long time ago, you fething idiot.'

Larkin chuckled. 'That row of tents. There was me and Bragg, and you, Feygor, Corbec. All set for a life in the Guard, we were. Young, stupid and full of piss and vinegar. Ready to set the galaxy burning.'

Rawne smiled slightly.

'Ready to set the galaxy burning and follow some off-world fether called Gaunt into the war. Now look at us. Bragg's gone, long gone, Feygor, dear old Colm, who always seemed like he'd live forever. Feth it, I'm not even here as completely as I'd have liked.'

Rawne's smile broadened.

'Just that little row of tents,' Larkin went on, pulling something else out of his jacket pocket, 'and we're all that's left of it. Does that make us lucky, or the unluckiest ones of all?'

'My money's on the latter,' said Rawne.

Larkin nodded and unstoppered the old bottle he'd produced. He poured a measure into each of the two tin cups.

'What's that?' Rawne asked.

'The really good stuff,' Larkin replied.

Rawne picked up his cup and sniffed it dubiously. 'That's sacra,' he said.

'That's not just sacra,' Larkin replied. 'Taste it.'

Rawne took a sip. A haunted smile transfixed his face. 'You old bastard,' he said. 'You kept a bottle of Bragg's recipe all this time.'

'No,' said Larkin, 'but if I told you where it really came from, you wouldn't believe me.' He took a sip. 'This is special stuff, for special occasions.'

'Who are we drinking to?' Rawne asked, getting to his feet with his cup in his hand.

Larkin got up to face him. A traditional Tanith toast took three parts.

'Old Ghosts,' said Larkin.

They clinked the cups together and drank.

'Staying alive,' said Rawne, and they clinked again. The stuff went down so smoothly, like velvet and liquid ice.

Larkin and Rawne looked at one another.

'Ibram Gaunt,' they both said at the same time.

'May the Emperor protect his mortal soul,' Larkin added.

They clinked again and emptied their cups.

IV

Rawne was asleep on the cot that had been Gaunt's. He didn't stir as Eszrah slipped into the room. The Nihtgane walked over to the desk and sat down. He stared at the power sword lying across the desk top.

It was the dead time before dawn. The wind was swirling around the fortress. Nahum Ludd had carefully explained to Eszrah what had happened, using those pieces of the partisan's ancient language that he'd studiously endeavoured to learn. Ludd's eyes had been red and tearful.

Eszrah had simply nodded and made no reaction. He had walked away softly and left Ludd to his misery.

Sleepwalkers showed no emotion. It was part of their way. There was no weeping, no grief, no mourning for a Gereon Nihtgane. Such behaviour was a waste of time.

Eszrah ap Niht understood he had failed. He had failed his father's last command to him. The man his father had given him to was dead because Eszrah had not discharged his duty to protect him.

That made Eszrah a dead man too, a shamed outcast, dishonoured. Eszrah wasn't sure why any of the Ghosts were still speaking to him, or acknowledging his presence. Surely they realised his state of disgrace and recognised that the only thing awaiting Eszrah was the *deada waeg*, the road of corpses. His life had no purpose any more, except that he should atone for the wrong he had allowed to happen.

Eszrah ran his fingers along the blade of the power sword. He knew what to do: recover the body for burial and avenge the death ten-fold.

He took off the sunshades that Varl had given him so many months before and laid them on the desk. He would need to see now, see like a hunting cat in the dark. He took up his reynbow and, as an afterthought, picked up the power sword too. Eszrah was no swordsman, but the nature and true ownership of the weapon was important to the ritual. It had to be the dead man's weapon.

Rawne snorted in his sleep and rolled over. He looked up, blinking.

He was alone in the room.

V

'I'M ASKING YOU just one thing,' said Dalin in a low whisper. 'Don't die too. Please, don't die too.'

He sat at Tona Criid's bedside, his head pressed against hers. She did not move.

'Come back to me. Caff's not going to, I know that, but you can. You gakking well can.'

Tona lay as she was, her mouth slack.

Noises disturbed the field station. The medics were still at work, treating the last and the least damaged of the casualties. Corpsmen hurried in and out with bundles of supplies, fresh dressings and bowls of water.

'It'll be all right, Dalin,' a man said. 'She'll be all right.'

Dalin looked up and saw Major Kolea standing beside him.

'Sir,' Dalin said, and began to rise.

'As you were, boy,' said Kolea.

Dalin knew the major had been close with his mother and Caff. There was something about Major Kolea that was at once reassuring and also alarming. Kolea treated Dalin oddly, not like Meryn and the other arseholes, overly respectful of Caffran's memory. Kolea was different. He reminded Dalin of someone he'd once known, long ago, an uncle or a family friend perhaps, back on Verghast before the war.

'Did my mother know you, sir?' he asked.

'What?'

'My birth mother, not Tona, back at Vervunhive, where I was born. You're Verghastite. Did you know my family?'

Kolea shrugged. 'Yes.'

'Really?'

'I knew them very well.'

'Why haven't you spoken to me about them before, sir? My memory of that time is only patchy, but if you knew them–'

'It's a long time ago, Dalin,' said Kolea, his voice thick. 'Tona's been your mother for as long as it counts.'

'I know that,' said Dalin, 'but... what were they like, my mother and father? You knew them. What were they like?'

Kolea turned away. He halted. 'They loved you,' he said. 'You and Yoncy both, very much. And they'd be proud to know a woman like Tona took you in and made you safe.'

'They died in the war, didn't they? My parents. They died in the Vervunhive war?' Dalin asked.

'They died in the war,' said Kolea.

VI

THE ELEVENTH DAWN came, without betraying any visible sign. The dust storm outside was so fierce that it blotted out the daylight and made the night linger. The whirring, almost buzzing moan of high wind and blowing dust droned along the hallways and corridors.

'Well, at least they won't be coming at us in this,' remarked Berenson, accepting a cup of caffeine from Baskevyl.

'Because?' Baskevyl asked.

Berenson shrugged, forgetting for a moment he had one arm in a sling, and winced. 'Zero visibility? They'd be mad to.'

'Have you fought the Blood Pact before, major?' Baskevyl asked, sipping from his own cup as he reviewed some transcripts his adjutant had delivered to him.

'Yesterday was my first time,' Berenson admitted.

'And did you see anything yesterday that remotely indicated they were sane?' Baskevyl asked.

Berenson was silent.

'They could come at any time, storm or no storm, dust or no dust,' Baskevyl said. 'They won't let anything stop them, unlike our own forces.'

'What's that supposed to mean?' Berenson asked.

'It means your reinforcements are supposed to be here in the next two days,' Rawne said as he joined them in the base chamber. 'This storm is bound to slow them down.'

Berenson frowned. His expression was alarmingly like the one Caffran used to display when his honour was insulted.

'Oh, relax,' said Rawne, pouring himself some caffeine. 'That wasn't a slur on your regiment's reputation or efficiency. This dust-out is going to slow any mechanised advance down to a crawl. No Guard commander's going to push on blind. They'd have to be mad.'

'I refer you to my previous remark,' Baskevyl said to Berenson.

Kolea, Mkoll, Daur, Theiss and Kolosim arrived in the base chamber, closely followed by Sloman, Kamori and Meryn. Rawne waited a few minutes more until all the company officers had congregated around him.

'Let's start,' he said. 'Munition status?'

'Not fantastic, sir,' said Arcuda. 'We're down to about forty-eight per cent of our supply. We're all right for the time being in terms of standard cells, and we can cook some up if necessary. But we expended solid ammo, charges and tube rockets like you wouldn't believe yesterday.'

'Running badly low on barrels for the long guns too,' Larkin put in.

'Order a supply drop,' Rawne told Beltayn, who was taking notes. 'Be very specific about what we need.'

'No supply drop's going to find us in this,' said Kamori darkly.

'And if it does...' Kolea began.

'If it does, *what*?' Rawne asked.

Kolea made a face. 'Dropping water into that courtyard was one thing. Dropping munitions? Charges and volatiles? That could turn out to be one feth of a big, bad idea.'

'So's sitting here without any support weapons or heavy firepower,' said Rawne, 'and that's where we'll be if we take another hit like yesterday's. Rifles and blades are not going to be sufficient disincentive against another storm assault.'

'Maybe we can find an alternate LZ?' Daur suggested. 'Providing the storm abates, of course.'

'Start working on alternative plans for safe receipt of a munitions drop,' said Rawne. 'Beltayn, request the drop anyway.'

'Yes, sir.'

'How's our link, by the way?'

Beltayn shook his head. 'We can't raise Elikon or... or anyone else at this time, sir, atmospherics are too harsh. I'll keep trying.'

'Do that,' said Rawne, 'and keep trying to link Major Berenson's mechanised, will you? An E.T.A. would be appreciated.'

'Sir.'

Rawne took another swig of caffeine, savouring the novelty of something warm to drink. He cleared his throat. 'Secure and hold is the order of the day. Vigilance is paramount. You all know your places and your areas. I want every rat-run, shutter and basement in this fething edifice locked up tight. Any contact, any attempt to penetrate, must be denied with our trademark lack of tolerance. Another full assault would be bad enough, but I've a hunch they may try stealth again.'

The officers nodded.

'Tell the men, make it clear to them,' Rawne said. 'I know the mood is grim, but we have to be twice as hard now. I don't want excuses. Make sure the men appreciate that any slip up today means that Gaunt will have died for nothing.'

There was a nasty pause. Varl sucked his breath in through his teeth in disapproval.

'You think that was callous?' Rawne asked. 'Then none of you know me very well. I'm not playing around because *they're* not playing around. And before you ask, that's the way he would have wanted it.'

Mkoll nodded. 'I don't doubt that for a moment,' he said.

'Good,' said Rawne. 'Who's securing the new area?'

'Two company's under me,' said Baskevyl.

'I want it clean and locked up in three hours,' said Rawne.

'Unless, of course, we find more new areas beyond the new area,' Baskevyl replied.

'Granted. Take Beltayn with you. A full report on that library and armoury, please.'

Baskevyl nodded.

'Then let's get to it,' said Rawne. The officers hesitated for a moment. Rawne stared at them and then sighed.

'Oh, and the Emperor protects and you're all going to live forever and all that...' he said with a wave of his hand. 'I don't do rousing or uplifting. Just get on with it.'

The men turned to go.

'One last thing, before I forget,' Rawne added, pulling them back in. 'Someone took Gaunt's sword from my office last night. Souvenir hunter, I'm guessing, or some sentimental idiot. I want it back. No excuses. And there will be severe discipline for whoever took it.'

'I'll handle that, major,' said Hark. At some point during the briefing, he had joined the back of the group. He was fully dressed, with his storm coat on, resting his bulk on a crutch made out of a stretcher pole. He looked pale and sick.

'Should you be up?' Rawne asked.

'No,' said Hark, 'but I am. This situation isn't going to wait for me to heal. Curth stuck me with enough painkiller to make you all seem like a lovely, smiley bunch of people. That'll wear off, I'm sure. Don't expect any rousing speeches from me, either, but Major Rawne is quite correct. We have to get this right today, and the next day, and the next, without feeling sorry for ourselves. Gaunt would hate it if we went to pieces now. Everything he spent his life working to achieve would be wasted.'

'Everyone got that?' Rawne asked. 'Good. Carry on.'

Day eleven. Sunrise at five plus two, dust out conditions, total, storm maintaining from last night. Worst storm yet.

I have to admire R. He has already met the task head on, handing out heavy work and duty loads to distract the men and officers both from the mortal blow we have suffered. He's right. This is the only way to continue. The ~~officiers~~ officers cannot afford to be squeamish or weak. There is no time for grief or despair. If we are lucky – very lucky – we may get a chance to mourn later.

The fact that we have water now is a boon. The munition/communication/reinforcement prospects are not so glorious. Given the present situation, I believe we may withstand one further attack.

~~I continue to hear odd noises and sounds in~~ I believe the drugs A.C. has given me to allow me to operate without pain may be having some side effects of a hallucinatory nature. I will ignore all such distractions.

I expect the enemy to assault again before the day is out, whether the storm blows out or not.

– field journal, V.H. fifth month, 778.

FIFTEEN

After the Storm, the Storm

I

BESIEGED BY THE storm, the house covered its eyes and mouth, and waited. Concussive waves of brown grit and loose white dust-vapour broke against the ramparts and sand-blasted the metal casemates. Shutters flapped and rattled, and some had to be tied down from within. From the vantage of the main gatehouse, the wind made a deep, raw voiced howl as it thundered up the approach pass.

In the base chambers, the voxcaster sets whined and yelped like injured animals as they hunted for a signal.

II

MERYN WAS CALLING to them. Dalin and Cullwoe finished checking the chamber with their lamp-packs and returned to the hallway.

'Anything?' Meryn asked.

'Empty, sir.'

'Move along. Keep it fast.'

'Yes, sir,' said Dalin. He led Cullwoe on towards the next doorway. Meryn stepped back to check the progress of the rest of his company, which had broken down into pairs to explore and secure the newly discovered sections of the house beyond the inner courtyard. He called out some instructions.

'Captain?' Baskevyl appeared behind him.

'Sir.'

'Find anything?'

Meryn shook his head. 'We've identified about eight or nine rooms so far, mostly leading off this hallway. There are more over that way, according to Sloman's men. We're mapping as we go.'

'Empty?'

'Everything's empty,' Meryn nodded. 'Not even any furniture.'

'This area may have been abandoned, I suppose,' said Baskevyl. 'I mean, Mkoll had to go through a wall panel to find it.'

Meryn glanced at him. 'Or hidden,' he said, 'deliberately hidden. There's that library place, and the weapons store. Why board that off?'

'I wish I had an answer for you, Meryn,' Baskevyl said. 'Any sense of this area's limits yet?'

'No, sir. Different in here, though, isn't it?' Meryn said.

'Different how?'

Meryn gestured towards the nearest wall light.

'The lighting glows amber, not white. It's lower intensity, but it doesn't come and go. It's as if it's on a different power feed from the rest of the place.'

'Or shut back to some emergency, energy conserving level,' said Baskevyl.

'Right.'

Baskevyl wrapped his camo-cloak around his shoulders. 'I'm going back to the library. Keep going here, and report to me with anything you find.'

'Don't get blown away,' said Meryn as he turned to go.

Baskevyl snorted as he moved off in the opposite direction. To get back to the library and armoury and, from there to the rest of the house, a man had to cross the inner courtyard. In the storm, that was not any kind of fun. Baskevyl pulled down his goggles, and edged out into the fury of the gale. The dust ripped into him with minute claws and pinpricks. He had to hold on to the courtyard wall and feel his way.

The wind made an odd, whooping, scraping sound as it formed a vortex in the courtyard. It sounded like–

No, it doesn't, he told himself.

He glanced up. Most of the dust storms they had endured since their arrival on Jago had been white-outs: blinding hazes of ash-white dust backlit by the sun's glow.

This was different, and had been different since springing up the night before. It was an abrasive darkness, the dust brown-black and noxious, and there was no light behind it, no promise of sun. High above, the sky seemed a tar-brown emptiness, banded and mottled with radiating bars of darkness. Though it was lightless, sparks of luminescence seemed to dart through it. Lightning, Baskevyl presumed, electrical discharge. The wind was making so much noise, he couldn't tell if he could hear thunder or not.

Just let it not be artillery, he thought.

He made it to the far side of the courtyard and blundered in between the two Ghosts posted there.

'Stay sharp,' he told them, and began to walk up the steps in the direction of the library and armoury, pulling off his goggles and shaking the dust out of his cape.

III

WHEN BASKEVYL WALKED into the gun room, Larkin and Maggs were busy examining some of the big antique weapons by the soft amber light.

'If only we had ammo,' Larkin was saying.

'We do,' said Bonin, leaning back against a rack on the far wall, his arms folded. He nodded at the armoured bunkers running down the middle space of the room.

'If only we had *useable* ammo,' Larkin corrected.

'Oh, there is that,' agreed Bonin. The back and left side of his neck were thickly dressed. The pain of his recent injury didn't appear to bother him.

Baskevyl knelt down and lifted the lid off one of the bunkers. He looked at the heap of brown satin pebbles inside.

'Do you think they charged them?' he wondered. 'Do you think they're rechargeable?'

'Coir reckoned they'd been in the coffers too long, Throne rest him,' Bonin replied. 'I reckon we could kill ourselves pretty quickly fething about with old, exotic ammunition.'

'Still,' said Larkin, picking up a brown pebble and holding it in his hand until it began to glow.

'Larks...' Bonin warned, pushing away from the wall and standing upright.

Baskevyl held up a hand. Larkin opened the heavy, mechanical lock of the rampart gun he was holding, dropped the glowing pebble into it, and snapped the action shut. He aimed the massive piece at the blank, end wall of the armoury, flexing his palm around the over-sized grip.

'This is not a good idea,' said Bonin.

'Coming to this bad rock wasn't a good idea in the first place,' Larkin replied. He adjusted his hold, judging how to balance the considerable weight of the wall-gun.

He pulled the trigger.

There was a perfunctory *fttppp!* and a disappointing fizzle of light around the gun's fat muzzle. Larkin clacked open the action and looked down at the dead, brown pebble inside.

'Well, it was worth a try,' Larkin said, lowering the hefty firearm. 'You'd need a slot too, to fire this beastie properly. A slot and a monopod stand.'

'Like this?' Maggs asked. The shelving under the main gunracks was full of slender brass tubes. He pulled one free. It telescoped out neatly to form a shoulder-high pole with a forked rest at the top.

'Exactly like that,' said Larkin.

'We've got everything,' said Maggs.

'Except ammunition, in which case we've got nothing,' said Bonin.

'Are you always such a glass-half-empty bloke, Mach?' Baskevyl asked.

'Actually, I'm a glass-half-broken-and-rammed-in-someone-else's-face bloke,' said Bonin.

'Good to know,' said Baskevyl. 'Keep looking around and see what you can find.'

'Hey,' said Maggs. He'd tugged at the brass gun rest again, an additional fifty centimetres had telescoped out. 'Why would you want it this tall?' he asked.

'For aiming upwards?' Baskevyl suggested with a shrug as he left the chamber. 'Carry on.'

IV

BASKEVYL CROSSED THE corridor to the library chamber where Beltayn, Fapes and two other adjutants were at work.

Beltayn looked up from the pile of books he was studying on the reading tables. Baskevyl didn't like the look on Beltayn's face.

'We're checking book to book, but it's either an old or non-human script, or it's code.'

'Everything?'

Beltayn patted the stack of books on the desk in front of him and then rolled his eyes meaningfully at the thousands of volumes and scrolls on the shelves around them.

Baskevyl nodded. 'All right. That was a stupid question. You've only just started.'

'By all means, help,' said the adjutant.

Baskevyl stood for a moment, listening to the slurring, scratch of the wind outside, a sound that seemed somehow to be coming from below him. Anything to take his mind off that.

He walked the length of one of the walls, running a fingertip along the lip of the elbow-high shelf. A fine billow of dust rippled out in a drowsy wake behind his moving finger. The books were a jumbled assortment, the spines frayed, worn and old. In some cases, it was clear from a collapsed knot of papers wedged between volumes that whole bindings had disintegrated. A few of the volumes bore embossed titles on their spines, but Baskevyl couldn't read any of them. Others seemed to be adorned with emblems or decorative motifs. He looked around at random for a book to start with.

'Is everything all right, sir?' Fapes asked him.

'Yes. Why?'

'Nothing, sir. You just made a sound like you were surprised at something.'

'Just clearing my throat, Fapes. This dust.'

Screw the dust, dust had nothing to do it. Nothing to do with the mumble of shock he'd been unable to stifle. Baskevyl swallowed and looked back at the shelf. It wasn't just the emblem his eyes had alighted on, it was also the fact that he'd been picking at random – *at random!* – and it had been right there waiting for him.

He stared at the spine of the book. It was bound in what looked like black leather, sheened and smooth, like–

Stop it.

Too late to stop it. Too late to stop his mind racing. The emblem, embossed in silver on the spine, glared at him. A snake, a serpent, a worm, its long, segmented body curled around in a circle, so that its jaws clenched its tail-tip to form a hoop.

He swallowed again, and reached out to take down the book. Deep in the recesses of his mind, he heard the scratching grow louder: the grunting, sloughing, scraping beneath his feet, beneath the floor, beneath the mountain itself, increasing as the daemon-worm writhed in pleasure and anticipation.

Baskevyl's hand wavered a few centimetres from the spine of the book.

Take it. Take it. Take it down. Look at it.

His fingers touched the black snakeskin binding just above the silver motif.

'Major?'

Baskevyl snatched his fingers away. 'Beltayn? What did you want?'

Beltayn had a large, leather bound folio open on the reading desk.

'You might want to see this, sir,' Beltayn said, leafing through the pages.

Glad of any excuse to leave the snakeskin book where it was, Beltayn moved around the desk behind Beltayn.

The folio Beltayn had found was big and loose-leaf, containing fragile pages almost half a metre square. Some were blocks of annotated text: copy-black blocks of script in an arcane tongue, decorated with faded penmanship that was even less intelligible.

The rest were illustrated plates. They were finely done, but the colours that had been used to hand tint them were just ghosts of their former strengths.

The plates were diagrams of fortress walls, bastions, emplacements, outworks for debauchment, casemate lines, trench systems, cloche groupings.

'Feth,' said Baskevyl. 'Is this… here?'

Beltayn nodded. 'I think it might be. Actually, I think this might be a record of Jago. That… that looks like Elikon, doesn't it?'

'Yes it does.'

'And that… that's way too big to be here. That's… well, it looks like a hundred kilometres long at least.'

'At least.' Baskevyl breathed deeply. 'Records of the fortress world, old records. I wonder how accurate they are?'

'Better than ours, I'll bet,' said Fapes, peering in over their shoulders.

'Throne bless you, Bel,' said Baskevyl, slapping Beltayn on the shoulder. 'You may have just found something truly important to the war. How many more volumes are there like this?'

'Er… four, six, eight…' Fapes said as he began to count. 'Twenty-three on this stack. There may be others.'

'Shit,' said Baskevyl.

'You're not wrong there,' said Beltayn. 'Look.'

He'd turned over another plate. This one wasn't a diagram, it was a picture, an illustration. It was a cut-away view, done in an antique style, of armoured men defending a casemate during action. Starry missiles, like ancient depictions of comets, arced down at them. Some lay dead, side on, at the foot of the page, their scale and attitudes disagreeing with the perspective of the picture. The men at the casemate were quite clearly armed with wall guns identical to the weapons stored not twenty metres away from where they stood.

'Fighting men,' said Baskevyl, 'at a gun slit.'

Beltayn turned another plate over and revealed another, similar image, a third. Then a fourth, which showed the warriors winding the shutters open for firing. The intricate shutter mechanisms were clearly shown.

'Are they?' Beltayn asked.

'Are they what?'

'*Are* they men?' Beltayn asked. 'Look closely.'

Baskevyl peered down. Beltayn was right. The warriors in the pictures were humanoid, but they were encased in intricate armour from head to foot. Their faces were covered with complex visors.

'They might not be men at all,' said Beltayn. 'Look how big they are in comparison to the casemate slots.'

'You can't say that. There's no perspective, no scale,' Baskevyl said.

'Then look how big they are compared to the guns,' said Fapes.

In the illustrations, the warriors at the casemate slots were holding the rampart weapons as if they were lasrifles. Some of them were shown using gun rests, but even so...

Baskevyl remembered Maggs slotting out that last fifty centimetres of telescoping brass pole.

'Oh holy Throne,' he murmured.

'What's the matter, major?' asked Fapes. 'You seem awfully jumpy today.'

Baskevyl touched his microbead. 'Sir, this is Baskevyl.'

'Go,' replied Rawne's voice.

'Can you get yourself down to that library we found? There's something I'd like to show you.'

'Ten minutes, Baskevyl. Can it wait that long?'

'It's waited I don't know how many centuries so far. I'm sure another ten minutes won't make any difference.'

V

HUNDREDS OF FOOTSTEPS echoed around the house. The watch shift was changing.

The wailing storm outside had outlasted the night and the first watch of the day. Mkoll strode down a corridor spur off the base chamber to check on the scout rotations. He passed the door to Gaunt's chamber. It was ajar.

Not Gaunt's, he told himself, not any more. Rawne's.

He stopped walking, and stepped back a pace or three until he could look in through the open door.

Oan Mkoll was a hard man, a man not given to displays of emotion. He would never have admitted to anyone how lost he felt without Gaunt. They were all feeling it, he knew that. Every last one of them was feeling the loss, and there was no point amplifying that misery. He certainly didn't want anybody commiserating with him.

But the centre of his universe had gone, just like that, even though he had always known it probably would one day. He'd give his life to the service of the Tanith First and, more importantly, to Ibram Gaunt. Mkoll knew war as more than a passing acquaintance. Given his particular role, Mkoll had always assumed he'd die long before Gaunt. Now that Gaunt had beaten him to the happy place, nothing seemed to matter any more.

He hated himself for feeling this way. He resented Gaunt for his passing. It wasn't right. All the while Gaunt had been alive, there'd been some purpose to living, some point to the endless catalogue of war zones and battles, some hope, some... *destination*.

Mkoll pushed the door open and walked into the room. He breathed in. He could smell Gaunt, the ghost of him. He could smell Gaunt's cologne, the starch of his uniform, his lingering body odour.

Rawne's belongings were strewn untidily around the room. Mkoll walked over to the desk. Rawne's announcement that morning that Gaunt's sword had been purloined had filled Mkoll with the deepest fury.

What a bastard, dishonourable thing to do. Steal a dead man's sword? That was low.

Mkoll stared down at the desk top. A few personal items lay on it: a data-slate, a button-brush, a tin of metal polish, a tin mug.

From the moment Mkoll had entered the gatehouse of Hinzerhaus, he hadn't been himself. He'd been jumpy, tense and terrified that he was off his game. He'd told Gaunt as much, that evening out on the crag top. Gaunt had tried to buck him up, but Mkoll had continued to feel it: the sloppiness, the doubt.

I can't trust myself. This place is making a fool out of me. And fools die faster than others.

That's what he'd said.

Mkoll was painfully sure that Gaunt would still be alive if Mkoll had been on form. Mkoll would have been up in upper west sixteen, leading the way, making sure Gaunt didn't *have* to lead the way.

I should have been there. I should have known where the real danger was. I should have been there and I should have saved Ibram, even if that meant I took a kill shot myself.

Mkoll sighed. *I failed you. I'm so sorry.*

He looked down at the desk again. Feth take Hark and his due process. *I'll find the bastard who lifted Gaunt's sword and I'll–*

Mkoll saw the sunshades. He picked them up and turned them over in his hands. They were cheap things, machine stamped out of some plas-tek mill on Urdesh or Rydol. He remembered Varl posing with them for a laugh on Herodor.

What he most clearly remembered was the fact that the sunshades had never once left the Nightgane's face from the moment Varl had given them to Eszrah on Gereon.

'Oh, you stupid feth,' Mkoll murmured to himself. 'What have you gone and done?'

VI

RAWNE ENTERED THE library.

'This had better be worth my time,' he said.

'Oh, it is,' Baskevyl replied. 'Look at this.'

'Look at what?' Hark asked, limping in behind Rawne.

'I–' Baskevyl began. He paused, and looked at Hark. 'Commissar? What's the matter?'

Hark had frowned suddenly, as if hearing something. When he spoke, his words came out in a short bark.

'Brace yourselves!'

They felt the shudder of the first shells falling on the house. One salvo, another. Some burst nearby, causing the floor to vibrate and dust to spill down from the ceiling.

'The storm is still blowing!' Beltayn complained. 'How can they range us?'

'They had us yesterday. That range still applies,' Rawne shouted back. 'Even firing blind!'

'But–' Beltayn began.

The next salvo felt as if it struck the bulk of the house directly overhead. Chunks of plasterwork and sections of brown satin panels spilled down out of the roof space. The lights flickered.

Rawne's eyes narrowed. *How do we fight an enemy we can't see and we can't reach? How do we fight an enemy that can pick us apart one piece at a time?*

VII

THE SHELLING CONTINUED for ten more minutes and then eased off. In another ten, it began again, like a summer rainstorm that comes and goes with the chasing clouds.

The house jarred in its rocky bedding. Several overlook casemates took square hits and were demolished, but there were few casualties as the Ghosts had withdrawn into the fortified heart of the house. The shell impacts sounded through the wailing drone of the wind, shrill and raucous, like the bleats of livestock going to slaughter.

Zweil had been conducting a service in the base chamber when the first shells started to land. As the men around him looked up in consternation, he hushed them down and carried on with his reading as if nothing was happening.

Nearby, on a lower landing of the same chamber, Rerval, Rafflan and other vox-officers had continued to apply themselves to their caster-sets, their constant, murmuring voices becoming a liturgical chorus to Zweil's confident voice.

Daur was in command of the watch on the main gatehouse. He knew that what they were hearing – and feeling – was harassing fire at best, a constant plugging away to weaken their resolve. No one, not even the Chaotic enemy, used artillery during a full-scale typhoon with any expectation of accurate, productive results. It was a wonder anything was hitting the house at all.

But even the whine of shells passing overhead, or the sound of a barrage landing within earshot, was enough to unsettle dug-in troops. It made them feel helpless and even more vulnerable than usual. It whittled away their hope and eroded their confidence.

Daur walked down through the huddles of muttering, wary men in the gatehouse and stood in front of the main hatch. His fingers traced the slight crease in the seam where the ram had done its work the day before. It wouldn't take much more to break the seal.

He placed the palm of his hand flat against the metal of the hatch and felt a slight, continuous vibration beneath his touch. Was that the pressure of the storm driving against the other side?

The shelling persisted for another half an hour and then died away again. There was no respite from the storm. High in the house, along those ill-fated uppermost halls and galleries, the fiercely moving air and dust outside made sounds against the metal domes of the cloches like claws on glass. Hastily tied or wired-down shutters juddered in their sockets. Sentry fire-teams waited in uneasy groups, listening, talking softly, playing at cards or dice, or gnawing on dried rations.

Mkoll toured the upper galleries, checking on the sentry teams. The men were glad to see him. Mkoll was a reassuring figure. As the shelling came and went, he told them not to worry, and to keep a close watch on the shutters and the trip-wires.

More than once, as if in passing, he casually asked, 'Do you happen to have seen the Nihtgane today?'

VIII

'You know what this is?'

'A royal pain, mister?' answered Cullwoe.

'Feth, yeah,' Dalin smiled, though his smile was not confident. Exploring and securing the new-found sections of the house was taking longer than projected: empty rooms opened unexpectedly into other empty rooms, and then into more besides, just when they were expecting to find a dead end or an external wall. The crump and rattle of falling shells simply added to the nervous tension.

Lamp-packs, fixed on the lugs under the barrels of their weapons, hunted through the amber gloom. The come and go of the soft white lights in the rest of the house, a detail that had been disturbing to begin with, seemed infinitely preferable to the low, steady orange burn of the wall lights in the new section.

Their microbeads clicked.

'Confirm click,' said Dalin into his mic. Atmospheric distortion had been causing false signals on the intervox all day.

'Confirm,' said Wheln. 'Can you get down here?'

They followed his signal along a boxy corridor that joined a larger hallway at right angles.

'Down here!' Wheln called, seeing their lights.

The robust, older Tanith was waiting for them at the southern end of the hallway. His search partner, Melwid, was with him.

'What have you found?' Dalin asked.

'Take a look, adjutant,' Wheln said. It was so odd. Wheln, like many others, seemed to have no hesitation whatsoever in accepting Dalin's new role, despite the age gap.

The hallway opened out into a wide flight of steps, eight deep, that descended onto the brown satin floor of a large, oblong chamber. There were no other doors or spur-exits. It was a dead end. Amber wall lights glowed along the side walls, but the wall facing the steps was just a panelled blank.

'End of the line,' said Cullwoe.

'Maybe. Look at that,' Wheln replied. He raised his hand and pointed out the carved wooden archway over the steps. It had been eaten away in prehistory by worms, and the carved figure work was impossible to read.

'So what?' asked Cullwoe. 'Are we making a note of interesting architectural features now?'

Melwid shook his head. Wheln ignored Cullwoe and looked straight at Dalin. 'Seen anything like it?' he asked.

Dalin nodded. 'Twice,' he replied. 'There's one at the end of the hallway between the main gate and the base chamber.'

'And another on the way into this part of the house, just as you're coming into the courtyard,' Wheln agreed.

Cullwoe shrugged. 'So?'

'Shush for a minute, Khet,' Dalin said.

'But–'

'Don't you get it?' Dalin asked. 'The other two arches like this mark entrances.'

Dalin crossed to the far wall of the dead end chamber, and ran his hand across the brown satin panelling. Then he struck his knuckles against it. The sound was dull.

'No echo,' said Melwid.

'Even so,' said Dalin, and clicked his microbead. 'Captain Meryn? Criid here, sir...'

IX

No sentries had been posted in the windcote. The belfry had been deemed, by everyone including Mkoll, too inaccessible for a scale assault. The shutters had been wired down and secured. It was an empty, gloomy roost where the wind got in through slits and crevices.

Eszrah ap Niht sat on the deck with his back to the metal tree and carefully applied *wode* to his face. When he had finished smearing the grey paste on, expertly banding it across his skin without the need of a mirror, he took another little gourd flask out of his tunic pocket and unscrewed the cap. One by one, he took up the iron darts laid out on the floor beside him, and dipped their tips into the flask, charging them with the lethal moth venom of the Untill. Then he wrapped the poisoned darts back up in their quiver, put the flask away and sat for a while in silence. Four items lay on the decking in front of him: a spool of rope, a bag of climbing hooks and pins, his reynbow and Gaunt's sword.

The moan of the wind outside was easing slightly, as if the gigantic storm was finally running out of power. Eszrah ignored the sporadic rumble of shell fire that echoed up from the southern face of the house behind him.

He rose to his feet in one smooth, unsupported uncrossing of his legs. He strapped the sword to his back and tied the reynbow over it, crosswise, to balance the weight. The bag went over his body so it hung down on his left hip. He put his right arm through the spool of rope.

The loose dust in the windcote air slowly began to settle. After several minutes, the faintest hint of pale daylight began to show around the lips of the brass hatches.

Eszrah walked over to a north-facing hatch, undid the wiring and opened it. He looked out into a cold twilight, a violet sky, smeared by cloud, hanging above a thick yellow blanket of slowly calming dust cover that obscured the mountainside below him and stretched out over the immensity of the badlands to the north.

The storm had ended. Daylight was fighting to take its place.

Eszrah slid out through the shutter without hesitation and let it flap shut behind him.

X

'Storm's dropped,' Daur was informed.

'Gate here,' he said, activating his intervox. 'Overlook? Anything?'

High in the house above, the spotters and lookouts were returning to their posts, and opening the shutters they had sealed against the storm to look out into the bruised half-light across a landscape that had not yet properly recovered its form.

'Nothing, gate. Will keep you advised.'

Daur took a swig of water.

'I don't like this,' he heard one of the troopers nearby murmur.

I know what I don't like, Daur thought. *I don't like the fact that the moment the storm died back, so did the shelling.*

In the base chamber, Rerval adjusted another dial and said, for the umpteenth time, 'Elikon M.P., Elikon M.P., this is Nalwood, this is Nalwood, do you receive, over?'

'Nalwood, this is Elikon, this is Elikon,' the voxcaster replied.

Rerval clapped his hands together. 'Someone tell Rawne!' he shouted. 'We've got a link!'

XI

SPLINTERING AND CRACKING, the old brown panelling came away. Wheln and Dalin levered at it with the pry-bars Meryn had brought. The void behind the satin brown panels was packed with dust and grit, and everyone was coughing and pulling their capes up over their mouths.

'It's just bare rock,' Meryn spat, 'just bare rock. It was worth checking, Dalin, but–'

Wheln reached into the space behind the partially demolished panelling. He pulled out a large chunk of dirty stone. 'It's not bare rock,' he said. 'It's loose rock. It's spoil packed in.'

'Clear it,' Meryn ordered.

They didn't have to clear much to see what was behind it. There was a metal hatch behind the wall, caked in crusts of earth-mould and dust, a hatch virtually identical in size and design to the one in the main gatehouse.

'A second gate,' said Dalin.

'Yes, but sealed up,' Meryn said.

'On *this* side, captain,' Dalin said.

'We didn't know this place had more than one gate,' Meryn said. 'Why would the enemy know any different?'

'Because they seem to know a lot more about this place than we do,' said Dalin.

'The boy's right,' said Rawne appearing in the hallway behind them. 'So we have to be sure. Captain, get three squads assembled in here, three squads with at least one flamer.'

'Sir.'

'On the double, Meryn. I want this hatch open.'

They all looked at Rawne.

'Anybody else know a way to find out what's behind it?' Rawne asked.

XII

HARK LET OUT a low whistle as he slowly turned the loose leaves of the folio over one by one.

'Important, right?' Baskevyl asked.

Hark nodded.

'Rawne didn't seem that impressed,' Baskevyl added.

'He's got more immediate problems,' Hark said. The images he was looking at were so astonishing, he'd almost forgotten about the throb of pain in his back.

He looked up at Baskevyl and Berenson. 'These need to be taken to Elikon M.P. as soon as possible.'

'Yes, commissar,' Berenson replied. 'I think it's vital.'

'Taken?' Baskevyl said.

'There's no other way of communicating them,' said Hark. 'We can't upload them.'

'No way of converting them at all?' Berenson asked.

'We may have a few pict-readers, but it would take weeks to scan all of the volumes. The quality would be poor.' Hark sighed. 'And our uplink isn't secure enough to transmit it, certainly not in this quantity. No, gentlemen, this is going to have to get to Elikon the old-fashioned way.'

'Rawne won't like it,' said Baskevyl.

'Major Rawne's going to have to lump it, then,' said Hark.

XIII

MKOLL CREPT UP the wooden stairs into the windcote. His keen senses were not mistaken. The Nihtgane was up there, or he'd been up there.

The dome space was empty. Mkoll looked around. There wasn't much to see. One of the brass shutters rattled in its frame as the breezes knocked at it.

He saw a faint grey smudge on the floor. He bent down, touched it, and sniffed his fingertip.

Wode, the smell of the deepest Untill.

He rose to his feet and went over to the rattling shutter. It had been unwired.

He stood for a long time, deep in thought.

XIV

'STAND BY, GATE,' the vox-link said in Daur's ear.

'Come on,' Daur fretted.

'There's still a lot of dust, gate,' the overlook observer said. 'Terrain is still obscured.'

'But you thought you saw something?'

'Can't confirm. Stand by.'

Daur breathed out. He was about to speak again when the hatch behind him shook. A deep, reverberative clang rang around the gatehouse.

'Never mind, overlook,' Daur said grimly. 'Rise and address!' he yelled to the men.

The ram resumed its steady beat against the other side of the hatch.

Elikon M.P., Elikon M.P., this is Nalwood, this is Nalwood. Request urgent munition resupply. Request urgent vox-to-vox link with field commander at earliest practical opportunity. Please advise soonest.

Nalwood out. (transmission ends)

- Transcript of vox message,
fifth month, 778.

SIXTEEN

The Third Assault

I

'CLEAR IT THERE! There!' Rawne called out. 'No, those rocks. They're jamming the hinge!'

Melwid scrambled into the gap and dug the rocks out of the way with both hands, strewing them back into the chamber behind him like a burrowing animal.

'Good!' Rawne yelled. 'Pull it now!'

The dry metal hinges of the hatch groaned in protest at being forced to move after such a long time. A shaft of grey daylight speared in around the edge, and white dust blew in with it.

'Squads ready!' Rawne ordered.

'Ready to address!' Meryn relayed.

The hatch opened to a gap of about half a metre and the cold outside light leaked more comprehensively into the chamber.

'Enough!' Rawne called. He held up his hand for quiet.

No one moved. No one spoke. The only sounds were the trickle of disturbed dirt, the soft hum of the wind outside and the hiss of Neskon's waiting flamer.

Using gestures, Rawne pulled Wheln, Melwid and Dalin back from the hatch, leaving Cullwoe and Harjeon behind the bulk of the door, ready to heft it shut again at a moment's notice.

Nothing came from outside, no sound of movement, no shots.

Rawne looked over at Bonin with a nod.

Bonin moved forwards, followed by his fellow scouts Livara and Jajjo. They reached the gap. Bonin took a quick look around it using one of the little, makeshift stick mirrors that Mkvenner had developed.

He signalled *clear.* Jajjo slipped past him, then Livara. Bonin followed them.

Rawne was the fourth man at the hatch. He was about to follow the scouts out when Meryn put a hand on his arm.

'Sir, I don't think–' Meryn whispered.

'Not now, Meryn.'

'We can't afford to lose two commanding officers in as many days.'

Rawne met Meryn's eyes for a moment, then he slid through the gap anyway.

Outside was a bleak place. The air smoked with lightly blown dust and the sky far above was stained the colour of an old bruise. The hatchway opened into a gulley, a high-sided ravine with slopes made of loose scree and tumbled boulders that centuries of gales had brought down the mountainside.

Rawne picked his way down towards the bottom of the gulley. He could see the three scouts moving ahead of him, low and careful. He turned slowly. He could see the craggy shelves of the house and the cliff face rising behind him, above the hatchway. The hatch itself was half-buried in scree. Before the hatch had opened, there would have been no obvious clue that there was a gate there at all.

The gulley was quite broad at the mouth, and it evidently lay adjacent to and separate from the main pass leading to the gatehouse: a side entrance, a secondary port. The enemy clearly didn't know about it, or they'd have used it during the last assault instead of climbing up and coming in over the roofs.

Rawne's bead clicked.

He moved down the gulley towards the mouth, where the scouts were waiting. He had almost reached them when the intervox in his ear shouted, 'Contact! Main gate!'

Rawne didn't reply. He started to run, and joined the scouts. They'd bellied down amongst the jumbled stones at the end of the gulley, looking right.

Rawne got down with them. Bonin handed him a scope and pointed.

As Rawne had surmised, the gulley opened out into the eastern side of the dust bowl in front of the main gate. The approach pass, grim and high-sided, lay to their left. The gatehouse was about five hundred metres west of them.

It was under attack.

Despite the sobbing moan of the wind and the curious acoustics of the pass, Rawne had been able to hear the noise of the attack from the moment he cleared the end of the gulley, the steady, gong-like beat of a ram against metal, intoning like a bell, the snarl and shout of men, the batter of drums.

More than a hundred Blood Pact warriors had gathered around the main gate, chanting and shouting as the ram-team heaved and swung their heavy device. Banners flapped in the mountain air.

Additional packs of enemy warriors were trudging in across the dust bowl to join the mass. Rawne could see the spiked ladders they were carrying, or dragging, across the dust. They were preparing for another scale assault.

Rawne opened his intervox. 'This is Rawne. Any contact from the top galleries? Anything from the north?'

'Negative, sir. It's quiet up there.'

'Keep watch. Full alert. They may come at any time. Be advised, the enemy is about to mount a scale assault of the south face. All defences are ordered to open fire only when they have clear targets on the wall. No wasting ammo.'

'Yes, sir.'

'I mean it.'

'Sir.'

Rawne paused. 'This is Rawne again. Who's commanding the gate?'

'Captain Daur, sir.'

'Get him some support, another company at least. I think he's about to need it.'

Rawne glanced at the three scouts.

'We could move in around them,' Bonin said.

'Go on.'

Bonin gestured back down the gulley at the new gate. 'Bring a company or two out this way, we could be into them from the right flank before they know it, and do a lot of hurt.'

Rawne nodded.

'Well?' asked Bonin.

Rawne took a deep breath. The idea was deliciously tempting. He could imagine how much damage a surprise counter-strike might do.

'No,' he said.

'No, sir?'

'No, Bonin. We hit them like that, they'll know we've found another way out. They'll come back this way and find the other gate.'

'But–'

'That second gate is our little secret. It's an advantage we didn't know we had, but we're only going to get one use out of it, so we've got to make it count. We have to use it at the right moment, for the best effect.'

'Isn't this the right moment, begging your pardon?' asked Jajjo.

'Feth, I wish it was,' said Rawne. 'I'd like to get my silver wet today. But I think we need to save it. Tactically, it could be much more important later.'

The three scouts nodded, but they didn't seem convinced.

'It's how Gaunt would have played it,' Rawne said.

'Really?' asked Bonin sceptically. 'How can you be so sure?'

'Because if he was here, he'd be telling us to wait, and I'd be the one telling him he was a fething idiot.'

There was a sudden burst of noise from the main gate. The first ladders had hooked up the walls, and the Blood Pact storming up them had been met with gunfire from the casemates and the overlooks above. Las-bolts spat down from the gunslots like bright rain, and many red-clad figures jerked and tumbled back down the lower cliffs, rolling and bouncing limply. Explosions began to bloom like desert flowers, brief gouts of fire that left fox-tails of black smoke trailing off into the sky when they had gone. Two spiked ladders, laden with enemy troopers, tore free and went slithering and cascading down the steep revetment of the lower house. Rawne could hear screams and yelling, voices raised in both pain and war cry. The firing grew more intense. Rockets banged off from the ground outside the gate and curled in to strike the upper casemates. Blood Pact crews with mortars and bomb-launchers had set up outside the gatehouse, and began to crank their machines to lob explosives up the walls. Fire and shrapnel skittered back down the cliff.

'Let's go back and secure the new gate,' said Rawne. 'We'll keep it open and under watch so we can see what's out here, and close it if we need to.'

'I'll stay put,' said Bonin. 'We could use a spotter. First sign of trouble, I can double time back to the gate and get it shut.'

'Just stay out of sight,' Rawne told him.

He headed back up the gulley with Livara and Jajjo. Behind him, he could distinctly hear the *Clang! Clang! Clang!* of the iron ram striking the main hatch.

II

'Where do you suppose you're going?' Hark asked.

He was limping down the hallway towards the main gate on his crutch, moving through the tail end of Daur's men. They were agitated, and some had risen to their feet instead of crouching by the walls as instructed.

'Get back down and get ready!' Hark ordered, thumping past. The repetitive slam of the ram up ahead was dismal and chilling, and he could appreciate why the men were close to snapping. Hark understood their fear, but lack of formation discipline simply couldn't be permitted. He drew his pistol.

'Get ready! Ready now! Glory of Tanith! Spirit of Verghast! Fury of Belladon! They're going to come at us and we're going to give them death! What will we give them?'

'Death!' the chorus came back.

'That's more like it!'

Some of the men cheered. Others shook themselves and tightened their grips on their weapons. Hark realised he was wishing, hoping, *begging* for the main gate *to just get on with it and cave in*. The waiting was the worst part. Give the Ghosts a fight and none of them would have time to think about running.

Brutal fighting was already underway. From above, through the thick rock of the roof, they heard the muffled noises of frantic las-fire and explosions reaching them from the scale assault. The floor shook occasionally, and dislodged dust seeped fitfully from the cracked ceiling.

Hark came up the tunnel to the gatehouse. The men were lined up against the wall. He saw Ban Daur, standing ready at the tunnel mouth. Daur had four flamers drawn up ready at his back, but there were over a dozen troopers positioned down in front of him around the tunnel steps and the inner hatch. Daur had cleared all his men out of the gatehouse chamber.

'Captain?' Hark said.

'Commissar.'

'Why the feth have you pulled out of the gatehouse, Daur?' Hark whispered in his ear. 'Why aren't your flamers front and centre?'

'Who's commanding this position, commissar?' Daur asked.

'Well, you, of course.'

'Thank you. I know what I'm about. The men know what's expected. Support me. Don't question me.'

Hark had never seen Daur so firm, so bloody determined.

'Absolutely,' Hark said, with a courteous nod.

The outer hatch was badly deformed. With each successive blow of the ram outside, it buckled even further, tearing away from its frame. They could hear, quite clearly, the shouts and bellows of the enemy right outside, clamouring to get in.

Clang! The hatch bent. *Clang!* The lip of it twisted inwards. *Clang!* A hinge began to shear. *Clang!* The middle of the hatch distended like a fat man's belly.

'We hold the outer hatch, we kill a few of them,' Daur whispered to Hark. 'I want to kill a lot of them. The gate chamber is our killing ground. It bottles them up and leaves them ready for slaughter.'

Hark nodded. He understood.

'You may tell the company to fix, commissar,' said Daur.

'G Company!' Hark yelled, turning to aim his voice back down the tunnel. 'Straight silver!'

A clatter of locking blades answered him.

'Fixed and ready!' Haller called back.

'Fixed and ready, captain,' Hark said.

'Any moment now!' Daur shouted. 'Remember who you are! And remember Ibram Gaunt!'

The company, to a man, roared its approval. The sound drowned out the beat of the ram.

The sound drowned out the metal screech of the hatch finally sundering.

Screaming like feral shades loosed from the depths of the warp, the Blood Pact stormed the gatehouse. The hatch had only partially fallen in, and they came pouring in, over and around its bulk, streaming, as it seemed to Hark, like rats, like a swarm of rodent vermin spewing out of a duct across the belly hold of a mass conveyance, flowing like a tide over any and all obstructions. Grim figures in red, their filthy uniforms adorned with strings of finger bones and human teeth, came scrambling through the opening, howling out of the mouth slits of their black iron masks, their eyes bright with bestial lust. Some fired weapons, others brandished trench axes and mauls. The reek and noise of them was appalling.

The first of their wild shots hit the floor, the roof, and the frame of the inner hatchway. A Ghost in the front rank went over.

'Fire!' Daur yelled.

The dozen or so Ghosts crouching around the inner hatchway opened fire, cutting into the front of the swarming tide as it surged towards them. Enemy warriors buckled and fell, or stumbled, wounded, and were promptly smashed down by the brute men rushing in behind them. There was a sudden stink of blood and crisped flesh. The Ghosts kept firing. Daur was firing too. Hark raised his pistol and lanced energy beams into the oncoming mass, incinerating some, violently dismembering others. In seconds, the leading ranks of the storm force were dead, just corpses carried forward by the press behind.

The tide faltered slightly. The Blood Pact warriors began struggling to clamber over bodies to reach their foe. Some tripped and fell. Las-fire knocked others off their feet. The close confines of the gate chamber degenerated a bewildering blur of bodies and yelling, motion and shots, almost incomprehensible in its violent confusion.

In the first ten seconds after the fall of the hatch, the Blood Pact lost forty warriors in the gate chamber, for the cost of only two Ghosts. Daur's killing ground had been expertly achieved.

But Ban Daur's ambitions were greater. As the gate chamber filled to capacity with storming enemy troops, with more shoving in behind, and the front of their assault almost at the inner hatch, Daur turned.

'Switch! Now!' he yelled above the din.

The Ghosts at the hatch who had been holding the enemy at bay with rifle fire suddenly rose and fell back, firing as they went. Daur pulled Hark to one side.

The flame-troopers stepped up, line abreast, and took their places, facing the charge.

'Flames, flames!' Brostin yelled.

He triggered his burner. At his side, Lubba, Dremmond and Lyse did the same. The result was devastating. The heat wash shock-sucked back down the tunnel and made Daur, Hark and the Ghosts around them gasp and shield their faces. The four flamers stood side by side in the inner hatch and streamed liquid fire into the entry chamber of the gatehouse.

There was nowhere to run or hide. There was nowhere to escape from the conflagration. The seething inferno ripped back across the chamber all the way to the broken hatch, and then blasted outside into the open, into the iron-masked faces of enemy warriors packed tight and clawing to get in.

Inside the furnace of the gate chamber, the monstrous destruction was stoked by grenades and ammo packs touching off and exploding. Stumbling, burning figures, ablaze from head to foot, blew apart as grenades in their packs and musette bags caught and detonated.

The fire made a whining, keening sound as it swirled around the chamber, spinning up to scorch the roof. It was licking, leaping and surging as if it was alive. It was almost too bright to look at, and the writhing black shapes inside it almost too terrible to bear. The scream of the fire reminded Hark of the shriek of the wind that punished Jago, day and night, eternal, primordial and hungry.

The burns across his back ached in blistering sympathy. It felt good to pay back that pain with flames.

III

The Ghost manning the slot to Kolea's left suddenly took three rapid steps backwards, swayed, and collapsed flat on his back.

'Medic!' Kolea yelled, continuing to fire down out of the slot at the enemy figures on the walls below him. His overlook wasn't the only one where someone was shouting for a doctor. Kolea had started the fight with five men in the box, and now only Derin and Obel's adjutant, Dafelbe, remained upright.

'Medic!' Kolea yelled again. 'Medic here!' He aimed out, saw a scrambling figure ascending through the smoke below, and squeezed off two shots. The enemy warrior crumbled and half fell, his arm snagging on the side of the storm ladder he'd been scaling. Hooked, the warrior struggled. Before Kolea could shoot again, the warrior's own comrades had heaved him off the ladder out of their way. He fell into the smoke. Derin put a round right through the face of the first man up behind him.

'Need ammo,' Derin growled.

'I know,' said Kolea.

'Soon,' Derin added.

A whooping rocket hit the top lip of their slot and showered them with grit as it exploded.

'Too close,' coughed Dafelbe.

Kolea looked out again, shots whining up past him. He saw the Blood Pact on the nearest ladder passing up another coiled length of scaling rungs, man to man, making ready to cast it up the next stretch of wall. Kolea fired at them.

The warrior at the top of the ladder, anxious to protect the ladder-bearers below him, unpinned a stick grenade and swung back to pitch it up at the slot.

'I don't think so,' said Kolea, taking a pot-shot.

The warrior toppled back off the ladder, and his grenade dropped in amongst the men immediately beneath him. The blast took the ladder away from the rock face in a thud of smoke and sparks.

Kolea had no time to feel satisfied. Heavy fire began to chop in from the right. The raiders had succeeded in getting another scaling ladder right up under the overlook next to them. The Blood Pact warriors at the top of it were fighting hand-to hand with the men in the slot, hacking to gain entry. Those lower down on the swaying ladder section were shooting sideways at Kolea's position.

'Feth it!' Kolea said, trying to return fire. The angle was poor.

'Derin! Do what you can!' Kolea cried, backing away from the window.

'Where are you going?'

'Just do it!'

Kolea ran out of the overlook, along the connecting hallway and into the adjacent casemate box.

The gunslot there was full of hacking, flailing limbs and snarling grotesks. Pabst, Vadim and Zayber were fighting to keep them out, but Pabst was wounded in the arm and Vadim could barely see for the blood streaming down his face.

'Shoot them!' Kolea cried, coming in behind them.

'No ammo!' Vadim screamed. A trench axe crunched into Zayber's neck and he staggered backwards, spewing blood.

Kolea snapped his carbine to full auto. 'Ghosts drop!' he yelled. Vadim lurched aside, pulling Pabst with him.

Kolea raked the gunslot with rapid las, blowing chunks and lumps out of the rockcrete sills. The enemy warriors choking the slot screamed and jerked as rounds ripped into them. Some fell out and disappeared instantly, others yowled and held on, clawing at the edges of the firing position, weighed down by the dead and wounded.

'Run! Get some ammo!' Kolea shouted at Pabst. He kept firing, blowing off fingers and hands, dislodging grips. A Blood Pact warrior tried to lunge bodily in through the slit, and Kolea blew him open across the shoulder, dropping his corpse onto the firestep inside the slot.

Kolea ran to the step and pulled two stick bombs out of the corpse's webbing panniers. He yanked the pins out and posted them out over the slit edge. There was a meaty double *thud*.

Pabst came running back in with a bag of clips. He was closely followed by Merrt, Vivvo and Tokar.

'What are you?' Kolea asked them.

'Gn...gn... gn... reinforcements,' said Merrt.

'Rawne sent a company down from topside to back you up,' said Vivvo.

'Get to the slot. Good to see you,' Kolea nodded. He went back into the corridor, moving through the fresh troops joining the overlook deck.

'Spread out! Fill the gaps!' he heard Corporal Chiria yelling down the smoke-washed run.

He went back to his original position, and found that Derin and Dafelbe had been joined by two Ghosts. One was Kaydey, a Belladon marksman firing a long-las. The other was Tona Criid.

The side of her head was bandaged. With grim concentration, she was firing snapshots from the corner of the slot.

'Welcome back to the Emperor's war, sergeant,' Kolea said to her as he resumed his place.

'I can't tell you how glad I am to be here,' she replied sardonically.

Kolea risked a look out as the others rattled away on either side of him. No fresh ladders had been attached, and the enemy forces were milling around at the foot of the casemate buttress in a disorganised rabble, swathed in smoke, contenting themselves with firing up at the boxes. A vast plume of dirty black smoke was fuming out of the gatehouse far below.

'I think Daur's done a day's work,' Dafelbe muttered.

'Looks that way,' Kolea agreed.

'Either that, or the fething fortress is alight,' Derin added, never one to trust a bright side.

'They're falling back!' Criid called out.

It was hard to see clearly through the thick, accumulating smoke seething up the southern face of the house, but the enemy did appear to be in retreat. Gunfire and rockets continued to come up at the gunboxes, though the rate grew thinner. Kolea could see groups of distant figures fleeing back across the dust bowl into the throat of the pass.

The last few shots were exchanged.

'This is Kolea,' Kolea said into his microbead. 'Report – did we hold the gate?'

Traffic snatched to and fro in brief clips.

'Say again?' Kolea said.

'Overlook, this is Daur. We have held the gate.'

Kolea looked at Derin and they both allowed weary grins to cross their dirty, unshaved faces.

'Sir!' Dafelbe called out.

Kolea turned.

Dafelbe was bending over Tona Criid. She had sagged down quietly in the corner where she had been standing. Kolea hurried over.

'Was she hit?' he asked.

'I don't think so,' Dafelbe replied. 'I think she just passed out.'

Tona stirred. 'I'm all right.' she mumbled.

'On your feet too soon,' Kolea said. 'Let's get you up.'

She didn't answer. She had blacked out again.

Day twelve. Sunrise at five plus eleven, clear. No contact overnight, no sign of enemy at daylight.

We weathered the third assault yesterday with precious few casualties considering. I am certain that if they had hit us on two fronts, as per the previous ~~assualt~~ assault, we would not have survived.

As it is, I intend to recommend B.D. for decoration for his sterling command in defence of the main gate (see accompanying citation).

Ammo very low. R. trying to arrange supply drop. He has a plan that he is not sharing with anyone at this stage. I have impressed upon him the vital nature of the documents discovered in the so-called library. We must preserve and secure them, or transport them clear, before this fortress finally succumbs.

One minor but troubling footnote. Master of Scouts Mkoll seems to have disappeared. I am trying to account for his whereabouts.

– field journal, V.H. fifth month, 778.

SEVENTEEN
The Ghosts

I

THE GHOSTS CLOSED *in. They have been there all the time, luminal things chained to the ancient place, just out of sight. Now they step closer, silent as whispers, elusive as voice fragments on a skipping vox-channel, soft as the brush of black lace against stone. They draw near.*

They are not invited. They are sent. They smell the mind-heat of the lost souls in the house at the end of the world and swoop down, like winged things returning to the windcote. They are the dust on the satin brown walls, the glow and fade of the lights, the scratch and rattle of something buried under the earth. They have the voices of friends. They are the voices of the dead. They are the darkest corner of the night, the coldest atoms of the cosmos, the moan of the wind. They are music, half-heard. They are dry skulls in a dusty valley.

The ghosts close in. Only in death may they move so freely. Only in the presence and the hour of death may they come so close.

They feel it. The end is coming: the end of Hinzerhaus and all those within its walls.

They gather in the empty halls and cold galleries. Slowly, slowly, they reach–

II

–OUT.

The light died. Rawne cursed, and flicked at the lamp-pack on his desk. He was sure the cell had been a fresh one, but it was dead.

'Rerval!'

His adjutant appeared at the door. 'Sir?'

'Get me a fething lamp-pack, would you?'

'Yes, sir.'

Rawne sat back. He was tired. He'd been studying some of the old books brought up from the library. Trying to work by the come and go radiance of the wall lights gave him a headache, so he'd trained a lamp-pack on the pages.

The books didn't interest Rawne much. He'd never had much time for history. History was dead, and Rawne was much more interested in being alive. However, the likes of Hark and Baskevyl believed the books to be important, so he'd made the effort.

It had also given him some occupation. The day had passed slowly, perhaps the slowest so far. Expecting attack at any moment, they'd all stayed on knife-edge nerves. That wore a body out. As Hark had said so often, waiting was the real killer.

The books, with their crumbling, loose leaf pages, had been diverting enough. Most of the plates made no sense, and Rawne had no way of knowing how accurate any of the charts were.

But he could see enough to know that Hark was right. The books had to be shown to someone who could assess their real worth. If there was any chance – *any chance* – that they were what they seemed to be, then they could be the difference between triumph and defeat.

A chill passed through the room, a draught from somewhere. Someone had come in, pushing the door open quietly.

'Have you got that fething lamp?' Rawne asked, looking up.

'One last fight,' said Colm Corbec, smiling sadly down at him.

Rawne got up so fast his chair fell over backwards with a bang.

He blinked fast. There was no one there. Rawne turned around sharply, shaking, then around again. The room was empty.

'Feth!' he hissed. 'What the *feth*...'

'Did you knock your chair over, sir?' asked Rerval mildly, walking into the room with a fresh lamp-pack in his hand.

Rawne strode right past him to the door, and glared up and down the hallway outside.

'Sir?'

'Was that someone's idea of a joke?' Rawne snarled.

'Was what, sir?' Reval asked, confused.

'That! The... the...' Rawne stopped talking. None of the men could have pulled that stunt. Only his mind could have played a trick like that. He was tired. That was it, just fatigue.

'Are you all right, sir?' asked Rerval.

Rawne walked back to the desk and righted his chair. 'Yes. Yes... just a little jumpy.'

Rerval held the lamp-pack out to Rawne. Rawne took it.

'Thanks.'

Rerval nodded. 'Beltayn says your link should be set up in the next half an hour.'

'Just give me a nod when it's ready. I'll take it here.'

'Yes, sir.'

Rerval walked out of the room and closed the door behind him. Rawne sat down and turned his attention back to the folio, clicking the lamp-pack on.

As he turned the pages, he kept one eye on the door.

III

THAT NIGHT, ALTHOUGH the weather had not turned, the house felt especially airless after dark. The air was dry and still, and the shadows seemed to be layered, as if they had piled up on top of one another like sheets of fine black lace.

Hark hobbled along a lower hallway, leaning heavily on his stick. His back hurt. He knew he'd been pushing himself too hard, and the pain was beginning to erode the sense of well being that Curth's drugs had briefly provided. His burns were not healing. They were still wet and raw, and moving made them worse.

He reached a short flight of steps and lowered himself carefully down onto them. Just sit for a minute, he thought, just a minute or two.

His skin was pale and clammy and sweat streaked his forehead. He breathed heavily. He heard the footsteps of an approaching patrol. Hark had no wish for any of the men to see him so ill-taken.

He drew his sidearm. The cell of his plasma pistol had been running low, so he'd taken a back-up from his holdall – a handsome, almost delicate bolt pistol of brushed steel with a saw-grip handle and engraved slide plates. He made a show of unloading and reloading it.

When the patrol came past, they nodded to him and he nodded back. Just Commissar Hark, taking five to prep his weapon.

He waited until they had gone. It seemed to take a long time, because apparently phantom footsteps rolled up and down the brown satin floor for several minutes after the men had disappeared.

'Is there anyone there?' Hark called out.

The footsteps stopped.

Hark shook his head. Since they'd taken up occupation of Hinzerhaus, he'd heard so many reports of ownerless footsteps.

'Throne take this place,' he muttered.

He put the pistol away, noticing how his real hand was shaking, not from fear. It was the pain doing that, the pain slowly gnawing away at his strength.

He got up and climbed the stairs like an old man. The scout billet was a little way along the next gallery.

Livara was standing by the doorway when Hark approached. He nodded to the commissar. Hark went inside. Most of the scouts present – Hwlan, Leyr, Caober and Mklane – were resting. Preed was playing a solo card game on an upturned box.

Bonin was sitting in the corner, cleaning dust out of his lasrifle with a vizzy-cloth. He saw Hark, put his weapon and cleaning kit down, and got up.

The skin of Bonin's face was raw, like sunburn. They'd had a scout out on watch at the end of the gulley since the discovery of the new gate, and Bonin had personally taken three of the shifts. The dust had scoured him relentlessly.

'You wanted to see me?' Hark asked as Bonin came over. Bonin nodded.

'On what matter?'

Bonin jerked his head and they went out into the corridor, away from the others. They walked along until they were out of earshot.

'Are you a man of honour?' Bonin asked. 'I've always assumed you were.'

'I'd like to think so,' said Hark.

'I need to report something. I need to report it to you as a man of honour, not as a commissar.'

'The two things are not separate,' said Hark.

Bonin sniffed. 'Do you understand what I'm saying? What I'm going to tell you, I won't have you jumping on it like a commissar.'

'I'll have to make that judgement,' Hark replied.

Bonin thought for a moment. Then he said, 'I hear you've been looking for Mkoll.'

'You hear correctly.'

As if it gave him great discomfort, Bonin reached his right hand into his grubby jacket and pulled out a crumpled piece of paper. He unfolded it and stared at it for a moment.

'I found this tucked into my bedroll this evening. Dunno how long it's been there. A day, maybe two.'

He handed the slip to Hark.

It was handwritten, a brief note. It said:

Mach–

There is something that must be done, a matter of honour for the regiment. It is the sword, I mean. It must be got back.

I have gone to get it. I know I have no orders to do so, but I have a moral duty. In conscience, I could not disappear without any word. I ask you to tell them where I've gone and what I plan to do. I hope they will understand the purpose of my actions.

The Emperor protect you.

Your friend,

Oan.

Hark read it twice. 'How long have you really had this, Bonin?' he asked.

Bonin didn't answer.

'Do you know where he's gone?'

'It says there.'

'I mean how and which direction?'

Bonin shrugged. 'There was rope gear and pegs missing from the store. North, I'd guess.'

'Why north, do you think?' asked Hark.

Again, Bonin didn't answer.

'He's gone after the sword,' said Hark, 'and the sword didn't leave by itself.'

'It doesn't say who took it,' said Bonin.

'It doesn't,' Hark agreed, 'but Mkoll's not the only one missing.'

Bonin looked sharply at the commissar. There was a long silence.

'What will you do?' Bonin asked.

Hark folded the paper up and put it in his coat pocket. 'I'll have to decide. This is troubling. By his own admission, Mkoll has abandoned his post and his duty. He's left the regiment's side without orders or permission. That's called desertion.'

'Feth you!' Bonin growled. 'I asked you if you were a man of honour! I didn't have to tell you this!'

'Oh, you really did.'

Bonin stared at Hark. 'Not his duty.'

'What?'

'You said he'd abandoned his duty. He hasn't.'

Hark sighed. 'I know full well that there was no one more loyal to Gaunt than Mkoll, but we can't afford to be sentimental. Gaunt's dead, his sword's gone, and we really, really needed Mkoll here, not away on some idealistic quest.'

Bonin shook his head sadly. 'You don't know the old man like I do. Since we arrived here, he's been off his game. Told me that himself. Hated the fact that he felt sloppy and ineffective. When... when Gaunt died, he took it personally. A personal failure. He doesn't believe he's any use to us here, not any more. A liability, more like. This is his way of making amends.'

'I will consider this carefully and decide what action needs to be taken,' said Hark. 'Without wishing to sound pessimistic, it may be rather academic. If Mkoll's gone north, alone, we'll probably never see him again. If that's the case, I won't tarnish his memory by going public with this. But I have to tell Rawne. I imagine he'll want you to take command of the scouts. He'll probably send for you before the night's out.'

'Yes, sir.'

Hark looked up at something.

'What?' asked Bonin.

'I thought I heard...' Hark began. 'No, my mistake.' He looked back at Bonin. 'As you were,' he said, and limped away.

IV

A CHOKE-HOLD was the last thing he expected.

Weary of the stifling air in the shuttered overlook, Larkin left Banda on watch and stepped out into the connecting hallway. It was no better out there. The air was cold, but still, unmoving, even though the wind crooned outside. Shadows clung to the walls, and the baleful white lights glowed and faded in a slow rhythm.

Larkin paced up and down, rubbing his hands. He took a sip of water from his flask, and was about to put it away again when an arm locked around his throat.

'You're dead, Tanith,' said a voice in his ear.

Larkin struggled but the grip did not slacken. He tried to speak. *Who...?*

'You know who I am, Tanith,' the voice whispered. 'Sure as sure.' Something cold and sharp pressed against Larkin's throat.

'We got Gaunt, so we did. Now I get to settle things with you.'

Larkin snarled and rammed backwards against the hallway wall, crushing the figure on his back against the brown satin panels.

Larkin landed on the ground.

'What the gak are you doing, Tanith?' Banda demanded, appearing at the door of the overlook. Larkin looked around. He was alone. On the floor beside him, his unstoppered water flask slowly glugged out its contents.

'Musta slipped,' he said.

Sure as sure.

Banda shook her head and went back to her post. Larkin struggled back up onto his feet.

A strong hand helped him up.

'I can't watch you all the time,' said Bragg.

Larkin turned. Bragg was just there, large as life. There was a great sadness in his genial eyes. He reached over and brushed dust off Larkin's shoulders and sleeves with his huge, gentle hands.

'I can't watch you all the time,' he repeated. 'You have to be careful, you know? Be careful, Larks, or the fether will get you.'

'Bragg,' Larkin whispered. He stretched out his hand, but there was nothing to touch. Bragg had gone, like a bubble bursting, like dust settling to nothing as a bad rock storm blew out.

Larkin bent over, his fists against his forehead.

'No, no, no, NO!'

He couldn't feel the headache or the nausea yet, but he knew they were coming.

It was the only explanation, the only explanation Larkin could tolerate, anyway.

V

'Do I HAVE to stay here?' Criid asked, toying with the bandage on the side of her head.

'You asked that the other day,' replied Dorden, unwrapping the blood pressure strap from her bared arm, 'and look what happened when I let you walk around.'

Criid shrugged and sat back on her cot. The field station was quiet. Far too many Ghosts lay silent and broken in the bunks on either side of her.

'What aren't you telling me?' she asked.

'It's concussion,' said Dorden.

'And?'

'Just concussion. But it's bad, and if you move around, you're going to feel ill and pass out. So you stay there, please, until I say otherwise.'

'Really? That's all?'

Dorden sat down on the edge of her bed. 'I won't lie to you, Tona. If we were in a proper medicae facility, with decent equipment, I'd run a deep scan to assess for oedema, meningial bleeds and pieces of skull pushing into your brain, just to be safe. But we're not, so I can't. And I am confident in my diagnosis: concussion. You still have pain?'

'It comes and goes.'

'Now?'

She nodded.

'I'll get you something,' he said.

Dorden walked down the length of the field station and crossed the hall into the side room where they had secured the drugs and dressing packs. It was gloomy, and poorly lit. He took out the lamp-pack he'd taken to carrying on his belt and clicked it on. It came on, then faded, as if the battery was drained. He clicked it on and off.

'Lesp!' he called.

He started to rummage in one of the dispensary cartons, looking for high dose tranq/anti-inflammatories.

He could hear something dripping.

'Lesp! Get in here! Bring a light!'

The orderly appeared in the doorway with a shining lamp.

'Doctor?'

'Get some light on me, I can't see a thing.'

Lesp shone his lamp down obediently.

'What's that sound?' he asked after a moment. He turned the beam away.

'Feth's sake, Lesp! I can't see!'

'Doctor?' Lesp murmured. 'Look.'

Dorden looked up. Lesp's lamp beam was illuminating the back wall of the little room. The wall was streaming with blood. It glistened black in the hard light.

'What in the name of–' Dorden stammered. 'Who did this? What fething idiot thought it would be funny to waste precious blood supplies?'

'It's coming out of the wall,' said Lesp.

'That's ridiculous! It's–'

Dorden stared. The blood was quite clearly oozing out between the brown satin panels.

'Get me a pry-bar,' said Dorden.

'What?'

'A pry-bar! A pry-bar!'

'What's going on in here?' Zweil snorted, entering the room behind him. 'You're waking the patients. Is that good medical practice? I don't believe so–'

'Get out, Zweil!'

'I will not!'

'Father, get out of this room now!'

'What are you staring at?' Zweil asked, pushing past them.

'The blood!' Lesp blurted. 'The blood on the wall!'

'What blood?' the old ayatani asked, touching the wall. 'It's just dust.'

Dorden snatched the lamp from Lesp's quivering hand and stepped closer. He could see it clearly. It wasn't blood running down the wall, it was dust, fine trickles of dust seeping out around the panels.

'Throne take me for an old fool,' Dorden muttered. He looked around at Lesp and punched him on the arm. 'And you for a young one.'

'It looked like blood,' said Lesp, ruefully.

It really had.

'Get me a ten mil dose of axotynide and shut up,' Dorden replied.

He walked back into the field station, aware that his pulse was still racing.

Criid's cot was empty.

'Where is she?' he asked, looking around. 'She was just here. Where is she?'

In a nearby cot, Twenzet shrugged. 'She just got up and went out. I told her not to. She said–'

'What did she say, trooper?'

'I dunno,' Twenzet replied.

'What did she say?' Dorden snarled.

Twenzet's eyes widened. 'I... I think she said something like "He's calling me". I thought she meant her boy.'

Dorden didn't believe that for a moment. He hurried back into the hallway. 'Tona!' he shouted. 'Tona!'

VI

LUDD STARTED TO hurry the moment he heard the angry voices up ahead. Then there was a rattling crack of gunfire and he broke into a run.

He burst into the billet hall, into the middle of a riot. On all sides, troopers were shouting, backing away, waving their hands. Wes Maggs stood with his lasrifle in his hands in the centre of the room. He was shaking, his eyes wide, his teeth clenched. Scorched holes in the wall panels ahead of him showed where his shots had gone in.

'Give me the gun, Wes,' Varl was saying calmly, moving round to face Maggs, his hands extended.

'She was right there! Right there! You all saw her, didn't you?'

'Give me the fething weapon, Wes!' Varl ordered.

'She was right there!' Maggs yelled. 'Right in fething front of me! I must have hit her!'

'That's enough,' said Ludd. No one paid him the slightest attention.

'I said, that's enough!' Ludd bellowed.

'Give me the gun!' Varl repeated, facing Maggs down.

'Stand back, sergeant,' said Ludd, trying to interpose himself between them.

'Get out of the way,' Varl warned him.

'That's not how this is going to work,' Ludd replied.

'She was right there!' Maggs insisted, his voice strangled with tension.

Varl lunged at Maggs.

'No!' Ludd cried.

Varl got his hands around Maggs's weapon and they grappled. Varl's augmetic strength forced the barrel up. A flurry of rounds fired off into the ceiling.

Nahum Ludd was neither especially large nor especially strong, but the Commissariate had trained him well in methods of self-defence and disarmament. Training took over.

He leapt forward, scoop-kicking Varl's legs out from under him. Simultaneously, he took hold of Maggs's weapon in his left hand, and chopped Maggs in the throat with the side of his right. Varl crashed down on his back to Ludd's left, and Maggs went over, gasping, to his right. Ludd was left standing between them, Maggs's lasrifle in his hand. He swung it around deftly and aimed it at Maggs.

'Stay the feth down!' he instructed.

'I didn't do any–'

'Stay down! Varl, don't even think of continuing this.'

'Hey,' said Varl, getting up, his hands raised. 'I was just trying to help.' He looked at Ludd, impressed. 'That was pretty fancy stuff, Ludd.'

'Commissar Ludd.'

Varl nodded, grinning. 'Fancy fething stuff, eh?' He looked around.

The Ghosts around them began to cheer and clap.

'Thanks, but shut up,' said Ludd. 'Melyr. Garond. Remove Trooper Maggs's other weapons and get him on his feet.'

'She was right there!' Maggs protested as the two Ghosts scooped him up and took his warknife and pistol away. 'I was just trying to protect us all!'

'From what?' Ludd asked.

'The old dam! The old dam!' Maggs cried bitterly.

An armed fire-team slammed into the billet hall behind them, led by Kolea. They had their weapons trained.

'Shots reported,' Kolea growled looking at Ludd and the others down the foresight of his carbine. 'Do we have contact?'

'False alarm, major,' Ludd said. 'Just a little domestic incident.'

Kolea lowered his gun and clicked his microbead. 'Kolea to all stations. Stand down, stand down. False contact.'

He looked back at Ludd. 'What happened?'

'Nothing I couldn't handle,' said Ludd. 'Can we find somewhere we can make Maggs secure for the time being?'

Kolea frowned. 'Lock him up, you mean?'

Ludd nodded.

'Is he on charges?'

'I think it's safe to say yes,' said Ludd.

Kolea whistled.

'I was only trying to protect us all,' said Maggs, quieter and calmer now. 'You've seen her, haven't you, Gol?'

'What's he talking about?' Kolea asked.

'Who the feth knows?' Varl replied.

VII

He hadn't been able to sleep, the air was so still. As he lay in his bedroll, it felt like he was being smothered. He got up and walked around, with no particular destination in mind.

That was a lie.

No particular destination at all.

The scratching under the floor knew he was lying.

Baskevyl wandered idly down through the lower levels of the house, nodding to sentry groups and watch positions as he went, stopping to share a few words.

All the while, he could hear the slithering underground, the mottled, slick, spinal cord thing moving through the rock beneath him, following him, following him.

No, not following, leading.

Baskevyl walked on, down a loop of stairs, passing lights that glowed and faded, glowed and faded, in time with the hideous scratching noise *down there.*

He reached the entry hole in the wall that led into the new section. The wall panels that had been pulled down had disappeared for firewood. Three troopers guarded the doorway: Karsk, Gunsfeld and Merrt.

'Quiet night, sir?' Gunsfeld asked.

'So, so.'

'We heard there was a thing just now, in one of the billet halls,' said Karsk.

'Nothing to worry about.'

'We thought it might have been another raid starting.'

'It wasn't,' said Baskevyl. 'You can relax. Not too much, mind. All right if I go through?'

Gunsfeld ushered him in. 'Help yourself, sir.'

Baskevyl smiled a thank you, and stepped through the hole into the amber glow of the new section. He'd gone a little way when he heard a voice call to him from behind. Trooper Merrt had followed him down the tunnel.

'What's up, Merrt?'

'I just gn... gn... gn... wanted to ask you something, sir,' Merrt said. He looked awkward and embarrassed.

'All right.'

Merrt held out his weapon. 'What does that say to you, sir?'

Baskevyl peered at the gun. 'It says... I think... er, "034TH".'

Merrt nodded. 'Right. Gn... gn... gn... thanks, sir.'

'Was that it?'

'Yes, sir.'

'Carry on, then.'

Merrt waited until Baskevyl was out of sight, then he looked at his rifle again. 034TH. That's what Gunsfeld had said too, when Merrt had asked him. Gunsfeld had looked as perplexed by the question as Baskevyl was.

The problem was, they were wrong. Merrt could understand that, because he'd been seeing 034TH too, for a long time.

But the more he'd studied the serial mark, the more he'd become convinced he'd been right all along.

It said DEATH. It absolutely, definitely said DEATH.

It slithered beneath him, so close to the surface, some of the brown satin floor panels seemed to lift slightly and drop back into place as it passed. He could hear it scratching and grinding, wet meat and bone on rock.

'All right,' he whispered. 'I'm doing it.'

The scratching fell silent.

Baskevyl entered the library. He walked along the stacks until he was facing the book. It was bound in black leather, sheened and smooth, with an emblem embossed in silver on the spine – a worm with its long, segmented body curled around in a circle, so that its jaws clenched its tail-tip to form a hoop.

He reached out to touch it. His fingers wavered.

He took the book off the shelf.

* * *

VIII

'WHAT DO YOU mean, you don't know where she is?' Dalin asked.

'She's just gone for a walk,' said Curth. 'We're looking for her.'

Dalin looked around at Cullwoe.

'She'll be all right,' Cullwoe said. 'She's tough.'

Dalin turned and walked back to where Meryn stood at the door of the billet.

'Permission to help search for Sergeant Criid, sir,' he said.

'Two fire-teams, out here with me,' Meryn called over his shoulder. 'Quick as you can.'

He turned back to face Dalin. 'We'll help you look, adjutant,' he said.

IX

'SO, IT'S TRUE then, Vawne?' Van Voytz's voice crackled over the poor link.

'That's Rawne, sir. Yes, it's true.'

Static hissed and buzzed. 'I'm losing you, general,' Rawne said, pulling the mic closer.

'I said that's a damn shame, Rawne. He was a good man, one of the best. I've known Ibram for years. Fine, fine officer. I'll miss him. How are you coping?'

'The circumstances here are not good. We need assistance urgently. Munitions mainly, but reinforcement would be very welcome.'

'It's coming, Rawne,' the voice on the link said. 'Hold tight. I'll try to arrange a munitions drop for you.'

'Sir, I've sent you particulars. Munition requirements, plus a plan for the drop.'

Static shrieked and moaned for a moment. '–in front of me.'

'Say again, Elikon?'

'I said, I've got your request right in front of me, Rawne. Looks do-able. You're sure about this drop site?'

'Confirmed, sir.'

'And you want an extraction too?'

'Yes, sir. If you read my communiqué, you'll see why.'

Rawne waited. The vox gurgled and fizzled like a dud grenade. The signal strength indicators kept dropping back to nothing.

'Did you hear me, Nalwood? Nalwood?'

'Here, sir.'

'I said I'll review this and try to set something up. I won't leave Gaunt's boys hanging out to dry. Expect contact from me around dawn.'

'Thank you, sir.'

'Ech'kkah.'

Rawne paused. 'Elikon, Elikon say again? Elikon, Elikon, this is Nalwood, this is Nalwood.'

The vox grunted and flared, letting out a sharp rising whine that made Rawne yank off his headset with a wince. The signal continued to flood out of the speakers.

'–ech'rakah koh'thet magir shett gohrr! Gohrr! GOOOOHHRRR! ECH'KHETT FF'TEH GOOOOHRRR ANARCH!'

The link went dead, cold and dead as hard rock.

'Beltayn!' Rawne yelled, leaping to his feet. 'What the feth was that?'

Fifty metres away in the base chamber, Beltayn urgently nursed his voxcaster, one headset cup pressed to his ear.

'Channel interference, sir!' he shouted back. 'I'm trying to recover the Elikon signal now!'

Rerval bent over Beltayn. 'Try 3:33 gain–'

'Thank you, I *am*.'

'That sounded like–'

'I know what it fething sounded like, Rerval!' Beltayn snapped.

Rerval went pale. 'Do you think... if we can hear them... can they hear us?'

Beltayn wasn't listening. He wound a dial over and threw two toggle switches. 'Think I've got it... I think I've got it back. Clean signal. Setting for balance.'

Beltayn sat back from the caster suddenly. 'Feth,' he said.

'Bel?' Rerval asked.

Beltayn handed him the headset. Rerval pressed it to his ear.

He heard the voice, distant but quite distinct. It said, 'Are we the last ones left alive? Are we? Someone, anyone, please? Are we? Is there anybody out there? Are we the last ones left alive?'

Rerval began to shake. 'Bel,' he said. 'That's *your* voice.'

'I know,' said Beltayn.

X

IT SEEMED A long way back to the base chamber. Hark wanted to lie down. More than that, he wanted painkillers. More than that, he wanted sleep.

He was limping along a corridor in the middle range of the house on the southern side. Individual inset box gunslits formed a row of windows looking out down the pass. He sat down on the firestep under one of them, careful not to lean back. Shifting around he managed to peer out into the darkness. It was well past midnight, local. The night was virtually calm and very clear. He could see the black walls of the pass against the maroon sky, and the small, fierce moon hanging above them. The moonlight lit up the lower slopes of the house and made the dust bowl beyond the gate glow like a snowfield. He watched the wind chase zephyrs of dust across the shining dunes.

He heard footsteps approaching.

He took out his pistol, pretending to load it again.

Someone walked past him, stirring the air. He looked up, but there was nobody around. Hark tensed. The air had suddenly gone very cold. The pain in his back flared and he realised he was quite incapable of standing up. He distinctly heard the sound of Tanith pipes. Fear prickled across him.

Tona Criid appeared, padding along in bare feet. She looked like she was sleepwalking.

'Tona?'

She turned her head slightly, but didn't seem to recognise him.

'Tona, can you help me?'

She kept walking, her feet making small, slapping noises on the brown satin flooring.

'Sergeant Criid, please,' he groaned. 'I can't stand, and there's something badly wrong here, something terrible.'

She stopped in her tracks and looked back at Hark.

'He's here,' she said. 'He's here.'

'Who is?'

'Caff,' she said. 'Look.'

She gestured ahead of her. Down the corridor, in the dark, a light had appeared. It was tiny at first, but then it grew brighter until it had become a twisting, jumping, flickering snake of intense, baleful luminosity. It danced and crackled. Hark felt the hairs on his neck rise and smelled ozone. He knew it for what it was: corposant, freak electrical discharge.

'Tona, get back,' he said, trying to get up, but his legs were too weak. 'Tona Criid, get back, now!'

'Look,' she said, smiling.

The light wasn't a light anymore. It was a figure, a human figure, radiating light from inside its form. Tona began to cry. Tears raced down her thin cheeks.

'Caff,' she sobbed.

'That's not Caffran!' Hark cried. He tried to rack the slide of his bolt pistol. It jammed. He fought at it, grinding it back and forth.

'Tona!'

The figure turned to face them slowly. It was tall. Its clothing was torn and ripped, and soaked with blood. It was quite dead, Hark saw that instantly. Gore caked its face and matted its short, blond hair.

It was Ibram Gaunt.

Criid uttered a cry of pain and disbelief. She lurched forwards and beat at Gaunt's chest with her fists.

'You're dead! You're dead!' she wailed, thumping at him. 'Where's Caff? You're dead! You're fething dead!'

The bloody figure reached out its arms to embrace her. She pulled back, terrified.

Hark finally cleared his gun. He found his feet at last and rose, taking a step forward.

'He's dead!' Criid screamed.

'I know,' Hark said. He grabbed her by the arm and pushed her back behind him. She did not resist. He faced the figure and raised his pistol.

'I don't know what you are,' he said. 'I know what you'd like us to think you are. Leave us alone.'

The figure opened its mouth, as if to reply, but the mouth did not stop opening. The jaws extended wider and wider in a hellish, silent scream, and noxious light shone out of the throat. The skin, the bloody lips, pulled back away from the widening maw, revealing teeth, revealing skull. Flesh and meat scurried backwards like acid-eaten fabric, stripping the face, the scalp, the throat down to muscle and sinew, then down to bare bone. Clothing rotted in a split second, decomposing back to dust, stripping the skeleton until it stood before them, gaunt and stark.

Its mouth was still wide open in that silent, endless scream. Its arms were still extended, the last gobbets of liquid flesh and tufts of rag dripping off them.

Then, and only then, it screamed aloud. The sound stripped out their minds and shivered their organs. It was a sound neither of them would ever forget.

Hark dropped his pistol and pulled Criid into his arms to protect her with the bulk of his body.

The screaming skeleton exploded.

They felt the shockwave rock them. They smelled dust and fried bone and, worst of all, Gaunt's cologne. Every wall lamp in the hall blew out and the light died.

Hark released Criid. They blinked in the darkness. They heard footsteps running up through the house to find them.

'What the feth was that?' Hark gasped.

Outside, the heavens lit up. Huge booming sounds echoed down the pass, the sound of a martial god's boundless wrath. Hark staggered to the nearest window slit and looked out. Bombardment fire had lit up the sky behind the pass, making it a jagged silhouette, flash after flash.

'What the feth was *that*?' Criid asked him.

'I don't know,' Hark replied quietly, watching the giant flares of light eat up the dark. 'But I think this is the end for us.'

Day thirteen. Four sixteen, before sunrise. Conditions good.

What am I saying? Conditions good? I mean the wind is down and it's clear. Nothing else is good.

Madness descended last night. Things happened that can't be accounted for. Men saw things, felt things, heard things. I saw things. I will not record them here, because I do not ~~know how~~ have any way to explain them.

I had a feeling about this place from the very start, a feeling that the rational part of my mind put aside. I can't ignore it any more. This place, this damn house, is evil. There is a presence here that is growing in strength. I believe it poses as great a threat to us as the enemy itself.

When we came here, when the rumours first started, G. had us ban words like 'cursed' and 'haunted'. I do not think such words can be ignored any more. We are in trouble, more trouble than we ever imagined.

The war reached us a few hours ago, in the middle of the night, at the height of the madness. Some kind of huge artillery battle is taking place beyond the pass, lighting up the sky.

This may mean the promised reinforcements are moving up to relieve us. Or it may mean we are about to be annihilated in the middle of a full scale offensive.

– field journal, V.H. fifth month, 778.

EIGHTEEN
The Last Chance

I

'THAT'S YOU THEN, is it?' Rawne asked, watching the light shock quake and shimmer the distant morning sky beyond the pass.

'Yes,' said Berenson. 'It's been confirmed, though details are scant. Vox-links are poor. But, yes. As of midnight local, last night, the advancing strengths of the Cadogus Fifty-Second engaged the enemy main force. At Banzie Pass, actually, just as predicted.'

'Throne bless the Tacticae,' said Kolea.

The three of them stood outside a cloche on the ridge line of the house, looking south through scopes. The day was bright and startlingly clear. The cloche domes studding the ridge on either side of them glowed gold like templum cupolas. The sky was selpic blue. Far away, beyond the crags and the western arm of the Altids, that blue buckled and quivered like silk in the wind. They could hear the *thoom thoom thoom* of heavy guns. It would have sounded like an approaching thunderstorm, except that the booming was too regular.

'Implications for us?' Rawne asked, lowering his scope.

'The prospect of relief at last,' said Berenson. 'If the Cadogus main force has reached Banzie Pass, then the reinforcement companies must be close at hand.'

'Right on time,' muttered Rawne. 'Three days, you said.'

'I did,' Berenson nodded.

'It's not going to be that easy,' said Kolea. 'They won't let us go that easily.'

'Why not?' asked Berenson.

'Because we've hurt them,' said Kolea. 'We've kept them out for days. They want this place, so they can secure the pass here. But that part is secondary. They'll want to make us pay.'

'You can read their minds, major?' Berenson sneered.

'I've fought them before,' said Kolea.

'Are we in a position to fight them now?' Berenson asked.

'No,' Rawne replied, 'but in a few hours, we might be. I've secured a munitions resupply. We can re-arm and hold on a little longer. As long as we have to.'

'When's the drop?' asked Kolea.

'Waiting for an ETA,' said Rawne. 'By noon, I hope.'

'Let's hope we're all still here come noon,' said Kolea.

Rawne looked around at him. 'What's that supposed to mean, Kolea?'

'You were here last night, weren't you?' Kolea replied. 'You saw the things that were happening. They're getting worse, these–'

'Are we ever going to use the word?' asked Rawne. 'Hauntings?'

'All right, hauntings,' said Kolea. 'They've been happening since the day we got here, but they're getting worse. And just because the sun's come up, it doesn't mean we're safe.'

II

ZWEIL PUT DOWN his psalter, licked his thumb and forefinger, and snuffed out the votive candle.

'You want me to do what?' he asked.

Hark sat facing him in the small room that Zweil had taken as his sanctuary.

'You heard me, father.'

'An exorcism? I'm an ayatani priest, not a wizard, you idiot.'

Hark breathed deeply. 'All right, setting to one side the fact you just called me an idiot – you really shouldn't do that, father, on account of the fact that I have a gun – I know what I'm asking is extreme. But you've seen what's going on.'

Zweil nodded. His gnarled, liver-spotted hands reached up and removed the ceremonial stole from around his neck, folded it and put it away in his satchel. 'I've seen,' he said. 'I've seen what I always see. Men in a dire circumstance. Men afraid. Men dying. Men *afraid* of dying. Tension, stress, battle fatigue...'

'It's more than that.'

'Piffle. This place is ghastly, the fighting's been miserable and we've lost a great deal. Worst of it is, everyone feels like we're penned in. Trapped, like we're in a cage. Like this house is our cage.'

'Father...'

Zweil glanced at Hark. 'There are no malign spirits here, Viktor. Just frightened soldiers in extremity. The human mind does all the rest. Last night, Dorden – a man as sound and sober as Dorden, Viktor – thought he saw blood running down a wall. It wasn't blood. It was dust.'

Hark drew his hand across his mouth and then, hesitantly, told the old priest what he and Criid had witnessed the previous night.

Zweil was silent for a long time after Hark had finished.

'Well, was that my imagination, father?' Hark asked.

'There will be some rational explanation,' Zweil replied.

Hark shook his head and rose to his feet. To do so, he had to lean heavily on his crutch. 'Let's say you're right, father, and it's all in our heads. Surely a blessing of prohibition from you would help psychologically if nothing else?'

'I don't do parlour tricks,' said Zweil. 'I won't have the Imperial creed diminished by empty theatrics.'

Hark turned and limped towards the chamber door. 'Your scepticism disappoints me, father ayatani. It's especially disappointing to hear it coming from a man who saw the Saint with his own eyes, and believed.'

'That was different,' said Zweil.

'Only because you wanted to believe then,' said Hark. 'You really don't want to believe in this, do you?'

III

Baskevyl's hands had been shaking as he'd opened the book for the first time. Now, as he closed it again, he felt like a fething idiot. His service pistol, which he had drawn and laid on the table beside the book just before opening it, only emphasised that idiocy. What exactly had he been expecting? That something was going to leap out of the pages at him? Had he actually been thinking he might have to shoot the book?

Idiot, idiot, idiot...

The book was nothing, an alien thing, as incomprehensible as some of the other texts Beltayn had pulled off the shelves to examine, a disappointment.

There had been pages of tightly packed text, which he couldn't read, and illustrated plates that seemed to be a mix of obscure diagrams, primitive zodiacs and charts. As he leafed through the pages, Baskevyl had turned the book the other way up several times, uncertain which end was the front and which the back. Neither way seemed convincing.

Baskevyl had borrowed Rawne's office for an hour while the commander walked his dawn tour of the house. Outside the door, the place was waking up. Men trudged past. Baskevyl heard glum, early morning voices, the voices of those who had woken up after far too little sleep mixing with the voices of those who had seen the small hours in, red-eyed, on watch. He smelled meal-cans warming on the cooking grate in the base chamber and caffeine steaming in metal jugs.

He got up and stretched. Maybe some food...

There was a knock at the door and Fapes came in. Hurriedly, foolishly, Baskevyl covered the book and the pistol with his jacket.

'Thought you might like a cup, sir,' said the adjutant, holding out a tin mug of caffeine.

'I'll have to report you to the Black Ships, Fapes,' Baskevyl smiled.

'Sir?'

'You're a mind-reader.'

Fapes grinned and brought the mug over to the desk.

'Last night, eh, sir?' he said. 'What was all that?'

'The barrage, you mean?'

Fapes shrugged. 'That, yeah. But the rest of the stuff. I heard Wes Maggs went nuts and there are all sorts of stories doing the rounds.'

'Stories?'

'Rumours, I suppose, sir.'

'You know the regiment's stance on rumours, Fapes.'

Fapes nodded.

Baskevyl picked up the mug and sipped. 'Still,' he said, 'between you and me?'

Fapes smiled again. 'They've been saying this place is, you know–'

'Haunted, Fapes?'

'I wouldn't like to comment, sir, but they've been saying it since we got here. Last night, feth, footsteps, lights, whispers. Bool swears he saw an old lady without a face.'

'A what?'

'Up in west six, sir. He told me himself. An old biddy in a long, black dress.'

'With no face?'

'Exactly.'

Baskevyl took another sip. 'How long has Bool been in charge of the regiment's sacra supply, Fapes?'

Fapes snorted, but Baskevyl could tell he was unsettled. The light-hearted approach, the easy manner, it was all Fapes's way of handling the matter. He was looking for reassurance.

Baskevyl was horribly afraid he wasn't in a position to offer any.

'Do you think,' Fapes began, 'do you think there really are ghosts here, sir?'

'Apart from us? Of course not, Fapes.'

Fapes nodded. 'If there are, sir, if there are... could they kill us?'

Baskevyl blinked. He wanted to blurt out *there's something under the rock here, right under us, that would kill us all in a second.*

Instead, he managed a simple 'No.'

'That's what Ludd said, sir. He said it was our imaginations getting to us.' Fapes didn't look particularly convinced.

'Ludd's right, Fapes,' said Baskevyl. 'One thing, though...'

'Sir?'

'It's *Commissar* Ludd.'

'Yes, sir. Of course, sir.'

There was a slightly awkward pause.

'Major Rawne has called a command briefing in half an hour,' Fapes said.

'In here?'

'Yes, sir.'

'I'd better clear my things. Go and get a pot of this stuff and some more cups. The officers will appreciate it.'

Fapes nodded and left the room. Sipping his caffeine, Baskevyl scooped up his jacket with his free hand. The sleeve caught on the book's cover and knocked it open.

Baskevyl put his cup down and pulled on his jacket. A draught slowly licked the open pages over like dry leaves. Baskevyl picked up his pistol and buckled it back into its holster.

He stopped and reached towards the book quickly. What was that he had just seen? He flipped back through the pages, reversing the draught's work. *Where was it? Surely he hadn't imagined it...*

He found the illustration. Baskevyl flattened the page with his hand and stared at it.

It was a drawing of a worm. A line drawing of a worm that, like the silver emblem embossed on the book's spine, had seized its own tail in its jaws to form a hoop with its lean, limbless body. The worm circle was surrounded by concentric rings of a certain design, and lines came in from various sides to intersect with the outer circles.

What the feth is this?

Baskevyl turned the page and saw another illustration. It seemed to show some kind of pin or bolt in cross-section, though it could easily have been a heraldic device. Further diagrammatic drawings showed other rings and systems of lines drawn in a rectilinear web and annotated.

He turned another page. Here was a diagram showing what appeared to be the hooded eye of a reptile.

But it wasn't. Baskevyl took a deep breath.

He knew exactly what it was a picture of.

IV

HALF AN HOUR later, with the ominous boom of the distant bombardment still echoing in the background, Rawne walked into the room. Hark, Ludd, and all the company officers who had survived well enough to stand were waiting for him.

'Commanding officer!' Ludd barked.

Everyone saluted without hesitation. Everyone shared the grim presentiment that this might be the last time the officers of the Tanith First gathered for such a meeting.

Rawne took the salute with a nod. Berenson was with him, and Rawne had also called in the senior adjutants.

'The sounds you've been hearing since midnight last night,' he began, 'are the sounds of the Cadogus Fifty-Second giving hell to the Archenemy in Banzie Pass.'

There was a general chorus of satisfaction.

'All that remains for us to do now is hold on,' Rawne said. 'Hold on and hold this fething place until they get to us.'

'How long will that be, sir?' asked Kamori.

Rawne glanced at Berenson.

'As soon as they can,' said Berenson. Several officers groaned.

'How many times have we been told that over the years?' asked Obel.

'Too many,' said Rawne. 'And it's always true.' He looked around at them all. 'We keep our heads and do what we do best, and we'll get out of this hole yet. That's my promise to you, and you know I don't make many promises.'

'Doesn't keeping that promise rather depend on the Blood Pact playing along?' asked Kamori, winning a few dark chuckles.

'No,' said Rawne. 'Maintain discipline and vigilance. Get ready to fight if you have to, and if you have to, fight like bastards. The Blood Pact can go feth itself.'

Larkin raised a hand.

'Is this a question about munitions, Larks?' Rawne asked.

'Yup,' Larkin nodded, lowering his hand.

'Then I've got good news. Beltayn?'

The senior adjutant stepped forwards. 'We received the confirmation signal from Elikon M.P. twenty minutes ago. Munition supply drop will be made in exactly two hours.'

Beltayn's announcement provoked a lot of chatter and noise.

'Quiet down,' said Rawne.

'How's that going to work, sir?' asked Daur. 'We land anything in the gate area, the enemy is going to be all over us in minutes. You know what happened with the water drop. I wouldn't want to be lugging munitions in under fire.'

'We're not going to be using the gate area, Daur,' said Rawne. He looked over at Bonin. The new chief of scouts frowned slightly, and then slowly nodded as he understood.

'This is that "right moment" you were talking about, isn't it?' Bonin asked.

'It is,' said Rawne. 'The transports have been instructed to set down in the gulley in front of the second gate. As far as we can tell, the enemy doesn't know about it, and the gulley gives us decent cover. The transport can land, and we can unload it in through the second gate before the enemy realises what's going on.'

Bonin nodded. 'That's good,' he said.

'It'll still be tight,' said Kolosim.

'Of course,' Rawne replied, 'but it's the best option and we'll make it work. I want volunteers. Two companies, one to unload, one to cover them and defend the gulley.'

Almost every hand was raised.

Rawne looked around. 'Thank you. Captain Meryn, your boys get defence. Captain Varaine, L Company will be unloading. Everyone else, full strength at every rampart, overlook and casemate, north and south. Kolosim, Obel? The main gate's yours this time. Talk to Daur, he knows how to hold a fething gate. Kolea, you get command of the south face. Baskevyl, upper galleries and north. Daur, Sloman, Chiria, I want your companies mobile and fluid, ready to move at short notice to any part of the house that needs support.'

The three of them nodded. Chiria, now holding the brevet rank of captain, had taken acting command of K Company in Domor's absence. She was taking her duties very seriously. She was determined not to let her beloved captain down.

'One last thing,' said Rawne. He looked over at Hark. 'The stuff we found in the library.'

'The stuff Beltayn found,' Hark corrected, shifting uncomfortably on his crutch.

'Indeed. Credit to him. Everyone needs to understand this. Getting that stuff out and clear is as important as getting the munition supplies in. The drop will be two transports, not one. The first bird will be empty, ready to extract a team carrying as many of those fething books as they can. In and out, fast scoop. Then the munitions lifter will come in and we'll get busy. The gulley's only big enough to take one transport at a time.'

'That's gonna spoil the element of surprise,' said Bonin.

'Yeah, a little, but we work with it. The books are too important,' said Rawne. 'I know this because Hark and Bask told me so.'

'Who gets to take the ride out?' asked Meryn.

'I've already chosen a team,' said Rawne, 'and I'm not going to brook any arguments on it. Hark.'

Hark frowned. 'I want to stay, major.'

'No arguments, I said. I need someone with clout to get those books to the attention of the proper people. Besides, and I hate to draw attention to this, Hark , you're hurting. Dorden says you need urgent graft work. Get the books to Elikon, and they can give you the treatment you need.'

'That's an order, then?' asked Hark morosely.

'Firm as any I've ever given,' said Rawne.

Hark shook his head sadly. 'I won't pretend I like it.'

'Major Berenson's going to ride with you. I need him to link up with command and fill them in. Criid, you're going too.'

Tona Criid glared at him. 'No way am I–'

'Did I imagine it, or did I say the "no arguments" bit out loud?' Rawne asked. 'Dorden advises me you need proper treatment too so, like Hark, you're going to be a courier.'

'There are dozens of Ghosts in the field station who need emergency evacuation to proper medicae facilities,' said Criid bluntly. 'I won't be chosen over them.'

'Oh, Throne,' said Rawne. 'I fething hate being surrounded by so many bloody heroes. You're going, Criid. The poor bastards in the field station will get evacuated soon enough.'

'Who else?' asked Hark.

'Twenzet, Klydo and Swaythe. I'm not being sentimental about this. They're all walking wounded, but they're able-bodied enough to carry stuff. I'd rather send men with light wounds than draw troopers from the active line.'

Hark nodded. 'Makes sense. All right.'

'Get ready. Beltayn, help Commissar Hark pack the books into kit bags. And do one last sweep of the book room to make sure we haven't missed anything vital.'

'Yes, sir,' Beltayn nodded.

'Ludd?' Rawne said.

'Yes, sir?'

'Once Hark's gone, you'll be more than acting commissar. You'll be commissar, plain and simple. You up to that?'

Ludd nodded.

Rawne turned to the others. 'Ludd's going to have an uphill battle. Help him. Reinforce his instruction and his authority. You see any trooper, any trooper, mock or piss-take or ignore him, come down on him like an Earthshaker shell, or I'll come down like an Earthshaker shell on you. Are we perfectly clear?'

'Yes,' the officers said.

Rawne smiled and half-frowned. 'I believe I'm in command. I'm in command, aren't I, Bel?'

'Last time I checked, sir,' said Beltayn.

'So?' asked Rawne, and let it hang.

'Yes, commander,' the officers said.

'Better,' said Rawne. 'Now get your arses moving and let's show the fething bastard enemy how to prosecute a war.'

V

THE OFFICERS FILED out, heading off to assemble their companies. Rawne pulled Ludd to one side.

'Yes, sir?'

'Get Maggs out of lock up. We're going to need every man we can get. Tell him he was an idiot, and tell him if he acts up again, I'll hunt him down and gut him like a larisel.'

'Yes, sir.'

'Something else, Ludd?'

Nahum Ludd shrugged. 'What's a larisel, sir?'

'Does it matter, Ludd? I think the simile speaks for itself.'

'Yes, sir. Thanks for–'

Rawne had turned away. 'Thanks for what, Ludd?'

'For speaking up for me, sir.'

'Just do your fething job and don't shame me, Ludd. Then I won't have to gut you like a larisel either.'

Rawne walked off down the busy hallway. He entered the base chamber. It was thronging with troops moving off to their positions. The last of the ammo was being doled out. 'That's it,' Rawne heard Ventnor shout. 'What you've got is all there is! Only things I have left are prayers and goodwill!'

Berenson stood on the main level. He held his left hand out to Rawne, his right still in its sling. Rawne took it.

'I may not get the chance later,' said Berenson. 'Good luck. Not that you'll need it.'

'Oh, we're going to need all the luck we can get,' said Rawne.

VI

BASKEVYL WALKED INTO the field station. He looked around, and then crossed to the bed where Shoggy Domor lay. Domor was a pale shell of his old self, thin and drawn by the pain of his wound and the traumatic surgery he had endured. The white skin of his chin and cheeks was prickled with black stubble. He looked asleep. No, he looked dead, dead and gone.

Baskevyl hesitated.

'You need something, major?' Curth asked as she hurried by.

'No, thanks. Just looking in,' Baskevyl replied.

When she'd gone, Baskevyl stayed a moment longer, staring down at Domor.

He turned away.

'Major?' a small, dry voice said.

Baskevyl looked back. Domor's eyes were open, half open, at least.

'Hey, Shoggy, I didn't mean to wake you.'

'I thought it was you.' Domor's voice was very thin and quiet, and his respiration made an awful, hissing sound, like a snake.

Baskevyl pulled up a rickety wooden chair and sat down beside the bed.

'How are things going?' Domor asked, his breath hissing in and out like old, dry, punctured bellows scratching and pumping. *Hiss-rasp. Hiss-rasp.*

'We're all right. Still here.'

'They won't tell me anything. They keep telling me not to worry.' *Hiss-rasp. Hiss-rasp.*

'Well, they're right about that. We'll be out of here soon. Trust me.'

'Is that what Gaunt reckons?' Domor whispered. *Hiss-rasp. Hiss-rasp.*

Baskevyl bit his lip. 'Yeah,' he nodded. 'That's what the commander reckons.'

Domor closed his eyes for a moment and smiled. *Hiss-rasp. Hiss-rasp.*

'Shoggy?'

Domor opened his eyes.

'Yes, major?' *Hiss-rasp. Hiss-rasp.*

'You feel up to looking at something for me?'

Domor made a slight, flinching movement that might have been a shrug. 'Like what?'

Baskevyl pulled the black-bound book out of his jacket and opened it. He thumbed through he pages to the ones he'd marked.

'What's that?' Domor asked. *Hiss-rasp. Hiss-rasp.*

'You're the closest thing we have to an engineer, Shoggy, right?'

'I suppose.'

'Then tell me, please,' said Baskevyl, holding the book open so Domor could see. 'What do you make of this?'

VII

THE MICROBEAD CLICKED.

'Airborne inbound. Two minutes,' Beltayn's voice said over the link.

In the doorway of the second gate, Varaine glanced at Meryn.

'Time to go,' he said.

Meryn nodded. He looked back in through the open hatch. 'E Company, get set!' he called. Behind him, Dalin relayed the order down the line.

Meryn looked down the gulley. The day was still clear and open, the sky blue and bright. Down at the end of the gulley, Meryn could see Preed and Caober, the scouts on watch.

'This is Meryn,' he said. 'Are we good?'

'Anytime you like,' Caober voxed back.

'E Company, go!' Meryn called. The Ghosts under his command began to flow out of the hatch and move down the gulley, jogging to their designated places. They huddled in along the west side of the ditch, some of them scrambling up the scree bank to take up firing positions, belly down.

Meryn shook Varaine's hand and hurried to join them.

'E Company is set,' Varaine voxed. He turned and looked back in through the hatch opening. 'L Company, stand ready. Commissar?'

Hark moved forwards and stepped out into the daylight. He was limping on his crutch, a heavy kit bag slung over his shoulder. Criid followed him, then Berenson, Twenzet, Klydo and Swathe, all bearing heavy kit bags of their own. There was no dust, but everyone was wearing brass goggles.

Hark looked at Varaine.

'Any time now, commissar,' Varaine said.

'See you at Elikon, captain,' Hark replied, with a thin smile.

'Yes, sir.'

Vox-click. 'Here she comes,' Caober called.

They heard the throaty howl of engines a second later. A lone Valkyrie shot into view over the cliffs of the pass, skimming low. Hark could see that its side doors were already slung open. It made no turn or preliminary pass around the site the way the water drop transports had done five days before. It had locked coordinates and it wasn't messing around. Hark could almost taste the pilot's desire not to stay on station any longer than necessary.

Halfway down the gulley bottom, a magnetic beacon was set up and began sending out its signal.

The Valkyrie droned in and began to bank around in a hover.

The cliffs facing the house across the dust bowl lit up. Most of it was small-arms fire, but there were rockets too. A storm of gunfire began to spit into the sky.

'They've seen it,' said Variane.

'Of course they have,' Hark replied.

The Valkyrie dropped lower, turbines squalling. Even at a distance, they could all hear the loose shots spanking and twanging off its hull and booms.

'Feth!' said Varaine.

Hark opened his link. 'Rawne, perhaps–'

'Already there,' Rawne replied. The Ghosts in the southern casemates and overlooks of the house opened fire, blasting out heavy cover in the direction of the cliffs. Hark heard hot shots and .50's rattling away.

So much ammo getting wasted.

The enemy shooting reduced slightly as the suppressing fire from the gunboxes forced them to take cover. The house continued to unload on the cliffs.

The Valkyrie corrected, nose down and circled in, its downwash lifting torrents of dust from the gulley area. Its jets began to scream as it came to a dead stop hover and its landing claws slid out. Wailing like the Jago wind, it came down and settled in the gulley. Varaine winced. The Valkyrie's stubby wingtips seemed about to brush the scree slopes on either side. The gulley had looked big until someone parked a Valkyrie in it.

'Go, go, go!' Varaine yelled.

Hark, Criid and the others set off towards the waiting Valkyrie, lugging the kit bags. The cargo officer, his head dwarfed by the helmet/goggles/headphones combo he was wearing, pulled the team in through the side hatch, one by one, taking the heavy bags from them.

'Hark's in,' Varaine voxed.

'Good. They're coming,' Meryn voxed back.

Despite the fusillades raining down from the casemates, squadrons of Blood Pact troops were streaming out of the cliffs across the dust bowl, heading for the gate and the more distant gulley.

'Feth!' Meryn voxed. 'There are thousands of them!'

'Hold your fire until it counts,' Varaine voxed back, signalling his own company to get ready.

'I know what to do.' Meryn's vox-reply was petulant.

The cargo officer waved to Varaine. Varaine waved back. Ducking inside, the cargo officer made a hasty, urgent signal to the pilot.

The Valkyrie, with a bellow of underthrust, hopped up out of the gulley, kicking back a deluge of jet wash and dust. It cleared the gulley line and began to turn. Enemy fire pinged and clicked off its fuselage.

It rose higher, banking hard to make its exit turn around the steep battlements of Hinzerhaus.

Down in the dust bowl, a host of enemy warriors was rushing forwards, like insects spilling from a nest, most of them charging for the gulley. Fire from the house was dropping dozens of them, but still they came.

'Locks off,' Meryn voxed. 'Here we fething well go.'

Varaine looked up. A new, heavier note was vibrating the air. The Destrier appeared, slightly off target, rushing down the throat of the pass with its burners blazing.

'K862, K862, inbound,' they heard the pilot vox.

'Hello, K862. Good to see you again,' Beltayn called over the link.

'Wish I could say the same,' replied the pilot of the heavy transport, his voice clipped by the transmission chop.

The Valkyrie was climbing and turning out, haloes of white fire surrounding its jet vents as it hunted for lift and speed. Below it, the Destrier galloped in, slower, louder and more ponderous. The mass of Blood Pact warriors crossing the open field was firing up at it wildly. The big lifter took several solid hits and thousands of light clips.

It lowered itself, correcting its flight path, its engine roar growing louder the slower and lower it got. It looked huge. Its shadow covered the entire gulley floor.

'Feth, that's never going to fit!' Varaine gasped. He knew he had to trust that it would. He looked back in through the hatch. 'Come on, you cheerful bastards!' he bellowed over the jet noise. 'Get ready to move in and unload this bloody thing!' The men began to file out, heads down in the punishing downwash.

'Down in five,' the pilot voxed. 'Stand by. Three, two, one–'

A surface-to-air rocket struck it in the belly and blew the Destrier's ribcage open in a searing ball of white flame.

'Oh, shit!' Varaine yelled. 'Back! Back! Get back inside!'

His men started to turn. They started to run. Varaine was running.

The Destrier quivered and bucked, flames and smoke streaming back out of its belly. It began to turn, trying to rise, to abort. Its engines flared deafeningly. Then it fell.

It fell with a sickening doomsday crunch. It hit the western side of the gulley in a vast spray of scree, crushing and killing over a dozen of Meryn's men. Still moving, sliding and slewing, it made a long, tortured metallic shriek as it tore out its underside along the rocks and dipped into the gulley.

'Oh shit. We're dead,' Varaine heard the pilot whisper on the link.

No power in the galaxy could have arrested the Destrier's death slide. One straining engine blew out, vomiting smoke and sparks into the air. It came on like a steamroller, like a battering ram, crushing and destroying everything in its path in a lethal blizzard of flying rock and splintering metal, eighty tonnes of steel moving at nearly forty kilometres a second. Scree winnowed out behind it in a gigantic, dirty, clattering wake, tonnes of loose stones torn up and flung out in a fan.

'Get inside! Get inside!' Varaine yelled to his men.

He turned.

The ploughing bulk of the Destrier crushed him to pulp. A second later, the huge, burning mass rammed headlong into the second gate. Metal tore.

Fuel lines broke. Stanchions snapped. The nose of the bulk lifter crumpled, and mashed the cockpit section to oblivion.

The transport gave one last shudder and finally stopped moving.

Then the munition payload it was carrying detonated.

VIII

RAWNE TOOK A step back from the casemate slot as if he'd been slapped. He lowered his scope from his wide eyes. He didn't need a scope to see the immense mushroom cloud of fire rushing up out of the gulley. They'd all felt the thump. It had shaken the stone walls and lintels of the house.

'Oh holy throne,' he whispered.

The enemy host down below let out a huge, exultant roar. It began to rain. The raindrops were stones and micro-debris streaming down out of the dry sky.

By Rawne's side, Kolea shook his head in disbelief.

'We were so close,' he said.

'Feth!' Rawne roared, and threw his scope against the casemate wall in rage. 'Feth! Feth! Feth!'

He looked at Kolea, his eyes wild and bright.

'It can't end like this,' Kolea told him.

'It won't,' Rawne growled. 'It fething well won't. I won't allow it!'

Kolea paused, hesitating. 'We could–' he began.

'We fight on with what we have,' Rawne said, cutting Kolea off. 'We fight on with what we have left, and then we keep fighting with fists and blades. We kill every fething one of them we can, and we hold this damn place until we're all dead!'

Kolea nodded. 'That's basically what I was going to say,' he replied.

'Spread the word, Gol,' said Rawne, snatching up his lasrifle. 'Spread the fething word. Make sure everyone understands. No quarter, no retreat, no surrender.' *One last fight*. That's what Corbec had told him. *One last fight*.

Kolea nodded again.

'And get Daur's company down to whatever's left of the second gate,' Rawne added. 'If that's been blown wide, the bastards will be inside before we know it.'

Kolea turned to go. Around them, the house was chattering with defensive gunfire and the sounds of squads running to their positions. Men were shouting. Some were moaning in loud dismay, having just seen their last chance go up in a ball of fire.

'What about–' Kolea said.

'What about what?' Rawne asked.

'The men left outside? Meryn's company?'

Rawne looked away. 'The Emperor protects,' he said.

IX

FOR ONE, DISTURBING moment, he couldn't remember his own name. His lungs were full of smoke and his mouth was full of dust. He woke up with a violent lurch, and coughed out blood and dusty grey phlegm.

Sounds rushed in at him as the ringing in his ears faded.

From nearby came the noise of crackling flames and the cries of wounded men. From further off came a swelling roar of animal howling.

Dalin got up. The north end of the gulley had become a crater, littered with burning shreds of debris and machine parts. There was no longer any sign of the gate. The destruction of the Destrier had blown a giant scar into the ground, and scorched the exposed rock pitch-black. Thick smoke plumed off the heart of the conflagration and made a kilometre-high column in the sky. Dalin coughed, his throat tightening at the stench of fyceline fumes and burnt propellants.

The transport's death slide had scored a deep furrow across and down the gulley. Sheared off hunks of fuselage and hull casing dotted the gouge, along with mangled bodies.

The transport had killed dozens of Meryn's company on its way in. Dozens more had been killed or crippled by the blast. Those Ghosts that, like Dalin, had been fortunate enough to survive were getting to their feet, stumbling around dazed, calling out, or trying to dress the wounds of the many casualties.

Fortunate. That didn't really seem to be the right word. Dalin picked up his rifle and struggled up to the top of the scree slope. He could see the enemy force through the smoke. Despite the heavy fire striking down at it from the house emplacements, the Blood Pact warhost was still rushing the gulley. They had faltered slightly at the blast, but now they gathered again, surging forwards, screaming.

'Get up! Get up!' Dalin yelled at the bewildered troops around him. 'Get up and get into position! They're on us! They're fething on us!'

A few men stumbled forwards and dropped on their bellies on the ridge top, aiming their weapons.

'Come on! Move it!' Dalin yelled. 'Form a line! Form a fething line!'

The first rounds sang over their heads from the charging mass. The remnants of E Company began to pick off shots in reply.

'Like you mean it!' Dalin bellowed. 'You men! Get up here! Find a place! Move your arses!'

'You heard him!' shouted Caober, running back down the gulley from the southern end. He was shoving men up the slope, kicking some from behind. 'Get in a line or die! Shift it!'

He caught Dalin's eye. They stared at one another for a second. There was no time – no point – in exchanging tactical suggestions. They both knew there was only one thing to do.

'Onto the ridge!' Caober yelled at the befuddled men scrambling to obey him. 'Onto the ridge! Fire at will!'

Dalin checked a couple of bodies for signs of life. He managed to rouse Luhan, who had been knocked out by a grazing head wound.

'Get on the ridge,' Dalin urged him. 'Don't ask questions. Just shoot.'

Dalin saw Meryn, lying face down near the bottom of the gulley where the blast had thrown him. He leapt down and shook Meryn roughly.

'Get up! Get up!'

Meryn stirred and looked blankly up at Dalin.

'Get up, sir! They're right on us!'

Meryn blinked. 'Ow,' he said.

Dalin saw his injury. Half a metre of thin metal tube, a piece of one of the Destrier's bristling UHF antennae, had impaled Meryn through the meat of his left thigh.

'Oh, feth,' Meryn whispered, looking down and seeing the wound.

'I'll find a corpsman,' Dalin started to say.

'Forget it. Just get me up. Just get me up there.'

Dalin hoisted Meryn to his feet. Meryn swore in pain. Dalin dragged him up the slope, sliding and slithering on the loose scree.

They reached the ridge line. Heavy fire stung in from the approaching enemy, slicing over their heads or scattering stones at the ridge crest.

'You woke me up for this?' Meryn groaned.

They both started to fire. Along the ridge, E Company blazed away with what was left of their ammunition.

The enemy was a rolling wall of dust with rushing red figures inside it. Banners and standards bobbed like jetsam carried along by a breaker. Weapons flashed and cracked. The Blood Pact was howling a victory chant as it closed on the side of the gulley, even though masked warriors bucked and twisted as E Company's shots found them. They fell and were trampled, their bodies left behind in the swirling dust.

'Full auto,' said Meryn.

'Full auto!' Dalin yelled out to the company.

'Straight silver,' said Meryn.

'Straight silver!' Dalin shouted at the top of his voice.

Meryn took aim. 'Time to die like men,' he said.

* * *

X

'DID YOU SEE that?' Hark shouted over the wail of the Valkyrie engines. 'Did you see that?'

'Stay in your seat, sir!' the cargo officer shouted back.

Hark was fumbling with his restraints. The lifter was banking hard in its climb, juddering violently, its turbines screaming. Wind rushed in through the open slide-hatches. The ground far below was brilliant white with glare. Twenzet and the other troopers, strapped in, were glancing around in alarm.

'That flash!' cried Hark. 'That was an explosion! That was the fething transport!'

'Get back into your seat!' the cargo officer bawled.

'Hark! Stop it!' Criid shouted. Occupying the seat next to Hark, she fought to keep his hands off the harness release. 'Stop it, for feth's sake!'

'Sit down, Hark!' Berenson shouted from his seat.

'That was the bloody transport!' Hark roared back. 'They got it! The bastards got the bloody lander!'

Criid grabbed Hark's chin with her hand and slammed his head back against the seat rest. 'Sit down! There's nothing you can do!'

The cargo officer undid his own harness and got up. Gripping an overhead rail, he glanced forwards. They could all hear the pilot's rapid chatter. The Valkyrie slowly turned until it came level, still bucking and shaking in the rough air.

An alarm sounded and a red light on the ceiling began to flash.

'What's that?' asked Swaythe.

'What the feth is that?' Twenzet demanded.

The cargo officer looked around. Criid saw fear in the eyes behind the large tinted visor.

'We–' he began.

There was a loud, stunning *thump*. The Valk lurched and dropped sharply. Part of the cargo section flooring blew in, and sparks ripped up in a flurry. The alarm note changed to a much more urgent shrill.

'Hold on!' the cargo officer cried.

A second explosion shook the airframe, a vicious *bang* that blinded them for a second. Hot metal shards whizzed around the compartment. One streaking nugget punched clean through the cargo officer's chest.

He let go of the handrail and fell out of the side hatch, his limp body instantly snatched away by the savage slipstream.

Smoke filled the compartment and rushed out through the hatches. Someone was screaming. The alarm shrieked.

The Valkyrie began to vibrate. The engines started to emit a terrible, labouring noise. Its nose tipped down and it fell into a steep dive, a dive that it would never pull out of.

Mach–

There is something that must be done, a matter of honour for the regiment. It is the sword, I mean. It must be got back.

I have gone to get it. I know I have no orders to do so, but I have a moral duty. In conscience, I could not disappear without any word. I ask you to tell them where I've gone and what I plan to do. I hope they will understand the purpose of my actions.

The Emperor protect you.

Your friend,

Oan.

– Personal correspondence, Tanith 1st, fifth month, 778.

NINETEEN
The Deada Waeg

I

North of the Banzie Altids, and the curtain of rock encasing Hinzerhaus, the badlands stretched out for a million square kilometres. The badlands were a trackless waste, a mosaic of inhospitable terrains: zones of dust, plains of wind-blown scree and boulder rubble, dry salt licks, and gleaming basins of air-polished calcites that shone bone-white in the sun. In open areas, the dust had collected in great seas of rippled grey dunes, punctuated every few hundred kilometres by jagged crags that sprouted from the desert floor, forming lonely outcrops and mesas surrounded by islands of jumbled stones.

It was a place to be lost in. Despite the passage of the sun, and the lay of the land, there seemed to be no reliable directions. It was a landscape of dry hell, scoured by the constant, angry wind and bleached by the hard light.

Mkoll woke. Two days out in the wastes had taught him that the middle part of the day was no time to move about in the badlands, so he had chosen that period to rest, curling up in the lea of an outcrop boulder. Early morning, late afternoon and night were the best times for travel.

Something had woken him. Gun ready, he swept the rocks, fearing he had been discovered by a passing patrol or scout party. There was no one around in the crag, no sign of activity. The dunes beyond the outcrop were empty.

He looked south.

Despite the dust haze, Mkoll could see the saw-edged ramparts of the Banzie Altids a dozen kilometres behind him. A pall of dark smoke was rising from the mountains, the blaze plume of some catastrophic explosion.

Mkoll turned away. He took a sip of water, ate half a ration bar, and tried not to think about what might have produced the smoke.

He had learned to stay focused. The decisions he had made, the course he had taken, they were hard things to reconcile. Mkoll was a man of infinite and honest loyalty. He knew that the moment he started thinking about the comrades he had left behind would be the moment he turned and started the long trek back to rejoin them. So he shut such thoughts out.

That wasn't difficult to do. Out in the wastes, every scrap of a man's concentration went on survival. You had to pick every footstep carefully to avoid sand falls and dust-choked holes. In places, the surface regolith was so fine and powdery, it could swallow you whole in seconds. You had to read the loose rocks in the scree fields so as not to twist or snap an ankle. You had to watch the wind, and learn its clues so you could get into cover before it rose and carried you away like a dead leaf, or shredded the flesh off your bones with a dust storm. You had to pace your water consumption and avoid excess exposure to the hard sun. Every waking moment was filled up with deliberate, calculated activity.

There were live hazards too. The Blood Pact was out in the wastes in force. Mkoll lay low when motorised patrols throbbed by in the distance. Twice, he'd hidden on top of a mesa and watched as a unit of troops and armour trundled by. The Blood Pact was moving south in considerable numbers. It wouldn't be long before Hinzerhaus faced an assault on its northern ramparts again.

Mkoll checked his kit, cased his lasrifle and prepared to move off. He would have liked to stay put for another hour or two, but there was a faint smudge along the eastern horizon, a blur that rippled like heat haze. That was another dust storm, rising out of the deep heart of the badlands. Mkoll figured he had about ninety minutes before it hit, and ninety minutes would see him reach another lonely mesa just in sight to the north-west.

He started out, picking his way through the loose white boulders at the foot of the crag. His boots lifted powder as he left the rock line and began to walk out across the dust flats. A light wind was blowing, and little eddies of dust danced and scurried over the undulating dunes.

He glanced behind him and saw that the footsteps he had left were already filling in and vanishing.

That reminded him, uncomfortably, that there was something else he was trying not to think about.

II

He had miscalculated. He was only a few minutes out, but that was enough to doom him.

The dust storm, a dark band of racing cloud, began to overtake him while he was still a good half a kilometre from the mesa. The first few gusts tugged at him and made him stagger. The wind force was huge. He began to run, but the wind blew him over several times and rolled him across the dunes. As the storm bit down, he tried to crawl on his hands and knees.

The wind tore at his clothes. The dust particles stung his exposed skin and abraded it until it started to bleed. The light died as the roiling dust mass, two kilometres high, blotted out the sun.

There was no way he was going to reach the mesa. He couldn't even see the mesa any more. He could barely breathe, there was so much dust in his mouth and nostrils. It blocked his ears until there was nothing audible except a dull, moaning sound.

Mkoll clawed his way over onto the leaward side of a large dune and began to dig with his hands, scooping out a hollow he could pull himself into and curl up. He used his own bodyweight to pin his camo cape into the depression, then dragged the loose, flapping side around to cocoon him. That shut out the dust and made a little, airless tent like a womb, where all he could hear was the howl of the gale and the frantic gasping of his own breath.

Trapped there, blind and half buried, he began to think about the things he had banished from his mind before. There was one thing he could not leave alone.

Oan Mkoll, master of scouts, was the best tracker in the regiment. His skills with spore and trace were company legend. No one could follow a path or a trail better than Mkoll, and no one had a keener natural sense of direction. His gifts in these areas, most of them self-taught techniques, seemed almost supernatural to many of his comrades.

Mkoll had no idea how he was tracking the Nihtgane. He knew he was, and he had the keenest sense he was closing on him, but he had no idea how.

This terrified him.

Jago was a tracker's nightmare. The combination of dust and wind erased all traces of a man's passing. It allowed for no footprints, no worn trail, and there was no undergrowth to read for marks. Scent was sometimes a useful tool, but on Jago the wind stole that away too.

Mkoll wasn't sure what exactly it was that he was following. He just knew, somehow, knew as sure as he knew night from day, that he was going the right way.

It was as if there was a road, a clearly defined route set out for him to follow.

It was as if someone or something was leading him.

In the two days since he'd set out, he had not questioned it for a moment, because he hadn't wanted to think about it. He had climbed down the northern face of the fortress cliff and set off into the wastes without a moment's consideration as to where Eszrah might have gone.

Caught in the lea of the dune, with the dust beginning to bury him, he had no choice but to dwell on it.

The thought that something unseen might be guiding him frightened Mkoll more than the prospect of a suffocating death.

III

THE STORM DIED after an hour, clearing as rapidly as it had come down. The light returned as the dust settled and the grey film drained out of the air. In its wake, the storm left a landscape of resculpted, remoulded dunes and an aching, barren silence.

A hole appeared in the slope of one dune, soft dust sucking down into a cavity, like sand in an hour glass. The hole broadened.

A hand reached out into the dry air.

Mkoll rose up out of his shallow grave, the dust streaming off him and fuming away into the breeze like smoke. He shook the clogging particles out of his sleeves and fatigues, and flapped out his cape. It took a few minutes to clean his brass goggles and wash out his mouth and nose. His throat was dry. His sinuses felt impacted. His vision was blurred, as if his corneas had been abraded.

He sat down and emptied his boots. The mesa he had been heading for, a crooked, flat-topped rock surrounded by an island of boulders, seemed ridiculously close. Mkoll re-laced his boots and was grateful he had chosen to carry his rifle cased. He looked south once more. The pall of smoke, smaller now, was still clearly visible.

He heard a *pop*.

He looked around sharply and heard two more. *Pop pop*, just small sounds, carried by the breeze. He got up and began to head towards the mesa.

More popping sounds reached him. They were coming from the other side of the outcrop. He slowed down and began to uncase his rifle. He sniffed the air. *Motor oil, warm metal, unwashed bodies.*

Mkoll stuffed the rifle case into his pack and ran into the boulder scree, head down. He moved from rock to rock, staying low, listening and sniffing.

Pop. Pop pop. Pop. Pop pop pop.

Gunshots, hollowed out by the wind. He checked his rifle cell and flicked off the safety.

It took five careful minutes to circle the mesa to the northern side. The sun was no longer overhead and he had shadows to play with, hard shadows cast by the boulders and the crag.

He ducked down at the first sight of movement, his back to a large rock. He pulled out his stick mirror and angled it for a look, taking care that it didn't catch the sun.

In it, he glimpsed a Blood Pact warrior clambering through the rocks, rifle in hand. The brute was panting, and sweating so profusely that his stained jacket had dark half-moons under the arms. Mkoll could smell him, he was so close. He could smell the rancid sweat and the stale blood-filth the warrior had coloured his jacket with.

How many of them were there? He kept watching.

The warrior stopped, and called out something. An answering cry came back. The warrior raised his rifle and squeezed two shots off at the overhanging crag.

Mkoll drew his warknife.

The Blood Pact warrior got up on a large boulder and looked around. Four of his comrades were toiling up the scree slope in a wide line below him. Behind them, out on the dunes, a rusty half-track sat with its engine running. A patrol, on a routine sweep.

'Voi shett! K'heg ar rath gfo!' the warrior on the rock shouted. Three more warriors jumped down from the half-track, one of them an officer with a gilded grotesk.

'Borr ko'dah, voi!' the officer yelled, waving his pistol. The trio entered the rock line and followed the other troopers up into the slopes under the crag. One trooper remained behind aboard the half-track with the driver, manning a pintle-mounted cannon.

The warrior nearby jumped down off the rock and looked around for an easy path up through the scree. A hand circled his throat from behind and a blade slid up under his shoulder blade into his heart. He died without a sound.

Mkoll lowered the body silently. He wiped the blade on the warrior's coat and helped himself to the cell clips in his webbing. He could hear the officer shouting down below.

Mkoll darted between the rocks, head low. He heard the crunch of boots nearby and froze. Another warrior clambered past, just a few metres away, calling out.

Mkoll crept forwards and finished the warrior as quickly and clinically as before.

A lasrifle started firing and Mkoll dropped, fearing he had been spotted. But the shots were zipping up at the crag, stitching puffs of dust across the bare rock.

There was a squall of pain and the firing ceased abruptly. Mkoll peered out and tried to see what was going on. The squad of Blood Pact warriors, urged on by their officer, was scrambling up through the rocks more urgently, and all of them had started firing up at the crag.

Mkoll put his knife away. There was no more time for subtlety.

He rested his rifle across a sloping rock and took aim. A Blood Pact trooper came into view, bounding from boulder to boulder. He rose up to fire his weapon and Mkoll took him out with a single shot. The trooper dropped back off the boulder.

Confusion seized the enemy squad. They'd all heard the shot and seen their comrade fall. They started shouting at one another and firing randomly. Mkoll rotated away from his firing position, scampered down a gap between two large stone blocks, and aimed again. He got a decent line on one of the remaining enemy troopers, but the man dropped out of sight as Mkoll fired and the shot went wide. Las-fire suddenly scuffed and pinged across Mkoll's cover. He was pinned. They had an angle on him from two sides.

He slid down into the shadows and began to crawl. Shots slammed and *thukked* off the rocks above him. A deflected las-bolt whined past his face. Mkoll switched on his intervox and began to wind the tuning control. It took him about thirty seconds to find the channel the Blood Pact was using.

The officer's hoarse barks filled his ears. He translated slowly. His fluency in the Archenemy tongue had diminished somewhat since the long stay on Gereon. Something about '...more than one fugitive. Find them both or I'll...'

Some visceral threat followed that Mkoll was happy not to translate, as it involved trench axes and fingers.

'Voi shett d'kha jehlna, dooktath!' Mkoll voxed, and stood up. The officer and the three other troopers were all looking the other way. No surprise, considering someone had just told them 'Look and take heed, there's one of them behind you, you ignorant rectums!', although rather more colloquially.

Mkoll shot the officer in the back of the head, retrained his aim, and killed one of the troopers too, before the officer had even hit the ground. The other two wheeled around and opened fire. One dropped, mysteriously, of his own accord, as if he had slipped over. Mkoll flattened the last one with a spray of shots.

The pintle-mounted cannon started to blast fire out across the rocks. The half-track's engine was revving furiously, and black exhaust coughed out of the tail pipes, as if the driver was in a sudden hurry to leave.

Mkoll took aim. The range wasn't good, but he was no slouch. He squeezed the trigger and held it down, pumping half a dozen shots at the half-track. The first few kissed the bodywork and bent the small shield plate fixed to a bracket around the cannon housing. The fifth or sixth bolt hit the gunner in the head and smacked him back out of the vehicle. The half-track jolted and started to move, its track sections squirming up clouds of dust as it turned. Mkoll stood up and raked the driver's door and windshield with shots. The vehicle lurched, slewed on, and lurched again before coming to a halt. Its engine over-revved wildly as if a deadweight was pressing on the throttle. Then it stalled and the engine died away with an unhealthy clatter.

Silence. Mkoll picked his way through the rocks, checking the bodies of the dead and stealing their ammunition. He found one he hadn't killed, though the manner of the warrior's death was quite evident.

Mkoll stopped moving. Slowly, he raised his hands. He knew instinctively that someone was aiming a weapon at his back.

'Eszrah?' he whispered.

'Hwat seyathee, sidthe?' asked the voice behind him.

IV

MKOLL TURNED SLOWLY. Eszrah ap Niht stood behind him, his reynbow aimed.

The Nihtgane was the colour of Jago. His clothing and the wode on his face had absorbed the pale grey of the bad rock somehow. Eszrah had employed some camouflage technique that Mkoll would have paid real money to learn.

'It's me,' Mkoll said. 'Histye.'

Esrah nodded. 'Histye, sidthe,' he acknowledged. His aim did not stir.

'You've always call me that,' Mkoll said. 'I don't understand your language the way Ven did. What does it mean?'

'Ghost,' Eszrah replied.

Mkoll smiled. 'You don't have to point that at me, soule,' he said.

'Cumenthee taek Eszrah backwey,' Eszrah replied, maintaining his aim.

'No,' said Mkoll.

'Cumenthee sidthe, cumenthee taek Eszrah bye Rawne his wyrd.'

'For Rawne? You think he ordered me to come and get you?' Mkoll shook his head. 'No, soule, no, no. That's not why I'm here.'

'No?' Eszrah echoed. 'Seyathee no?'

'I've come for the sword,' Mkoll said, gently pointing to the weapon lashed to the partisan's back. 'It wasn't yours to take, my friend. It belongs to the regiment.'

Eszrah slowly lowered the reynbow. 'Eszrah's ytis.'

'No, it isn't.'

'Eszrah's ytis,' the Nihtgane insisted. 'Soule Gaunt, daeda he. So walken thys daeda waeg Y go, bludtoll to maken.'

'Blood toll? Do you mean vengeance?'

Eszrah shrugged. 'Not ken Y wyrd, soule.'

'Revenge? Retribution? Payback? You're going to take lives for Gaunt's life?'

'Lyfes for Gaunt his lyfen, bludtoll so,' Eszrah nodded.

There was a long silence, broken only by the mournful song of the desert wind. Mkoll felt sudden, immeasurable sorrow: for the partisan, for Gaunt, for himself. This was how it was all going to end, and a poor, messy end it was. Loyalty and devotion, duty and love, all stretched out of shape and malformed until they were unrecognisable and tarnished.

'You think you failed him, don't you?' Mkoll asked quietly.

'Seyathee true, sidthe soule.'

Mkoll nodded. 'I know. That's how I feel too. I should have been there. I should have been there and...'

His voice trailed off.

'Feth!' he said. 'Throne, how he'd have laughed at us!'

Eszrah frowned. 'Gaunt laffen he?'

'Yes, at us! Two idiots in the middle of nowhere, both of us thinking we're doing the right thing! He doesn't care! Not now! He's dead, and we've made fools of ourselves!'

Eszrah was still frowning. 'The daeda waeg yt is the last waeg.'

'The what? What is the daeda waeg?'

Eszrah thought for a moment, struggling to find the words.

'Corpse. Road,' he said.

'And where does that lead?' Mkoll asked.

Eszrah gestured out towards the dune sea beyond them.

'Out there?' Mkoll asked, looking around. 'Forever?'

The partisan shook his head. 'Closen bye, sidthe soule. Bloodtoll wayten.'

Mkoll looked at Eszrah. 'Will you let me take the sword? Will you let me take Gaunt's sword back to the house?'

The Nihtgane shook his head. 'Yt must...' he began, wrestling with his words again, '...yt must be his sword. His weapon. For the bludtoll.'

Mkoll sighed. He had no wish to fight Eszrah ap Niht. He wasn't entirely sure he would win.

'All right. Then will you let me walk the daeda waeg with you? Will you let me help you make the blood toll?'

Eszrah nodded.

'Good, then.'

Side by side, they clambered down through the rocks onto the desert floor.

'How many of them do we have to kill?' Mkoll asked. 'To make the blood toll, I mean?'

Eszrah grinned. 'All of them, soule,' he said.

Day thirteen cont.

Under attack from two sides. Munition carrier lost, and our hopes with it. Heavy casualties at second gate. Basic estimates put the enemy numbers ten to one in their favour.

Ammunition virtually exhausted. Even R. acknowledges this is the endgame. I had always imagined a last stand to be a heroic thing, but this is just brutal, senseless. I suppose heroism and glory are things perceived later by those who did not have to endure the circumstances. We are going to die in the next few hours, one by one, in the most violent manner. They will not show us — nor do we expect — any mercy. Once they get in—

I am wasting time with such self-serving remarks. I may not get the chance to record this later, so let me commit this to the record now. It has been my honour to ~~servethe~~ serve the Tanith First and Only. Every man and woman has my respect, Tanith, Verghastite, Belladon. I hope this record survives us. I want the masters of this crusade to know how dearly the Tanith cost the Archenemy, when the time came. They are the best and the most devoted soldiers I have ever seen. I stand beside them with pride.

I pray my master, Viktor Hark, has made it clear of the house with the material from the library. It has been reported to me that several men saw a Valkyrie taken out by a surface to air rocket over the Banzie Pass earlier. If that is true, then our deaths here will ultimately mean nothing.

— Field journal, N.L. for V.H. fifth month, 778.

TWENTY

The Lost

I

As THE THIRTEENTH day began to end, they went into the fire with no hope or expectation of seeing another sunrise.

The sky had gone dark with smoke. Even in the depths of the house, there was no escape from the constant thunder of weapons and the howl of voices.

The Archenemy had descended upon Hinzerhaus in a force over ten thousand strong. In a drab, red mass like an old blood stain, they spread down out of the cliffs and the pass and filled the dust bowl, pressing in at the main gate and southern fortifications. They brought hundreds of light field guns and auto-mortars with them, and bombarded the fracturing rockcrete bulwarks with shells and rocket-propelled munitions. A large assault force, spearheaded by warriors carrying long, stave-flamers, drove in against the main gate. Spiked ladders and extending climbing poles clattered up against the lower earthworks, and raiders began to scale the walls. Some of the raiders, equipped with a spiked mace in each hand and toe-hooks on their boots, came up the walls without the need for ladders, hacking and gouging their own foot- and hand-holds like human spiders. The drums and horns in the host made a din that echoed down the pass.

There was no shortage of targets for the Ghosts. Firing from the casemates, overlooks and gunboxes, the Tanith First made hundreds of kills, but the Blood Pact was not going to be deterred. Oath-sworn warriors of Archon Gaur, the elite storm troops of the Great Adversary, they were too far gone with bloodlust to care about individual lives. They had been goaded and roused to berserker pitch by their sirdar commanders, until they had achieved a feverish state of zealous devotion and feral glee. Gol Kolea had been quite right – the Blood Pact intended to make the Imperial forces pay for their defiance. Some of the raiders had cast off their helmets and grotesk masks to reveal the ritual scars cut into their faces and scalps. They wanted the marks of their dedication to the Archon to be plainly visible to their victims.

'That's right, you mad fether,' murmured Larkin, 'take your shiny hat off. That'll make my job easier.'

Either side of him in the overlook, Banda and Nessa matched his rate of fire. Banda had already been forced to switch to a standard pattern las. There were no fresh barrels for the long-form variants left. Their ammo bag was alarmingly empty too. Out in the hallway behind the gunboxes, Ventnor and the other ammo runners had set up braziers to cook some life back into spent cells. It was risky work, and they could never hope to juice enough back into operation in time.

Kolea had placed the bulk of his flamers in the lowest level of embrasures, so that their weapons, short-range at best, could roast the scaling parties off the walls. In one gunbox, where the air was eye-stingingly acrid with promethium fumes, Brostin speared squealing gouts of flame down out of the slot while Lyse coupled a fresh tank to her set.

Brostin ducked back inside as las-bolts chipped off the lip of the gunslot.

'They seem awfully eager to say hello to Mr Yellow,' he said.

Lyse answered his grin with a thin smile.

'What's the matter?' Brostin asked.

'That was the last tank,' she replied.

FOUR FLOORS ABOVE, Kolea rushed along a busy, smoke-swamped communication hallway, coordinating the repulse. A mortar shell had just penetrated one of the casemates on seven, slaughtering the five Ghosts inside. Another gunbox had been blown out by grenade work, though thankfully without fatalities. Its defenders were now firing from the cover of the ruptured rockcrete socket.

The volume of fire striking against the outer walls sounded like a rotary saw eating through lumber. Corpsmen hurried by, carrying the wounded. Kolea saw Ludd.

'Is the gate holding?' he asked.

'I don't know,' Ludd replied numbly. Kolea saw the dazed look in Ludd's eyes. Everyone around him was beginning to look that way. It was the seeping shock of the noise trauma, the inexorable destruction of nerves and focus wrought by the constant aural assault.

'Get with it,' Kolea hissed to Ludd. 'You're no use to the men unless you're sharp.'

Ludd blinked. 'Yes, yes of course.'

'You know how you feel?' Kolea asked. 'Every last one of the Ghosts feels like that. You need to help them forget it, ignore it, shut it out, or this fiasco is going to end a lot sooner than it has to.'

Ludd summoned some reserve of willpower. He hadn't realised how far he'd flagged.

'I'm sorry, major,' he said.

'Don't apologise,' Kolea replied. 'Didn't Hark teach you anything? Commissars never apologise. That's why we hate them so much.'

Ludd laughed. It was the last laughter Kolea would hear that day.

Part of Chiria's company surged down the hallway, sent to reinforce the gunboxes. Ludd moved away smartly to oversee and direct their deployment.

The intervox suddenly clicked. 'Contact! Contact! Upper galleries!'

So they're coming in from the north side too, Kolea thought. *Fething fantastic.*

II

'Pick your targets!' Varl shouted, firing from one of the cloche slots. 'Conserve your fething ammunition or we might as well hold the shutters open and invite them in!'

The first Blood Pact grotesks had appeared over the cliff lip about two minutes earlier. Now all the cloches and casemates along upper east sixteen, east fifteen and west sixteen were busy firing on the raiders swarming up over the edge of the precipice.

'Seems a shame,' remarked Maggs, snapping off a shot that knocked a Blood Pact warrior twenty metres away back off the drop. 'Poor bastards have climbed such a long way.'

'My heart bleeds,' replied Varl.

He jumped down off the fire step and yelled down the hallway. 'Stay sharp! Don't give them a chance to establish a foothold!'

Kamori appeared, running down the hallway at the head of twenty men.

'Varl! Where's Baskevyl?'

Varl shrugged. 'I ain't seen him, sir.'

'But he's got command of this level!' Kamori exclaimed.

'Maybe he got a better offer,' Varl suggested. Kamori was not well known for his humour. Varl turned away quickly. 'Cant! Go and find Major Baskevyl!'

'Where will he be?' Cant asked, jumping down from the step.

'If I knew that, he wouldn't need finding, would he?' Varl replied. Cant hurried away down the hall. 'And don't come back if you're still an idiot!' Varl called after him.

'How's it looking?' Kamori asked him.

'Sunny, some cloud,' Varl said.

Kamori's eyes narrowed.

Varl sighed. 'Oh, come on, Vigo. If you can't make light in the face of certain death, what can you do?' he asked.

'Punch you in the face,' Kamori proposed, and pushed past Varl to the firestep. He got up and looked out. Maggs and the other men in the cloche were firing sporadically, but the hits ringing off the cloche dome were growing more persistent.

'They're on the cliffs right below us,' said Maggs. 'You can bet they've come in force. They're pushing over the top a few at a time, but all they need is one lucky break.'

'Or one lousy mistake,' Kamori replied. He jumped off the step and clicked his microbead. 'Commander? Kamori, topside. It's holding here, but it's going to get hotter.'

'What's Baskevyl's estimation?' Rawne came back.

'We can't actually locate him at the moment, sir.'

'Say again, Kamori. For a moment there, you sounded like a fething halfwit.'

'I said we can't locate Major Baskevyl at this time, sir,' Kamori stated flatly, grimacing at Varl.

'Not what I want to hear, Kamori,' Rawne replied. 'Take charge up there and keep me advised.'

'Looks like you get to do the shouting, then,' Varl said to Kamori. Kamori nodded. He turned to the men he'd brought with him. 'Fill some gaps! Come on, shift! Sonorote, get each of the cloches on this level and the one below to sound off with a situation report. Make it fast, man.'

Cant reappeared, looking glum.

'I can't find Major Baskevyl, sir,' he said.

'Oh, you can't, can you, Cant?' asked Varl.

'Go feth yourself, Varl!' Cant snapped.

'Shut up, both of you!' Kamori growled. 'Get to a hole and start shooting out of it!'

A gritty blast blew down the hallway as Blood Pact grenades found an open slot on a nearby cloche.

'Move!' Kamori yelled. 'Hold the line and deny them!'

III

'LUDD! LUDD!' RAWNE yelled, striding through the smoke of lower east six.

'Yes, commander!'

'Major Baskevyl has deserted his post.'

'Sir?'

'You heard me, Ludd!' Rawne snapped.

'Sir, I'm sure there must be some explanation. Major Baskevyl is–'

'Does this look like a game to you any more, Ludd?' Rawne yelled. 'I don't want to hear you make excuses! I just want you to nod! Can you do that?'

Ludd nodded.

'Good. Major Baskevyl has deserted his post. Deal with it.'

Ludd nodded.

IV

BASKEVYL PAUSED AT the top of a stairway to let a fire-team race past him, double-time, heading towards the upper level. As he stepped to one side, he set down the heavy kit bag he was carrying.

He was about to make his way down when another squad hurried up the staircase towards him.

'I need one of your men,' Baskevyl told Posetine, the squad leader.

'We're all directed upstairs, sir,' Posetine said apologetically. 'Commander's orders.'

'Well, I understand that, but here's one of mine. I need the help of one of your men.'

Posetine looked awkward, but he guessed he would be in trouble if he tried to argue with the senior Belladon officer. He looked back at his men reluctantly.

'Merrt, step out and go with Major Baskevyl.'

Merrt glowered and stood to one side. He knew Posetine had picked him because he was no bloody good.

'Thank you, Posetine,' Beskevyl said. He hefted up his kit bag and ran down the stairs past the troops. 'With me, Merrt.'

'Major!' Posetine called out after them. 'Major, do you know they're trying to reach you on the link? They've been calling for a few minutes now.'

'I know!' Baskevyl yelled back. He'd taken his microbead off and stuffed it into a pocket precisely so he couldn't hear the intervox. 'Carry on, Posetine!'

'But–' Posetine began. Baskevyl had vanished.

'Shift it,' Posetine told his squad and they began to move again. Posetine adjusted his own microbead. 'Squad eight six moving up to west five. If you're looking for Major Baskevyl, we just saw him heading down into the basement levels.'

'What are we gn... gn... gn... doing?' Merrt asked, jogging to keep up with Baskevyl.

'I'll explain when we get there.'

'What's that book?'

'Just follow me, Merrt.'

Merrt hesitated. 'This leads down to the gn... gn... gn... power room,' he said dubiously.

'Come on man!'

No one had been left to guard the power room. The chamber was as Baskevyl remembered it. He could smell energy, and feel the slow pulse of the glowing iron power hub. Baskevyl put his kit bag down, took a few steps forwards and touched the warm metal.

'Major?'

'Wait,' Baskevyl said, holding a hand up. He pulled the black-bound book out from under his arm, set it on the floor and knelt down over it, turning the pages.

He looked up abruptly. The scratching sound was quite loud. It was coming from just below them and through the walls around them.

'Merrt?' Baskevyl whispered. 'Do you hear that?'

'Yeah,' Merrt replied. 'Do you see that?' He pointed.

Baskevyl saw the faces that had been drawn in the dust on the walls, eyeless faces with open mouths. He knew they hadn't been there when he and Merrt had entered the room.

'This place is cursed,' he said.

'I know it,' Merrt replied.

'There's something here. It's been here forever. It's trapped us here.'

'It wants us dead,' said Merrt.

Baskevyl shook his head. 'I think it wants us to stay. I think it wants company.'

'Forever?' Merrt asked.

'Yeah.'

'Then isn't that the gn... gn... gn... same thing?'

V

She was standing on the cliff edge, right out in the open, staring in at the cloche hatches. The desert wind was tugging at her black lace skirts.

Maggs shot at the next few Blood Pact warriors attempting to rush the dome.

'Why don't you take them instead?' he yelled out of the shutter at the old dam.

'Who the feth are you yelling at, Maggs?' Varl shouted from the neighbouring slot.

'Her,' Maggs replied.

'Oh, don't start with the–' Varl started to say. He shut up. 'Feth me, Wes.'

'You can see her?'

'Shit, yes.'

'Then it must be time. Throne, this must be it.' Maggs leaned forwards and yelled out of the shutter at the dark figure waiting silently at the edge of the cliff. 'Is that it, you old witch? Is it time now? Is this the end of it all? Is it?'

Very slowly, the awful meat-wound face nodded.

VI

WHEN NESSA TOOK a hit to the shoulder, Banda dragged her out into the hall to find a corpsman and left Larkin alone in the gunbox. His long-las had finally given up and he was using a standard pattern rifle. Looking out of the slot, it was distressing to see how far up the outer walls and bulwarks the Blood Pact had managed to climb. They were attacking the lower casemates. Larkin heard grenades and the bitter zing of nail bombs. The enemy would be inside in minutes, if they weren't already.

He peppered those in range with shots. 'Fire support here!' he called out. 'I need shooters at this slot!'

'You're on your own, Tanith,' said the voice.

Larkin turned around. He knew what he would see.

Lijah Cuu stood in the doorway of the gunbox facing him. His thin, scar-split face was drawn in a leer. His uniform was filthy and marked with rot and smears of soil.

Cuu had his warblade in his hand.

'All alone, sure as sure.'

Larkin shivered. Sheet ice was creeping across the inside walls of the overlook, creaking like flexing glass. Larkin could smell rich putrefaction and decay.

'I've killed you once, you son of a bitch,' Larkin whispered. 'I can do it all over again.'

'It doesn't work like that, Tanith,' said Cuu. 'Not this time around.'

'I'll tell you how it fething works,' Larkin replied. 'You're just a phantom from my crazy old brain. You're not real, so get the feth away from me! I'm busy!'

He turned his back on Cuu and began to fire out of the slot.

Slowly, steadily, the footsteps came up behind him.

VII

ZWEIL HOBBLED INTO the field chamber. He had been drawn from his prayers by curious sounds, sounds that were more than the usual moans and cries of anguish.

In disarray, the chamber had come to an odd halt. The wounded men, in their cots, were staring out in bewilderment. Corpsmen and stretcher bearers, bringing in the latest casualties from the repulse, had also stopped in their tracks, open-mouthed. Some were making the sign of the aquila. Others had dropped to their knees.

Zweil felt his guts turn to ice.

The dead had come back to them. The lost were all around them, thin grey shapes, shadows made of dust, transparent spectral figures cut from twilight. They lingered by bedsides, or hovered in the central aisle of the chamber, like silent mourners gathering for a funeral.

Some men were speaking to them out loud, crying out in fear or wonder, greeting old friends and fallen comrades, weeping at the sight of long lost loved ones. To them, the vague figures were wives and sweethearts, parents and children, brothers and sister, warriors of Tanith, Verghast and Belladon who had fallen on the long march to this dismal last battle.

Zweil saw men close their eyes or cover their faces with their arms, saw others open their arms wide for embraces that would never come. Some of the wounded men were trying to get out of their beds to reach the shades standing over them.

'No,' Zweil whispered. 'No, no, no...'

Dorden was beside him, his eyes streaming with tears. He gripped Zweil's arm tightly. 'My son,' he gasped. 'Mikal, my son.' Dorden pointed. Zweil saw nothing except a shadow that should not have been.

Zweil stepped forwards, pulling free of the old medicae's grasp. He raised his rod and held up the heavy silver eagle he wore on a chain around his reedy neck.

'I abjure thee,' he began. 'I command thee, be gone hence and be at peace–'

Voices rose in protest all around him, calling him a fool, a meddler, begging him to stop.

'I abjure thee now, by the light that is the Golden Throne of Terra,' Zweil cried.

'It's my son!' Dorden yelled.

'No, it isn't,' said Zweil firmly. Hark had been right, feth him, and Zweil had been a fool not to pay heed. Hinzerhaus was a place of damned souls, where the dead gathered to drag the living down into the lightless places.

'I command thee, daemons, be gone from here!'

Dorden clawed at Zweil, and the old priest pushed him away. Someone was screaming.

The shadows were thickening, becoming darker.

Blood, not dust at all, was streaming down the chamber walls.

VIII

THEY HAD HELD on to the gulley ridge for fifteen minutes, a period that had felt like centuries. Only eighteen members of E Company remained, and most of them were wounded. Unable to maintain a viable line, the survivors had drawn back into the throat of the gulley, until they were in amongst the wreckage of the crashed transport.

Dalin was down to his last clip. He fired his rifle with one hand, holding Meryn upright with his other arm. Meryn was almost comatose from blood loss.

He dragged the captain across the scree, shots lacing the air around him. The Blood Pact was streaming in over the top of the ridge, crashing down across the bank of loose stones, sliding and running. The warriors were uttering loud war cries and brandishing pikes and axes.

Cullwoe closed in beside Dalin, snapping off rounds from the hip. He nailed two of the charging warriors and sent them sliding down the loose stone slope on their faces.

'You know what this is, right?' Cullwoe cried.

Dalin didn't have time to reply. The bolt from a las-lock exploded Khet Cullwoe's midriff. He collapsed in a spatter of his own blood, ribs poking from his smouldering abdomen.

'I know what this is,' snarled Neskon. 'It's a fething bastard way to die!' His flamer roared and enveloped six enemy troopers in a sheet of white-hot combustion. They ignited, thrashed, and fell. One wandered a long way on fire before falling to the ground.

'Come on, boy!' Neskon shouted, ripping off another cone of fire. His flamer was beginning to splutter, its tanks all but done.

Dalin emptied the last of his clip and threw his rifle aside. Steadying Meryn, he bent down and took Cullwoe's rifle, and the last fresh clip Cullwoe had tucked into his belt loop.

'Come the feth on!' Neskon yelled. His flamer dried. He pumped it and worked the feed, but it was dead.

'Help me with the captain!' Dalin cried.

Neskon turned, pulling off his tanks and dropping them with a clatter. A las-round hit him in the hip.

'Fething hell!' he barked. Neskon did not fall down. He drew his service pistol and showed himself to be a damn good shot with a regular firearm. No one ever expected subtlety from a flame-trooper. Neskon banged off two rounds and blew a warrior with a pike over onto his back.

Neskon grabbed hold of Meryn and slung the man over his shoulder.

'Back to the gate!' he said, his voice hoarse with pain.

'There is no gate, Nesk!'

'Oh, we can pretend,' Neskon advised him. Together, they backed away through the burning wreckage of the Destrier, firing at the oncoming line of raiders.

'You can do this,' Caffran said.

Dalin glanced around. His father smiled and nodded to him. Then he was gone, and Caober, Preed and Wheln were beside him, adding their firepower to the hopeless retreat.

'First-and-Only!' Wheln yelled.

All four of them sang out a response, blasting their last shots into the faces of the enemy. In all the noise and fury, it sounded to Dalin as if the entire regiment was with them, shouting the war cry at the top of their lungs.

'Come on! Make for the hatch! The hatch!'

Dalin glanced over his shoulder. He saw Ban Daur and an awful lot of Ghosts behind him.

'Sacred feth!' he whispered in disbelief.

'Come on!' Daur yelled to them. 'Have I got to come and get you?'

The Blood Pact surged down the gulley. G Company came pouring out of the second gate and waited there to greet them, weapons raised.

IX

Trying to ignore the sheet ice slowly caking the power room walls, the scratching from under the floor and the fizzle of corposant scudding over the ceiling, Baskevyl tried to lift the lid off the power hub.

'There's a gn… gn… gn…' Merrt said.

'A what? A bloody what? Spit it out, man!'

'A latch! There!'

'Yes, all right. I've got it. Now lift.'

The lid came up, It was heavy, and they struggled with it as they lifted it clear. Hot, fetid air, as musty as–

dry skulls in a dusty valley

–the most barren, sun-baked desert, wafted out of the kettle.

'Now what?' Merrt asked.

Baskevyl looked into the hub.

It was a deep, hemispheric cavity. The bowl of it was covered in a rind of dust that looked like limescale or some mineral deposit manufactured alchemically deep under the earth.

The worm was inside the kettle.

It was a circular band of machinery, about two metres in diameter, segmented like a snake's scaled body, and it sat inside the waist of the cavity. It was rotating very slowly, pausing and juddering hesitantly, emitting a soft glow. Each pause and judder corresponded to a dip in the brightness of the wall lights.

Baskevyl stared at it. Where the segmented hoop was joined, there was a metal clasp that looked for all the world like a snake biting the tip of its own tail. It matched exactly the embossed emblem on the spine of the book.

Baskevyl reached into the kettle and felt the slowly moving hoop brush his fingertips.

'It's dry,' he said.

'This entire fething bad rock is gn... gn... gn... dry,' Merrt retorted.

'No, the kettle's dry. It's run dry, after centuries, used up its... I don't know... fuel. Its working on the very last of its reserves.'

'How do you know all this?' Merrt asked.

'I don't,' said Baskevyl, 'but Domor, he can read schematics. Apparently, this is essentially a basic cold fusion plant.'

'What's that?' Merrt asked.

'Fethed if I know.' Baskevyl walked over to his kit bag. 'Help me with this,' he said.

'With what?'

Baskevyl started to pull canteen bottles from the bag. Merrt approached.

'What's in the bottles?' he asked.

'Water,' said Baskevyl.

They heard a sound behind them and turned.

Ludd came down the steps into the power room, aiming his pistol at Baskevyl.

'Major Baskevyl,' he began, 'you are found derelict of your post, and have acted contrary to the express orders of the commander...'

Elikon M.P., Elikon M.P., this is Nalwood, this is Nalwood. Please respond. Please respond. We are under sustained and massive attack. Cannot hold out much longer. Casualties high. No ammunition remaining. Please, Elikon, can you hear us?

Nalwood out. (transmission ends)

- Transcript of vox message, fifth month, 778.

TWENTY-ONE

The Worm Turns

I

It was a camp, all right. In the dwindling daylight, with the mauve cast of evening covering the sky and lengthening the shadows, they watched the flickering fires from the cover of a salt-lick three quarters of a kilometre away.

'I see tents, prefabs,' said Mkoll, slowly scanning with his scope, 'about fifteen vehicles. There must be, I dunno, a hundred or more of the bastards in there.'

'Y haf an score bow shottes,' Eszrah replied.

'So do the maths.'

'Then thissen sword Y haf, afftyr bow shottes dun.'

Mkoll shook his head and laughed. 'You think we can take them? I admire your confidence, Eszrah.'

'Hwat seyathee, sidthe soule?'

Mkoll went back to his scope. 'Wait now,' he muttered, panning it around. 'That's a vox mast they've got set up there. High gain amp. You don't need a UHF voxcaster unless you're giving orders out, long range. This has got to be a command station. Someone pretty important, maybe a sirdar commander. An etogaur, even.'

'Hwat seyathee?'

Mkoll looked at Eszrah. 'You want your payback, don't you?'

Eszrah nodded. 'Paye bak,' he smiled.

'And I just want to do something useful before I die.' Mkoll pulled off his musette bag and sorted through the contents: two clips, four tube charges, one small-pattern cell spare for his pistol, a spool of det-tape, a grenade. He placed the items one by one into his webbing and pouches for easy access.

Eszrah watched him closely, intrigued.

Mkoll scooped up a handful of dust from the rim of the lick and wiped it across his cheeks and forehead. Eszrah laughed, and took out a gourd flask.

'You can do better?' Mkoll asked.

Carefully, ritually, the Nihtgane smeared grey paste across Mkoll's thin, dirty face. Then he nodded.

'Are we done?'

Eszrah pointed to Mkoll's warknife and held out his hand. Mkoll gave him the knife. Eszrah wiped concentrated moth venom along the edges of the thirty-centimetre silver blade.

'Dun,' he said, handing it back to Mkoll.

'Let's do it, then,' Mkoll said. He held out his hand. Eszrah looked at the proffered hand and then clasped it, bemused.

'It's been good knowing you, Eszrah ap Niht,' Mkoll said.

'Seyathee true, soule.'

They got up, heads down and hunched, and tracked off across the dust towards the distant fires.

II

THE VALKYRIE WAS burning. It was just a shell, a cage of black metal wrapped in a turmoil of fire.

Hark got to his feet. He assumed he had been thrown clear at the point of impact. If so, the dust, the benighted dust of bad rock Jago, had saved him. He could remember plunging down, and then tumbling over in the thick, soft cushion of the regolith.

He was not quite intact, though. His back throbbed mercilessly, and he could feel blood weeping down his legs. His head was gashed. Something, Hark had no idea what, had severed his augmetic arm at the elbow, leaving a sparking stump of wires that dribbled lubricant instead of blood.

He limped towards the wreck. Several of the kit bags had fallen clear. Two had split open, and ancient pages were fluttering away in the wind. He knelt down and tried to gather them together.

'Need a hand?'

Hark looked up. Twenzet, his face covered in blood, stood behind him. When Twenzet saw the snapped stump of Hark's mechanical arm, he baulked.

'I honestly didn't mean anything by that, sir,' he said.

'I never thought you did, trooper,' Hark said. 'Help me.'

Twenzet dropped to his knees and started to gather the loose pages in, stuffing them back into the kit bags.

'Thrown clear?' Hark asked him.

Twenzet shrugged. 'I woke up over there, if that's what you mean,' he said.

He looked at Hark. 'Where are we?'

'Couldn't say.'

'Are the others dead?'

Hark sat back on his heels and looked at the blazing wreck. Heat-stiffened, black silhouettes sat in their restraints in the heart of the fire. Hark looked away.

'Yes,' he said.

'Not all of them,' said Tona Criid, limping up behind them. She was clutching a lasrifle across her belly with her left hand. Her right arm hung limp and mangled. Most of her right hand was missing. Blood dripped out onto the dust.

'We came in hard,' she said.

'I remember that much,' said Hark.

'I threw you clear,' she told Twenzet. 'I tried to get back for Swaythe and Klydo, but–'

Her voice faltered. She sank down onto her knees.

Hark got up. They were in a broad valley, a pass surrounded by soaring walls of rock. Night was falling, giving everything a violet cast.

'Listen,' Twenzet said.

Hark heard nothing at first, then made out a sound like the hum of a voxcaster on standby. The hum became the grumble of faraway thunder, and then the thunder became the rumble of turbine power plants. Lights were approaching down the gut of the pass. Heavy, full beam lamps, shone in the dusk.

'Pick up the bags,' he said.

'Sir?' Twenzet asked.

'Pick up the bags and move,' Hark growled.

Twenzet hauled the bags onto his back. Hark helped Criid to her feet. They skirted the burning wreck of the flier, and headed up the shallow incline of boulders and drifted dust.

'Where are we going?' Twenzet asked, panting from the effort of carrying the heavy bags.

'Away from the wreck,' Hark replied.

The noise behind them grew louder. They could hear the clanking rattle of track sections.

'Up here,' Hark told them. They'd gone a decent way from the crash site. At his urgings, they clambered up onto a shelving outcrop of rock and got down.

Down below, two Leman Russ battle tanks rolled into view, lamps blazing. Dust wafted from their churning treads. Behind them, a Hydra flak tank, its quartet of long autocannons raised to the sky, clattered to a halt. Figures moved in the dust, infantrymen escorting the armour on foot.

'Fifty-two,' Twenzet said. 'Look, on the hull! Fifty-two. It's a Cadogus unit. Bless the Throne!' He started to get up. Hark pulled him down flat.

'Look again,' Hark whispered.

The hull plating on the two large tanks was gouged and scorched in places. Neither vehicle seemed to be in the best repair. They appeared to have kit bags or sacking strapped to their prows.

Twenzet peered more closely.

The objects weren't kit bags. They were the brutalised corpses of men in khaki battledress, strung across the front fenders of the tanks with barbed wire, like trophies. The bodies lolled and jerked as the tanks ground to a standstill.

The infantry moved on, past the waiting tanks, towards the burning shell of the Valkyrie. The twilight made their long coats and fatigue jackets look mauve.

Twenzet saw the iron masks covering their faces.

III

G Company held its ground for ten minutes until the Blood Pact advancing down the gulley realised the futility of charge tactics. They began to pull back and take up static firing positions, intending to clear Daur's men out of the way with prolonged and concentrated shooting. They left dozens of their kind dead in the bottom of the gulley, or littering the slopes.

As soon as the pressure of the assault waves broke, Daur ordered his company to pull back under bounding fire towards the gate.

The gate hatch had not survived the demise of the Destrier, and the opening had been buried by rock debris. Daur's men had cleared the way to get out, and now Daur intended to bury it again.

'There's no door to shut in their faces,' he said to Caober as they clambered in through the ruined doorway, 'and we don't have the ammo to hold them off.' Vivvo, Haller and Vadim were busy setting tube-charges in the portico of the gatehouse.

Corpsmen had already carried Meryn away, and Neskon had wandered off somewhere. Dalin felt lost and aimless. He kept looking around for Cullwoe, forgetting he wouldn't be there any more. Dalin was exhausted.

His hands were shaking and he was having to fight the urge to fold up and collapse in a corner somewhere.

The last of G Company came in through the gate. Heavy fire chased them. The Blood Pact outside were closing in, and they'd had time to bring up support weapons. Machine cannons pummelled the doorway with explosive shells, raising a fog of pulverised stone. The enemy was tearing through ammo box after ammo box. They were evidently not short of supplies.

'Set!' Vivvo called out.

'Clear the chamber!' Daur ordered. 'Fall back through, three rooms back at least! That's the way! Come on!'

The tail-enders, who had been maintaining a steady suppression fire from the doorway to keep the enemy back, picked themselves up and ran for the inner rooms.

Daur stayed until they were all moving and accounted for. 'Right the way back!' he yelled, repeatedly sweeping with his arm.

Daur touched his microbead. 'Commander, sealing the second gate at this time,' he reported.

'Understood,' Rawne voxed back.

Daur got into cover and nodded to Vivvo, who was clutching the trigger box.

Gunfire squirted in through the doorway, heavy and sustained. A moment later, the first Blood Pact warriors clambered in, scanning the empty chamber with guns ready.

The world blew out from under them in a flash of supernova light, and the mountain fell on their heads.

IV

'Put that away,' Baskevyl said softly.

'Up against the wall. Lose the firearm,' Ludd said. 'You too, Merrt.' His aim did not waver.

'I admire your dedication, Ludd,' Baskevyl said, steadfastly not moving, 'and I know you have a duty to perform and a lot to prove, but this isn't the time.'

'That's enough!' said Ludd. 'You left your post, Baskevyl. You ignored a direct order! In the middle of this shit-storm!'

'Listen to me,' Baskevyl said firmly, 'we're going to lose. We're going to die here unless something fething miraculous happens.'

'And that's why you came down here? To find yourself a miracle?'

'Maybe,' said Baskevyl. 'Perhaps not a miracle, but a long shot, at least. A chance.'

'Gn... gn... gn... listen to him!' Merrt growled.

'That's enough from you,' said Ludd.

'Look at the book, Ludd. Look at that book there,' Baskevyl pointed. 'I found it in the library. I showed it to Domor and he agreed with me. It's a set of schematics. It's the operation instructions for the house's power hub.'

Ludd glanced at the book open on the floor. 'It's gibberish,' he said.

'The text is. But the drawings are what matter. Look... let me show you.'

Ludd hesitated, and then gestured with his pistol. 'You've got one minute.'

Baskevyl bent down and picked up the book. He held it out to show Ludd. 'Look, here. That's the hub. See? It's quite clearly this hub. Here, that's a diagram of the locking mechanism holding the lid down.'

He flipped a page over. 'This is a plan of the light trunking systems. That's a wall light, see? It's unmistakable.'

'What were you... going to do?' Ludd asked.

'Restart it,' said Baskevyl, 'if I could. It's running on the very last dregs of its reserve. I think most of the systems have long since died, or failed. The lighting ring is running on low-level emergency power.'

'But how were you going to restart it?' asked Ludd.

'It's a cold fusion plant. It's pretty much dry. I was going to empty those canteens into it, give it something to start its reaction off.'

Ludd stared at him. He edged to the side of the open kettle and looked in at the labouring rotation of the hoop.

He holstered his pistol.

'Do it,' he said. 'You're not off the hook, Baskevyl, but you're right. This is worth a try.'

Baskevyl and Merrt hurried to the kit bag and gathered up armfuls of canteens. Ludd watched for a moment and then helped them. Baskevyl emptied the first canteen into the dry cup of the open hub and tossed the flask away. Merrt passed him another, the top already unstoppered.

The kettle took an astonishing quantity without seeming to fill. Eight canteens, and there was just a shallow puddle in the bottom of the basin.

'Keep going,' said Baskevyl.

Baskevyl had brought thirty canteens altogether. There was probably some charge pending for misuse of so much of the precious water ration. He emptied the last one into the kettle. The basin was barely a quarter full.

'Better than nothing,' Baskevyl said.

'Yeah, and nothing is what's happening,' said Merrt.

Baskevyl peered in again. The hoop actually seemed to be slowing down. 'Show me the book again,' he said.

Ludd passed the black-bound book over.

'All right,' said Baskevyl, studying the pages. 'Domor said we could expect this. Its probably been set, or has set itself, to conservation running. There's a...' he paused, turning the book on its side to follow the diagram. 'Yeah, there.'

Baskevyl reached into the hub again and adjusted the nurled calibrations on the head of the snake.

The hoop stopped spinning all together.

'No,' Baskevyl breathed. 'No, no, come on...'

They stared at it.

The hoop quivered slightly. Mechanisms deep inside the kettle base and its adjoining apparatus whirred and clicked. They made grinding, scratching noises that Baskevyl knew only too well.

The hoop started to turn again. It turned in the opposite direction to before. Its rotations were steady this time, and it gathered speed until it was spinning like a gaming wheel. The water in the bottom of the basin began to froth and gurgle. Then the water turned milky white and started to shine.

'Throne alive,' murmured Ludd.

'The lid,' said Baskevyl. 'Help me get the lid back on.'

The three of them manhandled the lid back into place and latched it shut. The kettle was humming quite loudly, and bright white light shone out of the grilled slits in its sides.

'What now?' asked Ludd.

'Well, here's the piece of this plan that's really an act of faith on my part. Follow me.'

He paused. 'Is that all right, commissar? Will you indulge me one last time? Or do you just want to shoot me now?'

V

THEY RAN UP the stairs from the power room and followed the inner hallways in the direction of the newly opened house sections. Outside and above them, the bedlam of the savage battle was quite distinct. Baskevyl faltered for a moment, looking up.

'Feth, you're right, Ludd. Listen to that. I should never have left my post in this. I was so... obsessed. I–'

Ludd held up his hand. 'Look,' he said. 'Look at that!'

The slow, mesmeric pulse and fade of the wall lights had stopped. All down the hallway, as far as they could see, the wall-strung lights were growing steadily brighter, replacing the satin brown gloom with a cool, bright radiance.

Merrt started to make a strange noise. Ludd and Baskevyl realised he was laughing.

Baskevyl broke into a run and they chased after him.

AS THEY ENTERED the new section of the house, they met Daur's company pulling back through. Daur had set five squads to watch the vulnerable courtyard, and was despatching the rest up to the main southern overlooks.

Daur's face was drawn and haggard. 'They're in,' he told Baskevyl. 'I just heard it on the vox. They're in at the main gate, and in some of the lower levels. It's hand-to hand now. Rawne says all munitions are pretty much spent.'

Baskevyl nodded. He pulled his microbead out of his pocket and plugged it back in. 'Did Rawne say anything else?'

'He told us to draw silver and become ghosts, ghosts in the house. Keep in the shadows and kill as many of the bastards as we could.'

'What shadows, captain?' Ludd asked.

Daur was so weary, so deadened by fatigue and the prospect of the final, bloody grind, he hadn't noticed the lights. The previously amber glimmer of the lighting in the new section had been replaced by a firm, bright white.

'What,' Daur began, 'what's going on?'

Baskevyl pushed past him and entered the armoury.

He opened the lid of one of the bunkers that ran down the middle of the chamber. The pebbles inside were all shining brightly, like tiny stars.

He clicked his microbead. 'This is Baskevyl,' he said. 'Daur, get the men in here.'

VI

LARKIN'S GUN DRY clicked. The cell was dead. He tossed the useless weapon aside and got up from the gunslot, drawing his blade. There were scaling ladders barely ten metres below the overlook that he could do nothing about, aside from spit at them.

The sound of the battle had changed. Larkin realised that there was virtually no gunfire coming from the casemates. It was all coming *at* them.

He turned around. There was no Cuu. The presence had remained behind Larkin for some minutes while he meted out the last of his shots, unwilling or unable to strike as it had threatened.

There was no Cuu, but Larkin could still feel him, the wretched essence of him, hanging around him like a mist.

'You don't frighten me any more,' he said out loud. 'You hear me? I'm not scared of you. You're just a ghost. Sure as fething sure. You want to kill me, you get in line, because there's a whole bunch of bastards at the gates after my blood.'

There was no answer. It seemed to Larkin that it was much brighter suddenly.

He limped towards the door. 'Stay out of my way, Cuu,' he growled at the empty air. 'I've got to go away and die with the real Ghosts now.'

VII

THE BLOOD PACT warriors were milling around the burning Valkyrie. Some of them were beginning to spread out, searching the immediate area. An officer got up from the turret of one of the captured tanks and shouted some orders.

'Stay down,' Hark whispered to the others. They were flat on their faces on the rock. Hark slowly reached for his bolt pistol.

A whisker of lightning laced the purple sky above the pass. Slow thunder rolled, like mountains grating together. Down below, the enemy soldiers were suddenly agitated. They shouted to one another.

The air temperature had dropped by several degrees.

Twenzet whimpered. 'W-what is that?' he whispered.

Hark didn't answer. He could feel it too, a creeping dread, unfathomable and unnameable, that made his flesh crawl and his ravaged back bleed.

Something terrible, some unutterable horror, was approaching.

Help me

TWENTY-TWO

Only in Death

I

THE VOX MAST, poking up into the enormous night sky, was emitting a string of clicks and beeps into the darkness, like some fidgeting nocturnal insect. The dust-proof tents, pitched in a wide ring, were internally lit by oil lamps and small, portable lights, so they glowed golden like paper lanterns. Braziers had been lit on the outer rim of the camp and brass storm cressets hung from poles. Figures moved about in the fire-lit spaces of the inner encampment. Voices came out of the night, along with the smell of cooking.

Two perimeter sentries, their patrol circuits crossing, paused to exchange a few words, then carried on along their routes, moving away from one another.

One paused and looked around. There was no sign of his comrade. The grey desert flat stretched away, empty, into the night.

He began to retrace his path, about to call out, and that became the final action of his life: a foot raised to take a step, his mouth open to call a name.

Mkoll lowered the body into the dust and wiped his knife. He nodded once, though his fellow infiltrator was invisible to him.

Low to the ground, Mkoll scurried forwards, dropping onto his belly for the last stretch where the lamp light extended.

Veiled by the dust-shroud of a tent, Mkoll rose, and stepped carefully over the guy wires. He waited as two thuggish men with scarred faces passed by. They were talking casually. One had a long-necked bottle.

When they'd gone, he slipped between two more of the tents and entered a darker area where the vehicles were parked. Half-tracks and cargo-8 transports made angular blue shadows against the sky. Mkoll dropped down, slid under the first vehicle, and went to work. Feeling, blind, he found the fuel line and cut a slit in it with his warknife. In under three minutes, two other vehicles had been bled in the same way, their fuel loads slowly, quietly pattering away onto the dust beneath them.

Mkoll prised the fuel cap off one of the crippled trucks and packed the pipe with strips of material sliced off the hem of his camo-cloak. Then he poked a strip of det-tape into the wadding with his finger.

He wondered how far Eszrah had got.

Mkoll fixed his warknife to the lug of his rifle and tore the ignition patch off the det-tape.

II

A CLAMMY SENSATION of evil engulfed them. The night air seemed to bristle with it, like a static charge. Twenzet started to moan, but Criid clamped his mouth shut with her good hand. She looked at Hark. His eyes were wide. A pulse was pounding in his temple.

Below them, the commotion amongst the Blood Pact warriors had died away. They were standing stock still, gazing into the distance with their rifles in their hands. They could feel it too. There was no sound except the idling murmur of the tank engines and the dying crackle of flames as the Valkyrie burned out.

The night wind stirred. The ground, the air, reality itself, seemed to tremble for a second.

They heard howling. It was a pitiful, yowling noise, like an animal in pain, and it appeared to come from all around them. The Blood Pact warriors started, turning, hunting for the source.

They began shouting again as they realised the howling was coming from one of their own. The stricken warrior tore off his helmet and his grotesk. He was shaking, as if experiencing the initial spasms of a seizure. Two of his comrades moved to help him.

He killed them.

His autorifle made a hard, cracking sound in the night air. He kept firing, cutting down two more men who were backing away, waving their arms in protest. Stray shots pinged off the sponson armour of the nearest tank. The tank commander, yelling in rage, stood up in his turret hatch and shot the howling maniac with his pistol. The man flopped over, arched his back, and died.

The officer continued shouting as he climbed down from his machine. Warriors who had ducked for cover when the shooting started slowly began to rise to their feet. The officer strode over to the lunatic's corpse, fiercely rebuking each cowering soldier as he went by. He stood over the body and put four more rounds into it.

A blinding fork of electrical discharge leapt out of the corpse and struck the officer's pistol with a shower of sparks. The officer was hurled backwards through the air by the massive shock. He hit the track guards of his tank with such force, his back snapped. The electrical discharge, blue-white like ice and as bright as a las-bolt, lit up the tank's hull in a crackling, sizzling display of raw voltage. Then it leapt again, striking the nearest warrior in the face.

The warrior bucked and twitched as the power overloaded his central nervous system. The energy let him go and, before his limp body had time to topple over, the forking blue charge had jumped to another victim, then another, then another. Each one died, his last seconds spent as a spastic, dancing puppet.

The commander of the second tank emerged from his hatch and started yelling at the rest of the foot troops to fall back. In the general panic, no one noticed the four, long barrels of the flak tank's cannon array slowly lowering to the horizontal plane.

The flak tank opened fire with a deafening, prolonged blurt of noise. Its quad autocannons were built for anti-aircraft operations, and delivered streams of explosive shells at an extremely high rate of fire. All four guns unloaded into the rear of the nearest tank from a range of about ten metres.

Despite its heavy plating and monumental chassis strength, the larger tank shredded. Its hull ripped like wet paper, and a billion slivers of torn metal flew out in a lethal blizzard. Less than a second after the tank began to disintegrate, auguring flak shells found its magazine.

The sun came out, and everything died.

THE OVERPRESSURE OF the gigantic blast knocked Hark and Twenzet off the top of the rock. Criid managed to hold on. An expanding fireball raced out and scorched the air above her, and dust slammed out in a shockwave wall. Small pieces of debris and rock rained down out of the night sky.

Criid got up. The area below was a litter of fire. All three armoured fighting machines had been obliterated.

'Hark?' she yelled. 'Hark?'

He was below her in the shadow of the rock. Twenzet was sprawled beside him. Hark clambered to his feet.

'Are you all right?' he shouted up.

'I can see lights!' she yelled back, pointing to the south. 'I can see lights coming this way!'

Hark got up onto a boulder and stared. Vehicles were approaching fast, their lights bobbing as they rode over the dunes and scree on their tracks.

'Throne help us,' Hark murmured, and wondered if his microbead still worked.

III

RAWNE COULD HEAR the squealing rasp of flamers echoing down the tunnel from the main gate. Ghosts, many of them wounded, were pouring back out of the tunnel into the base chamber all around him.

'Obel!'

Obel limped up the steps to the first landing where Rawne stood. 'Main gate's done for. It was all well and good while we had ammo left, but...' he shrugged and looked at Rawne. 'They're leading in with flamers, sir. We had no choice but to pull back.'

Rawne nodded. He had one clip left for his pistol. He was already holding his warknife.

'Anyone with ammo left, send them back to defend the field station for as long as possible. There are men there we can't move. Everyone else digs in. Tell them to spread out and go deep into the place. Find a corner, a nook, a hiding place, and stay there until something comes their way that they can kill.'

Obel saluted and turned to spread the instructions to his men.

'Beltayn!' Rawne roared. Below him, the vox-officers were packing up the last of the casters. 'Get them all clear, now!' Rawne yelled.

'Yes, sir!'

'Kolea?'

'Rawne?' Kolea replied over the link. His signal was patchy, and washed out by lots of background noise.

'How does it stand?'

'Lost east four, five and seven. It's hand to hand in the tunnels and getting worse. They're pouring in. Any word from topside?'

'Negative,' said Rawne. The signals from Kamori and the other officers running the cliff repulse had gone ominously quiet about six minutes earlier.

Rawne looked up at the deep stone vault of the base chamber, the vast wooden staircase rising like a mature nalwood in its centre, its landings extending into the adjacent hallways on each level like branches. Ghosts were running in all directions, fleeing into the house, carrying packs of supplies, caster-sets and wounded comrades. They were heading for bolt-holes, for sub cellars and attics, for corridors and stairwells where they could make their final stands, alone or in small groups, stabbing their straight silvers in defiance at death as it overran the house at the end of the world. Whatever corner of Hinzerhaus they went to, Rawne hoped they would find endings to their lives that were as quick as they were brave. One thing was certain: none of them would find a way out.

There was no more time for reflection. The vocal roar of the enemy outside threatened to tear down the house all on its own.

Flames scoured into the base chamber from the tunnel. On the lower steps, Mkfeyd, Mosark and Vril were caught and engulfed. Their thrashing forms crashed backwards down the stairs. Flames caught at the wooden staircase and scorched the stained brown floor panels. An abandoned voxcaster caught light and blew up.

'Move!' Rawne yelled. 'Move!'

Another belch of flame came rushing into the base chamber. Then the first of the Blood Pact flame-troopers appeared, sooty devils in heavy smocks wielding long firelances. Storm troops followed them, cracking shots up into the landings. Wooden steps splintered. Railings exploded like matchwood. Struck by las-fire, a Ghost plunged from an upper landing.

Rawne turned and fired his pistol at the invading figures. The last remaining troopers around him, Beltayn included, opened fire with their handguns as they retreated up the staircase. Rawne's first shots clipped a flame-trooper, and he went over, his lance thrashing out of control like a fire-drake, scorching several warriors and forcing them back.

Blood Pact gunfire filled the air with ribbons and darts of light. Tokar, standing right beside Rawne, fell backwards, the top of his skull blown off. Folore collapsed on the first landing, almost cut in two by autofire. Pabst was hit so hard he smashed backwards through the landing rail and dropped out of sight.

'Get back! Back!' Rawne shouted. He scrambled back up the staircase towards the second landing, pushing men ahead of him. 'Out of the chamber! Out of the chamber!'

Creach fell on his hands and knees, blood gushing from his mouth. Beltayn tried to pick him up and carry him on. A hail of shots cut them both down.

'Bastards!' Rawne bawled, and fired down into the advancing raiders. He reached Beltayn and Creach. The latter was dead. Beltayn had been hit in the side and thigh, and his uniform was soaked with blood. He blinked up at Rawne, his face peppered with blood spots.

'Something's awry,' he said.

'You've been shot you silly bastard,' Rawne told him. He started to hoist Beltayn up.

'Major!' Rattundo yelled from a few steps higher. The Belladon was firing down over Rawne's head.

Rawne swung round, Beltayn over his shoulder, and saw the Blood Pact storm troops thundering up the flight behind him. He shot the first one in the belly, and the second one in the hand and the forehead. The third fired his carbine from the hip. A round creased Rawne's cheek with stunning force. Behind him, Rattundo took the full force of the burst and fell against the stair rail.

Rawne fired again, but his pistol was finally dead. With a bellow of fury, he hurled it at the storm trooper and bounced the heavy sidearm off the man's face with enough force to knock him over.

Hands grabbed at Rawne and Beltayn from behind. Rerval, Nehn and Garond dragged them back up the staircase to the third landing. Bonin and Leyr, both of them firing a laspistol in each hand, hammered shots down the steps to cover them.

They made it into a side hallway and began to head in the direction of the field station. Nehn and Rerval took Beltayn from Rawne and carried him between them. The rattle of gunfire rolled after them, interspersed with the *crump* of grenades and the *rasp* of flamers. The air filled with the stench of burning.

They're going to burn the place down around us, Rawne thought, burn us like rats. And all that'll be left of us will be dry skulls in a dusty valley.

'Keep going,' Corbec said.

Rawne stopped and turned.

'Come the feth on, major!' Bonin yelled. 'What are you waiting for?'

Rawne stared into Corbec's twinkling eyes.

'You're just a ghost,' he said.

'No such thing as just a Ghost,' Corbec replied.

Then Corbec wasn't there. Las-bolts whipped along the hallway past Rawne. He started to run after the others. Blood Pact storm troopers thundered down the hallway behind him, yelling and firing.

Rawne saw Daur, Haller and Caober ahead of him. They were facing him, blocking the hallway.

'Back!' Rawne yelled as he closed on them. 'Get back!'

'Get down,' Daur replied.

* * *

IV

THE PARKED VEHICLES at the edge of the encampment went up in a satisfyingly dramatic *whoosh* of flame. In the seconds that followed, the site went into a frenzy. Enemy troopers and support crews ran in all directions, shouting and assembling extinguisher gear. The glare from the blazing vehicles lit the whole camp and threw long, leaping shadows. A fourth vehicle caught fire as flames raced along the fuel-soaked dust.

In all the commotion, few of the rushing enemy personnel noticed that some of them were falling down. Iron darts shot silently from the shadows. A trooper fell on his face. A mechanic with a hose tumbled onto his side. A junior officer flopped back into the side-screen of a tent.

Eszrah kept moving. Weaving from point of cover to point of cover, he fired his quarrels one at a time and made every one count. Where possible, he reclaimed his darts, wrenching them out of dead flesh, and slotted them back into his reynbow's barrel. He ran past a large tent, pausing briefly to fire two bolts through the backlit canvas. The silhouetted men inside convulsed and went sprawling.

Eszrah kicked over braziers as he went, rolling the sparking, sputtering cans onto ground sheets and into the hems of tents where the spilled coals ignited the canvas. A warrior with a trench axe came barrelling out of one tent, and took a wild swing at the Nihtgane. Eszrah thumped a quarrel into his sternum at point-blank range.

Eszrah ran on. Behind him, another large blast split the night.

Mkoll was employing the first of his tube charges. He took out a storage tent with it and then ran on in the direction of the vox mast. Every time an enemy figure appeared in his path, he fired snapshots from the hip, knocking them down. A few rounds of fire came his way as the enemy began to gather their wits.

Mkoll ducked behind a row of tents. At each one, he slit the back sheet open with his bayonet and shot at anyone inside. Halfway through this surgical, methodical exercise, Blood Pact troopers appeared at the end of the tent row and opened fire on him.

Las-rounds zipped past him. Mkoll leapt into a tent through the slit he had just ripped. Inside, an officer with a gruesome mass of scar-tissue for a face was reaching for his bolt pistol. Mkoll broke his head with the butt of his rifle and kept running. More las-rounds scorched indiscriminately through the flapping canvas wall behind him.

He came out through the front of the tent. A hard round hit him in the left shoulder and knocked him over. Mkoll rolled and raked off a quick burst of fire on auto that did for the pair of enemy troopers rushing at him.

He got up again. Several tents were alight. Random shouting and blurts of gunfire echoed around the camp. He heard pursuers crashing in through the tent behind him, and tossed his grenade in through the flaps. There was a flash and the sides of the tent bulged and tore. Smoke gusted out through the rips.

He had three tube-charges left. *Enough for the vox mast,* he thought.

The encampment's main shelters, a pair of large prefabs, lay close to the mast, which was mounted on a lashed-down field carriage platform. Mkoll reasoned that while he was still alive, he could silence both the mast and the bastard issuing orders through it.

He ran towards the prefabs. As he ran, he realised, without a shred of doubt, that something was still urging him forwards. Something was telling him the prefabs were more important than anything else.

Eszrah was out of bolts. His last shot had slain a large mechanic who had tried to attack him with a sledgehammer. Eszrah dropped the reynbow and drew Gaunt's sword. It felt clumsy and unfamiliar. Swords had never been part of his arsenal. Still running, he lit the blade and felt it throb with power. An enemy trooper emerged from behind a burning tent, and Eszrah cut him down without breaking stride. The blade went clean through the man's torso. Two more troopers appeared, and one saw the partisan in time to squeeze off a shot with his rifle. The round ripped through Eszrah's left side just above the waist. Before either of them could take another shot, he was into them, swinging the bright blade. The first slice cut a rifle in half and the second decapitated its owner. Eszrah shoulder barged the other man onto the ground and ran him through. As a swordsman, he made up in efficiency what he lacked in finesse.

Shots ripped past him. The air was full of streaming smoke. Eszrah slashed open the side of a tent, ran through it, and cut his way out of the far wall. The fully armed warrior standing on the other side turned in surprise and Eszrah chopped the blade down through the crown of his helmet. The blade slid out easily. The warrior, split in two to the breastbone, folded up in a heap. One more for the bludtoll.

Eszrah saw a large, prefab structure ahead of him. The wound in his side was bleeding profusely. He didn't slow down. Slowing down just gave the enemy a better target.

He stormed into the prefab.

It was a long hut, a command space, filled with stowage chests, collapsible furniture and chart tables. Brass lamps hung from the support poles. A junior Blood Pact officer just inside the entrance turned in surprise to block the intruder, pulling his pistol out of its holster. Eszrah delivered a scything blow with both hands that sent the officer crashing backwards over a campaign chest. A second junior officer, yelling out in dismay, came at Eszrah with a punch-grip dagger and effectively ran onto Eszrah's turning blade.

The encampment commander held the noble rank of damogaur. He had absolute control over eight sirdar brigades, and answered only to the etogaur of his consanguinity, and the Gaur who ruled above them all.

He was a being of massive stature. Men only advanced through the ranks of the Pact if they were capable of fighting off any rivals. He rose from his seat at the far end of the hut and faced Eszrah. His crimson battledress was reinforced with steel plates and adorned with gold frogging and hundreds of pillaged and defaced Imperial medals. His face was hidden behind a smiling grotesk of polished silver.

The damogaur reached for the nearest weapon. It was a huge, two-handed chainsword, a type popularly known in the Guard as an 'eviscerator'.

Activating his weapon, the damogaur thundered down the hut, bellowing the challenge cry of his consanguinity.

Eszrah held his ground and brought the power sword up defensively.

In seconds, the partisan realised that while a good sword cuts well, a man with no proper schooling in bladecraft could never hope to best a formally trained swordsman.

Eszrah ap Niht had reached the end of the daeda waeg.

V

THE LEAD VEHICLES of the Cadogus Fifty-Second mechanised squadron rocked to a halt, their engines running. Dust spumed around, glowing like smoke in the headlamps. An officer jumped down from the tailboard of a Salamander command vehicle and ran forward.

'Commissar Hark?'

'Yes,' Hark called back, limping into the glare of the headlights, shielding his eyes. He could see that the lead vehicles were just the tip of a significant armoured column.

'Colonel Bacler, third mech, Cadogus Fifty-Second. I didn't think we'd find you alive.'

'You were looking for me?' Hark asked.

'We were advised your bird had come down in this vicinity, sir. Elikon Command diverted us this way in the hope of finding survivors.'

'I've got injured with me,' said Hark.

'Medics to the front!' Bacler yelled into his voice mic.

'It wasn't survivors Elikon hoped you'd find, colonel,' said Hark. 'We're carrying critical documents in paper form.'

'I understand, commissar,' said Bacler. 'Did any of it survive the crash?'

Teams of corpsmen were running forwards to help Criid and Twenzet. 'Those kit bags with my people,' said Hark. 'We managed to get that much out of the wreck.'

'My orders are to get it back to Elikon as fast as possible.'

'Carry on,' Hark told him. Bacler ordered some troopers to gather up the kit bags.

'What's the state of things, colonel?' Hark asked.

Bacler shrugged. 'In the balance. The Cadogus has slammed up the Altid passes and blocked the enemy in three zones. It's tooth and nail in all of them. There's a hell of a tank fight going on about six kilometres north of us. That's where we were heading when the call to divert came in. This whole valley is crawling with rogue enemy units that have slipped past the main line. As you discovered.'

'What's your strength?' Hark asked.

'Forty main, twenty-five light, plus a thousand troops in carriers and sanctioned support. It was the sanctioned support that saved you, you realise?'

'Yes,' said Hark. 'I understood that's what it was.'

'I'll split the group up and send most of it on down the valley to the sharp end,' Bacler went on. 'A fast, light section under my personal command will carry you and your documents back to Elikon.'

'Thank you,' said Hark. 'What about Hinzerhaus?'

'I'm sorry, sir, I don't know anything about that. I believe there was a relief section on its way there as of this morning, but I can't confirm.'

Hark was silent for a while. He felt light-headed and unworthy. The chances were suddenly good he would get out of the zone alive. That didn't feel right, not when the Ghosts... wouldn't.

'Are you all right, commissar?' Bacler asked, frowning at him.

'Yes. I just remembered. It is with regret I have to inform you that your Major Berenson was killed in the line of duty.'

'Yes, that was a bloody shame,' Bacler replied.

Hark nodded towards the blackened shell of the Valkyrie on the slope behind them. 'I wanted to pull him clear, but it was too late,' he said. Bacler looked at him oddly.

'Did I say something wrong, colonel?' Hark asked.

'Major Berenson was lost when his Valkyrie was brought down en route to Hinzerhaus five days ago,' said Bacler.

VI

DAUR, HALLER AND Caober raised the weighty, antique weapons they were holding and aimed them. Rawne threw himself flat against the hallway wall. The three men fired.

The wall guns made noises like the amplified shrieks of eagles. Each one spat a fat, continuous beam of white searing light. At the far end of the hallway, the beams struck the Blood Pact troopers charging them.

The enemy figures weren't simply hit, they were destroyed. Bodies vaporised in clouds of atomised tissue. The streaming beams blew clean through the front rank, explosively dismembering them, and atomised the row behind.

The three men stopped firing and the beams vanished. 'Reload!' Daur yelled. They opened the heavy locks of the old weapons, ejecting the spent, black pebbles inside, and dropped in glowing white lumps they'd taken from their pockets. The locks snapped shut. Rawne had scrambled in behind the three men.

'What the feth?' he stammered.

Stunned for a moment by the fury of the first strike against them, the Blood Pact were pressing their assault again, blasting wildly as they poured into the hallway.

'Fire!' Daur ordered.

The wall guns shrieked again. Bright beams flashed the length of the hall and bodies disintegrated in puffs of wet matter. The hallway air misted with blood particles.

Rawne leaned back against the brown satin wall, breathing hard. Behind the firing line, he saw dozens of other Ghosts from G Company moving forwards with wall guns in their hands. Other troopers, in paired teams, had fashioned slings out of their camo-capes and were lugging four or five wall guns at a time into the nearest stairwell like stretcher bearers. Guardsmen with water cans and cooking pots followed them. The pots were full of shining white pebbles.

'How did you get them to work?' Rawne asked.

Daur stepped out of the line and gestured for the nearest trooper to take his place. Merrt hurried forwards. 034TH hung on its sling over his shoulder. He took his place next to Caober and raised the massive wall gun in his hands.

Merrt squeezed the trigger and felt the heavy, pleasing kick of the old weapon for the first time.

'Baskevyl did it,' Daur said, ducking in beside Rawne. He held his wall gun upright, its stock resting on the floor. 'He powered the system up.'

'Holy Throne,' Rawne murmured.

'I'm trying to get them distributed through the house. Ammo too. Baskevyl's leading Sloman's company topside to get them armed. Chiria's trying to cut through the house on level eight to relieve the southern face. It's not over yet. This is probably just a stay of execution rather than a reprieve, but we can make it count. We can give those bastards one feth of a show before we're done.'

'Ban,' said Rawne.

'Yes, sir?'

'I want one of those things.'

'I thought you might,' said Daur.

THE RAMPART LINE of cloche domes and casemates along the top of the house was on fire. Several domes had been blown entirely open, and flames and sparks guttered up into the cold night sky. H and B Companies had held the enemy back for as long as possible, but once the Blood Pact had penetrated the first of the domes, things deteriorated rapidly. The raiders had no shortage of grenades. They'd even lugged flamers up the sheer north cliff face. They showed no signs of fatigue after their arduous climb. Varl suspected they were too high on bloodlust and glanded stimms.

Vigo Kamori was killed by a nail bomb in upper west sixteen about five minutes before the last of the rifle cells packed up. He died not far from where Gaunt had fallen. To Varl, it seemed like a curse repeating itself. He had witnessed both deaths. He tried to raise Rawne on his bead, but the intervox had been dead for some time.

Kamori had not flinched in his duty. He had commanded the action from the front throughout, even when it descended into bestial melees in the burning hallways. Varl, forced to rely on his service pistol, found the men looking to him for leadership.

'Kamori's dead! Kamori's dead!' Cant screamed. 'What do we do?'

'Well, stop yelling in my ear would be a start,' Varl growled, cracking off a round to stop a charging storm trooper with an axe.

'Maybe we can hold them in the next gallery,' Maggs suggested.

'Yeah, good,' said Varl. 'Close up!' he yelled. 'Close up and fall back! Nice and steady! Do you hear me?'

Firing their pistols or clutching dead rifles with fixed blades, the men around him shouted back in affirmation.

'Just keep firing,' Varl called. 'Pick your targets and keep firing. You can do that, can't you, Cant?'

Cant looked at him. 'You fething watch me,' he replied.

'That's what I like to hear,' Varl grinned.

'You heard the sergeant!' Maggs yelled. 'If she wants us, she can bloody wait for us!'

She wanted them. Shots were punching into them. On either side of Varl and Maggs, men were falling and dying. Sonorote took a round in the mouth that blew out the back of his head. Fenix lost an arm and an ear to a raking line of tracer shots, and bled out before anyone could get to him. Ezlan was thrown backwards by an impact to the belly. When Gunsfeld reached his side to help him, he found that Ezlan had a live rocket grenade sticking out of his stomach wall. Ezlan was wailing in pain.

'It's a dud! Ezlan, it's a dud,' Gunsfeld yelled at him. 'It misfired!'

'Get it out! Get it out!' Ezlan screamed. Gunsfeld took hold of the projectile and tugged.

It wasn't a dud. The blast killed Ezlan, Gunsfeld and Destra outright and blinded Dickerson, the famous seamster and darner of socks.

Varl's pistol dry clicked. He searched in his pockets, certain that he must have one last cell left. He always kept one around for what he called 'emergency work', which translated as a headshot for himself if the situation ever got too bad.

Like now, he thought.

His pockets were conspicuously empty. In the turmoil, he'd torn through every cell on his person. He reached into his hip pouch and yanked out the old autopistol he carried as a last ditch. He racked the slide. Nine rounds and one in the pipe.

'Come on, back! Back!' Varl shouted. He fired the pistol. The bullet deflected off the grotesk of an advancing storm trooper.

'You useless fething object!' Varl shouted at his weapon.

Cant cannoned into Varl and pushed him against the hallway wall. 'What are you doing?' Varl began to exclaim.

There was a shriek like an eagle's call. A bright, colimnated beam of energy burned down the hallway past him and reduced two Blood Pact raiders to clouds of swirling organic debris. Several more beams followed it, bursting enemy soldiers like ripe ploins stuffed with det-tape.

The last thing Varl had expected to see was reinforcements. Baskevyl stormed past him, hefting a huge long-gun. Other men followed, similarly armed. One of them was Dalin Criid, a look of grim determination on his young face. They paused and sent more beams down the tunnel.

'Varl?'

Ludd appeared, leading a second block of men all armed with the antique weapons. Ludd was carrying his pistol.

'Commissar.'

'Pull your men back as best you can to the stairwell on fourteen. Preed's waiting there with weapons to hand out.'

'I like the sound of that,' said Varl.

Ludd turned and raised his voice. 'Men of Tanith!' he yelled. 'Do you want to live forever?'

VII

Eszrah staggered backwards. He was gashed on the right arm, the left thigh and the left shoulder. So much blood soaked his grey clothing, he might easily have been mistaken for a member of the Blood Pact cadre. He tried to swing the sword.

The damogaur clipped its threat away with his whirring chainsword and rammed the blade into the side of Eszrah's head. The Nihtgane crashed over, breaking a chart table.

The damogaur took a step forwards, holding the chainsword's elongated grip with both hands. He chuckled, a deep, throaty sound. He was playing with Eszrah. He had knocked him down with the flat of his blade. Eszrah clawed for the handle of the sword, but the damogaur put his foot down on Eszrah's forearm. Bones creaked. Eszrah gasped in pain. The damogaur, tiring of his sport, raised the eviscerator for the kill stroke. The teeth of the blade whirred.

A tiny silver point, no bigger than a fingernail, emerged from the damogaur's Adam's apple. A single drop of blood glittered on it. The damogaur pitched forwards, revealing Mkoll, teeth clenched, both fists clamped around the grip of the warknife he had rammed into the back of the damogaur's neck.

'Hwat seyathee, soule?' Mkoll asked.

Eszrah managed a feeble, pain-drawn grin. 'Y seyathee sacred feth,' he whispered.

Mkoll yanked his silver out of the corpse. 'I've set charges to the mast,' he told Eszrah as he helped him up. 'We've got four minutes.'

Eszrah nodded and picked up the sword.

'We can still get out of here,' Mkoll said. 'Get out of here and head out into the desert while this place burns and they all run around looking for their arses with both hands.'

Eszrah shook his head. He raised the sword and pointed towards the back of the prefab, where a canvas flap led through into the adjoining shelter.

Mkoll knew what he meant. He was feeling the same thing, the same urge.

They moved down the prefab. Mkoll had unslung his rifle and held it ready to fire.

Near the doorway, a man was cowering in the shadows. He was a plump, wretched thing with scars on his bloated face. He wore a stinking leather apron smeared with blood both old and fresh. His hands were cased in rough leather gauntlets. He looked like a worker from a meat processing plant; the denizen of some infernal abattoir.

As they approached, he whimpered and held out a dirty spiked goad to threaten them.

Mkoll shot him in the head.

They moved past his twitching corpse, pulled back the canvas drop sheet and smelled blood.

VIII

THE ROCKING SALAMANDER sped back down the length of the Cadogus column, kicking dust. Hark sat in a pull down seat in the cab, lost in thought. Criid and Twenzet followed in a second Salamander. Bacler, riding in the cab beside Hark, had told them they would pick up their escort at the rear of the column. Bacler was busy on the cab vox-set, issuing instructions to the officers who would be taking charge of the mechanised squadron when he left it.

In the distance, the night sky was underlit by the pummelling flashes of an artillery duel ten kilometres north. Tanks and armoured vehicles flashed past as they rode down the centre of the advancing lines of Bacler's battalion.

Hark was oblivious to the passing vehicles and lines of men. Pain and fatigue had all but conquered him. He swayed in his seat, burned out and lost, lost, like the Tanith First. His broken machine arm ached, and he found the pain faintly ridiculous.

Deep inside his head, the pipes started to play. They were Tanith pipes and they played as only Brin Milo could play them. They played the way they had often played in his haunted dreams those past few years.

He stood up, steadying himself.

'Commissar?' Bacler asked.

'Something's going to happen,' Hark said.

'What?'

'Tell the driver to stop,' Hark said. 'Something's going to happen. Whenever the pipes play, it's a sign.'

'Commissar, you're tired. You've been through a lot–'

'Stop the vehicle! I can hear the pipes playing.'

Bacler smiled awkwardly. 'There are no pipes, sir. I hear nothing.'

Hark looked at him. 'You're not supposed to, colonel. I think they've always been meant for me. Will you please tell the driver to stop?'

'Cut the engines,' Bacler called into the driver's compartment. The commissar was clearly deranged, but that was hardly surprising. There was no harm humouring him for a minute or two.

The Salamander came to a halt, rocking on its tracks. Criid's ride came to a halt behind it, engine revving. 'Everything all right, sir?' the officer aboard the second Salamander voxed crisply.

'Stand by, Leyden,' said Bacler into his mic.

Hark dismounted, jumping down into the dust. He took a few paces forward. The melody hung in the air, or in his head, he couldn't decide which. He felt a sudden, terrible feeling of sadness and regret. It was like a dream breaking, a buried dream he could finally remember.

He looked back at the other Salamander. Criid and Twenzet had dismounted and were staring at him.

'Hark?' Criid called out.

'Just... just a minute, Tona,' he called back. He started forwards, walking down the line of the column ahead, past rows of tanks with idling engines and Cadogus troopers sitting at ease on the tops of transports. They watched him walk by, amused by the sight of the ragged, one-armed commissar with the hopeless look on his face.

Hark.

Hark walked on, gathering speed, past the tank and transport elements into the next section of the waiting column. He walked between two rows of Trojan tractors towing canisters of fuel on low-loader trailers. Their engines throbbed, but did not drown out the thin, floating melody.

Hark.

The Trojan drivers, sitting up in the top hatches, watched him stride past through the dust. Several more Trojan tractors stood in a line behind the fuel carriers. The machines were painted black and towed a far more volatile cargo in their trailers. A cluster of men in caps and black leather coats stepped out in front of Hark. They were commissars wearing Special Attachment emblems on their collars and epaulettes.

'Let me pass,' said Hark.

They hesitated, and then stood aside.

Help me.

Heavy cages with thick, iron bars sat on the trailers towed by the ominous black tractors. Dark, spavined shapes lurked behind the bars, chained hand and foot, lashed to bare metal frames in the centre of each cage. Some of the cages were studded with spikes and barbs that pointed inwards. Despite the stink of exhaust wafting from the tractors, Hark could smell the pain. Blood, sweat, faeces, gangrene and the wretched tang of static filled the night air.

The pipes grew louder.

Each cage was attended by dark, silent figures: Special Attachment commissars, servitors, armed guards in black uniforms with curiously full helmets, their visors down, and men and women in dark robes armed with handling poles and electric prods. Pale, grim faces and closed visors followed him as he toiled along the line.

Help me, Hark.

Hark came to a halt. He realised there were tears running down his face. The sadness that had eaten away at him for years had finally broken out, cracking the frozen surface of his emotional reserve. He looked up at the cage in front of him. The inward turned spikes were matted with dried blood.

A hunchbacked man in black leather came and stood in front of Hark. 'You cannot approach the cage,' he hissed through rotten teeth.

'Go feth yourself,' said Hark.

A woman stepped forwards beside the hunchback. She was old and stiff, her thin face disfigured with a large red birthmark. She wore a long, austere dress of black lace that rustled in the desert wind.

'Custodian Culcus is quite correct,' she said. 'You may not approach the cage or the specimen. These are the rules of the Sanctioned Division. It is for your own safety, sir. Psykers, even sanctioned ones, are dangerous animals.'

'Get out of my way,' said Hark.

'Let him pass.'

Hark looked around. Bacler had followed him up the line of vehicles with Criid limping at his side. Criid had tears in her eyes. She can probably hear the frail, plaintive music too, Hark thought.

'Let him pass,' Bacler repeated.

The old dam in the black lace dress nodded and backed away, pulling the hunchback aside.

Hark clambered up onto the greasy bed of the trailer. He knelt down in front of the cage, his hands clutching the filthy bars.

'I'm sorry,' he whispered.

The thing inside the cage stirred. It was just a sack of meat, rotting and sagging. Heavy shackles pinned its wasted limbs to the cage frame. Hark could see that it had undergone extensive surgery. Sutured scars criss-crossed its dirty scalp and augmetic devices had been implanted in its neck, chest and throat. Its ears had been clipped off with shears and its eyes had been sewn shut. It slumped naked in a pool of its own waste. Open, weeping sores covered the flesh of its torso.

It's all right.

'No,' said Hark. 'It isn't.'

This is my life now.

'This is no life,' said Hark.

The thing in the cage stirred. The chains holding its cadaverous limbs rattled.

I felt you here.

'I know. I understand that now.'

I felt you close. All of you. My friends. My old friends. I tried to reach you.

'I'm afraid you hurt us. We didn't understand.'

I'm sorry, Hark. I just wanted to help you. Help you to survive.

'I know.'

I just wanted you to hear me.

'I heard you. We all heard you, in our dreams, in the things that haunted us.' Hark wiped his nose on his cuff.

I just wanted you to hear me. I just wanted to help you. You were so far away, in such danger, but I could feel you. I tried to reach you–

'You reached us,' Hark said.

The thing inside the cage shuddered. It gurgled. Slime dripped from the slit that had once been its mouth. It was laughing.

It's not a precise art, this thing I do. Not cut and dried, neat and tidy, like smeltery work or soldiering. I miss both of my old professions. What I do is not precise, Hark. You were so far away, I could only reach you through your memories.

'You reached us,' Hark repeated.

Thunder rolled. Frost had formed on the bars of the cage.

'That's enough now!' the old dam in the black lace dress called. Bacler put a hand on her shoulder and whispered to her. She fell silent.

My handlers are unhappy. They think I might act up now you're here. They think your presence might provoke me. They think I might kill you.

'I know you're not going to do that,' said Hark. 'Although if you did, I wouldn't blame you.'

I only wanted to help you.

'I know.'

I only wanted you to help me. Help me. Please, Hark, help me. I can't stand this any more.

The thing inside the cage rattled its chains again. Icicles had formed along the roof bars.

'I'll help you,' Hark whispered, pushing his face against the bars.

You have to make it look right, Hark. Commissar-style, you know? Otherwise they'll charge you for all sorts of crimes. They'll hang you out to dry.

'I know what to do. Trust me. And forgive me.'

There's nothing to forgive. Just help me.

Hark rose to his feet. He drew his engraved bolt pistol and racked the slide.

'By the grace of the Emperor!' he declared, loud enough for the handlers down below to hear him, 'You're dead and I can't let this go on. You're killing my men with your ghosts.'

He let the slide snap back and aimed the weapon between the bars of the cage.

'He can't do that!' the old dam cried.

'Yes, he fething well can,' snarled Criid behind her.

'Is there anything else you want to say to me?' Hark whispered, his hand trembling.

Only the same thing I've been trying to tell you all these last few days.

'What's that?'

He's alive. He's in terrible pain, but he's alive.

Hark paused.

'Be at peace,' he said.

The wretched thing that had once been called Agun Soric looked up at him with sewn-up eyes through the bars of the cage.

Hark fired.

He jumped down off the trailer. The sound of the pipes had faded, forever. Hark felt sick.

'What did you do?' the old dam screamed at him.

Hark shoved her aside.

'I gave him what he needed,' Hark said.

'You killed him!' the hunchback stammered, outraged.

'Only in death does duty end,' Hark replied, 'and he had done his duty a thousand times over.'

He walked away from the trailer, the bolt pistol hanging in his grip. Behind him, Bacler and Criid were arguing with the handlers.

Hark's foot disturbed something lying in the dust. He bent down.

It was a brass message shell.

Hark picked it up and unscrewed it.

There was nothing inside.

IX

Mkoll and the partisan entered the second prefab. The sour, metallic smell of blood hung in the air. A dozen prisoners were strung up on crude wooden frames along the tent space. It was obvious they had been subjected to intense interrogation under torture.

The scene was appalling, even to a hardened veteran like Mkoll. He stopped in his tracks, breathing hard. The limp, naked bodies suspended on the frames were slick with blood and covered with black, clotted wounds. The torture had been vindictive, cruel and utterly typical of Blood Pact methods. Some of the prisoners had suffered amputations or organ removal. Others had been nailed to the frames by their soft tissue. The hideous tools of the torturers' trade, goads and nails and skewers, lay in blood-stained trays on stands around the room. Branding irons stood in fuming braziers.

Mkoll went down the line of prisoners, quickly and mercifully putting each one out of his or her misery. The deep urge he had felt to come there and enter the place had vanished as suddenly and mysteriously as it had come. He just wanted to get out and make a run for it. But he wasn't going to leave before he'd spared these miserable beings further agonies.

It was simple to do. Just pressing the edge of his venom-smeared blade against an open wound let toxins into the blood stream. A swift, numbing death resulted, without the need for shots or further wounding.

He touched his blade against an open wound in the belly of a heavy-set man who had been partly skinned. The man opened his eyes briefly. He smiled at Mkoll as he died. Mkoll felt as if he was an ayatani priest, delivering a last comforting touch and a blessing.

He moved to the next dangling body and reached out with his ministering blade.

Eszrah caught his hand and pulled it back.

'What?' Mkoll asked.

'Not him,' Eszrah said.

Mkoll looked up at the hanging body. The man had been whipped and flayed several times. His skin was hanging off in places. His face, hanging low, was drenched in blood. The cords holding him spread-eagled to the frame were biting into his wrists and ankles.

'I need to help him,' Mkoll said. 'I need to end his pain.'

Eszrah shook his head. Mkoll looked at the ruined man again. He saw the old, deep scars across his belly, the mark of a chainsword wound suffered many years before.

'Oh feth,' he murmured.

They cut him down quickly, cradling his limp body. His eyes opened. He looked at them, blood trickling out of his mouth. Mkoll realised that he had been blinded.

'Are we the last ones left alive?' he asked, turning his head towards the sound of them. 'Are we? Someone, anyone, please? Are we? Is there anybody out there? Are we the last ones left alive?'

Nalwood, Nalwood, this is Elikon M.P., this is Elikon M.P. Please respond. Please respond. Can you hear, Nalwood? What is your status? Please respond.

Elikon out. (transmission ends)

- Transcript of vox message, fifth month, 778.

TWENTY-THREE

The End of the World at the House

I

Late on the fourteenth day, the mechanised unit Berenson, or some warp-whisper they had known as Berenson, had promised finally fought its way up the pass to Hinzerhaus. Twenty items of armour, with troop support in the van, and air cover from a string of Vulture gunships, blasted into the rear of the Blood Pact host besieging the house and scattered it in a battle that lasted fifty-eight minutes. The last twenty minutes were little more than a massacre. The Blood Pact fled into the cracks in the mountains, leaving over four thousand dead on the dust bowl and the lower escarpments of the house.

Hinzerhaus itself was a dismaying ruin. Clotted smoke drifted up into the desert sky from a hundred separate fires. Overlooks and gunboxes had been blown out and destroyed. Several sections of the southern face had collapsed, exposing the rockcrete bunkers buried in the rock to the sky. The walls were pockmarked and chipped with hundreds of thousands of gunshots. The main gatehouse had been totally demolished. The topside ramparts along the cliff lay in ruins, each and every cloche dome ruptured and burst. Fire spewed steadily and out of control from slots of the lower casemates. The cliff walls were cratered and dimpled with the scorched impacts of heavy shelling.

Major Kallard, commanding the relief force, clambered down from his vehicle in front of the gates and gazed at the ruin. The Vultures shrieked overhead, making another pass before peeling off to hunt for fleeing enemy units in the upper gorges of the range.

'Holy Throne,' muttered Kallard, surveying the burning structure. He looked around at his adjutant, a boy-faced man named Seevan.

'Anything?' he asked.

Seevan tried his caster again and looked up at Kallard with a shake of his head.

'Nothing. Link's dead.'

Kallard spat a curse. He waved the first detachment of his infantry forward into the place, pretty certain he knew what they would find.

'Look, sir!' one of the point men yelled.

Kallard turned and looked.

Figures were emerging from the demolished ruin of the gatehouse. Their dark uniforms were in tatters and their faces were plastered in dirt. They carried strange-looking, heavy rifles, which some had hefted up on their shoulders like yokes. They walked out across the dust towards Kallard.

He watched them approach, straightening his cap. There was something about them that demanded respect.

They came to a halt before him.

'I didn't think there'd be anyone left alive,' Kallard spluttered.

'It comes as something of a surprise to me too,' replied the gaunt, dark-haired man in front of him.

'Major Kallard, Cadogus Fifty-Second Mechanised,' Kallard said, making the sign of the aquila. The bad rock wind moaned.

'Major Rawne, commander, First-and-Only,' the man replied, throwing a half-hearted salute. 'These are my men... Kolea, Larkin, Daur, Commissar Ludd, Baskevyl, Bonin.'

The men behind him nodded in turn, and showed no sign of lowering the hefty antique weapons they carried.

'How... how did you manage to hold out for so long?' Kallard asked.

Rawne shrugged. 'We just decided we wouldn't die,' he replied.

Kallard gathered his wits. 'What are your losses, sir?'

'Forty-seven per cent dead. Eighteen per cent wounded,' Rawne said. 'I have two medicaes in there fighting to cope with the casualties.'

'Medics forwards and in!' Kallard yelled, waving his hand. Corpsmen and surgeons from the column hurried past him into the house.

'Might I ask, sir, what are those weapons?' Kallard asked.

Rawne took the wall gun off his shoulder and held it out for Kallard's inspection. 'They're what kept us alive. I have a feeling the Ordo Xenos will want to look at them.'

'I think they might,' said Kallard. He crunched around on the dust and gestured. 'I have transports waiting to ferry you out,' he said. 'Will you follow me?'

Rawne looked around at Kolea and Daur. 'Lead the way. Get moving. I'm not leaving until the last man is clear.'

Behind Rawne, a chunk of the southern cliff collapsed with a crunch and a gust of powder.

'Go.'

Rawne turned and walked back towards the house. Ludd followed him.

'You can leave now, Ludd,' Rawne said.

'I'll leave when my duty's done, sir,' Ludd replied. 'Let's get the men out.'

II

THEY FILED OUT along the burned out corridor that joined the base chamber to the gatehouse. Man after man, carrying their wounded with them. Curth and Dorden escorted the procession, tending to the most severely injured.

In the base chamber, Zweil cast a final blessing to the walls, and turned to hobble out of the place.

Merrt was one of the last troopers to leave. He left 034TH leaning against a wall in the base chamber.

'Don't you want that?' Dalin asked.

'It doesn't belong to me,' Merrt replied.

III

'MAJOR! MAJOR RAWNE!' Kallard yelled, running up the pass towards the line of Chimeras.

Rawne turned.

'I'm sorry, major, I quite forgot. There was a signal for you, from Van Votyz at Elikon.'

Kallard handed the slip of paper to Rawne.

Rawne read it. He turned to look at the Ghosts mounting the transports along the pass.

'Gaunt's alive!' Rawne yelled to them. 'He's fething well alive!'

One by one, they began to shout.

EPILOGUE
Elikon

I

SEVERAL SETS OF boots came marching down the stone hallway. Sentries presented arms as the figures marched by.

The boots crunched to a halt outside a ward room. The medicae on duty saluted and opened the door.

'Is that you, Barthol?' the man on the bed asked, turning his head from one side to the other. His eyes were bandaged.

'How did you know, Ibram?' General Barthol Van Voytz asked, sitting down beside the bed.

'I could smell acceptable losses.'

'Uhm,' Van Voytz replied. He looked over his shoulder at Biota and the escort guards. 'Out,' he said.

They made themselves scarce. The door closed behind them.

'I'm glad you're alive, Ibram,' Van Voytz said.

'As I understand it, that's thanks to Mkoll and Eszrah and a five-hour desert drive in a captured enemy half-track.'

'You surround yourself with good people, good things happen,' the general said.

Gaunt sat back. It was going to take many months of skin grafts to repair his body.

'I have always surrounded myself with good people, Barthol. Why do think I've lived this long?'

Van Voytz chuckled.

'You sent me to the end of the world, Barthol. You sent me to a death trap,' Gaunt said. 'Me and all my men. Barely half of them came out alive.'

'I'm sorry, Ibram,' Van Voytz said. 'Listen, we've spared no expense. Your new eyes will be the best aug–'

'My Ghosts, Barthol. My Ghosts, and you saw fit to let half of them die.'

'It wasn't like that, Ibram. It was vital to hold the enemy back for as long as possible. A delay was ess–'

'Here's what I want you to do, Barthol. Never ask that of me and my men again.'

II

FARAWAY, THE HOUSE *at the end of the world expires. The worm ceases its subterranean scratching. The old dam stops walking fretfully along the empty halls, biding her time and waiting, her black lace dress brushing the satin brown floors.*

A standard-pattern infantry rifle, serial 034TH, standing in the corner of a smoke-blackened room, begins to rust.

HINZERHAUS FALLS SILENT. *The wall lights flare and then dim away to nothing. In death, the house sleeps, waiting for the next soldiers to arrive out of the wind and dust, and the next battle to begin, one day, in ages to come.*

Day eighteen.

Sunrise at ~~something~~ dawn. No dust.

According to sources at the Tacticae, the documents retrieved from the library archive have proven remarkably helpful to the Jago campaign. I am told the war to reconquer Jago might be shortened by two or three years.

I am tired of this bad rock. It has cost us too much. My arm hurts. My mouth is constantly dry. ~~I miss the music in~~

When I told Rawne that Gaunt was alive, he looked as if he was going to cry. Just the dust, I suspect. The dust got into everything on Jago.

– Field journal, V.H. fifth month, 778.

ABOUT THE AUTHOR

Dan Abnett lives and works in Maidstone, Kent, in England. Well known for his comic work, he has written everything from the *Mr Men* to the *X-Men*.

His work for the Black Library includes the best-selling Gaunt's Ghosts novels, the Inquisitor Eisenhorn and Ravenor trilogies, and the acclaimed Horus Heresy novel, *Horus Rising*. He's also worked on the popular strips *Titan* and *Darkblade*, and, together with Mike Lee, the Darkblade novel series.

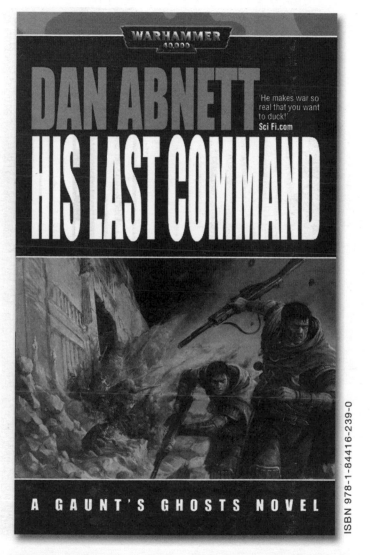

THE ARMOUR OF CONTEMPT

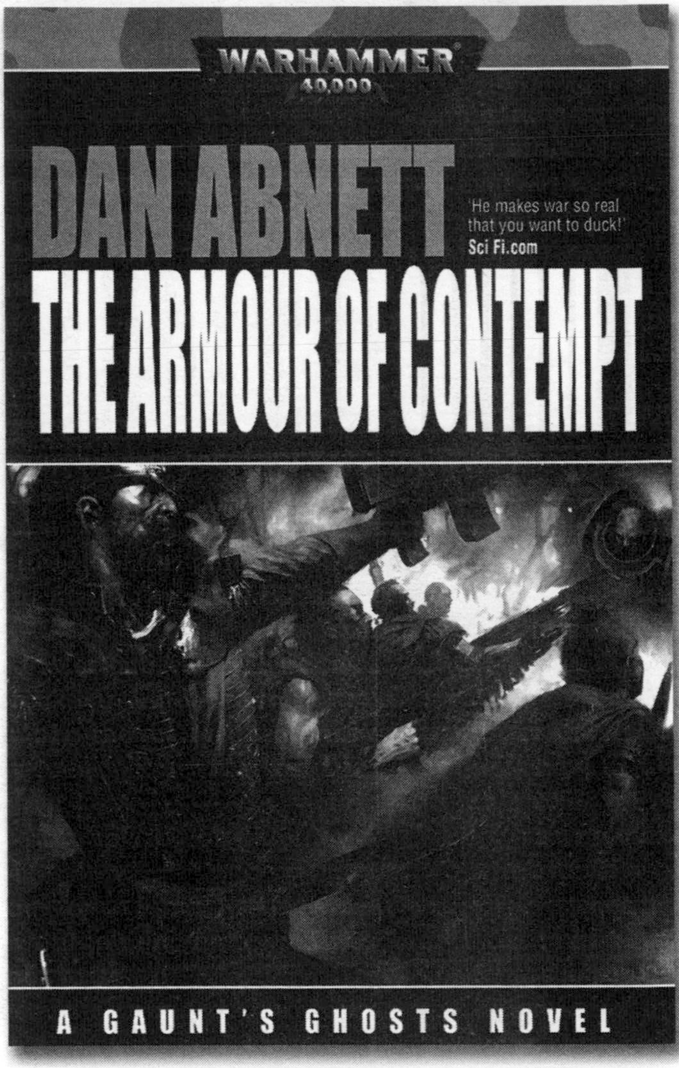

ISBN 978-1-84416-400-4

In the war-torn Sabbat World's crusade, Commissar Gaunt returns to the Chaos-held planet of Gereon to confront his personal demons!

Buy now from *www.blacklibrary.com* or download the first chapter for free!
Also available in all good bookshops and game stores

DOUBLE EAGLE

ISBN 978-1-84416-090-7

The Imperial world of Enothis stands on the brink of destruction and only the brave men and women of the Phantine fighter corps can halt the Chaos advance

Buy now from *www.blacklibrary.com* or download the first chapter for free!
Also available in all good bookshops and game stores

BROTHERS OF THE SNAKE

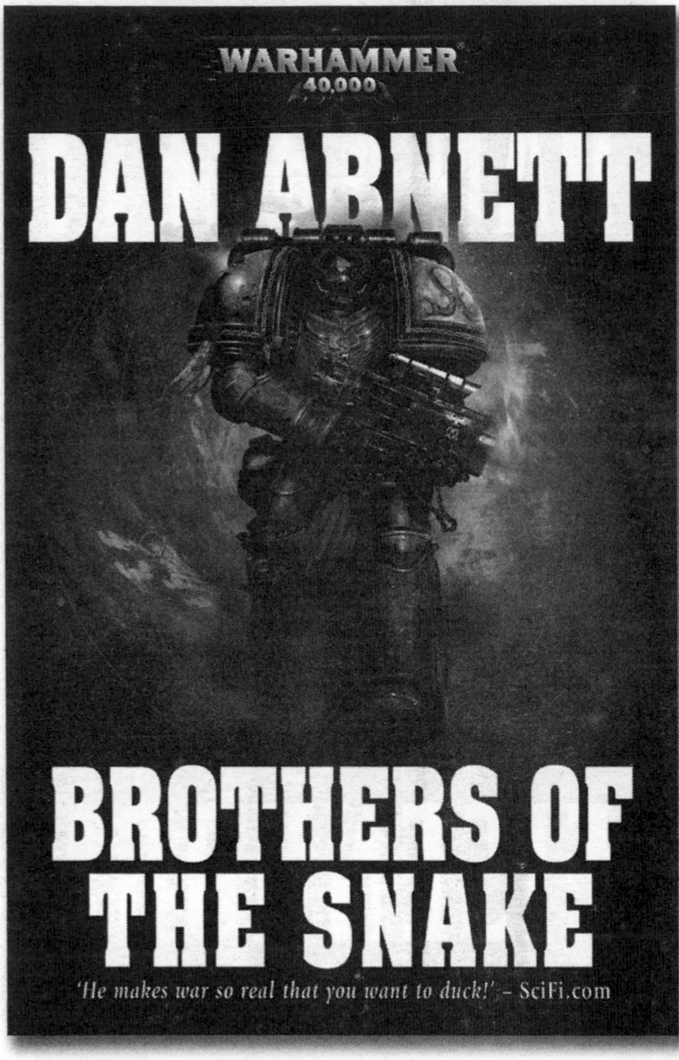

ISBN 978-1-84416-475-2

Dan Abnett turns his hand to the mighty Space Marines! *Brothers of the Snake* follows the exploits of the Iron Snakes Marines as they battle against the enemies of mankind

Buy now from *www.blacklibrary.com* or download the first chapter for free! Also available in all good bookshops and game stores

RAVENOR ROGUE

ISBN 978-1-84416-185-0

Inquisitor Gideon Ravenor, proud servant of the Ordo Hereticus, continues his fight against the dark forces that threaten mankind.

Buy now from *www.blacklibrary.com* or download the first chapter for free!
Also available in all good bookshops and game stores